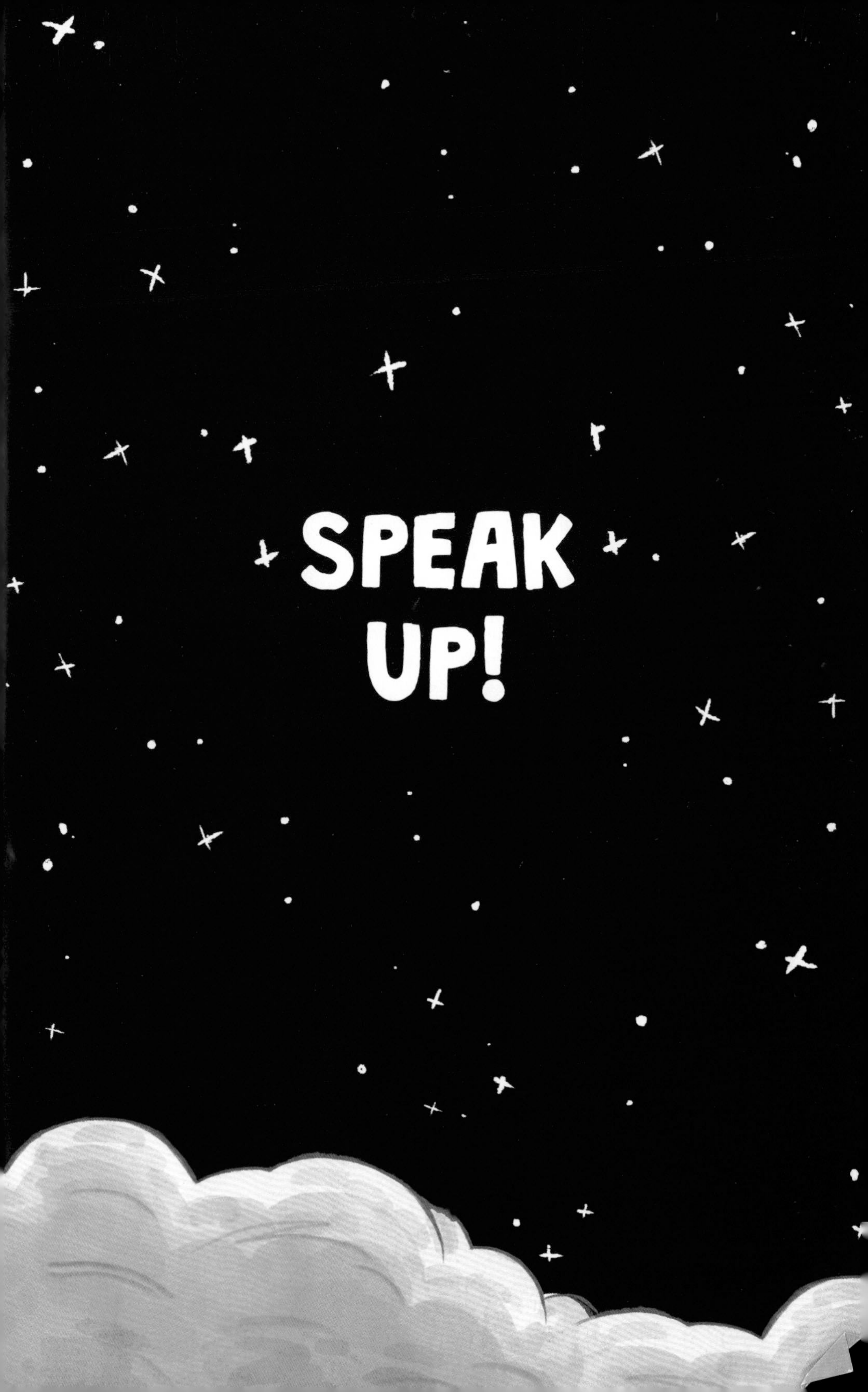
SPEAK
UP!

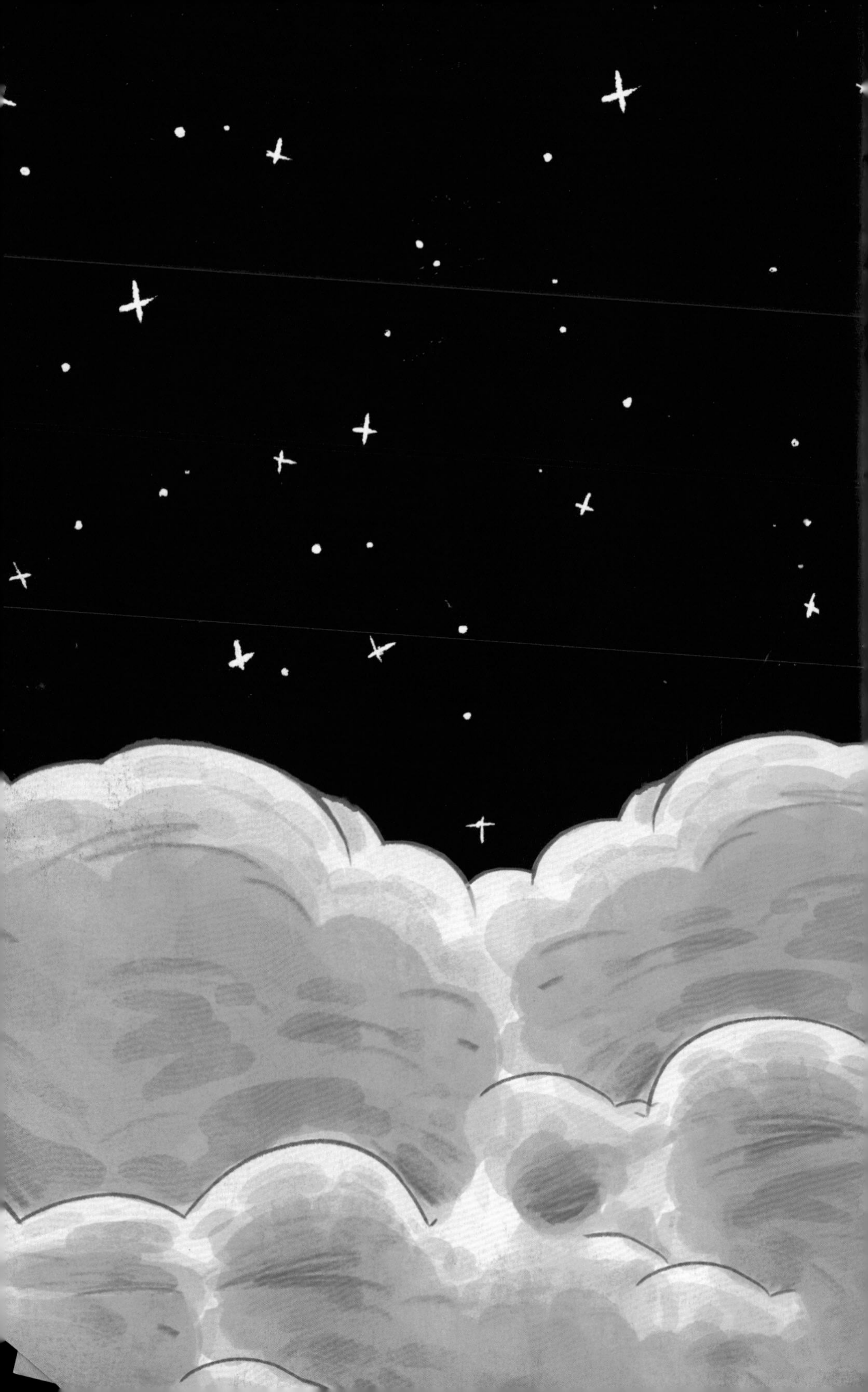

# SPEAK UP!

## REBECCA BURGESS

Quill Tree Books
Imprints of HarperCollinsPublishers

Quill Tree Books is an imprint of HarperCollins Publishers.
HarperAlley is an imprint of HarperCollins Publishers.

Speak Up!
information address HarperCollins Children's Books, a division of
HarperCollins Publishers, 195 Broadway, New York, NY 10007.
www.harperalley.com

Library of Congress Control Number: 2022934043
ISBN 978-0-06-308119-2 (paperback)
ISBN 978-0-06-308120-8 (hardcover)

The artist used Photoshop to create the illustrations for this book.
22 23 24 25 26   RTLO   10 9 8 7 6 5 4 3 2 1
❖
First Edition

FOR AMANDA, LAURA, KATE, AND MOTH—
AS WE'VE GROWN UP TOGETHER, I'VE SEEN
YOU ALL FIND YOUR VOICES TOO!

# CHAPTER ONE

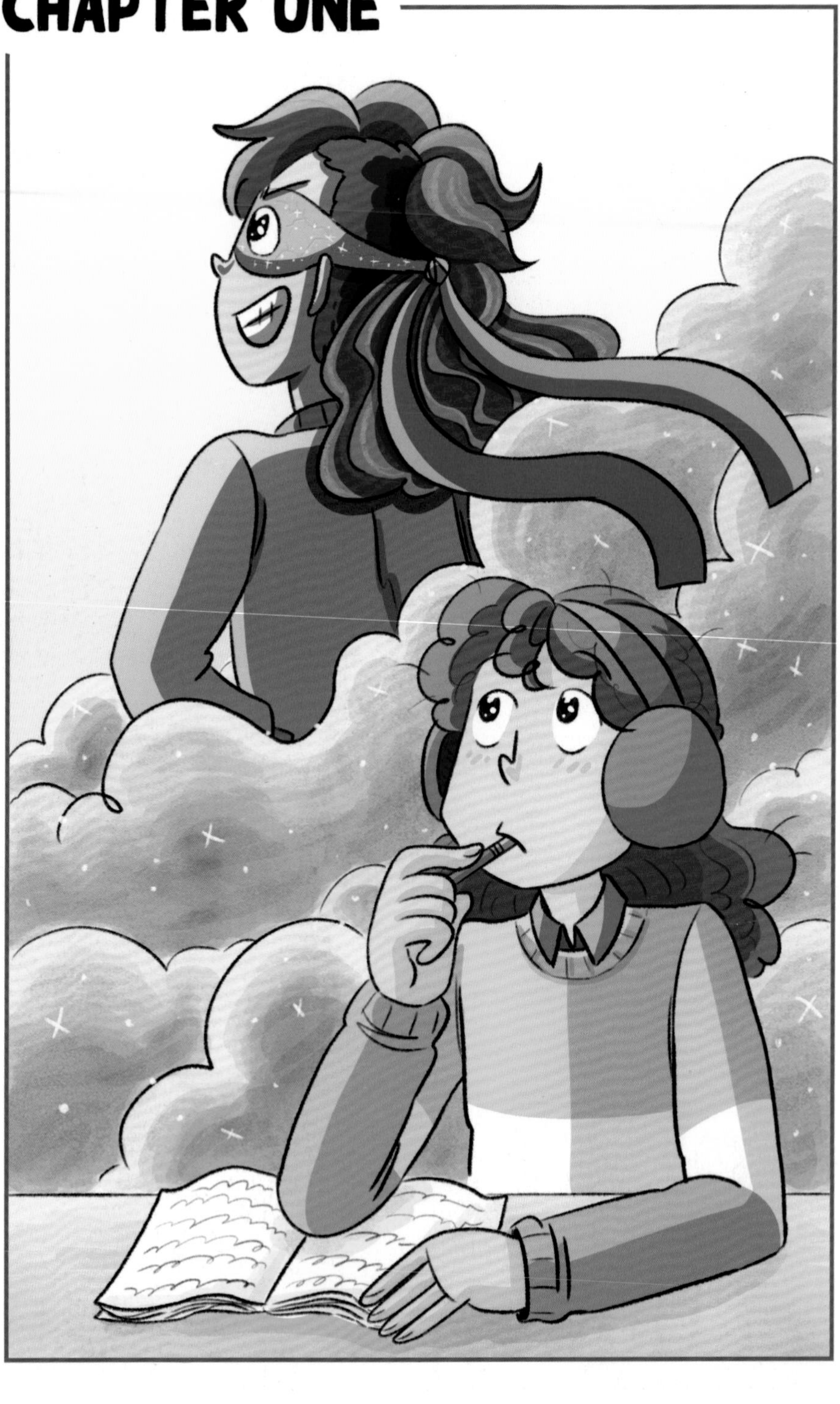

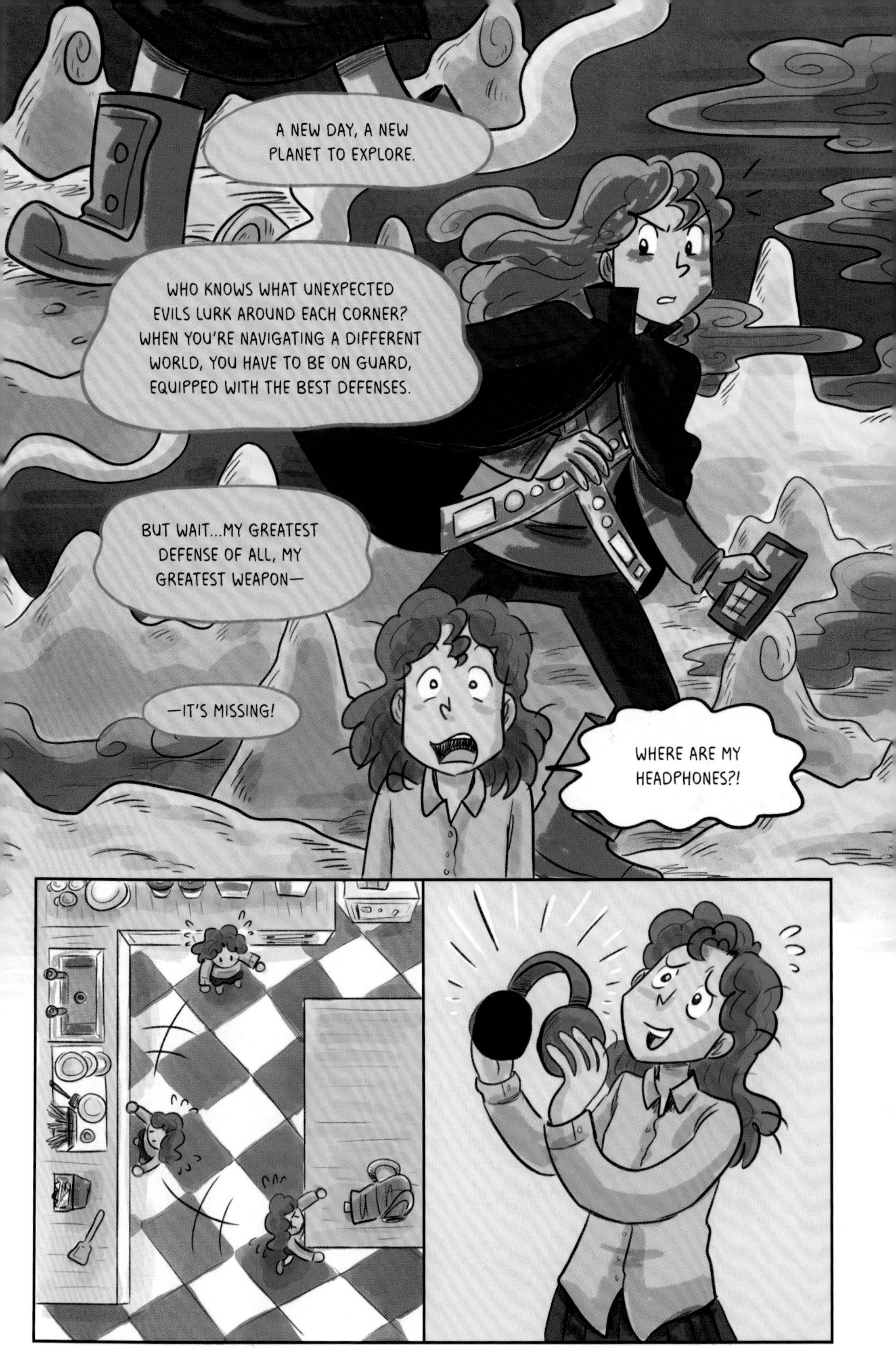
A NEW DAY, A NEW PLANET TO EXPLORE.
WHO KNOWS WHAT UNEXPECTED EVILS LURK AROUND EACH CORNER? WHEN YOU'RE NAVIGATING A DIFFERENT WORLD, YOU HAVE TO BE ON GUARD, EQUIPPED WITH THE BEST DEFENSES.
BUT WAIT...MY GREATEST DEFENSE OF ALL, MY GREATEST WEAPON—
—IT'S MISSING!
WHERE ARE MY HEADPHONES?!

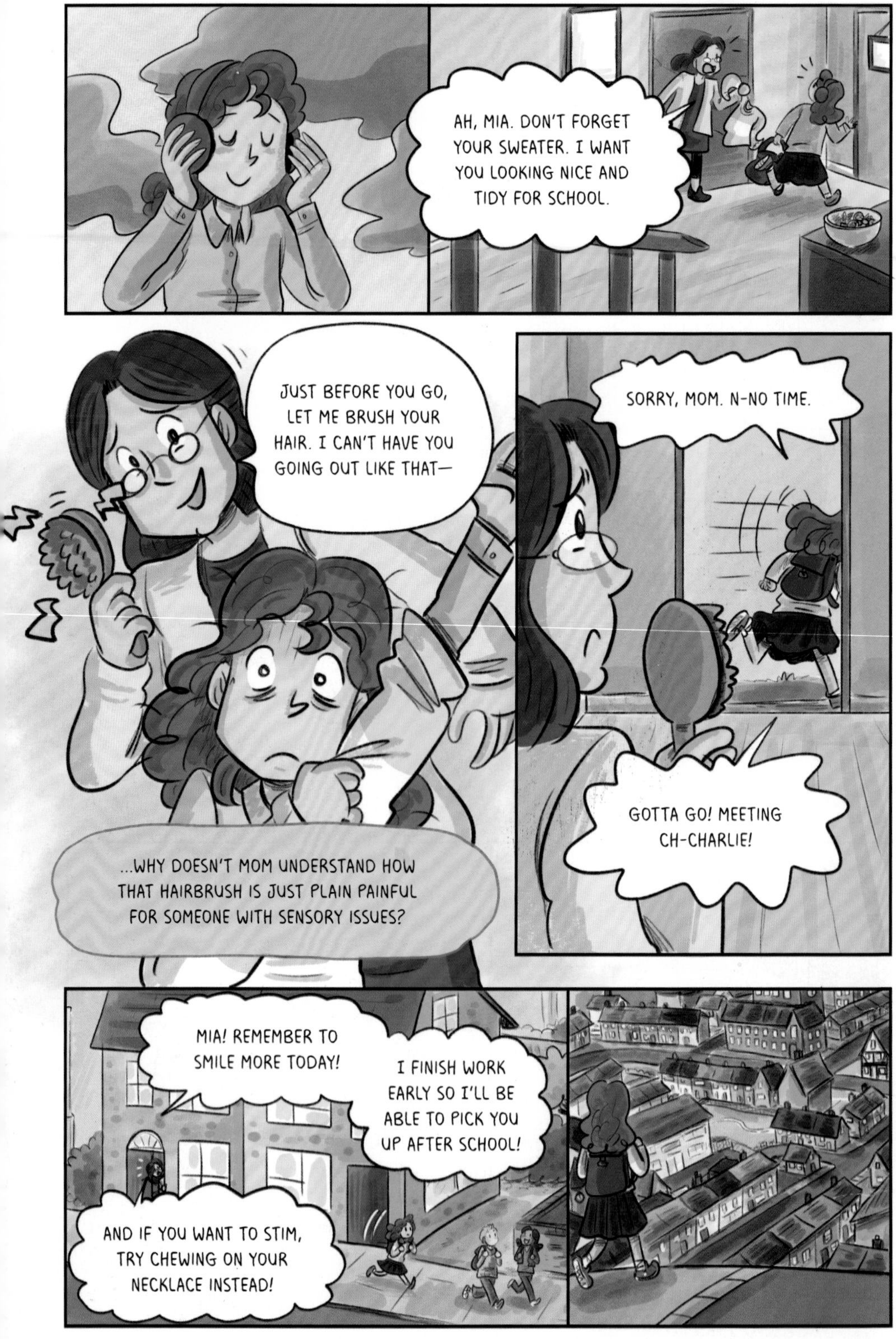
AH, MIA. DON'T FORGET YOUR SWEATER. I WANT YOU LOOKING NICE AND TIDY FOR SCHOOL.
JUST BEFORE YOU GO, LET ME BRUSH YOUR HAIR. I CAN'T HAVE YOU GOING OUT LIKE THAT—
...WHY DOESN'T MOM UNDERSTAND HOW THAT HAIRBRUSH IS JUST PLAIN PAINFUL FOR SOMEONE WITH SENSORY ISSUES?
SORRY, MOM. N-NO TIME.
GOTTA GO! MEETING CH-CHARLIE!
MIA! REMEMBER TO SMILE MORE TODAY!
I FINISH WORK EARLY SO I'LL BE ABLE TO PICK YOU UP AFTER SCHOOL!
AND IF YOU WANT TO STIM, TRY CHEWING ON YOUR NECKLACE INSTEAD!

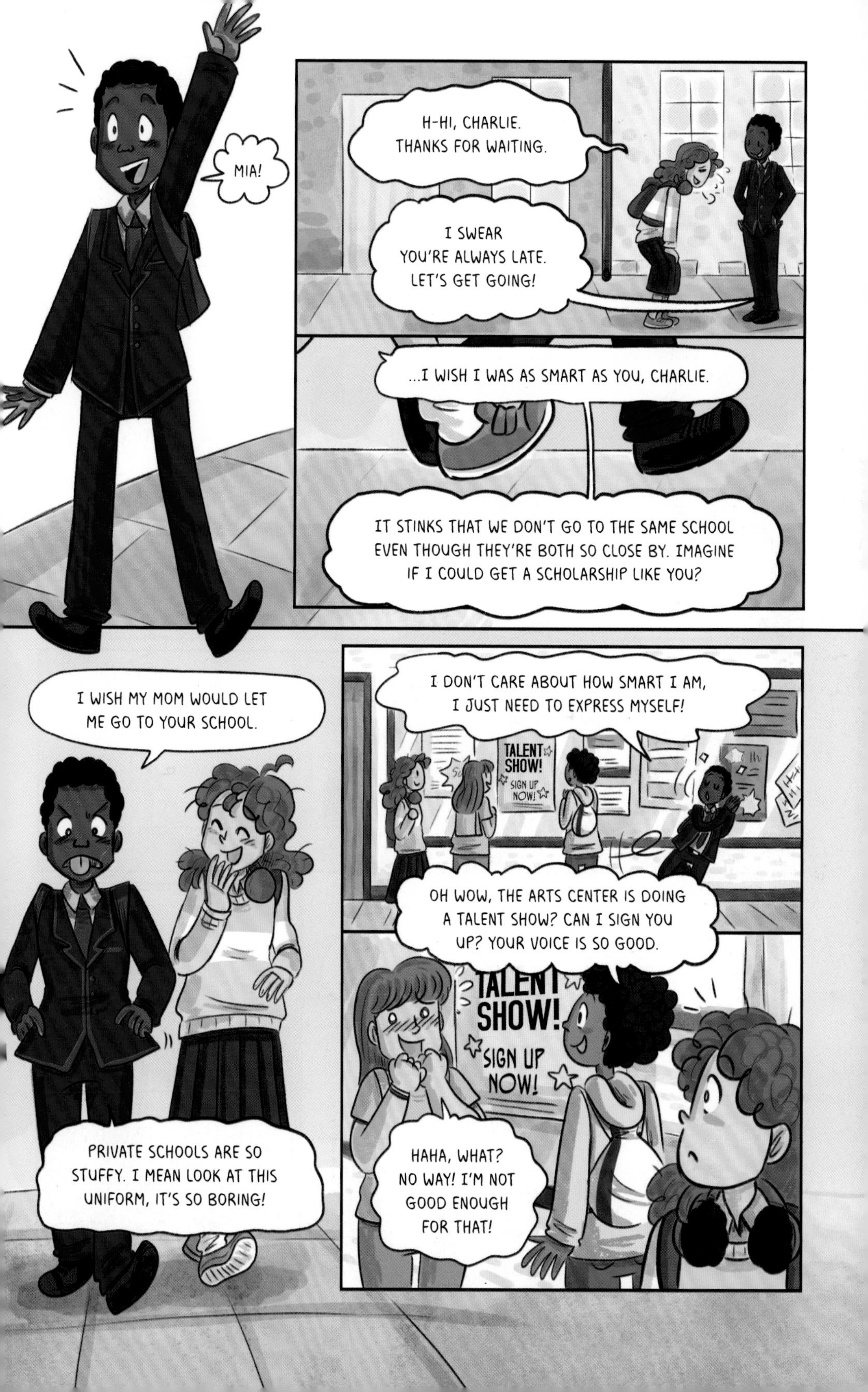
MIA!
H-HI, CHARLIE. THANKS FOR WAITING.
I SWEAR YOU'RE ALWAYS LATE. LET'S GET GOING!
...I WISH I WAS AS SMART AS YOU, CHARLIE.
IT STINKS THAT WE DON'T GO TO THE SAME SCHOOL EVEN THOUGH THEY'RE BOTH SO CLOSE BY. IMAGINE IF I COULD GET A SCHOLARSHIP LIKE YOU?
I WISH MY MOM WOULD LET ME GO TO YOUR SCHOOL.
PRIVATE SCHOOLS ARE SO STUFFY. I MEAN LOOK AT THIS UNIFORM, IT'S SO BORING!
I DON'T CARE ABOUT HOW SMART I AM, I JUST NEED TO EXPRESS MYSELF!
TALENT SHOW! SIGN UP NOW!
OH WOW, THE ARTS CENTER IS DOING A TALENT SHOW? CAN I SIGN YOU UP? YOUR VOICE IS SO GOOD.
TALENT SHOW! SIGN UP NOW!
HAHA, WHAT? NO WAY! I'M NOT GOOD ENOUGH FOR THAT!

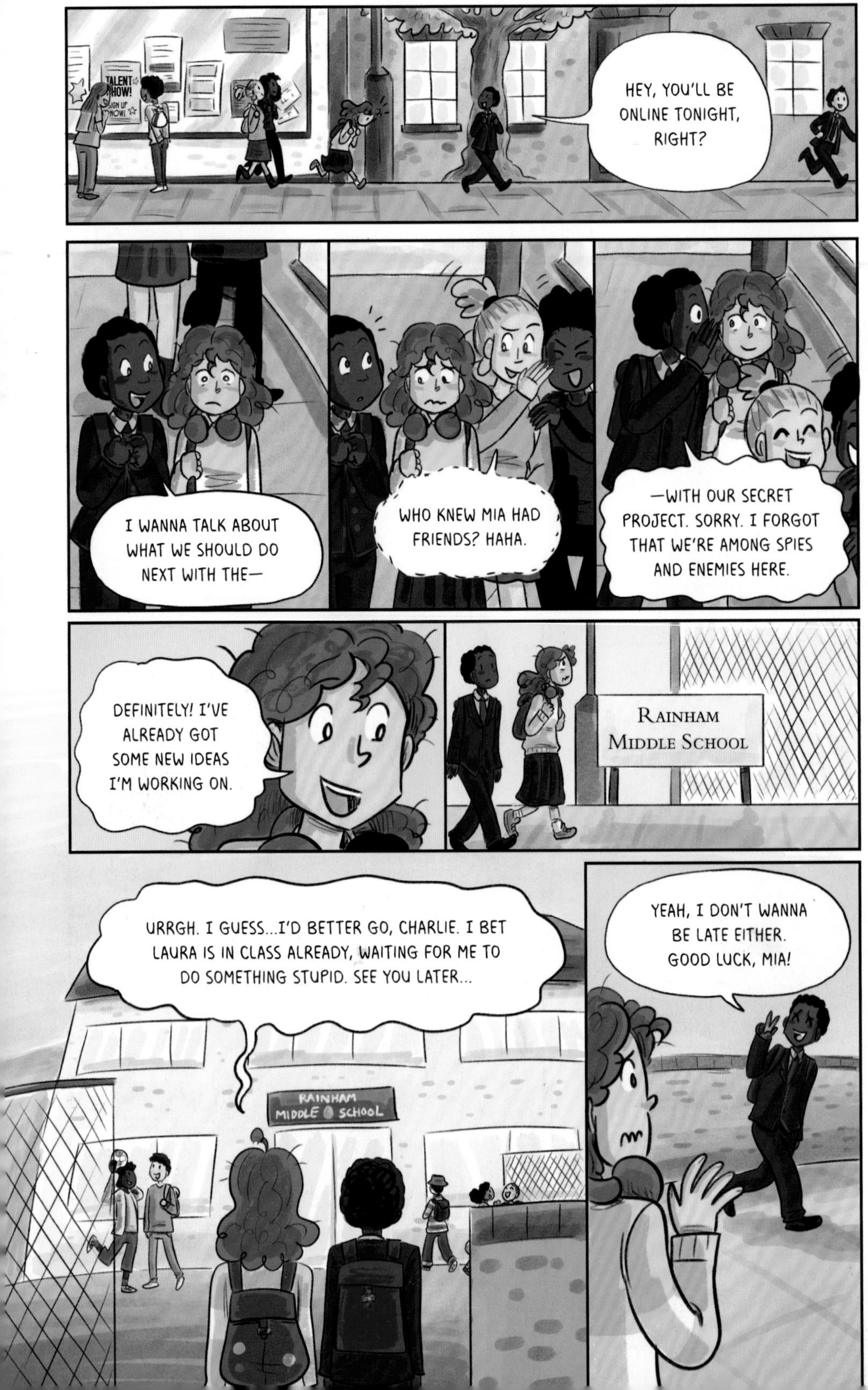
TALENT SHOW!
SIGN UP NOW!
HEY, YOU'LL BE ONLINE TONIGHT, RIGHT?
I WANNA TALK ABOUT WHAT WE SHOULD DO NEXT WITH THE—
WHO KNEW MIA HAD FRIENDS? HAHA.
—WITH OUR SECRET PROJECT. SORRY. I FORGOT THAT WE'RE AMONG SPIES AND ENEMIES HERE.
DEFINITELY! I'VE ALREADY GOT SOME NEW IDEAS I'M WORKING ON.
RAINHAM MIDDLE SCHOOL
URRGH. I GUESS...I'D BETTER GO, CHARLIE. I BET LAURA IS IN CLASS ALREADY, WAITING FOR ME TO DO SOMETHING STUPID. SEE YOU LATER...
RAINHAM MIDDLE SCHOOL
YEAH, I DON'T WANNA BE LATE EITHER. GOOD LUCK, MIA!

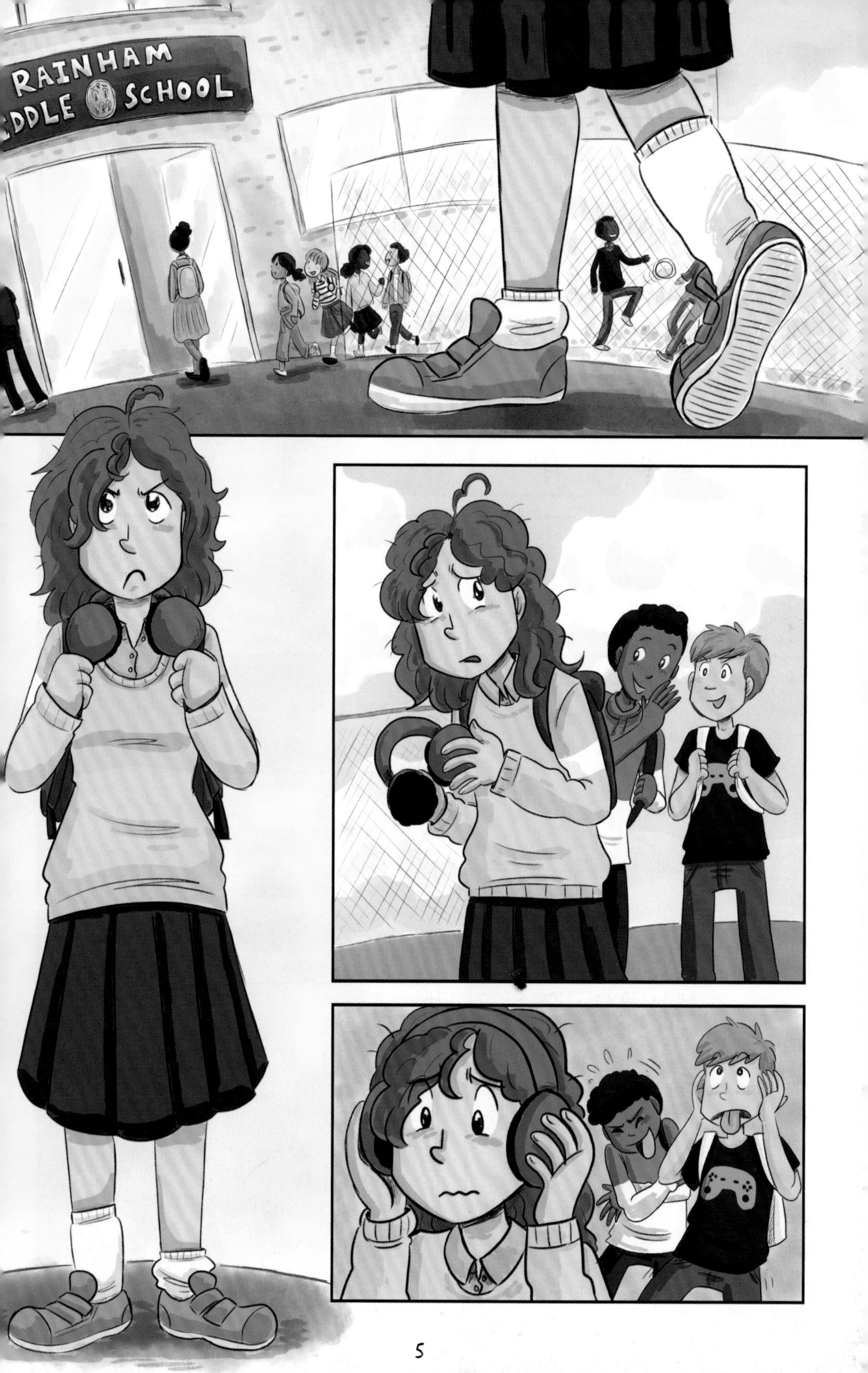
RAINHAM
DDLE SCHOOL

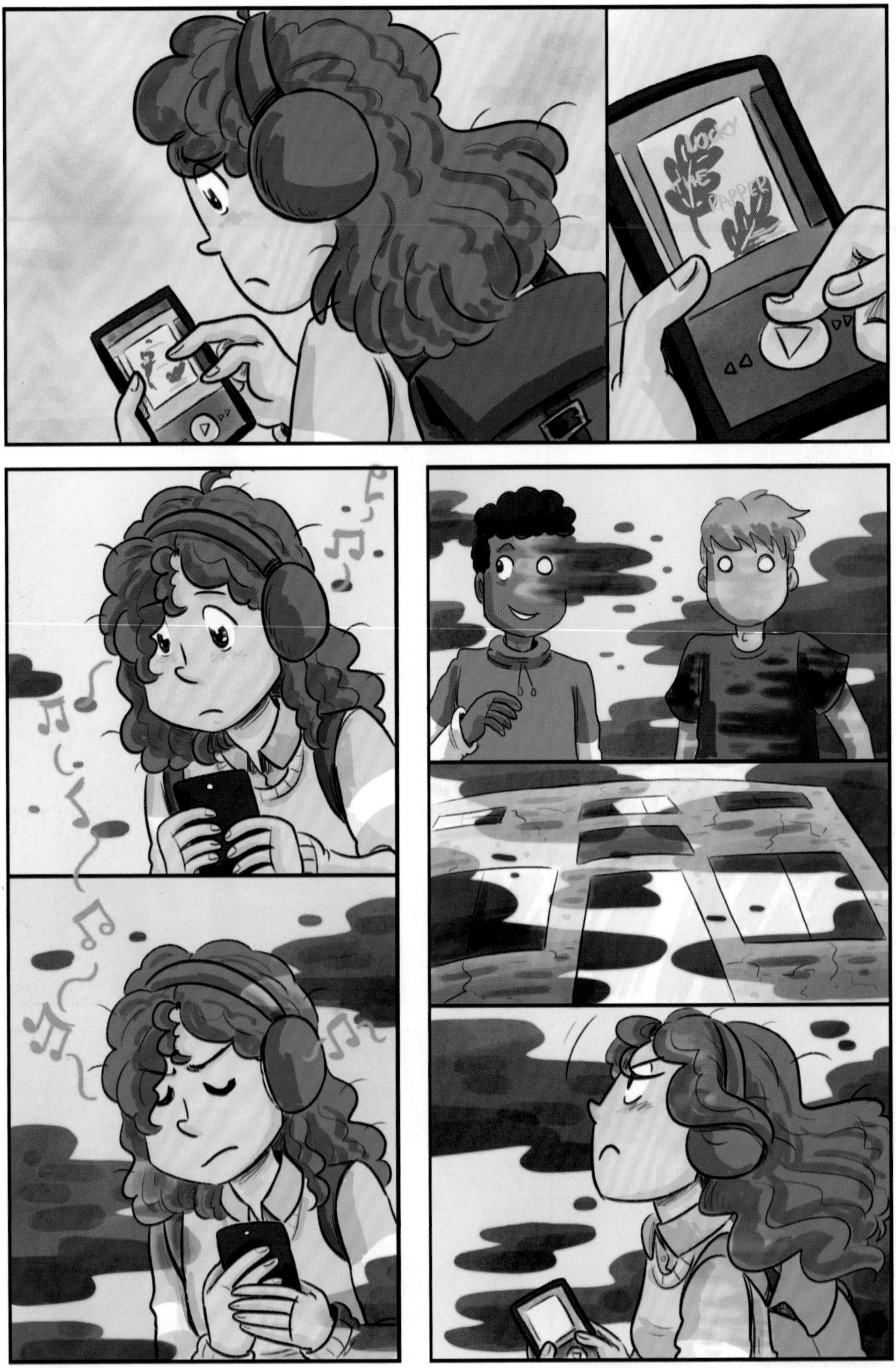
LOCKY THE RAPPER

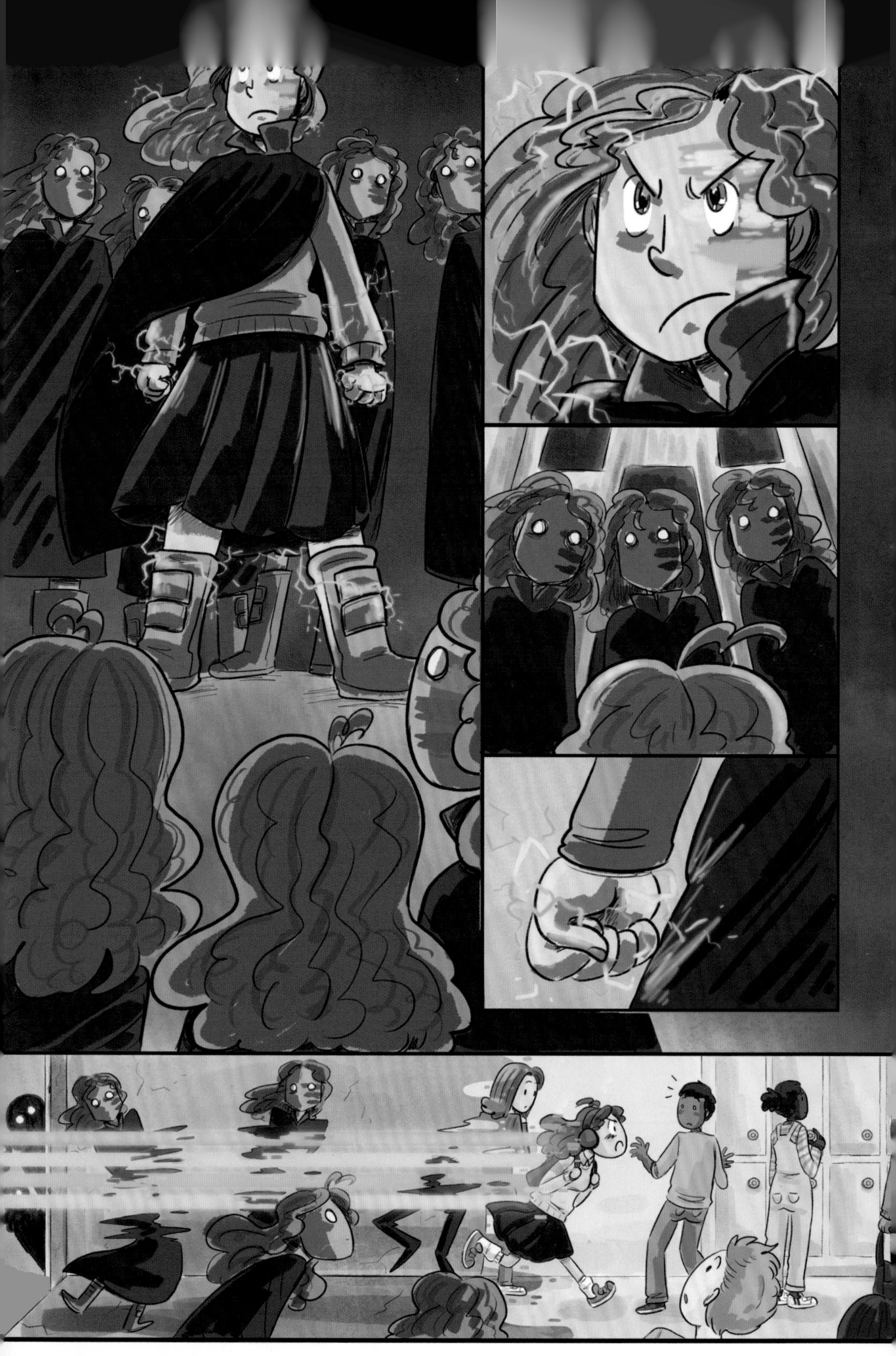

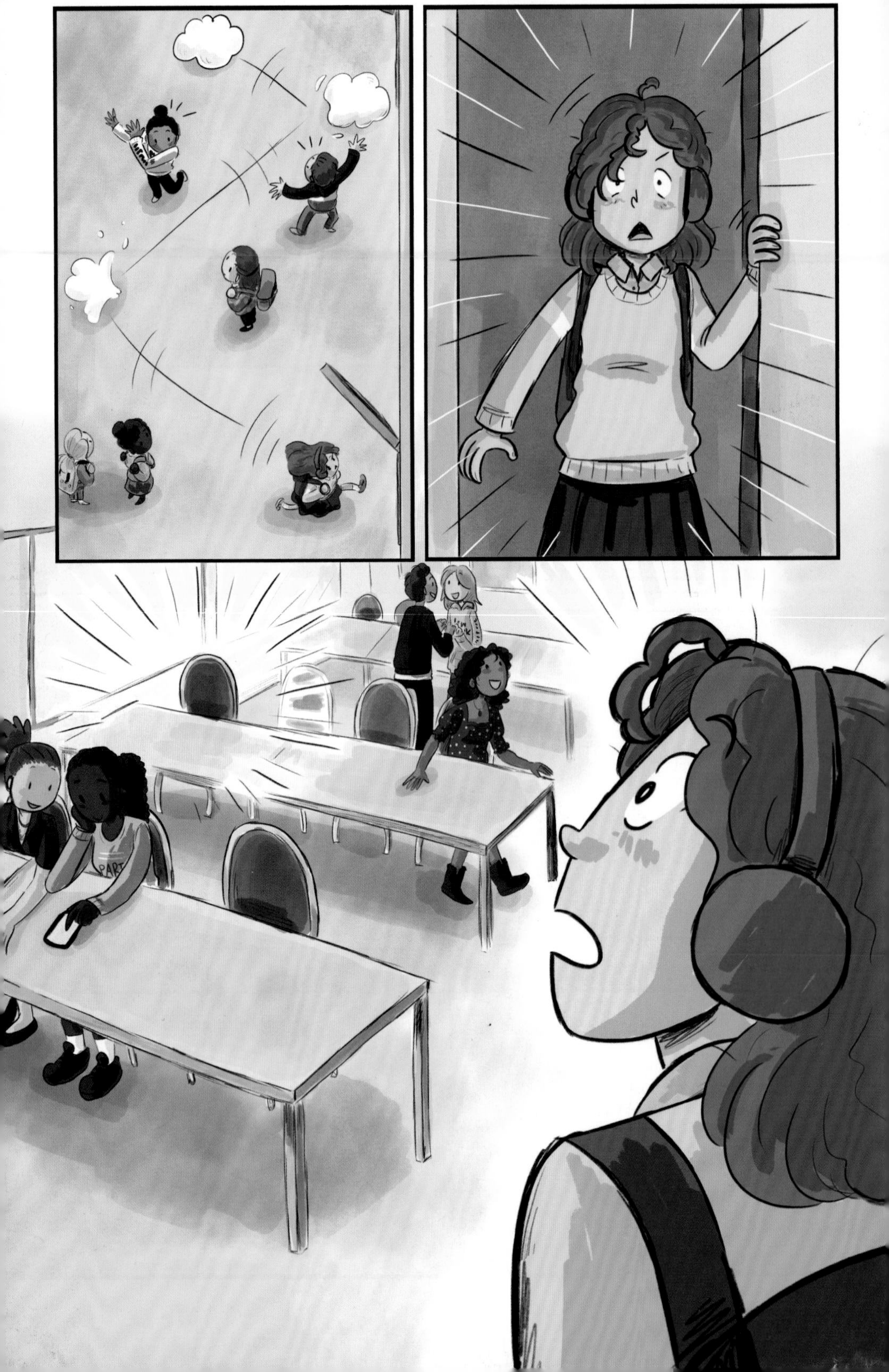

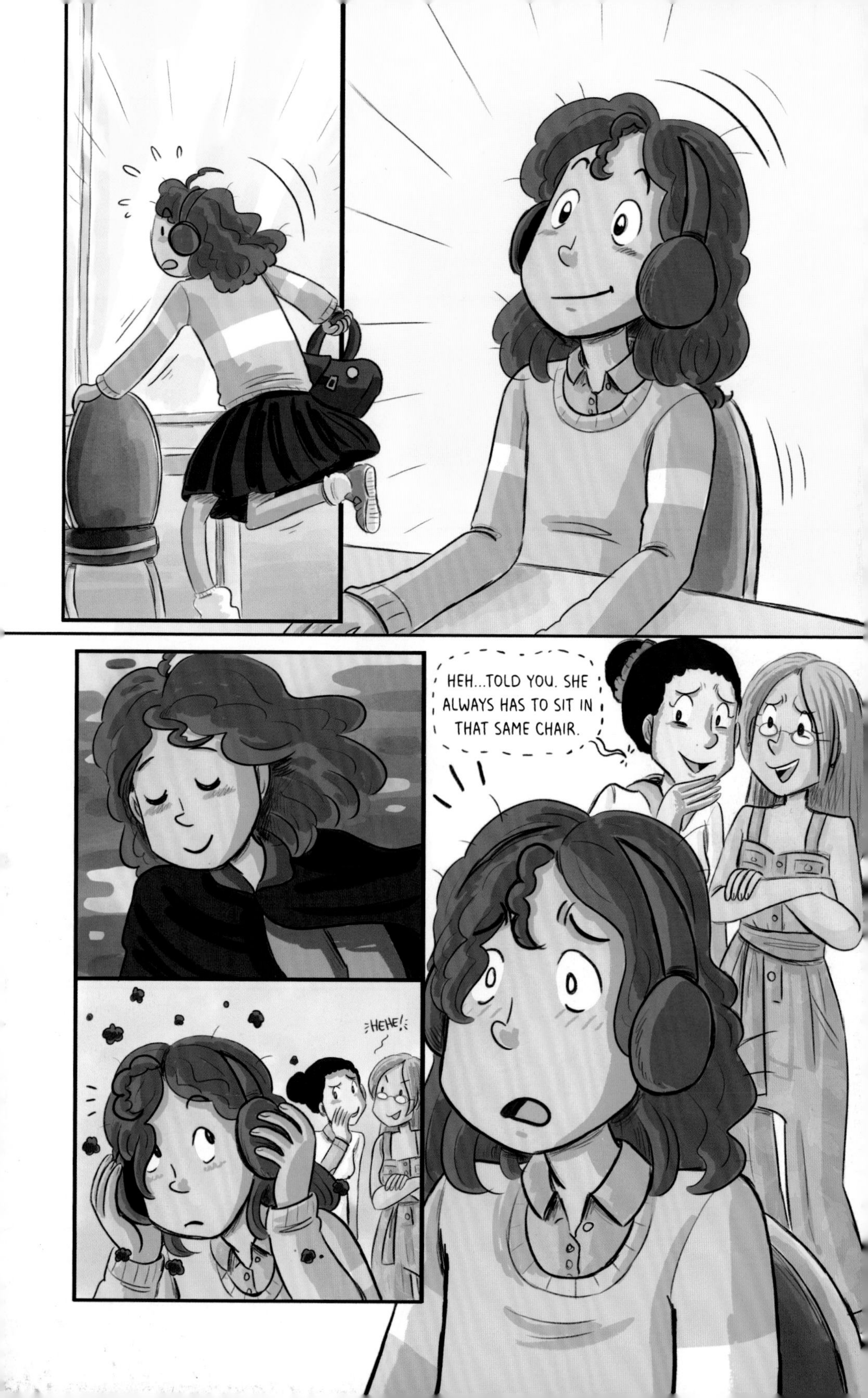
HEH...TOLD YOU. SHE ALWAYS HAS TO SIT IN THAT SAME CHAIR.
HEHE!

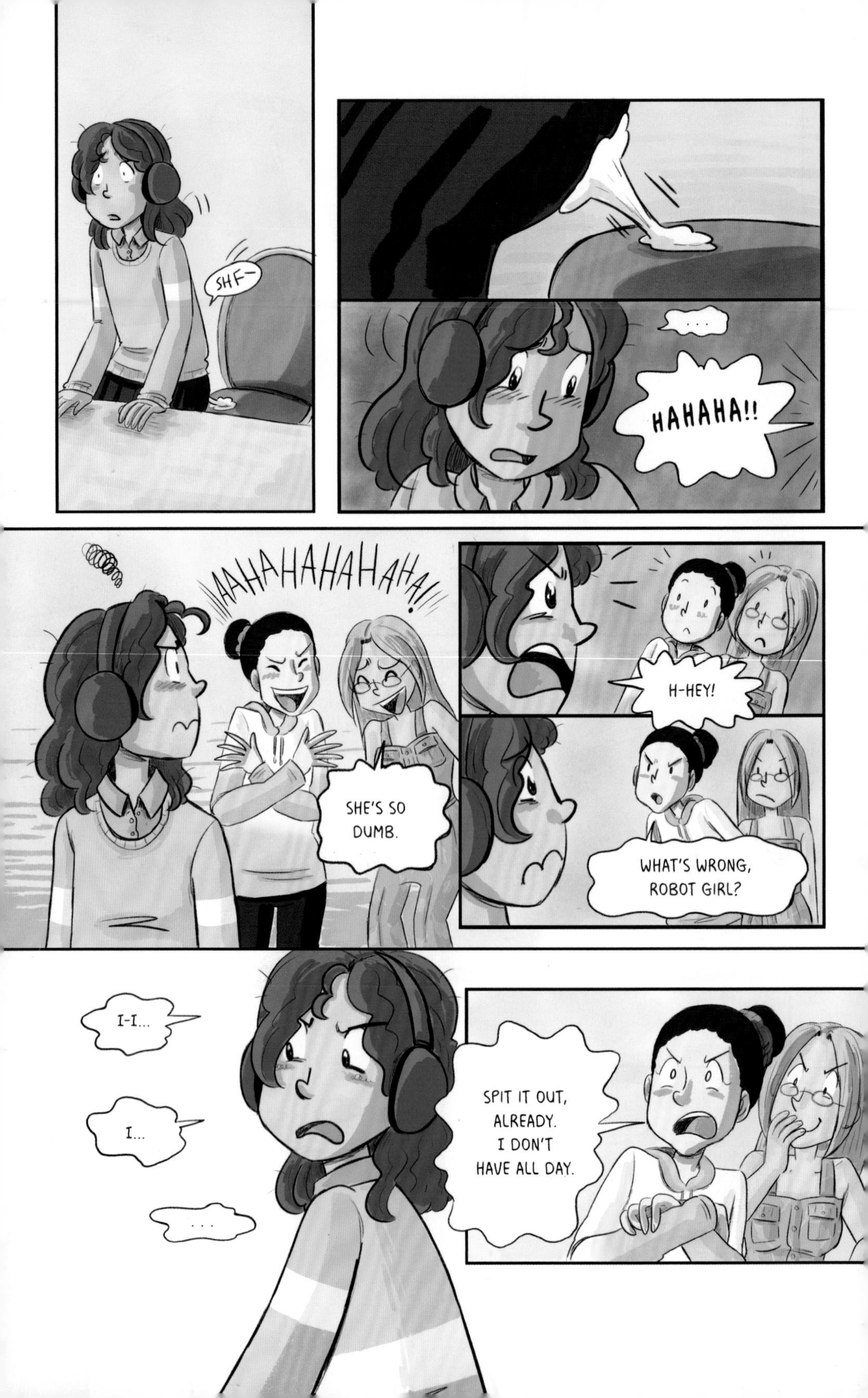
SHF-
...
HAHAHA!!
AHAHAHAHAHAHA!
SHE'S SO DUMB.
H-HEY!
WHAT'S WRONG, ROBOT GIRL?
I-I...
I...
...
SPIT IT OUT, ALREADY. I DON'T HAVE ALL DAY.

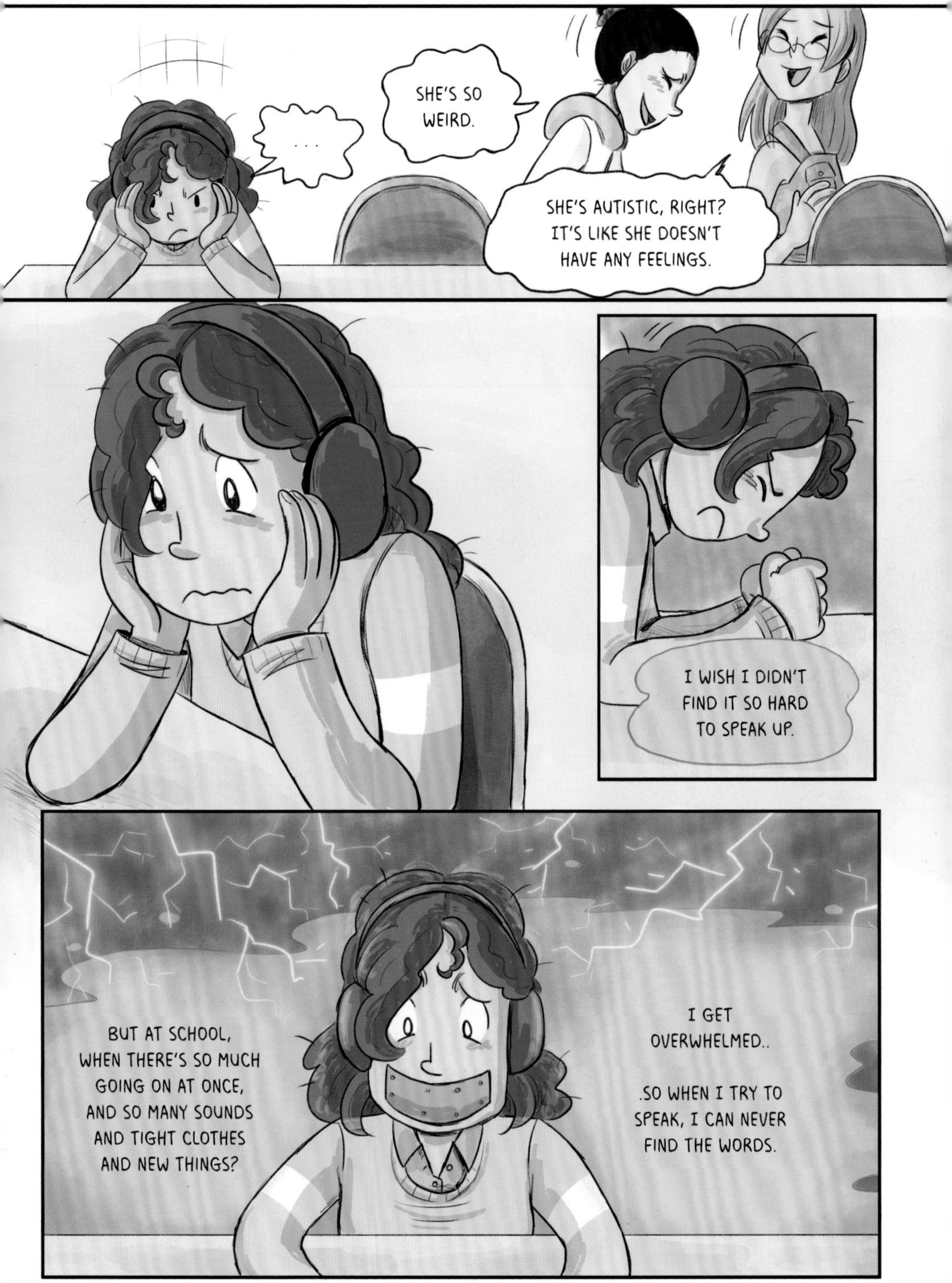
. . .
SHE'S SO WEIRD.
SHE'S AUTISTIC, RIGHT? IT'S LIKE SHE DOESN'T HAVE ANY FEELINGS.
I WISH I DIDN'T FIND IT SO HARD TO SPEAK UP.
BUT AT SCHOOL, WHEN THERE'S SO MUCH GOING ON AT ONCE, AND SO MANY SOUNDS AND TIGHT CLOTHES AND NEW THINGS?
I GET OVERWHELMED..
.SO WHEN I TRY TO SPEAK, I CAN NEVER FIND THE WORDS.

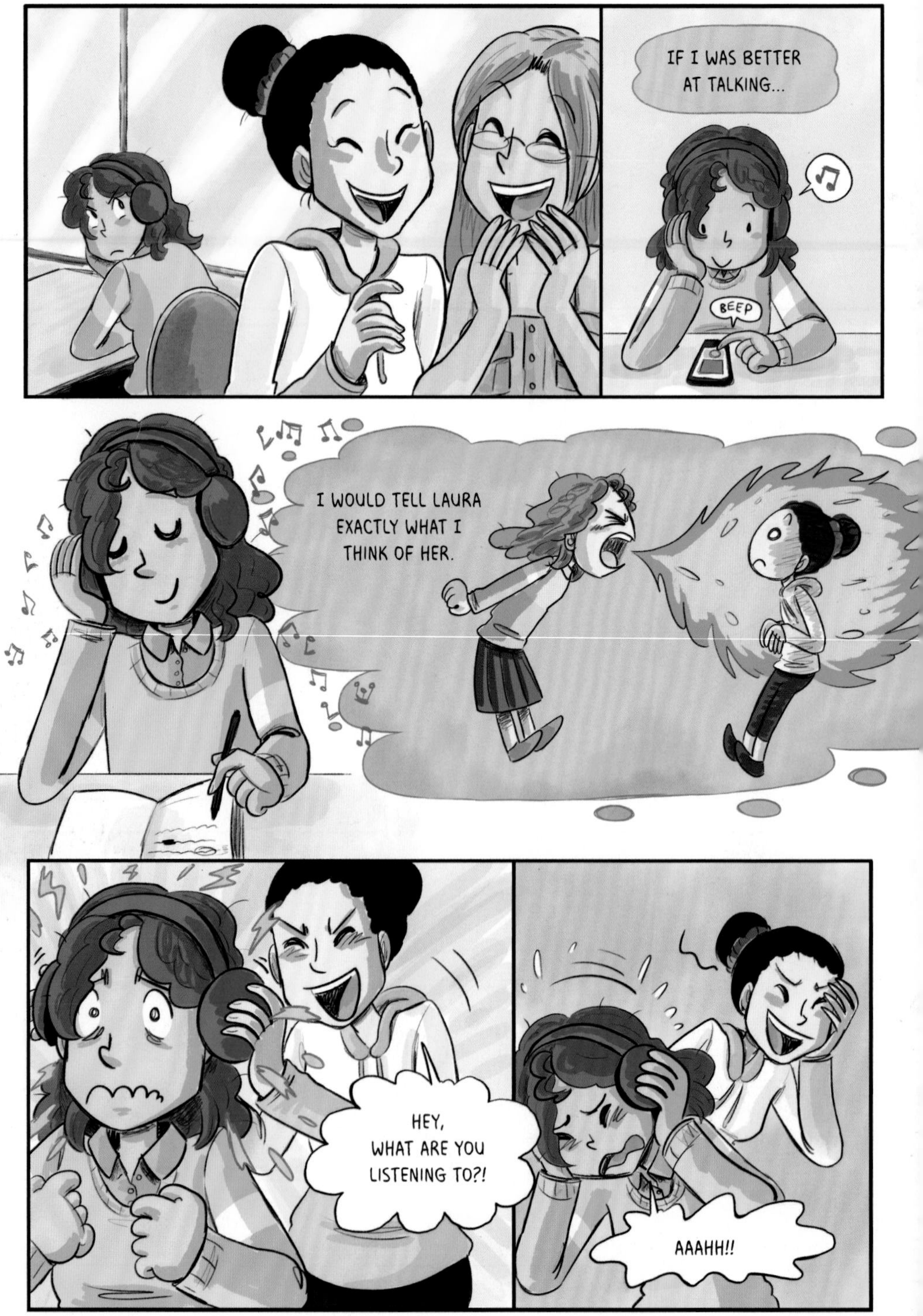
IF I WAS BETTER
AT TALKING...
BEEP
I WOULD TELL LAURA
EXACTLY WHAT I
THINK OF HER.
HEY,
WHAT ARE YOU
LISTENING TO?!
AAAHH!!

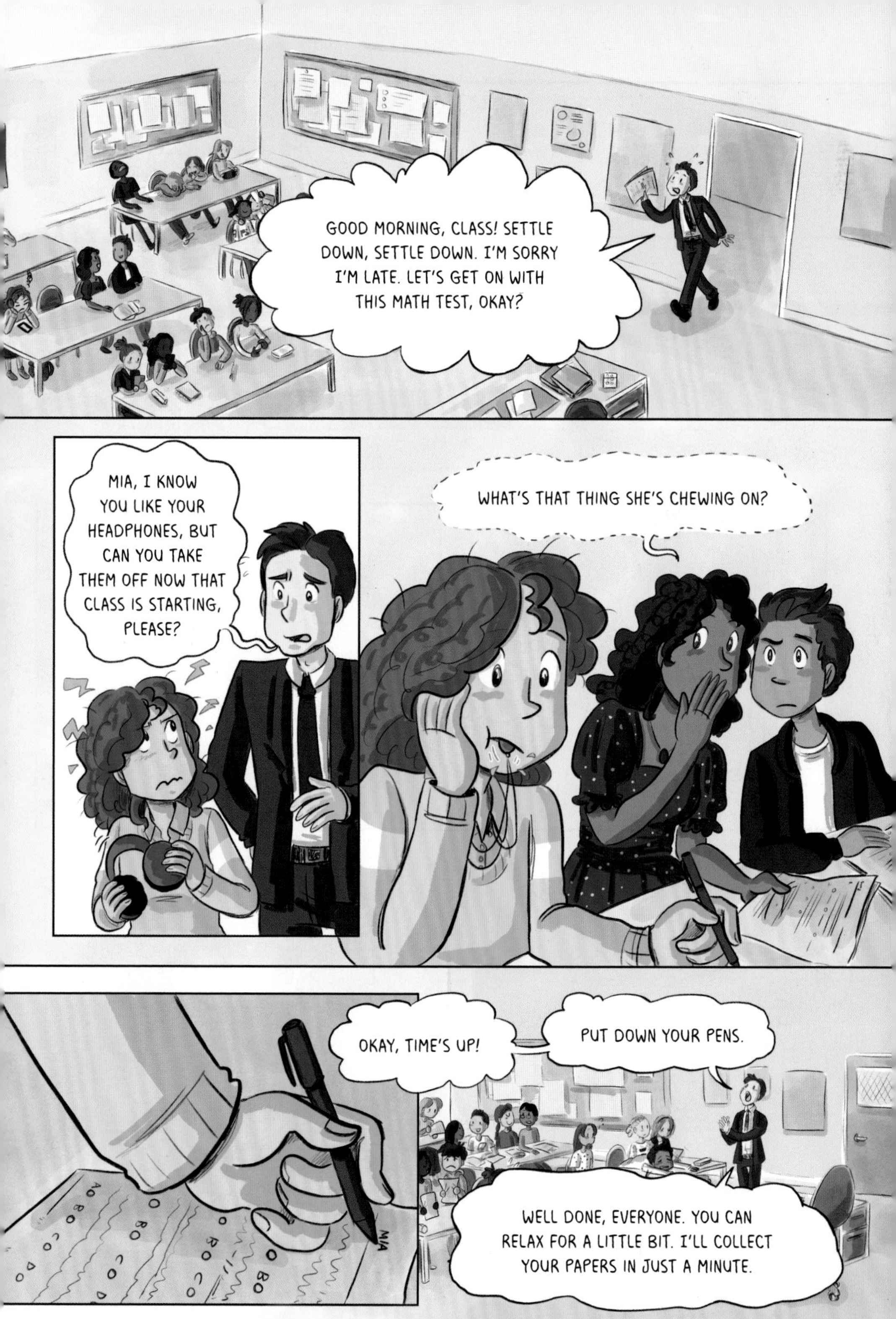
GOOD MORNING, CLASS! SETTLE DOWN, SETTLE DOWN. I'M SORRY I'M LATE. LET'S GET ON WITH THIS MATH TEST, OKAY?
MIA, I KNOW YOU LIKE YOUR HEADPHONES, BUT CAN YOU TAKE THEM OFF NOW THAT CLASS IS STARTING, PLEASE?
WHAT'S THAT THING SHE'S CHEWING ON?
MIA
OKAY, TIME'S UP!
PUT DOWN YOUR PENS.
WELL DONE, EVERYONE. YOU CAN RELAX FOR A LITTLE BIT. I'LL COLLECT YOUR PAPERS IN JUST A MINUTE.

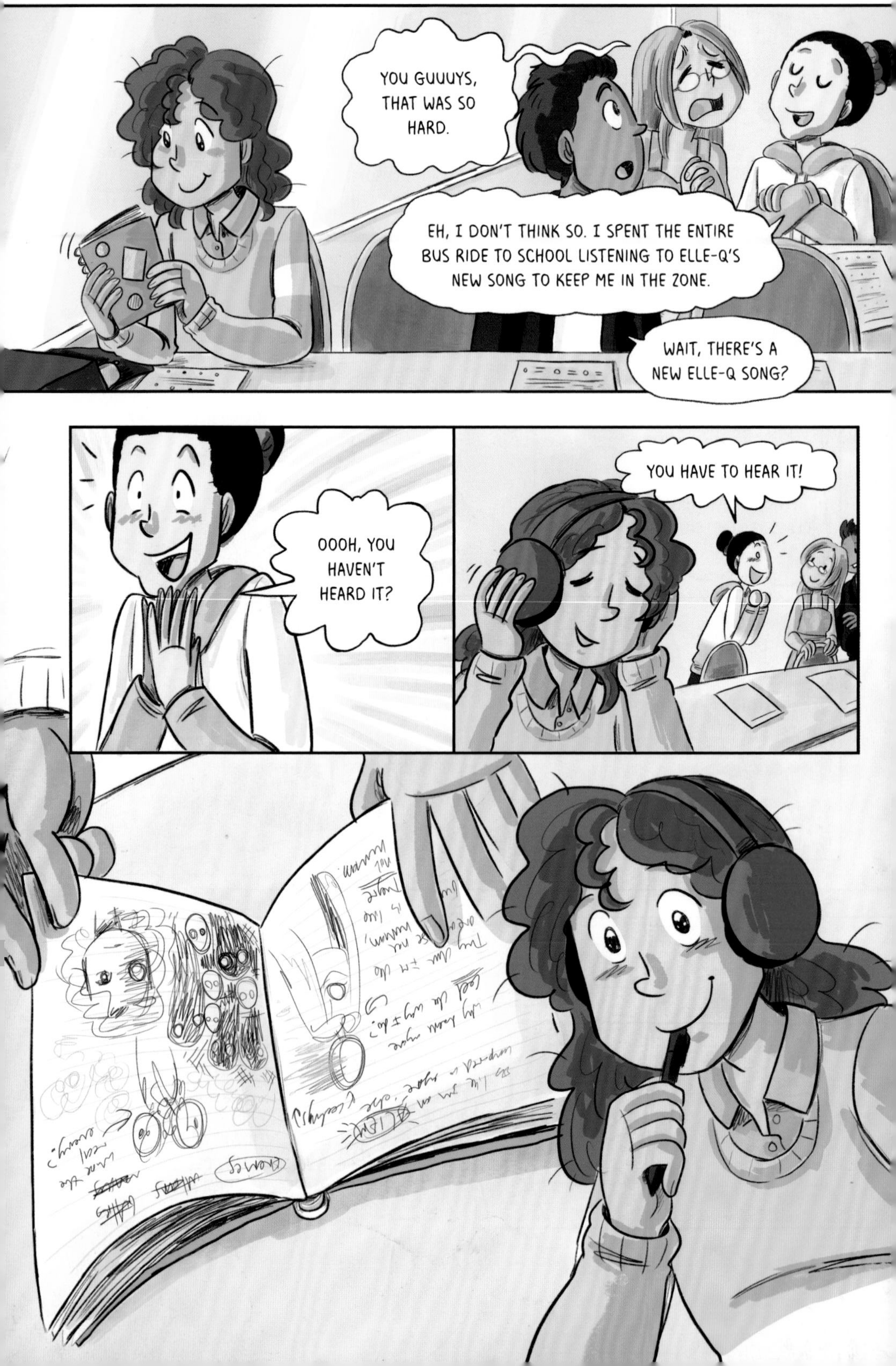
YOU GUUUYS, THAT WAS SO HARD.
EH, I DON'T THINK SO. I SPENT THE ENTIRE BUS RIDE TO SCHOOL LISTENING TO ELLE-Q'S NEW SONG TO KEEP ME IN THE ZONE.
WAIT, THERE'S A NEW ELLE-Q SONG?
OOOH, YOU HAVEN'T HEARD IT?
YOU HAVE TO HEAR IT!

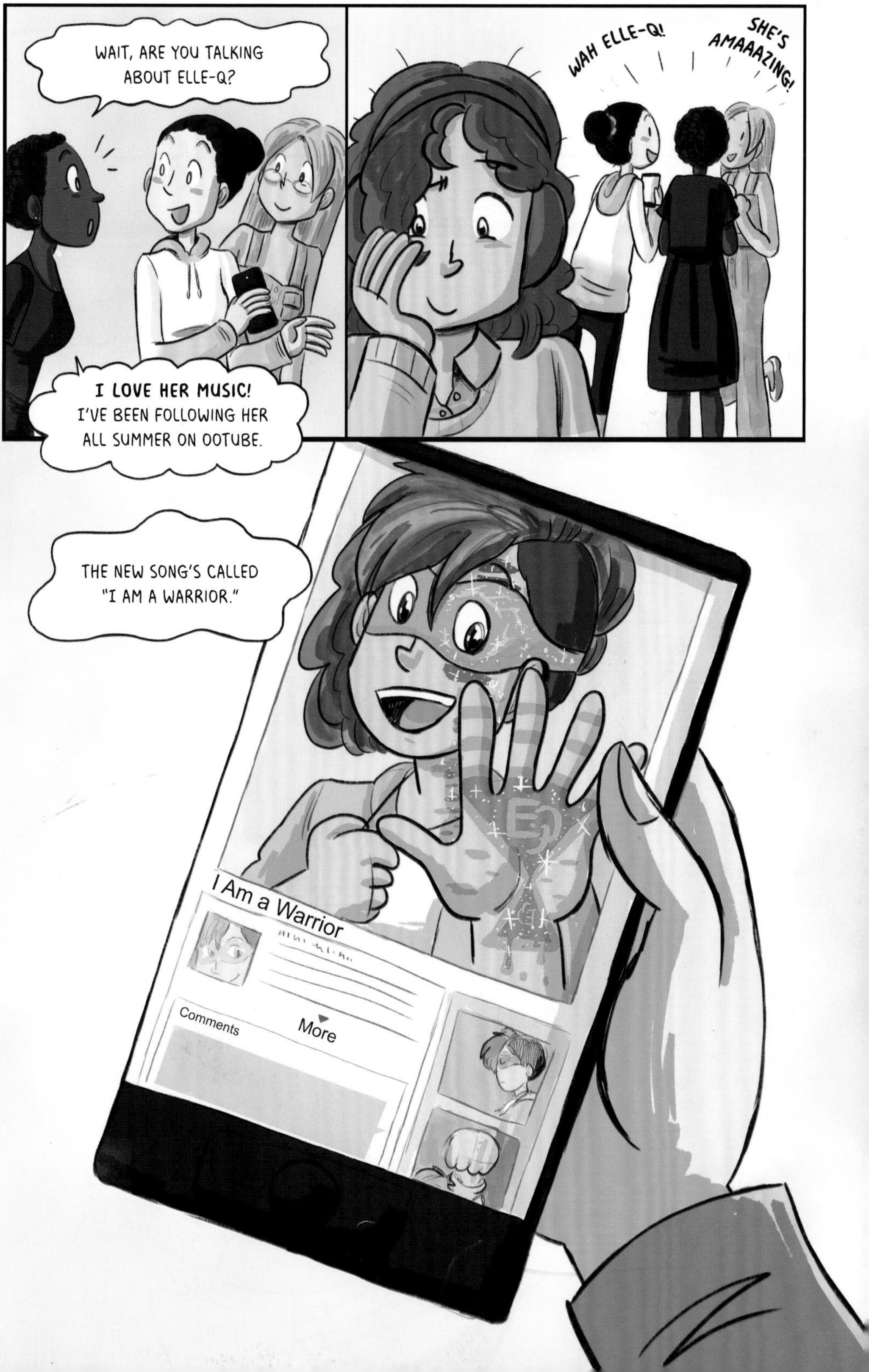
WAIT, ARE YOU TALKING ABOUT ELLE-Q?
I LOVE HER MUSIC! I'VE BEEN FOLLOWING HER ALL SUMMER ON OOTUBE.
WAH ELLE-Q!
SHE'S AMAAAZING!
THE NEW SONG'S CALLED "I AM A WARRIOR."
I Am a Warrior
Comments
More

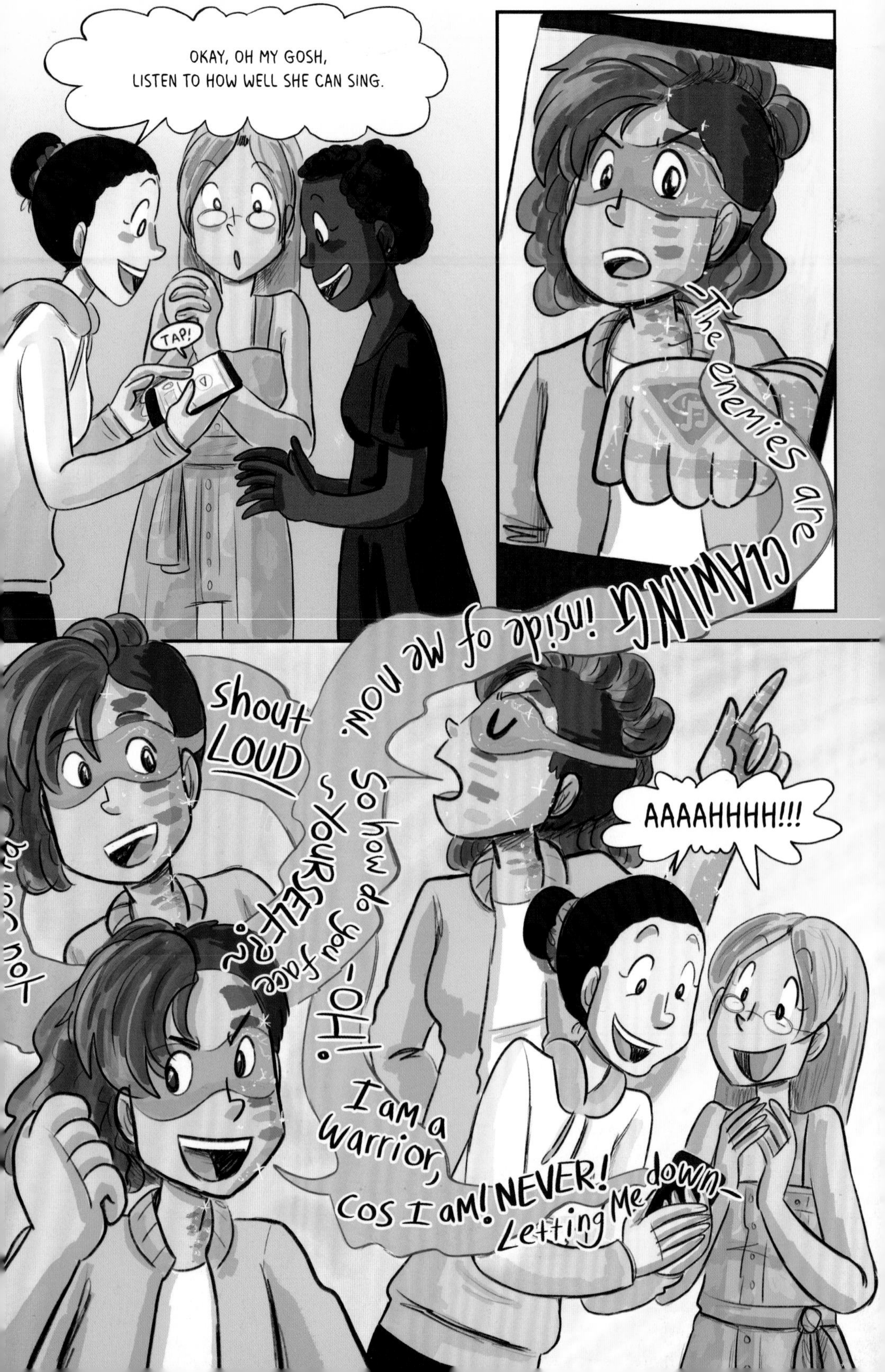
OKAY, OH MY GOSH,
LISTEN TO HOW WELL SHE CAN SING.
TAP!
The enemies are CLAWING inside of me now.
So how do you face ~YOURSELF??~
-OH!
shout LOUD
AAAAHHHH!!!
I am a warrior,
cos I am! NEVER! Letting Me down—

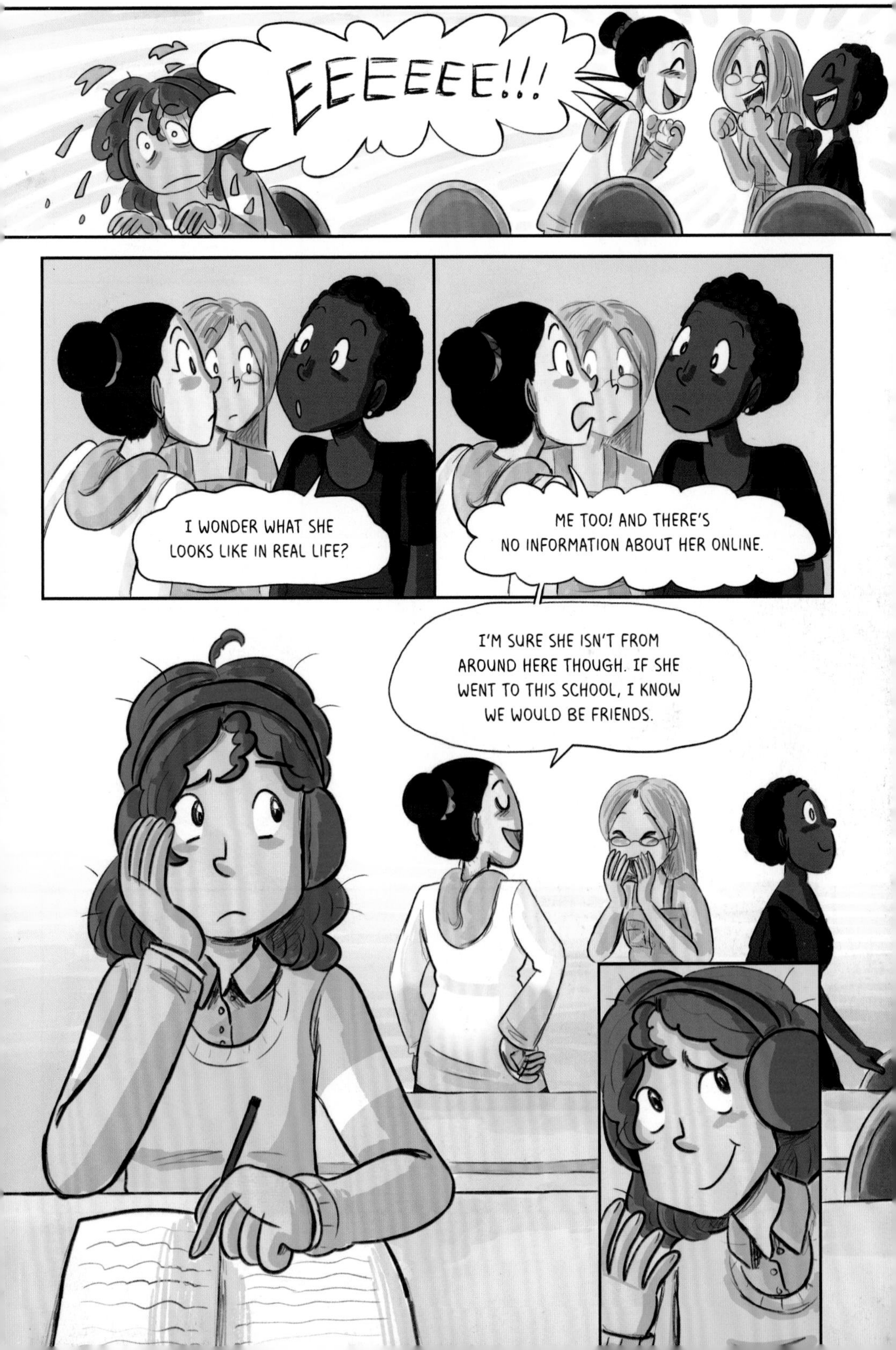
EEEEEE!!!
I WONDER WHAT SHE LOOKS LIKE IN REAL LIFE?
ME TOO! AND THERE'S NO INFORMATION ABOUT HER ONLINE.
I'M SURE SHE ISN'T FROM AROUND HERE THOUGH. IF SHE WENT TO THIS SCHOOL, I KNOW WE WOULD BE FRIENDS.

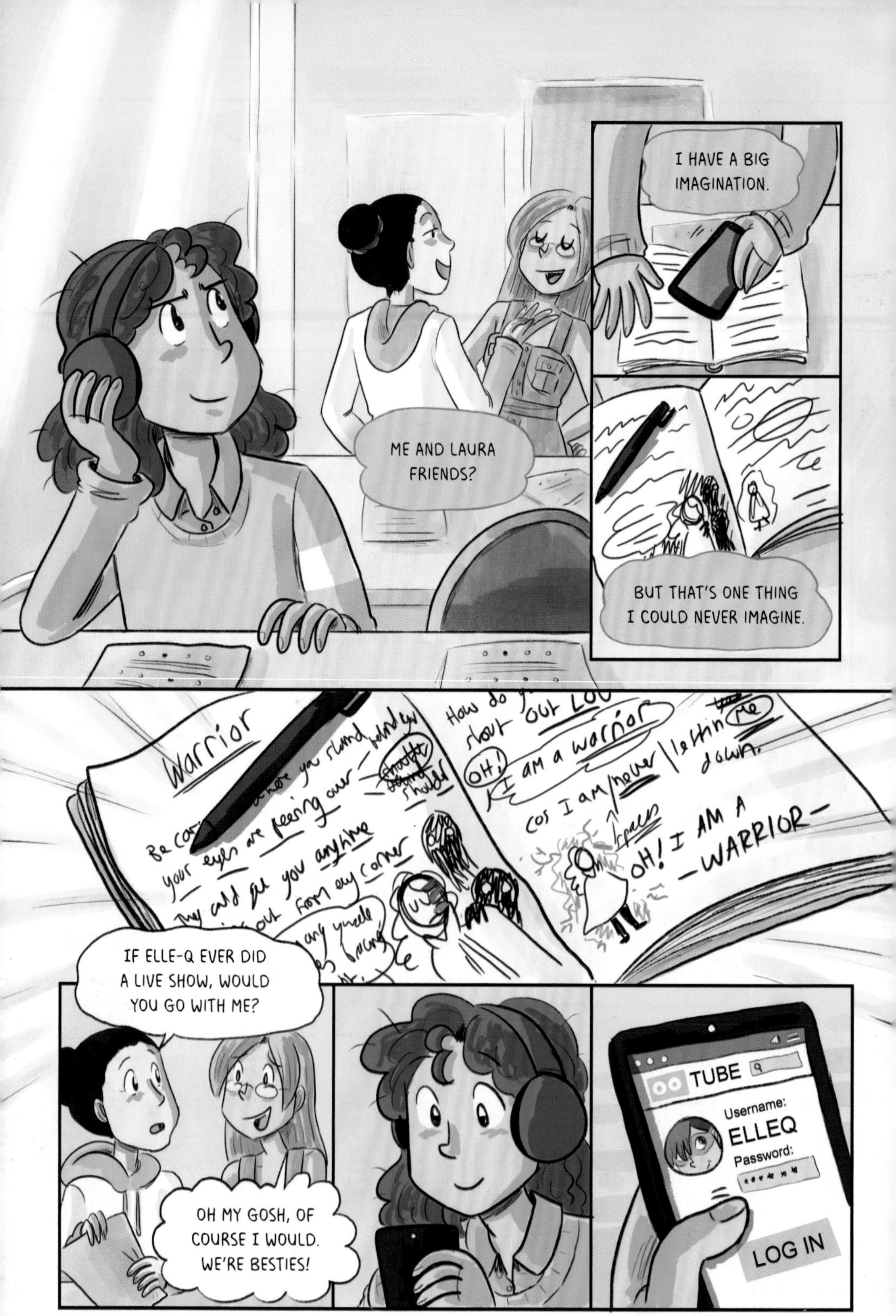
ME AND LAURA FRIENDS?
I HAVE A BIG IMAGINATION.
BUT THAT'S ONE THING I COULD NEVER IMAGINE.
Warrior
OH! I AM A WARRIOR
IF ELLE-Q EVER DID A LIVE SHOW, WOULD YOU GO WITH ME?
OH MY GOSH, OF COURSE I WOULD. WE'RE BESTIES!
TUBE
Username:
ELLEQ
Password:
LOG IN

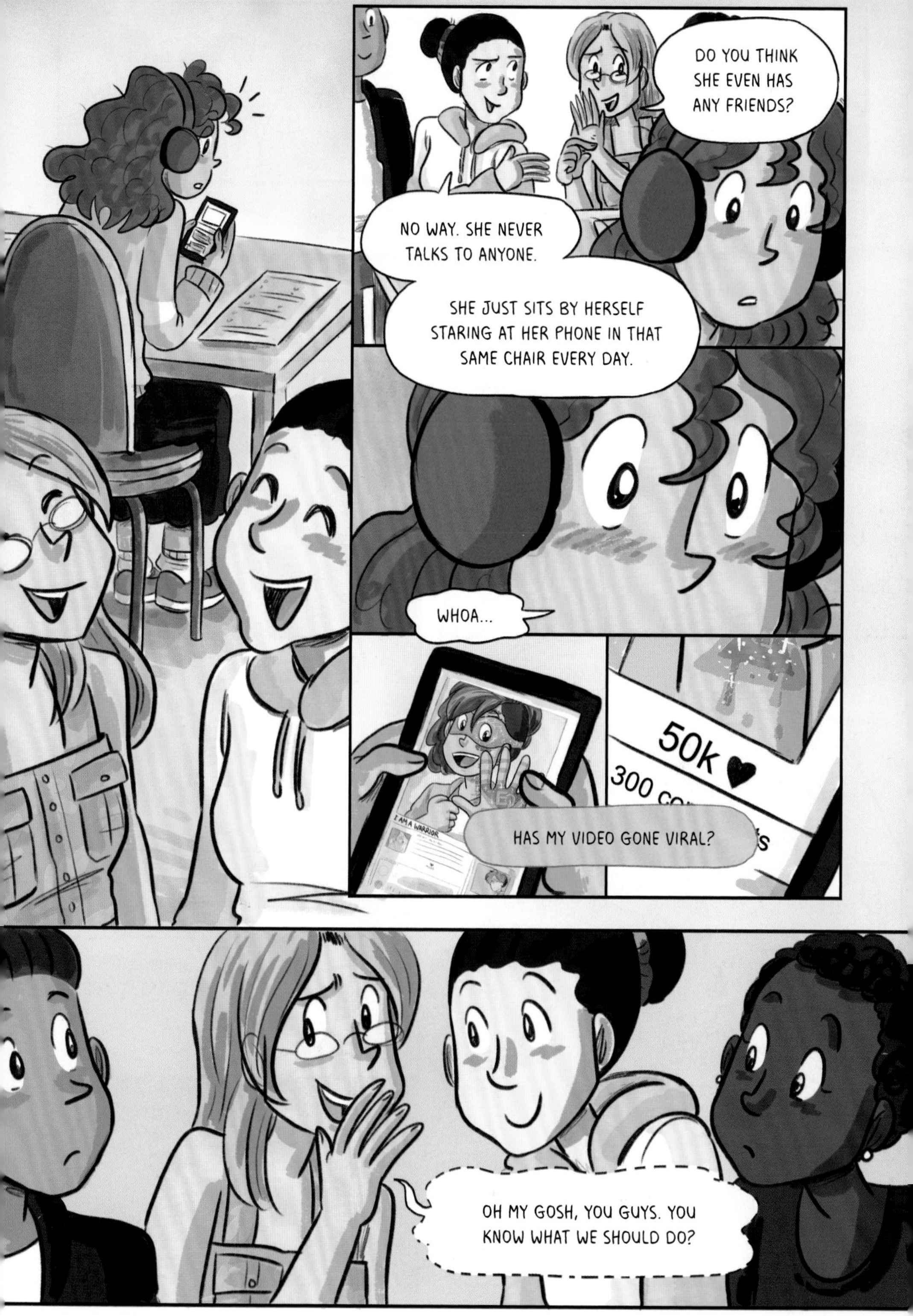
DO YOU THINK SHE EVEN HAS ANY FRIENDS?
NO WAY. SHE NEVER TALKS TO ANYONE.
SHE JUST SITS BY HERSELF STARING AT HER PHONE IN THAT SAME CHAIR EVERY DAY.
WHOA...
50K ♥
HAS MY VIDEO GONE VIRAL?
OH MY GOSH, YOU GUYS. YOU KNOW WHAT WE SHOULD DO?

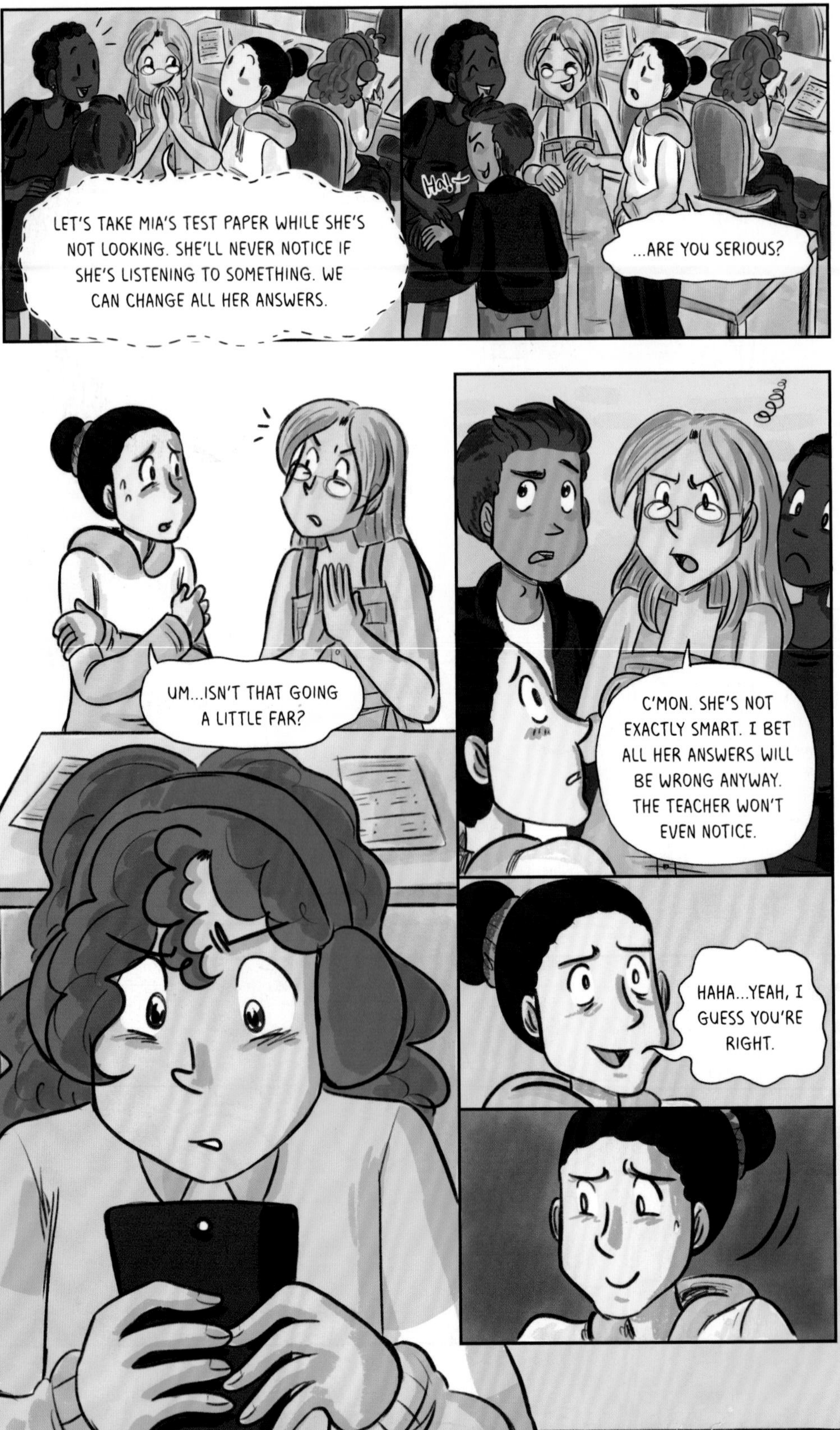
LET'S TAKE MIA'S TEST PAPER WHILE SHE'S NOT LOOKING. SHE'LL NEVER NOTICE IF SHE'S LISTENING TO SOMETHING. WE CAN CHANGE ALL HER ANSWERS.
Ha!
...ARE YOU SERIOUS?
UM...ISN'T THAT GOING A LITTLE FAR?
C'MON. SHE'S NOT EXACTLY SMART. I BET ALL HER ANSWERS WILL BE WRONG ANYWAY. THE TEACHER WON'T EVEN NOTICE.
HAHA...YEAH, I GUESS YOU'RE RIGHT.

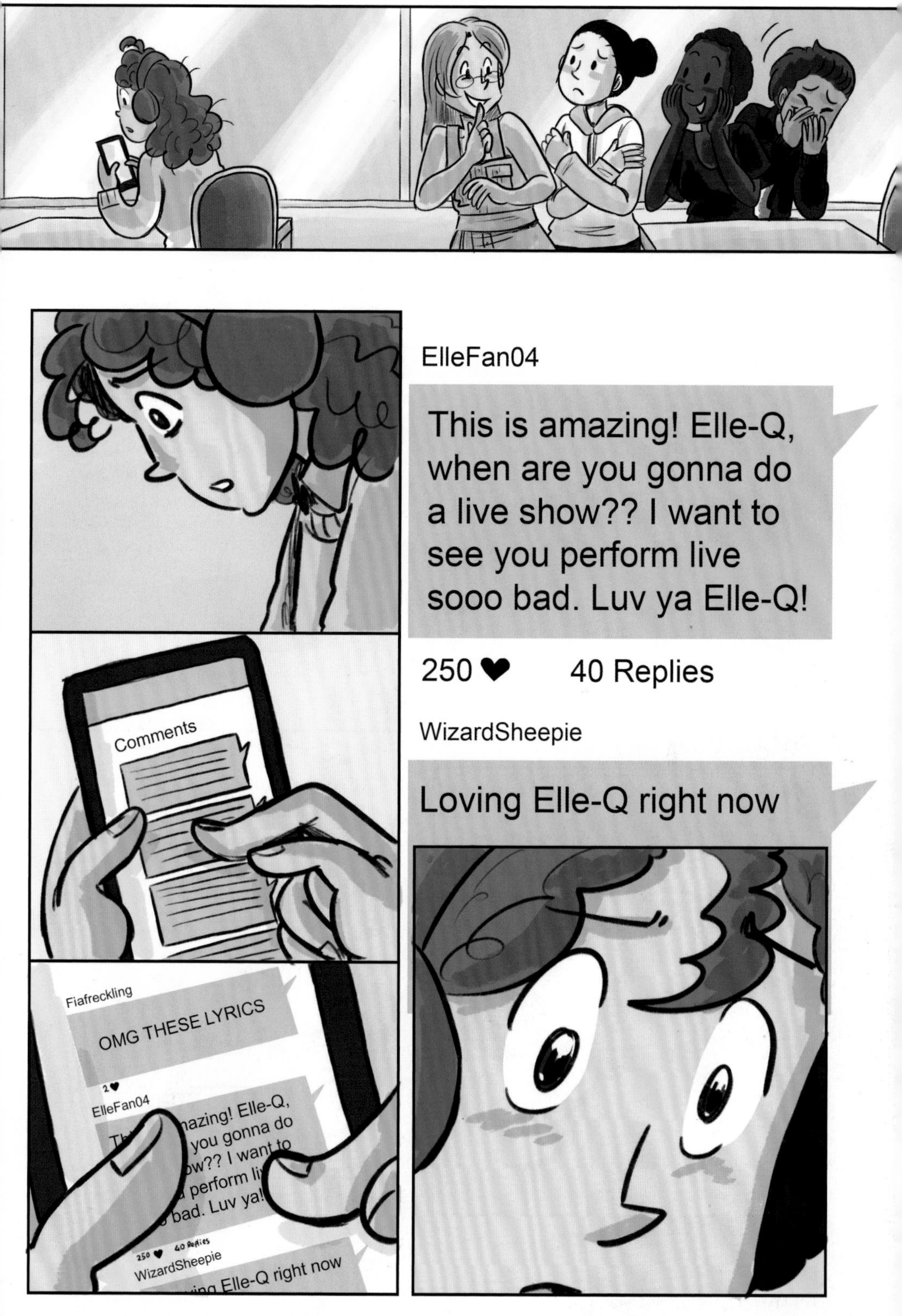

Comments
ElleFan04
This is amazing! Elle-Q, when are you gonna do a live show?? I want to see you perform live sooo bad. Luv ya Elle-Q!
250 ❤ 40 Replies
WizardSheepie
Loving Elle-Q right now
Fiafreckling
OMG THESE LYRICS
2 ❤
ElleFan04
250 ❤ 40 Replies
WizardSheepie

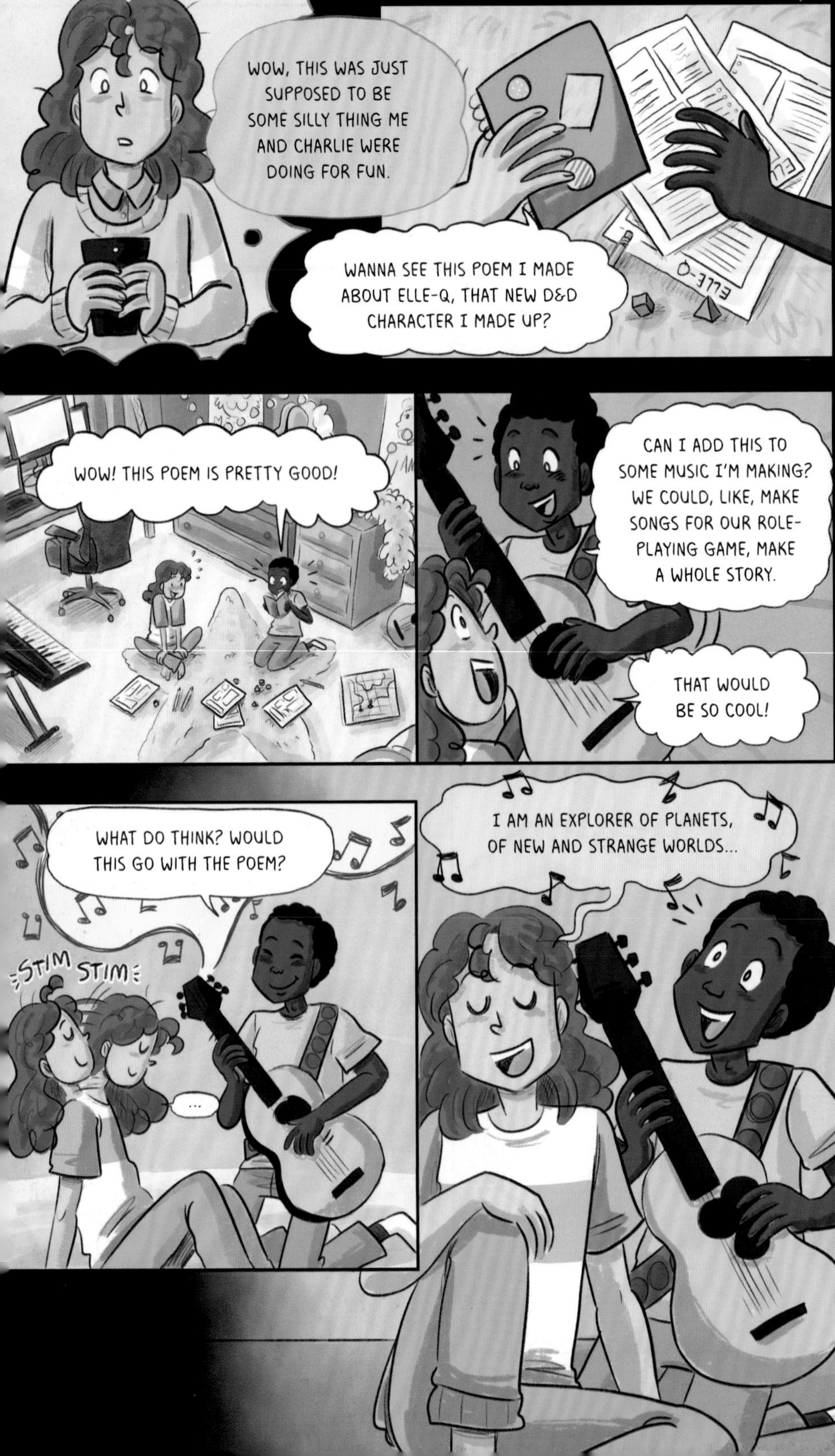
WOW, THIS WAS JUST SUPPOSED TO BE SOME SILLY THING ME AND CHARLIE WERE DOING FOR FUN.
WANNA SEE THIS POEM I MADE ABOUT ELLE-Q, THAT NEW D&D CHARACTER I MADE UP?
ELLE-Q
WOW! THIS POEM IS PRETTY GOOD!
CAN I ADD THIS TO SOME MUSIC I'M MAKING? WE COULD, LIKE, MAKE SONGS FOR OUR ROLE-PLAYING GAME, MAKE A WHOLE STORY.
THAT WOULD BE SO COOL!
WHAT DO THINK? WOULD THIS GO WITH THE POEM?
STIM STIM
...
I AM AN EXPLORER OF PLANETS, OF NEW AND STRANGE WORLDS...

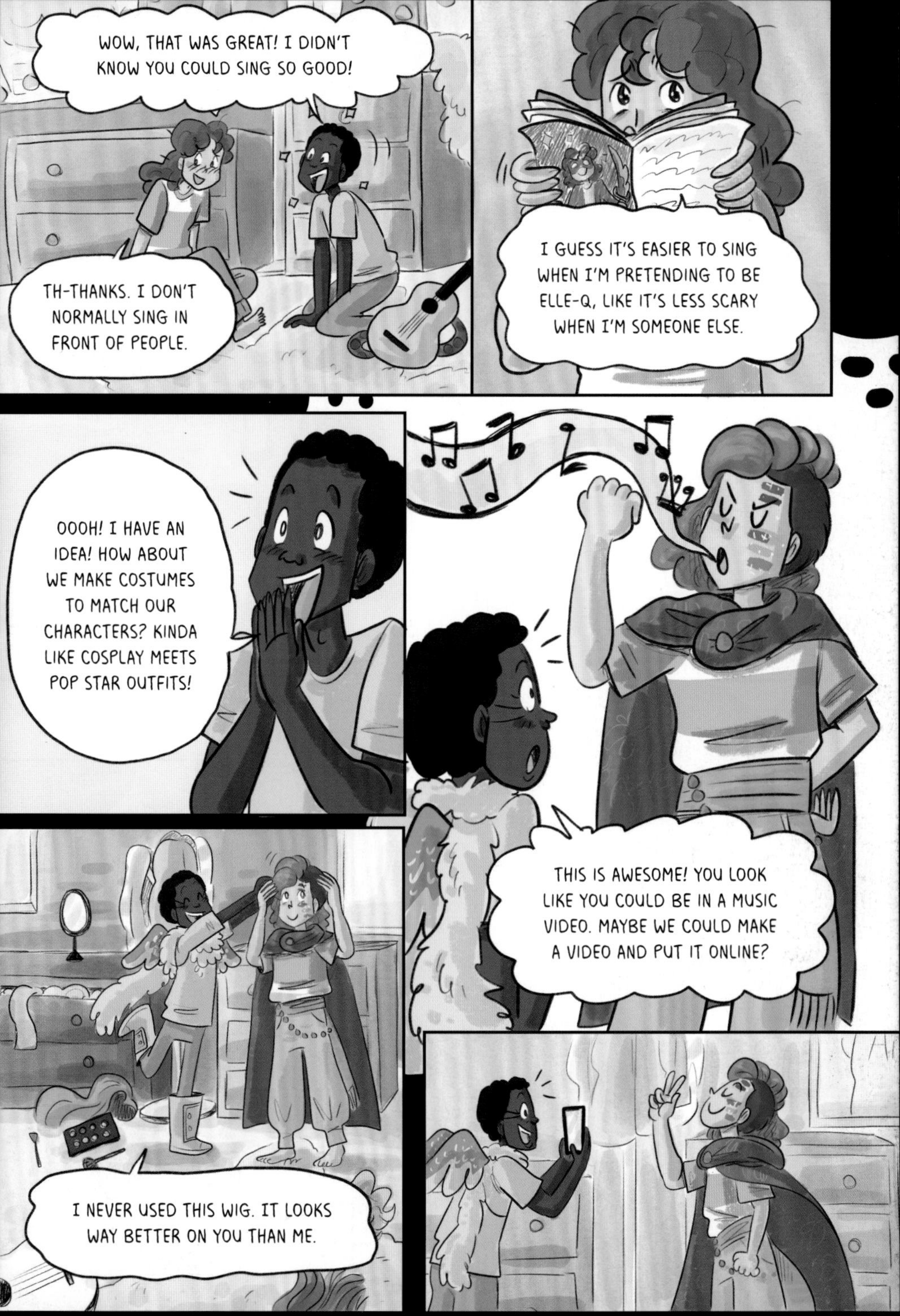
WOW, THAT WAS GREAT! I DIDN'T KNOW YOU COULD SING SO GOOD!
TH-THANKS. I DON'T NORMALLY SING IN FRONT OF PEOPLE.
I GUESS IT'S EASIER TO SING WHEN I'M PRETENDING TO BE ELLE-Q, LIKE IT'S LESS SCARY WHEN I'M SOMEONE ELSE.
OOOH! I HAVE AN IDEA! HOW ABOUT WE MAKE COSTUMES TO MATCH OUR CHARACTERS? KINDA LIKE COSPLAY MEETS POP STAR OUTFITS!
THIS IS AWESOME! YOU LOOK LIKE YOU COULD BE IN A MUSIC VIDEO. MAYBE WE COULD MAKE A VIDEO AND PUT IT ONLINE?
I NEVER USED THIS WIG. IT LOOKS WAY BETTER ON YOU THAN ME.

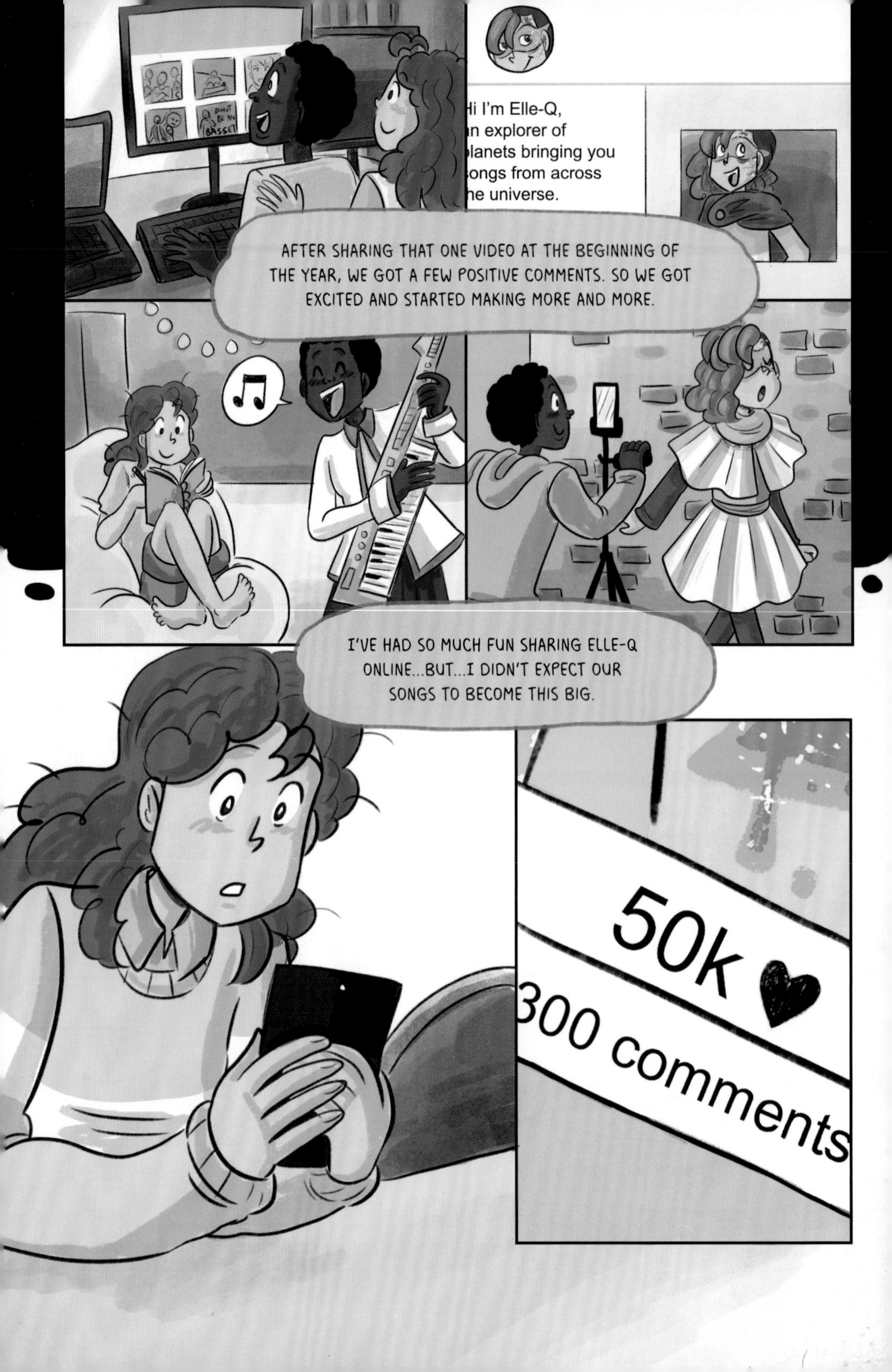

i I'm Elle-Q,
n explorer of
lanets bringing you
ongs from across
e universe.
AFTER SHARING THAT ONE VIDEO AT THE BEGINNING OF THE YEAR, WE GOT A FEW POSITIVE COMMENTS. SO WE GOT EXCITED AND STARTED MAKING MORE AND MORE.
I'VE HAD SO MUCH FUN SHARING ELLE-Q ONLINE...BUT...I DIDN'T EXPECT OUR SONGS TO BECOME THIS BIG.
50k
300 comments

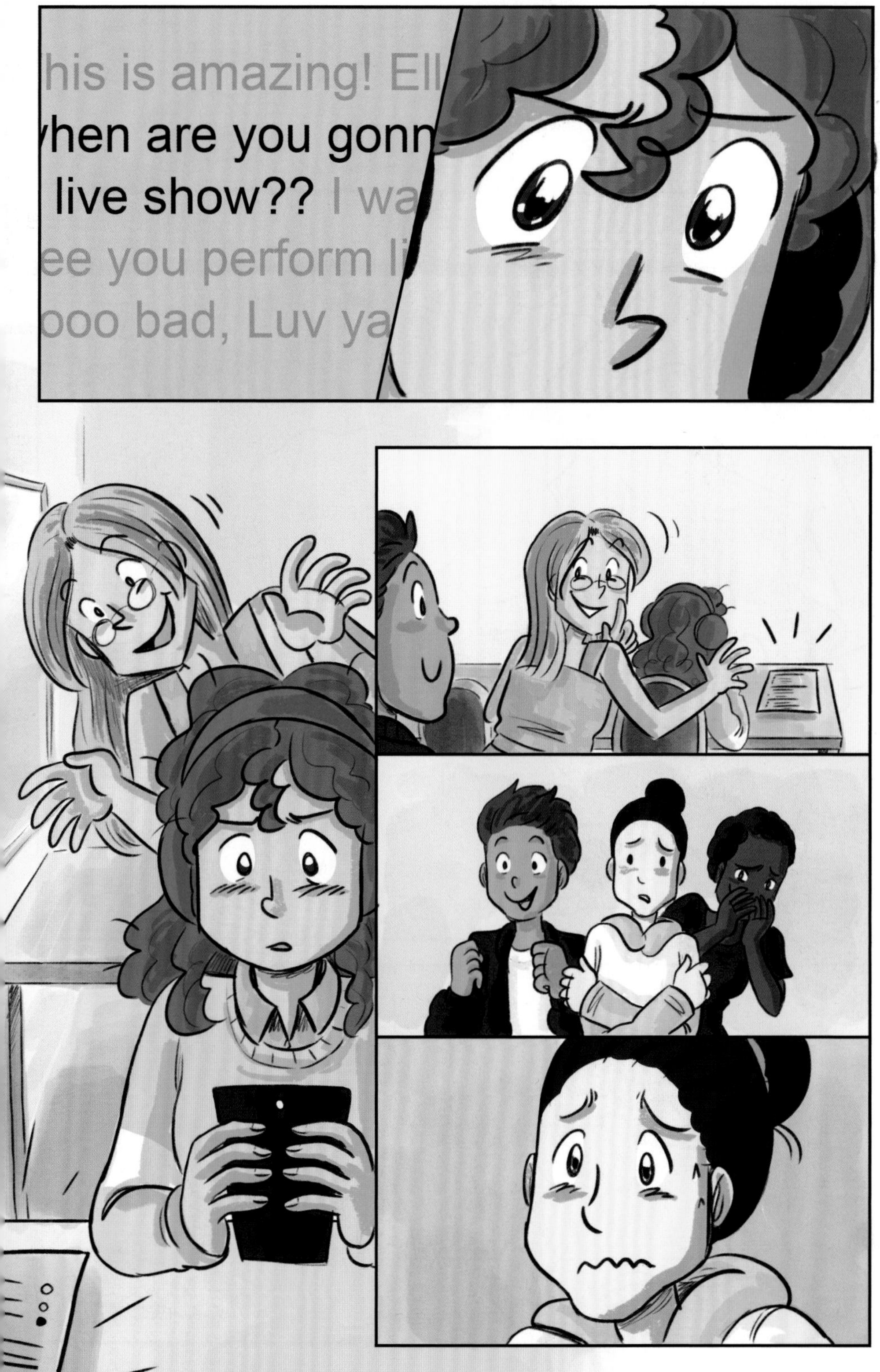
his is amazing! Ell
hen are you gonn
live show?? I wa
ee you perform li
ooo bad, Luv ya

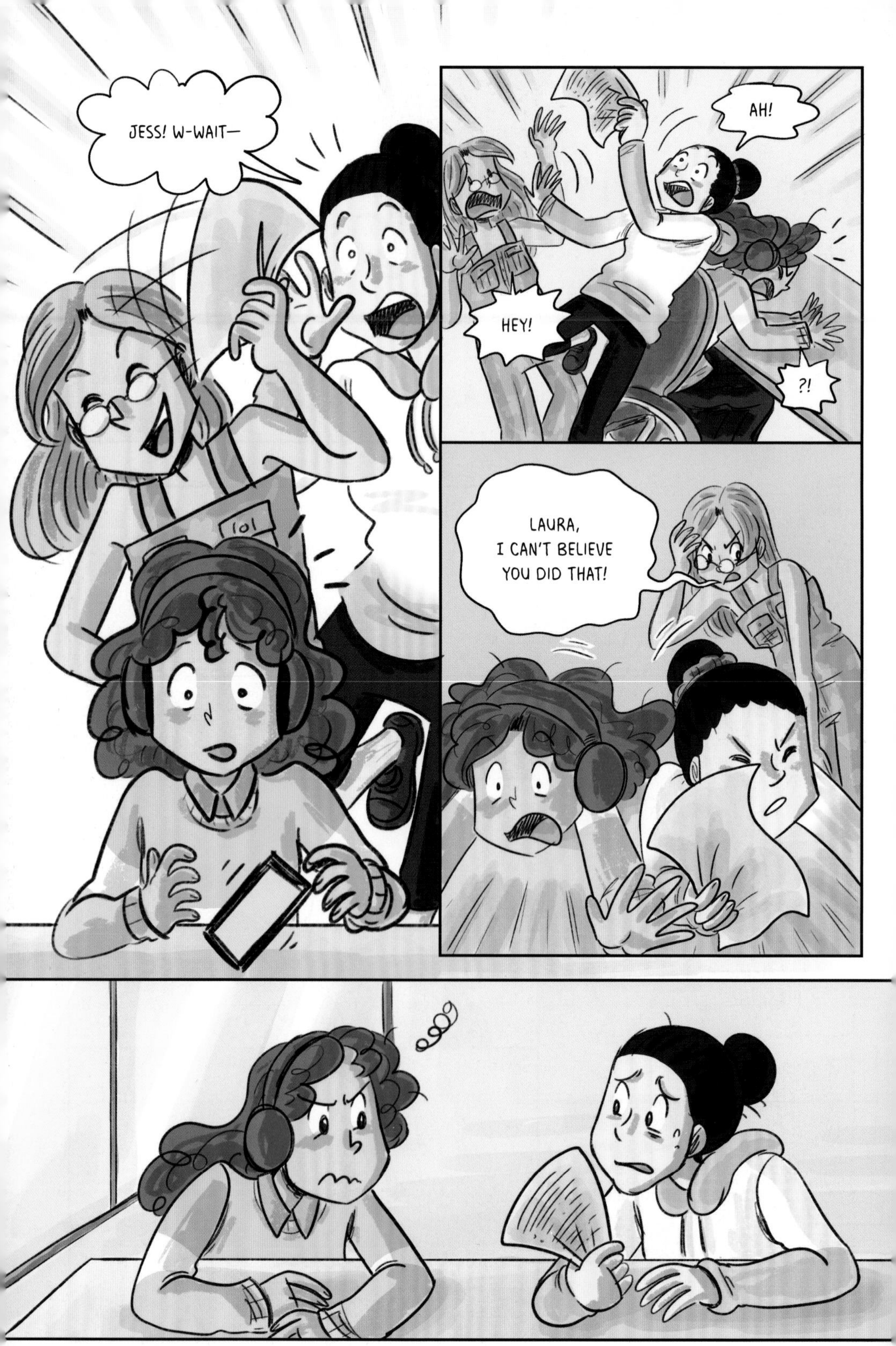
JESS! W-WAIT—
AH!
HEY!
?!
LAURA,
I CAN'T BELIEVE
YOU DID THAT!

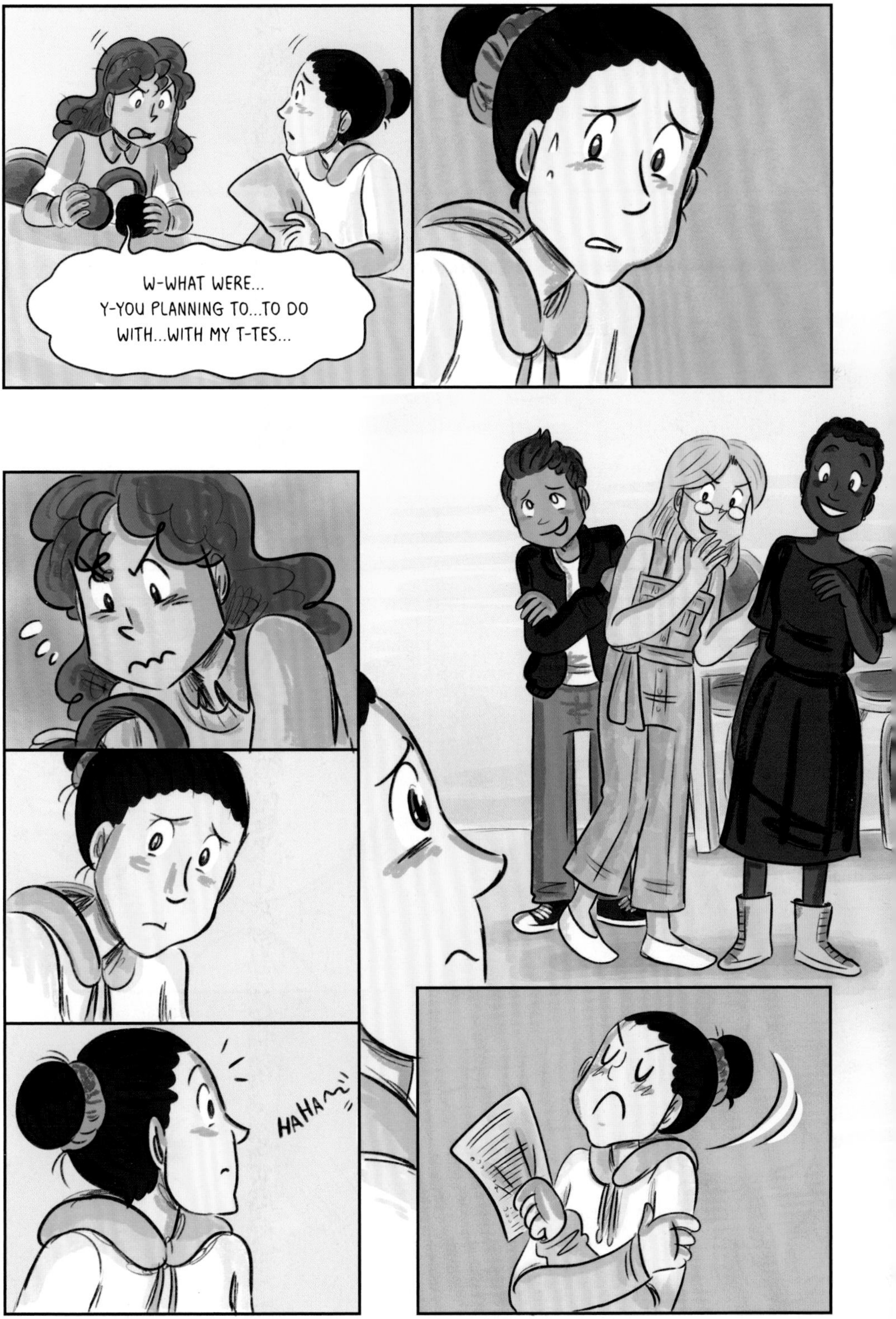
W-WHAT WERE... Y-YOU PLANNING TO...TO DO WITH...WITH MY T-TES...
HAHA

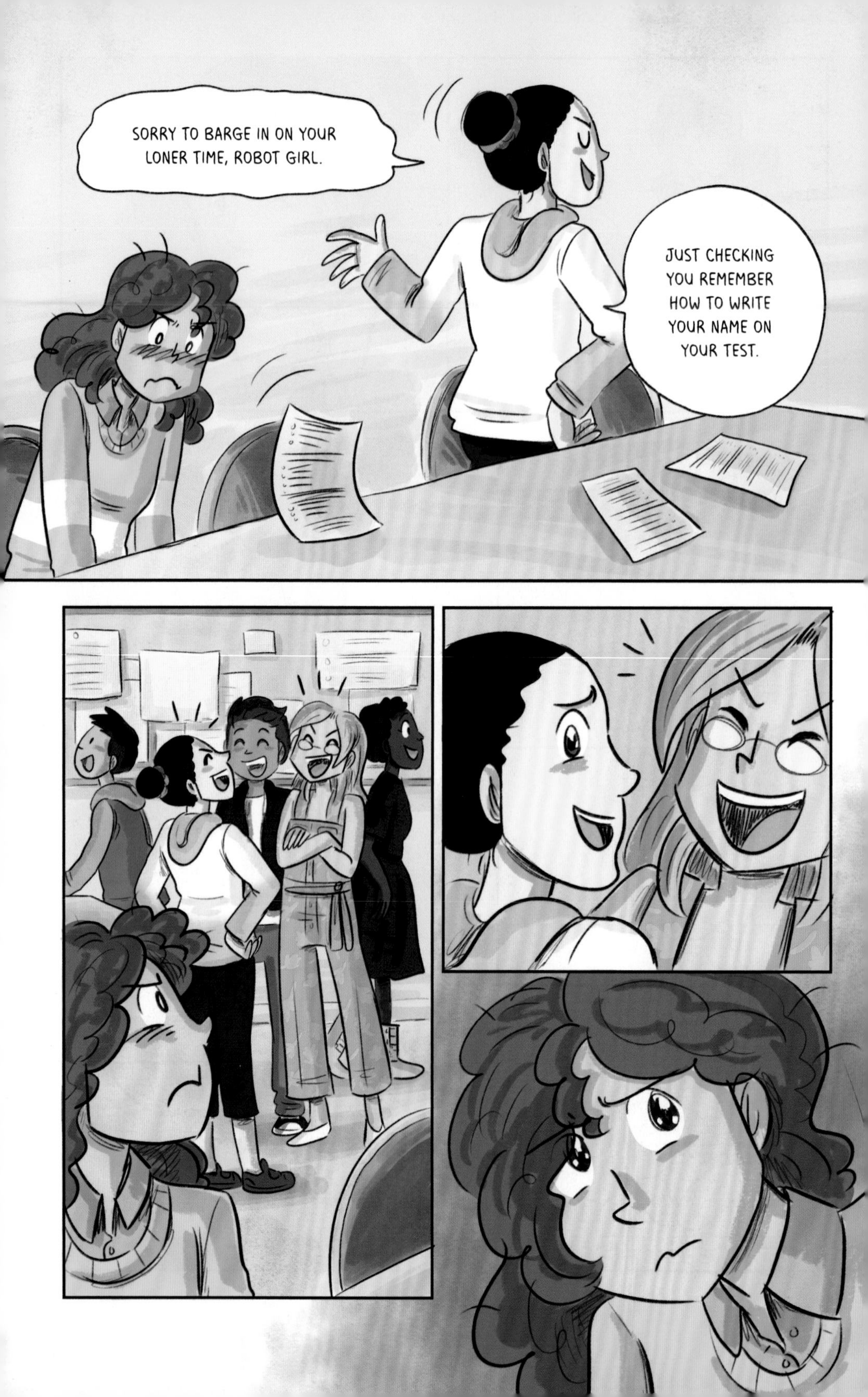
SORRY TO BARGE IN ON YOUR LONER TIME, ROBOT GIRL.
JUST CHECKING YOU REMEMBER HOW TO WRITE YOUR NAME ON YOUR TEST.

# CHAPTER TWO

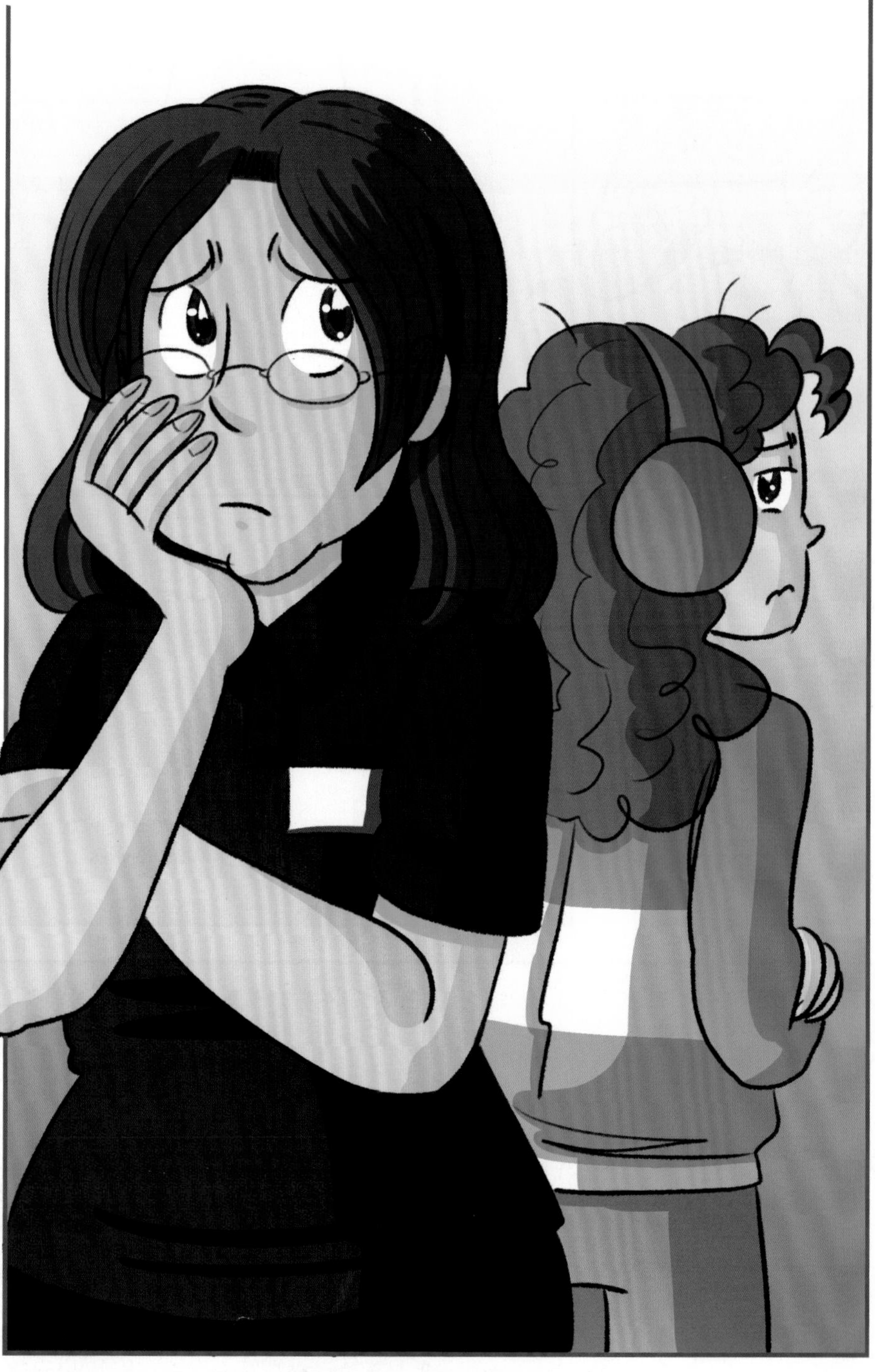

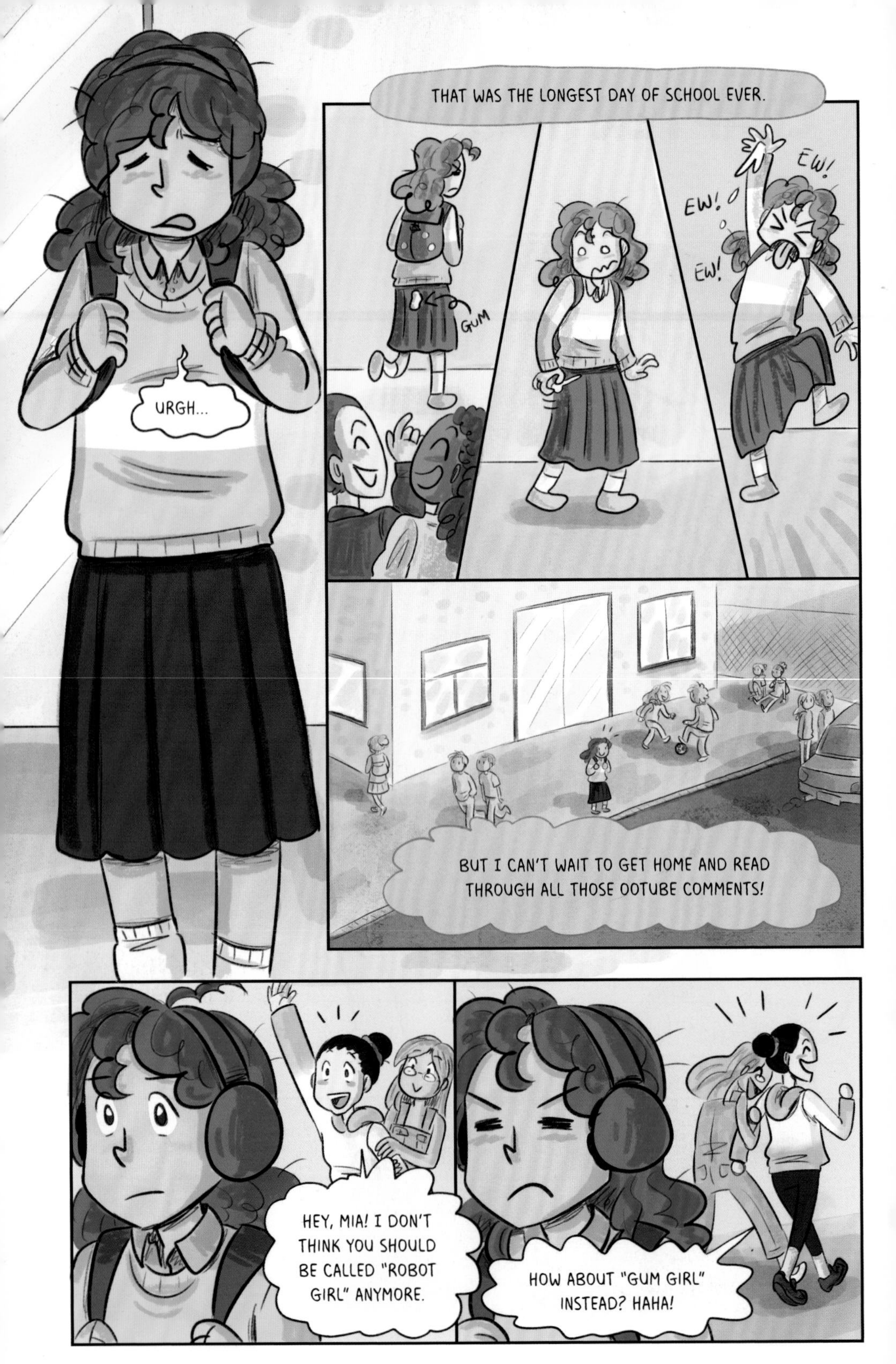
URGH...
THAT WAS THE LONGEST DAY OF SCHOOL EVER.
GUM
EW!
EW!
EW!
BUT I CAN'T WAIT TO GET HOME AND READ THROUGH ALL THOSE OOTUBE COMMENTS!
HEY, MIA! I DON'T THINK YOU SHOULD BE CALLED "ROBOT GIRL" ANYMORE.
HOW ABOUT "GUM GIRL" INSTEAD? HAHA!

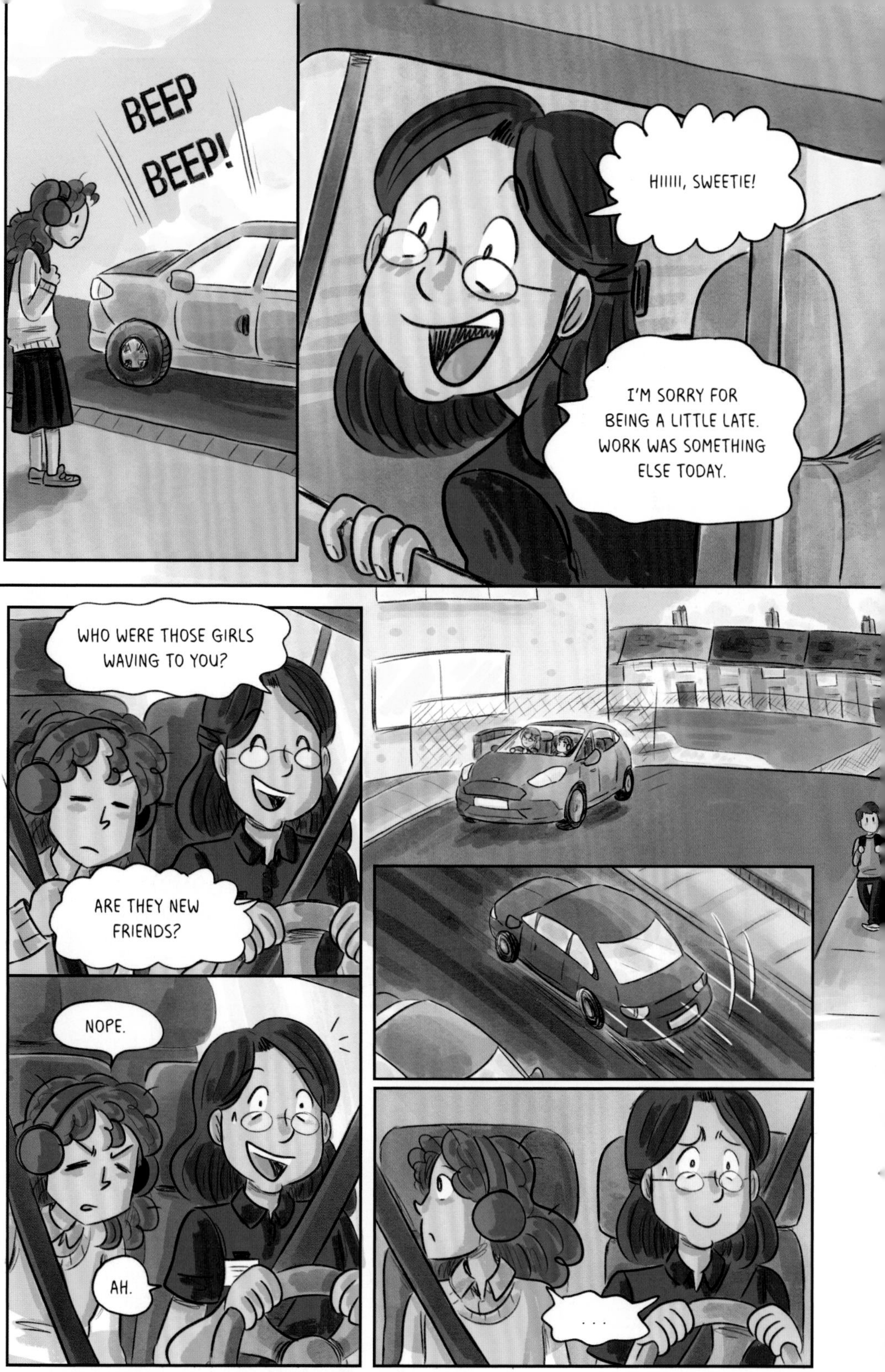
BEEP BEEP!
HIIIII, SWEETIE!
I'M SORRY FOR BEING A LITTLE LATE. WORK WAS SOMETHING ELSE TODAY.
WHO WERE THOSE GIRLS WAVING TO YOU?
ARE THEY NEW FRIENDS?
NOPE.
AH.
. . .

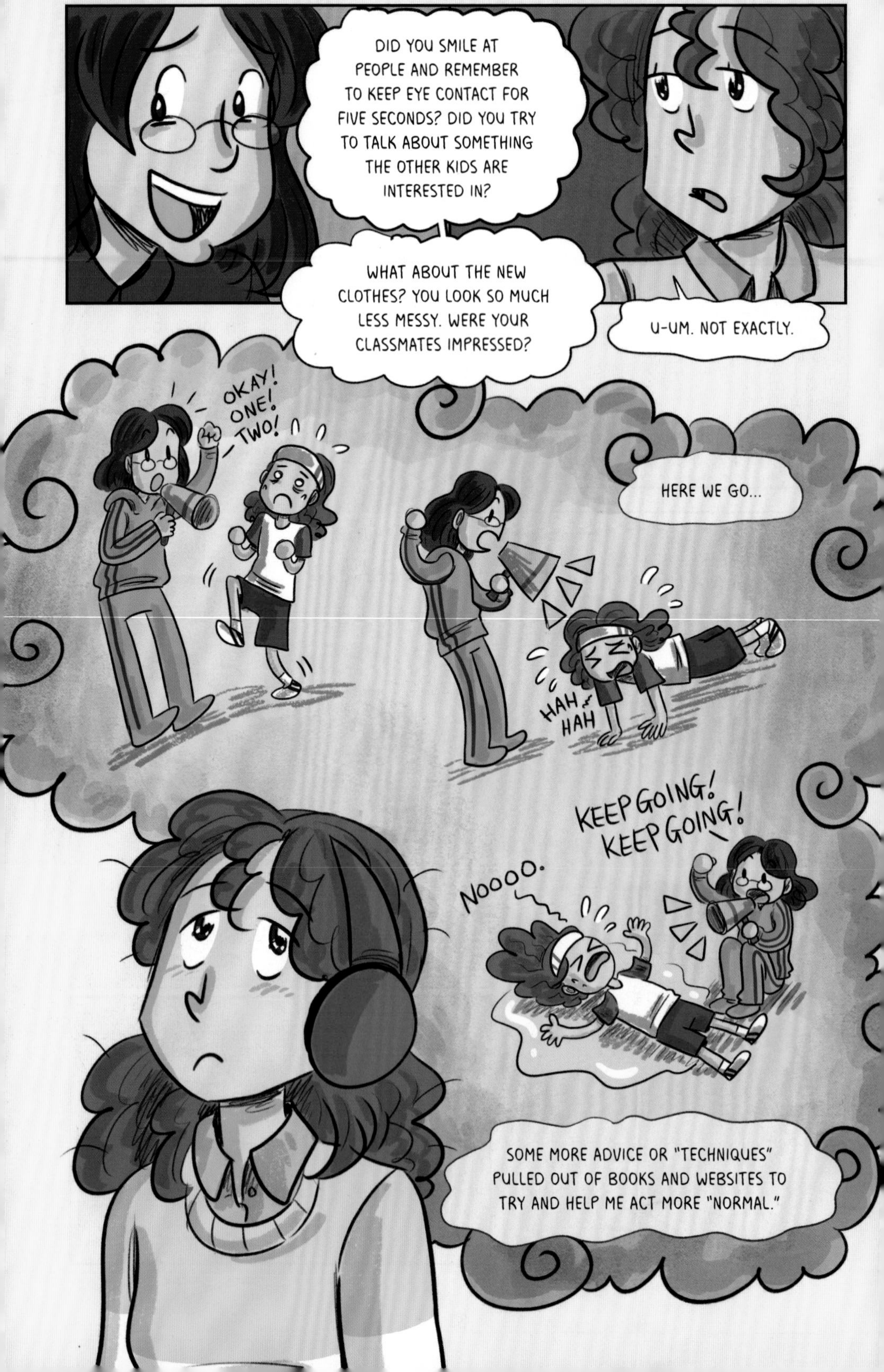

DID YOU SMILE AT PEOPLE AND REMEMBER TO KEEP EYE CONTACT FOR FIVE SECONDS? DID YOU TRY TO TALK ABOUT SOMETHING THE OTHER KIDS ARE INTERESTED IN?
WHAT ABOUT THE NEW CLOTHES? YOU LOOK SO MUCH LESS MESSY. WERE YOUR CLASSMATES IMPRESSED?
U-UM. NOT EXACTLY.
OKAY! ONE! TWO!
HERE WE GO...
HAH HAH
KEEP GOING! KEEP GOING!
NOOOO.
SOME MORE ADVICE OR "TECHNIQUES" PULLED OUT OF BOOKS AND WEBSITES TO TRY AND HELP ME ACT MORE "NORMAL."

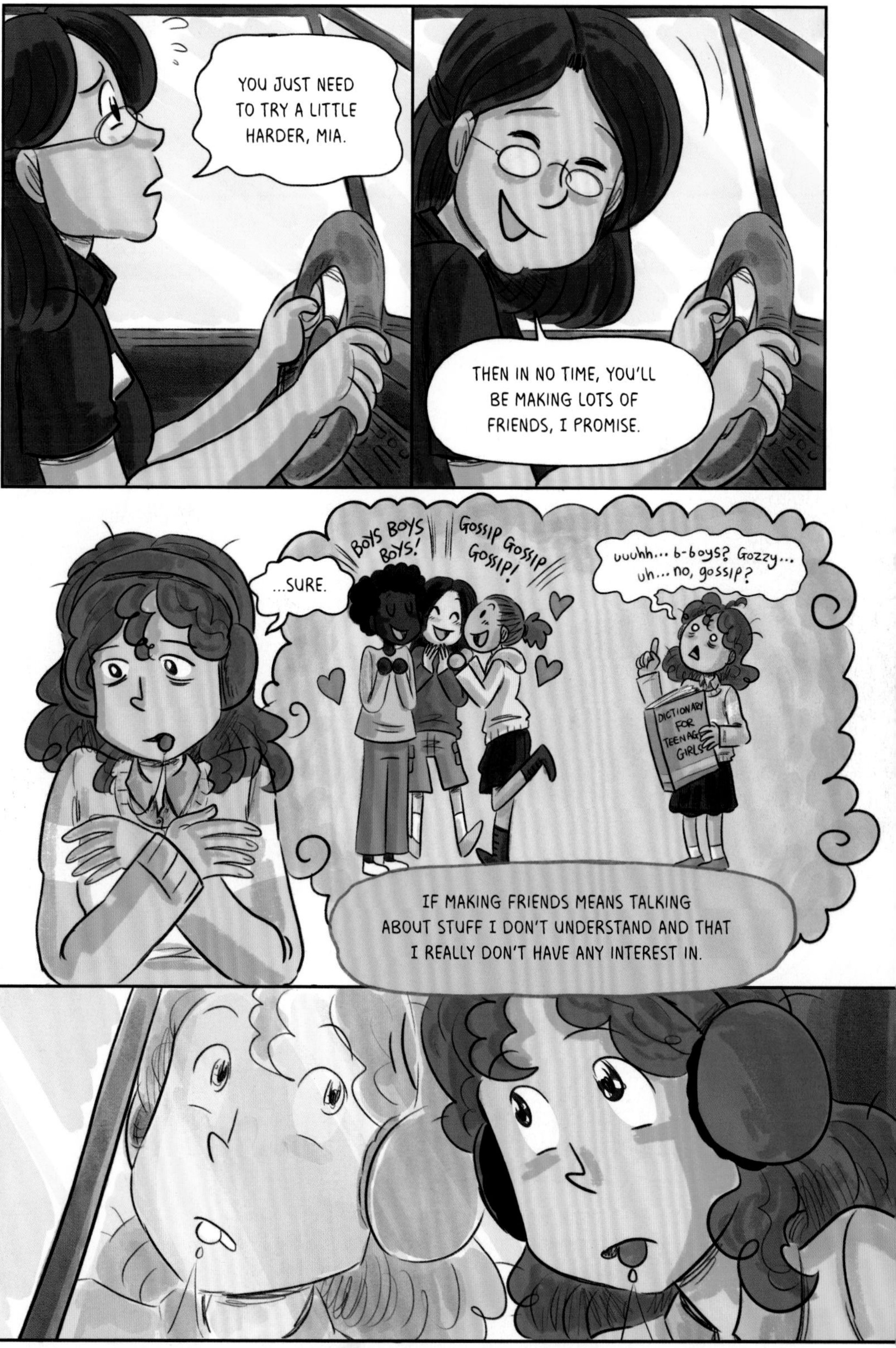
YOU JUST NEED TO TRY A LITTLE HARDER, MIA.
THEN IN NO TIME, YOU'LL BE MAKING LOTS OF FRIENDS, I PROMISE.
...SURE.
BOYS BOYS BOYS!
GOSSIP GOSSIP GOSSIP!
uuuhh... b-boys? Gozzy... uh... no, gossip?
DICTIONARY FOR TEENAGE GIRLS
IF MAKING FRIENDS MEANS TALKING ABOUT STUFF I DON'T UNDERSTAND AND THAT I REALLY DON'T HAVE ANY INTEREST IN.

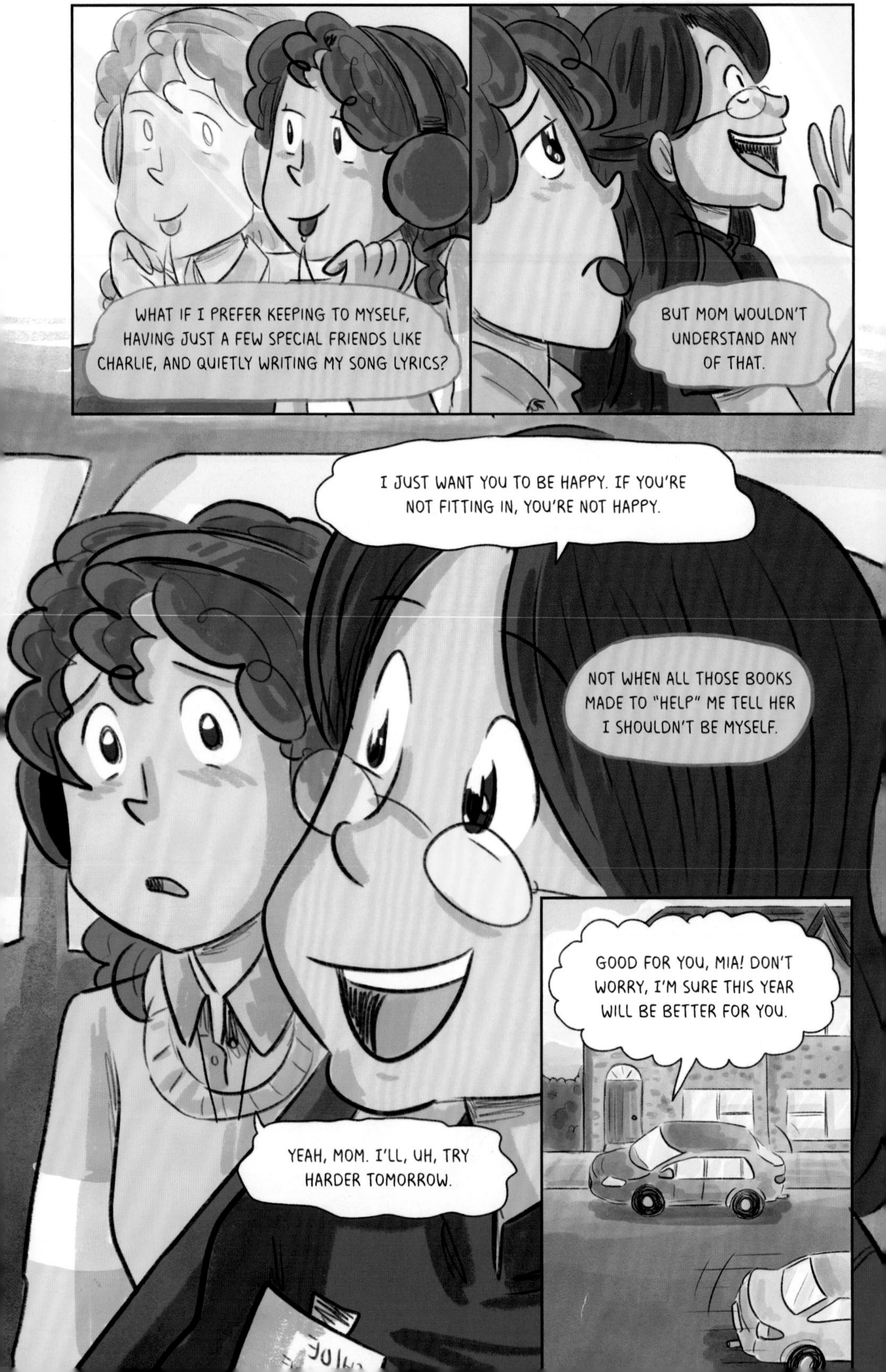

WHAT IF I PREFER KEEPING TO MYSELF, HAVING JUST A FEW SPECIAL FRIENDS LIKE CHARLIE, AND QUIETLY WRITING MY SONG LYRICS?
BUT MOM WOULDN'T UNDERSTAND ANY OF THAT.
I JUST WANT YOU TO BE HAPPY. IF YOU'RE NOT FITTING IN, YOU'RE NOT HAPPY.
NOT WHEN ALL THOSE BOOKS MADE TO "HELP" ME TELL HER I SHOULDN'T BE MYSELF.
YEAH, MOM. I'LL, UH, TRY HARDER TOMORROW.
GOOD FOR YOU, MIA! DON'T WORRY, I'M SURE THIS YEAR WILL BE BETTER FOR YOU.

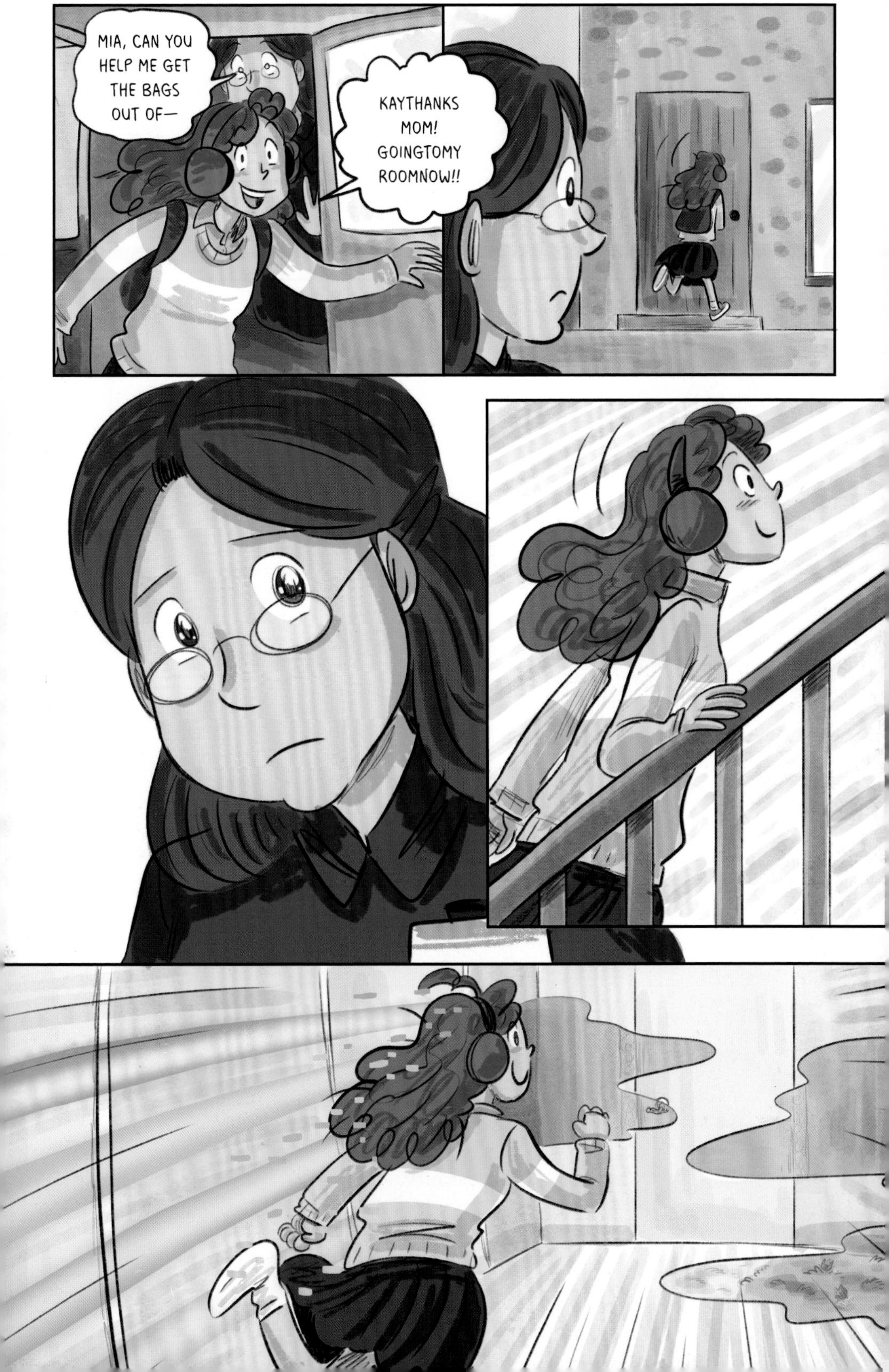
MIA, CAN YOU HELP ME GET THE BAGS OUT OF—
KAYTHANKS MOM! GOINGTOMY ROOMNOW!!

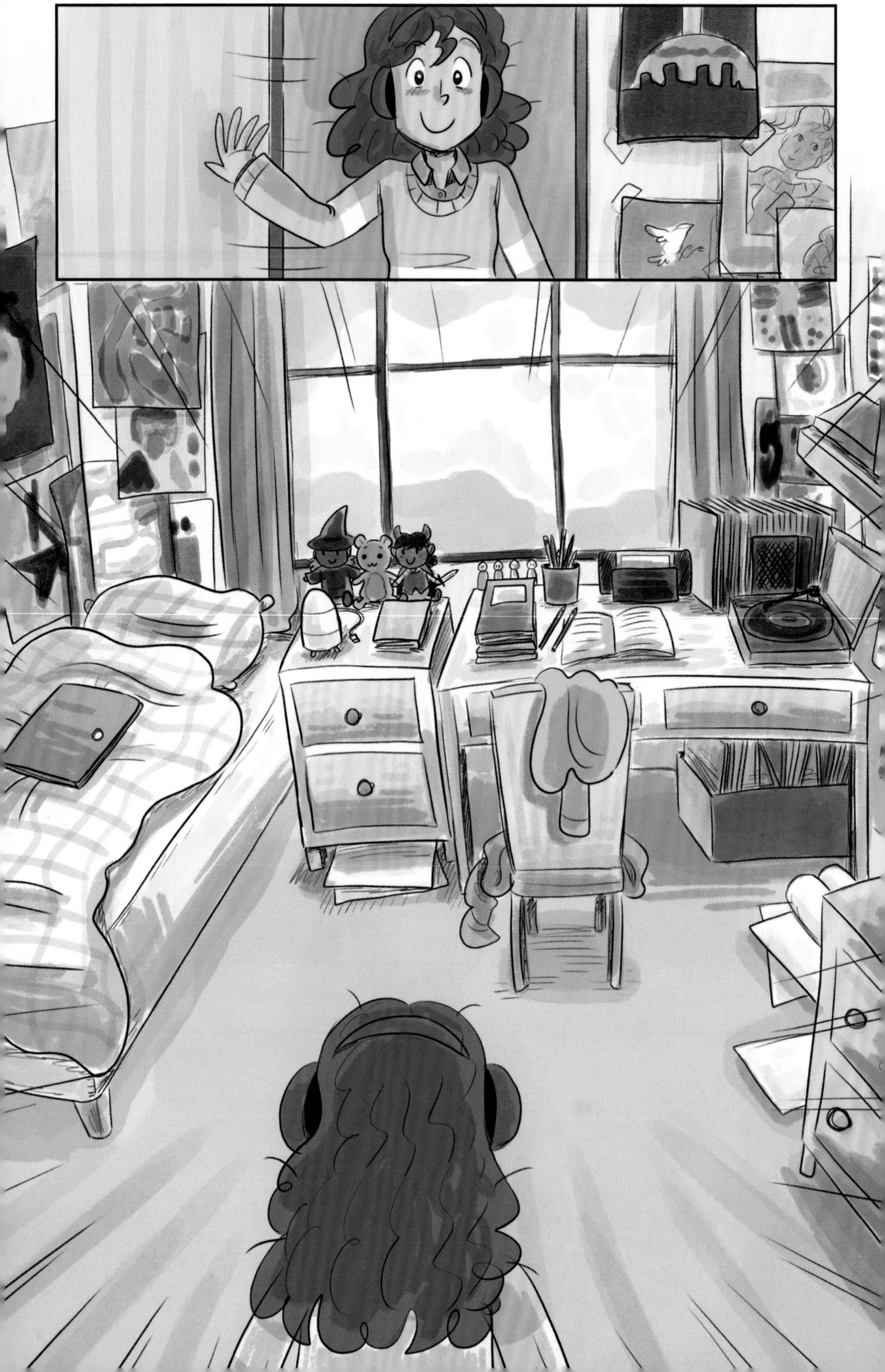

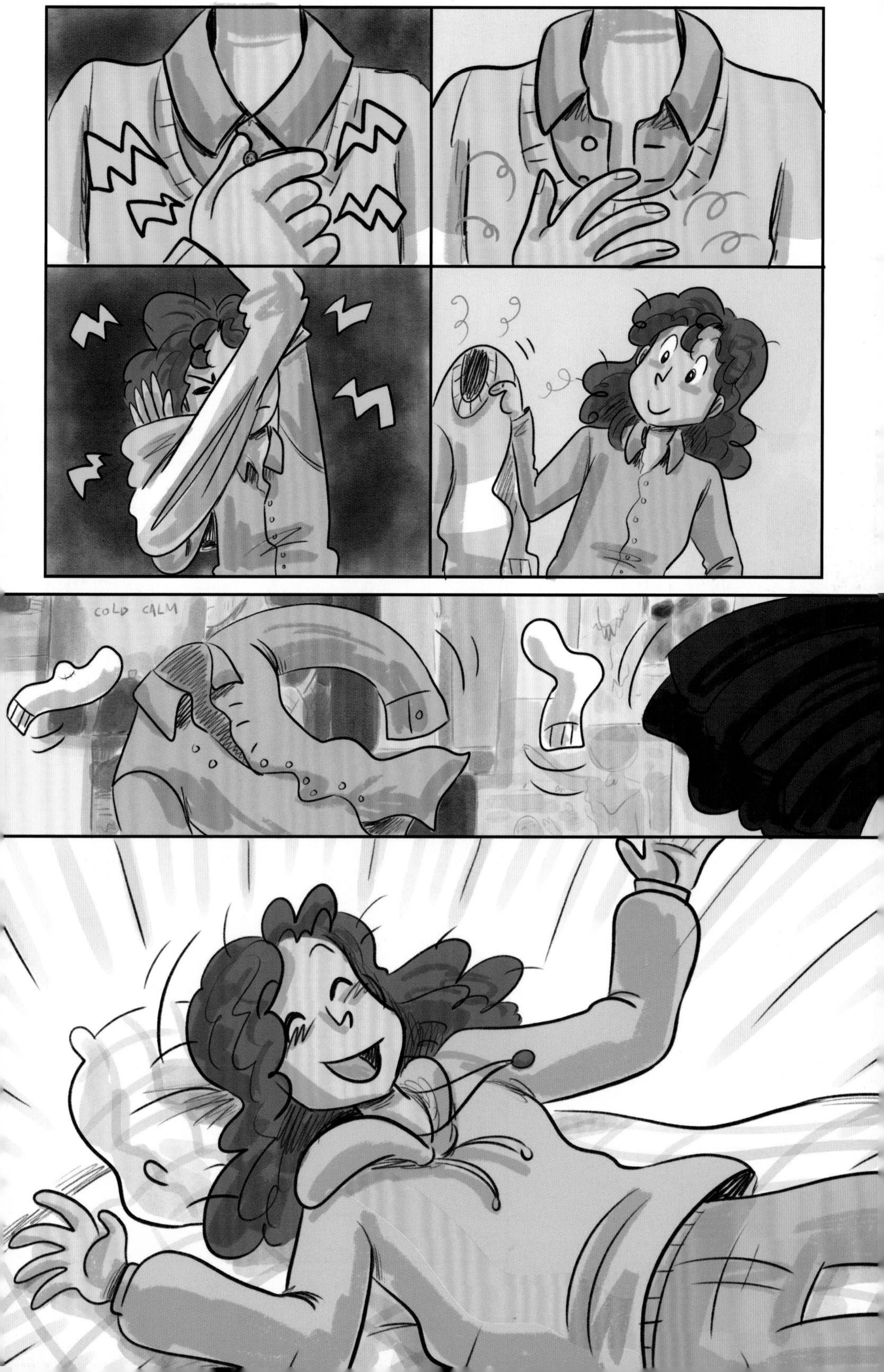
COLD CALM

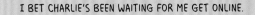

I BET CHARLIE'S BEEN WAITING FOR ME GET ONLINE.

24 messages

HAHA! YUP!

# Charlie

Mia OMG

Our new song is GOING VIRAL

Mia I can't believe it, our new song.

we're awesome.

MIA wHeRe Are yOu??

mmmmiiiiaaaaa

You gotta look at the Elle-Q page it's amazingg

omg mia it's been like AN HOUR

okayyy maybe more like 10 mins

HOW CAN I BE THE ONE DOING THE SINGING FOR ELLE-Q? YOU'RE THE ONE WHO DOES ALL THE TALKING.

Sorry, Mom was late picking me up. Let's talk on video chat?

Tap
Tap

Tap
Tap

38

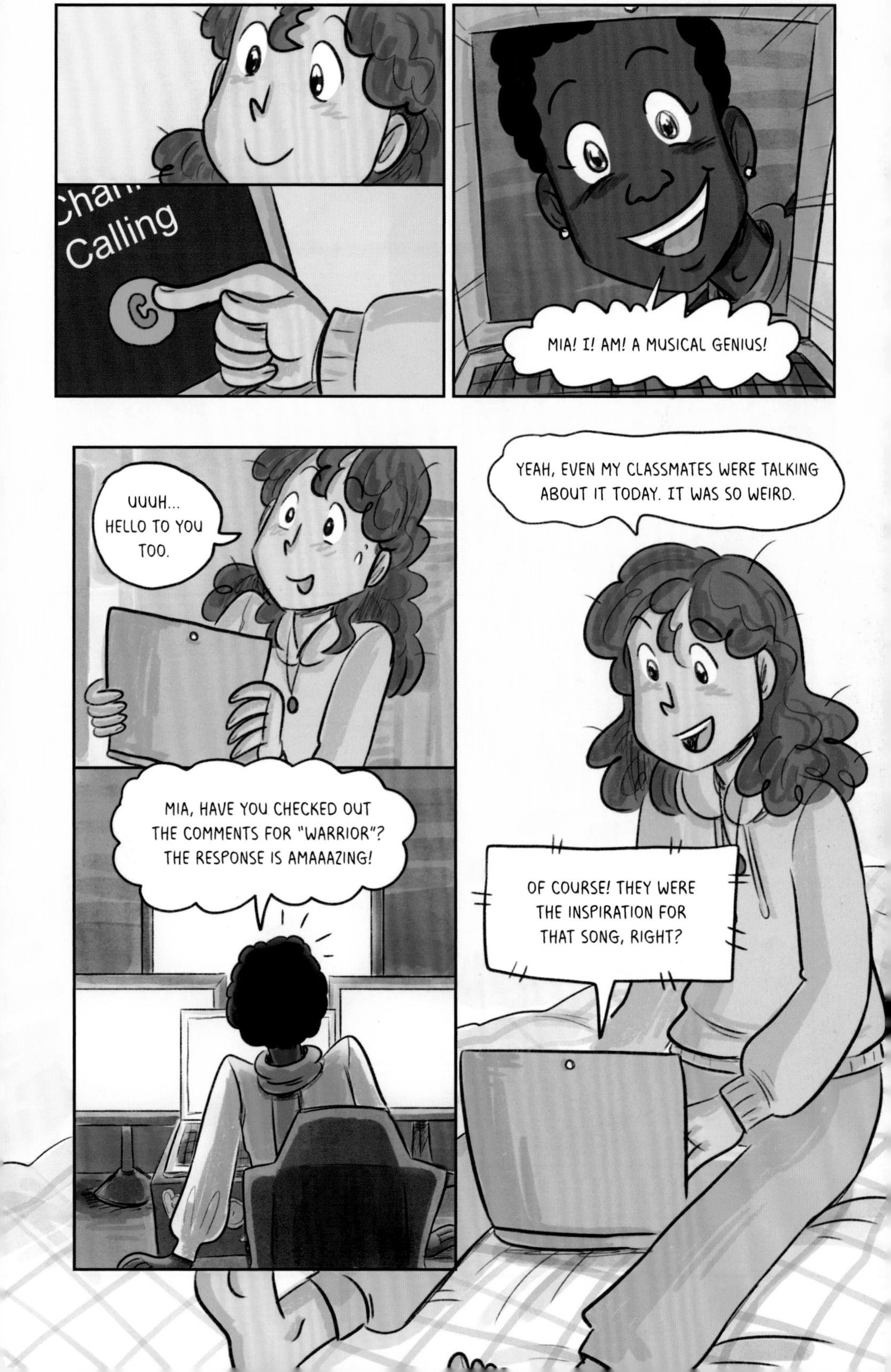
Calling
MIA! I! AM! A MUSICAL GENIUS!
UUUH... HELLO TO YOU TOO.
MIA, HAVE YOU CHECKED OUT THE COMMENTS FOR "WARRIOR"? THE RESPONSE IS AMAAAZING!
YEAH, EVEN MY CLASSMATES WERE TALKING ABOUT IT TODAY. IT WAS SO WEIRD.
OF COURSE! THEY WERE THE INSPIRATION FOR THAT SONG, RIGHT?

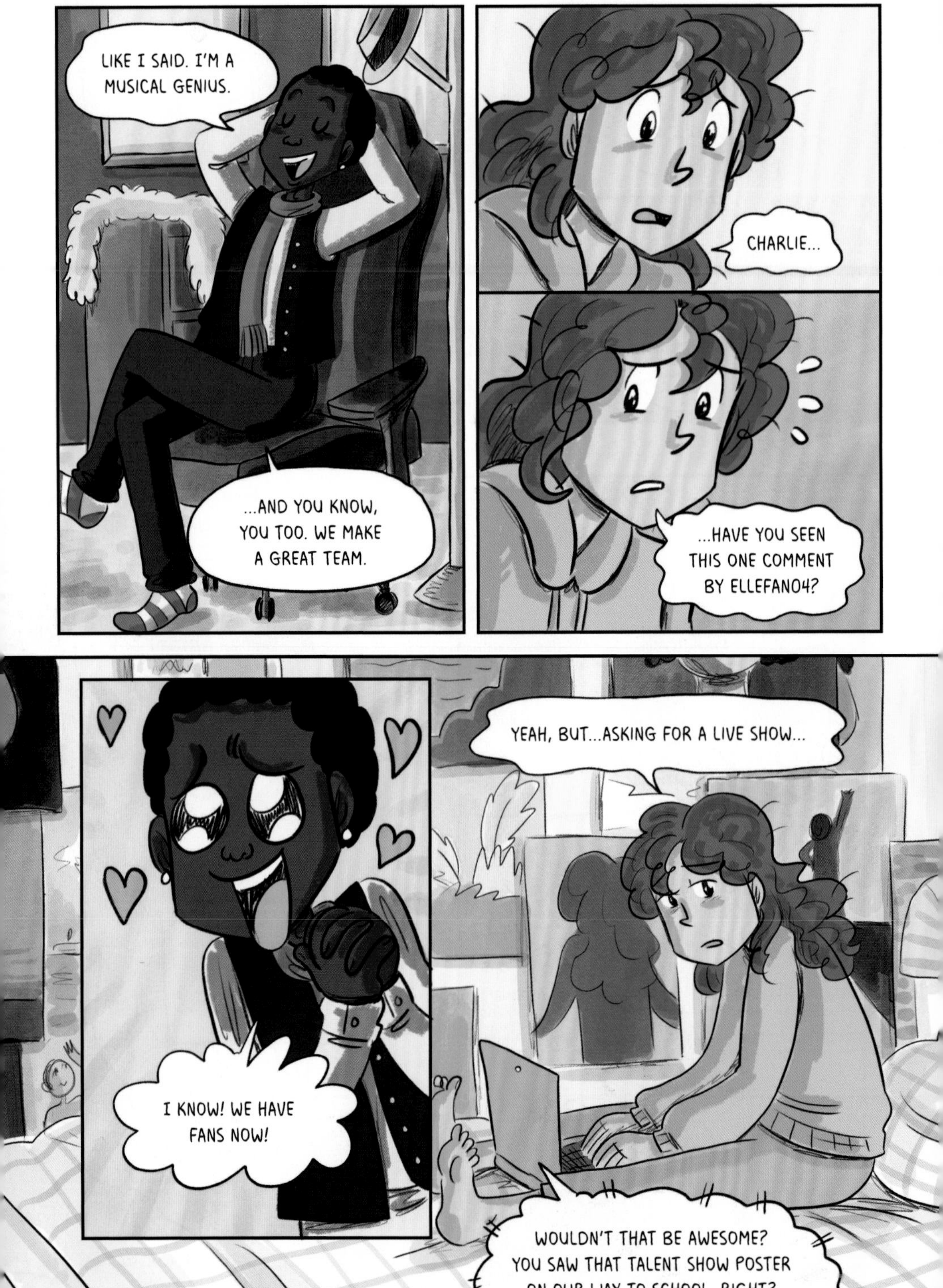
LIKE I SAID. I'M A MUSICAL GENIUS.
...AND YOU KNOW, YOU TOO. WE MAKE A GREAT TEAM.
CHARLIE...
...HAVE YOU SEEN THIS ONE COMMENT BY ELLEFAN04?
I KNOW! WE HAVE FANS NOW!
YEAH, BUT...ASKING FOR A LIVE SHOW...
WOULDN'T THAT BE AWESOME? YOU SAW THAT TALENT SHOW POSTER ON OUR WAY TO SCHOOL, RIGHT?

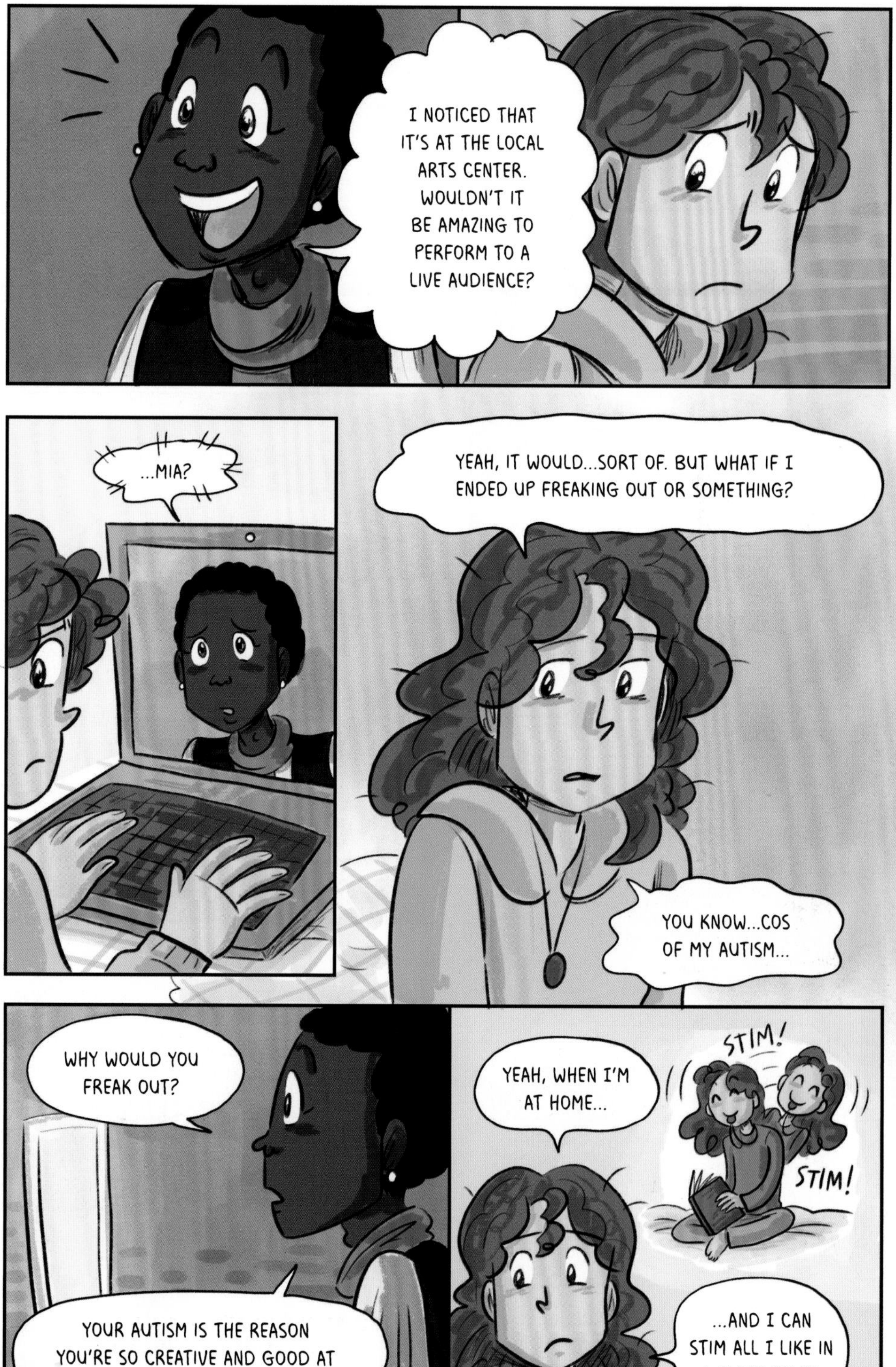
I NOTICED THAT IT'S AT THE LOCAL ARTS CENTER. WOULDN'T IT BE AMAZING TO PERFORM TO A LIVE AUDIENCE?
...MIA?
YEAH, IT WOULD...SORT OF. BUT WHAT IF I ENDED UP FREAKING OUT OR SOMETHING?
YOU KNOW...COS OF MY AUTISM...
WHY WOULD YOU FREAK OUT?
YOUR AUTISM IS THE REASON YOU'RE SO CREATIVE AND GOOD AT MEMORIZING YOUR LYRICS.
YEAH, WHEN I'M AT HOME...
STIM!
STIM!
...AND I CAN STIM ALL I LIKE IN A QUIET SPACE.

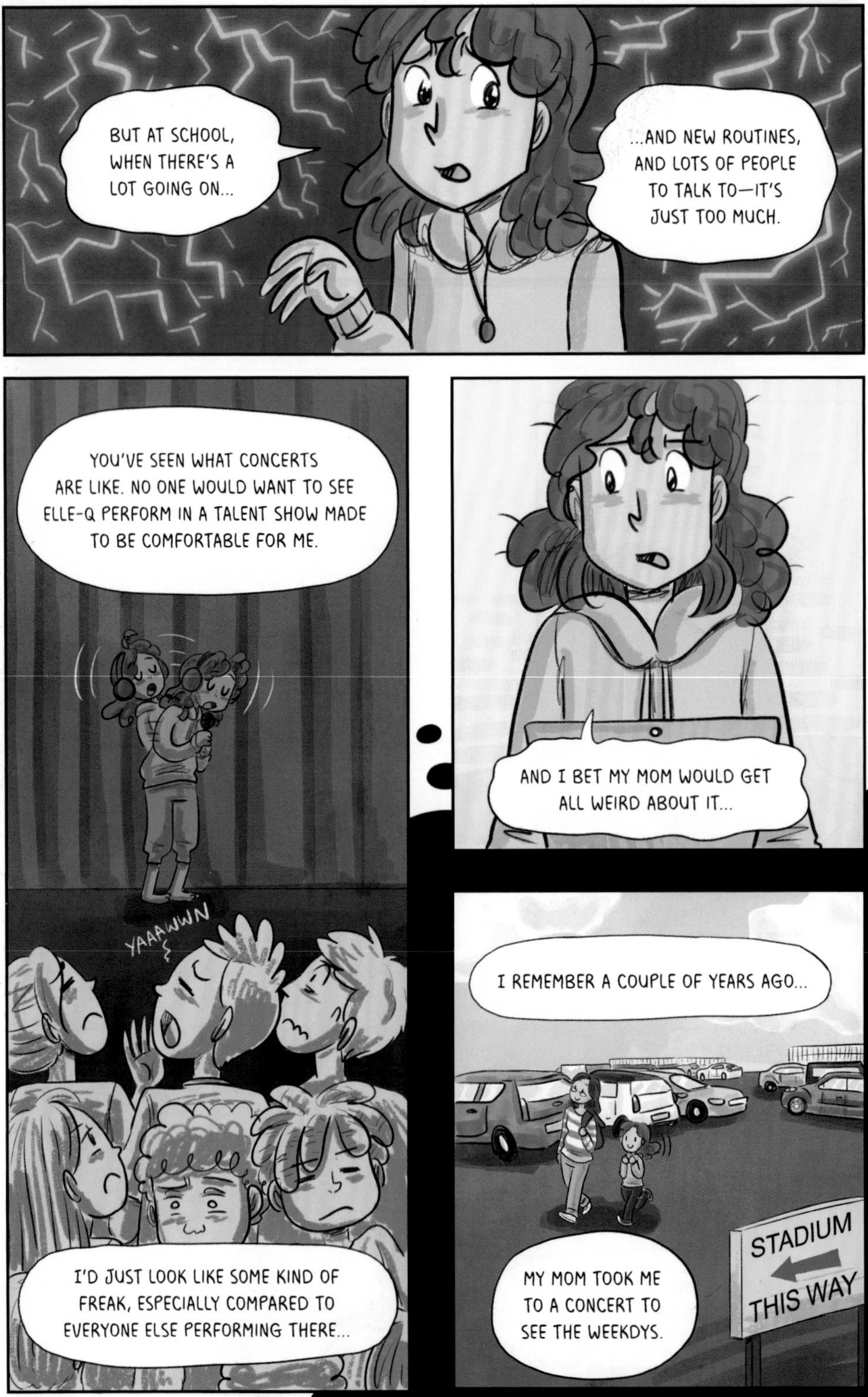
BUT AT SCHOOL, WHEN THERE'S A LOT GOING ON...
...AND NEW ROUTINES, AND LOTS OF PEOPLE TO TALK TO—IT'S JUST TOO MUCH.
YOU'VE SEEN WHAT CONCERTS ARE LIKE. NO ONE WOULD WANT TO SEE ELLE-Q PERFORM IN A TALENT SHOW MADE TO BE COMFORTABLE FOR ME.
YAAAWWN
I'D JUST LOOK LIKE SOME KIND OF FREAK, ESPECIALLY COMPARED TO EVERYONE ELSE PERFORMING THERE...
AND I BET MY MOM WOULD GET ALL WEIRD ABOUT IT...
I REMEMBER A COUPLE OF YEARS AGO...
MY MOM TOOK ME TO A CONCERT TO SEE THE WEEKDYS.
STADIUM
THIS WAY

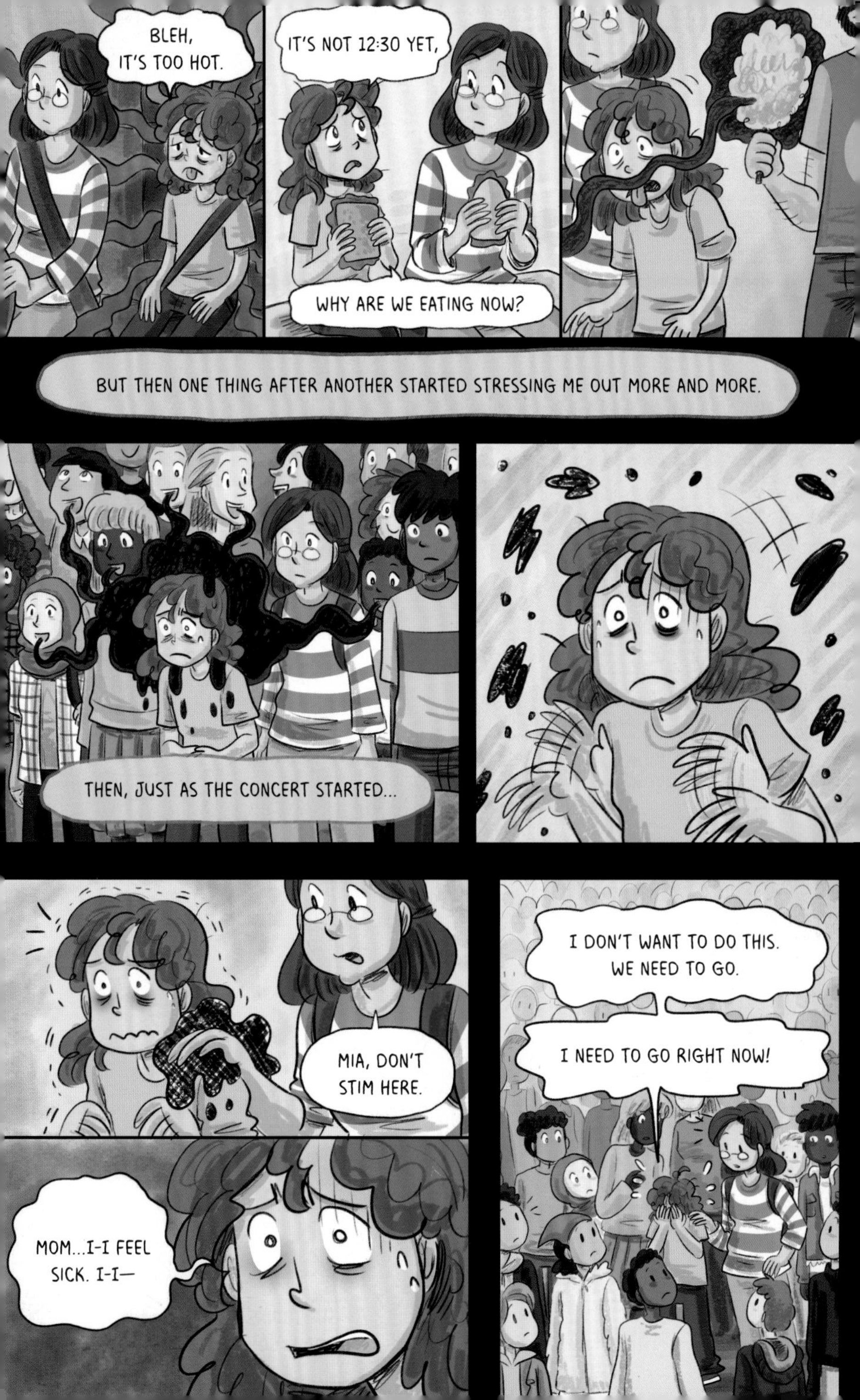
BLEH, IT'S TOO HOT.
IT'S NOT 12:30 YET,
WHY ARE WE EATING NOW?
BUT THEN ONE THING AFTER ANOTHER STARTED STRESSING ME OUT MORE AND MORE.
THEN, JUST AS THE CONCERT STARTED...
MIA, DON'T STIM HERE.
MOM...I-I FEEL SICK. I-I—
I DON'T WANT TO DO THIS. WE NEED TO GO.
I NEED TO GO RIGHT NOW!

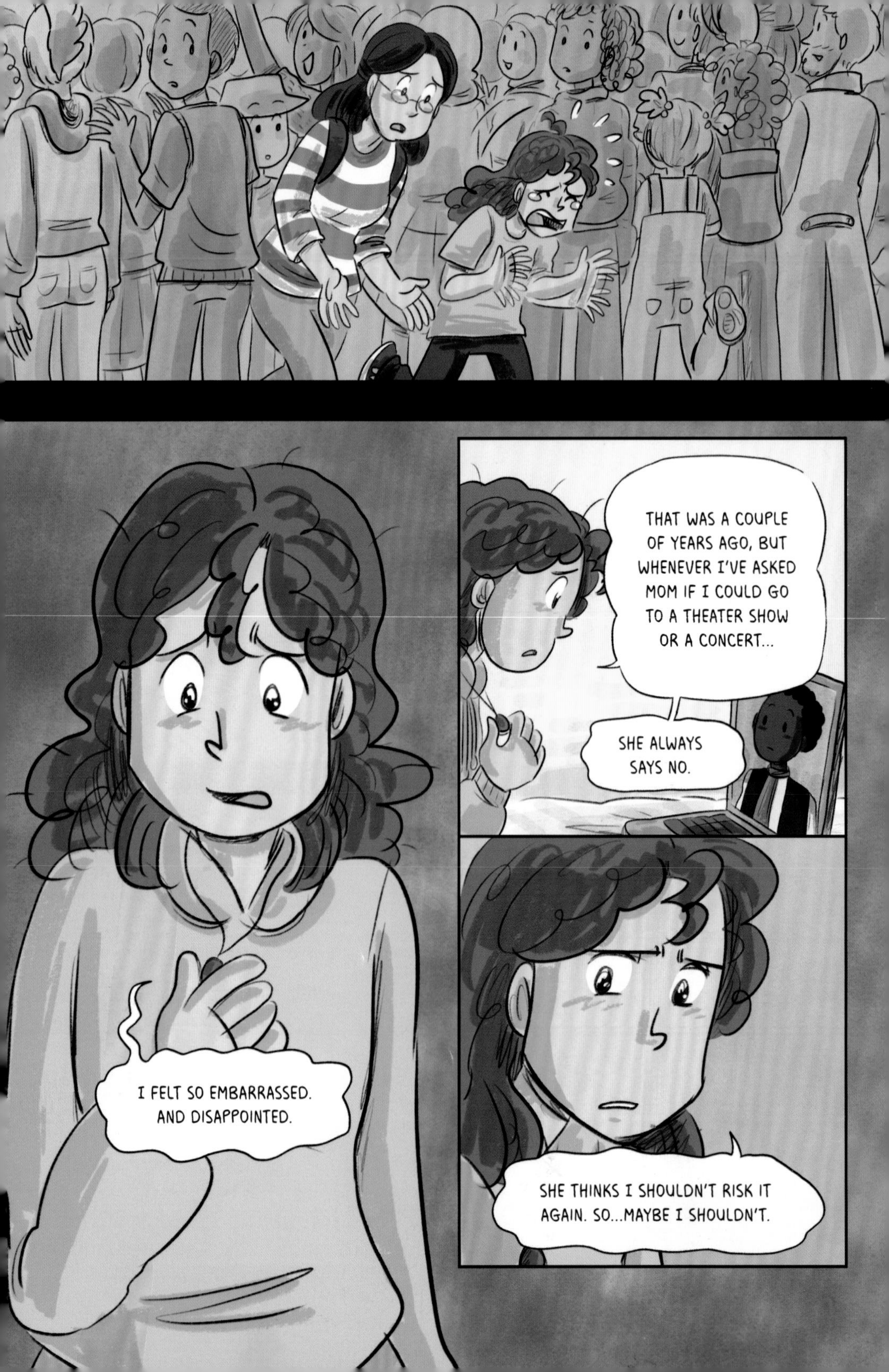
I FELT SO EMBARRASSED. AND DISAPPOINTED.
THAT WAS A COUPLE OF YEARS AGO, BUT WHENEVER I'VE ASKED MOM IF I COULD GO TO A THEATER SHOW OR A CONCERT...
SHE ALWAYS SAYS NO.
SHE THINKS I SHOULDN'T RISK IT AGAIN. SO...MAYBE I SHOULDN'T.

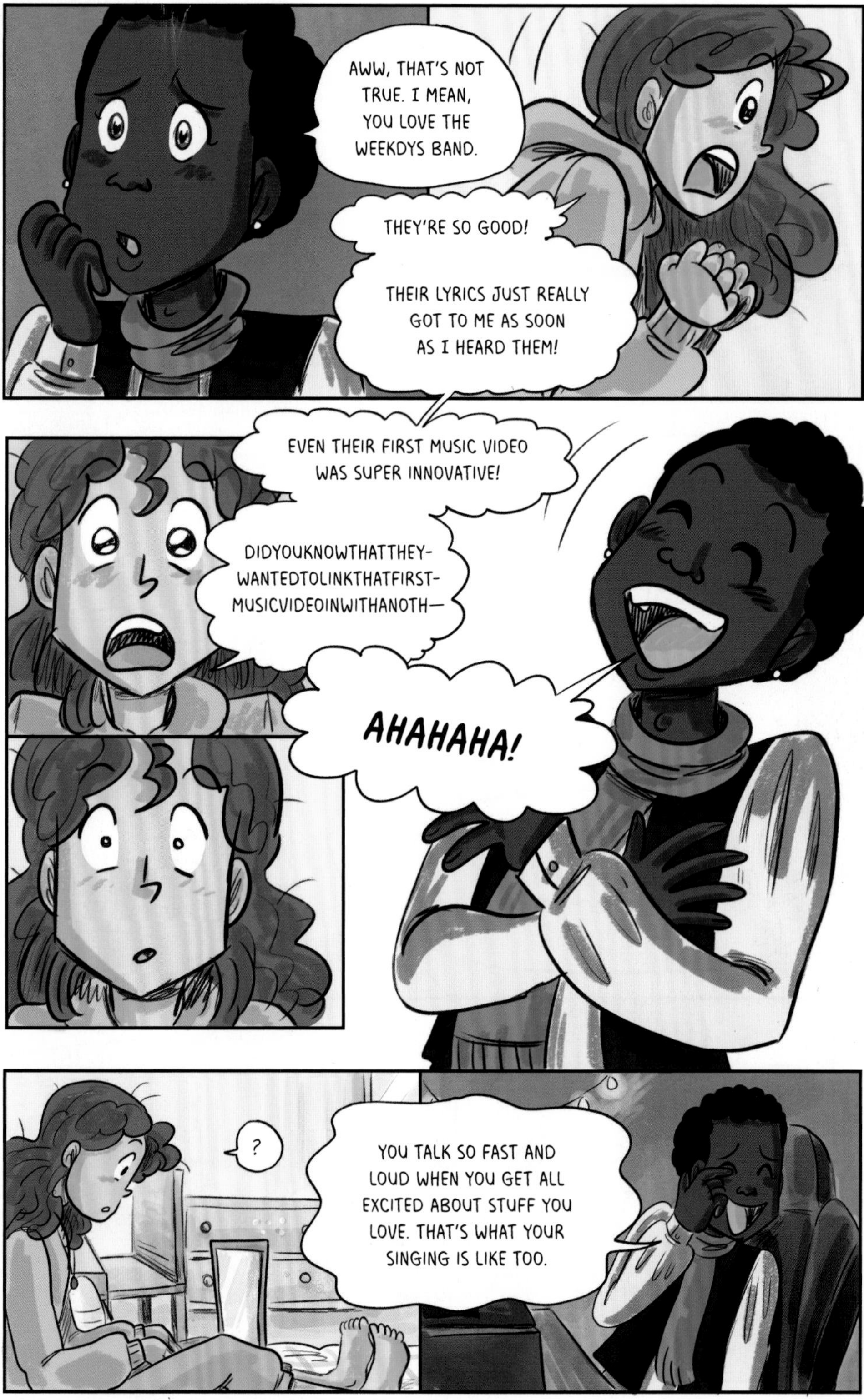
AWW, THAT'S NOT TRUE. I MEAN, YOU LOVE THE WEEKDYS BAND.
THEY'RE SO GOOD!
THEIR LYRICS JUST REALLY GOT TO ME AS SOON AS I HEARD THEM!
EVEN THEIR FIRST MUSIC VIDEO WAS SUPER INNOVATIVE!
DIDYOUKNOWTHATTHEY-WANTEDTOLINKTHATFIRST-MUSICVIDEOINWITHANOTH—
AHAHAHA!
?
YOU TALK SO FAST AND LOUD WHEN YOU GET ALL EXCITED ABOUT STUFF YOU LOVE. THAT'S WHAT YOUR SINGING IS LIKE TOO.

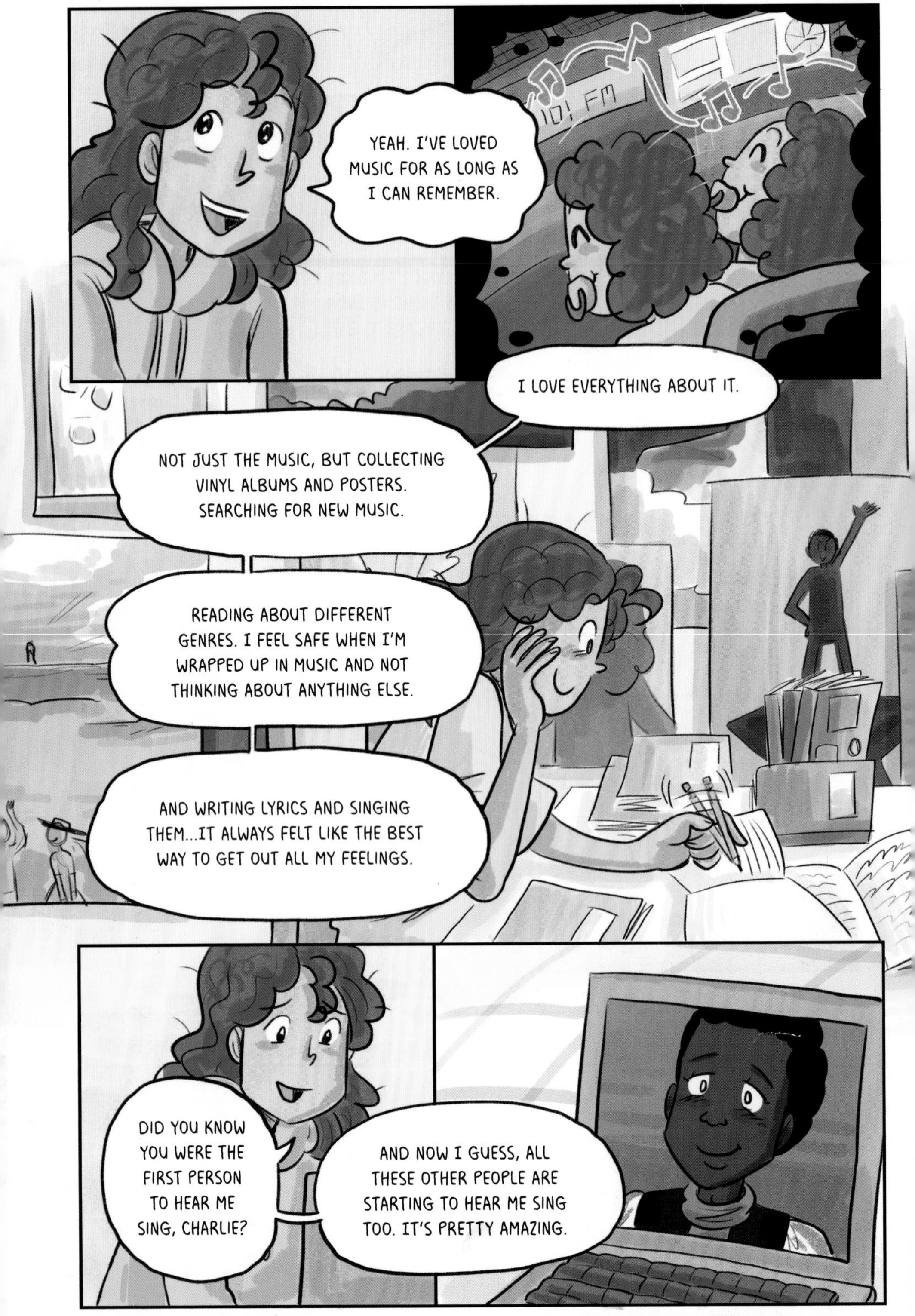
YEAH. I'VE LOVED MUSIC FOR AS LONG AS I CAN REMEMBER.
101 FM
I LOVE EVERYTHING ABOUT IT.
NOT JUST THE MUSIC, BUT COLLECTING VINYL ALBUMS AND POSTERS. SEARCHING FOR NEW MUSIC.
READING ABOUT DIFFERENT GENRES. I FEEL SAFE WHEN I'M WRAPPED UP IN MUSIC AND NOT THINKING ABOUT ANYTHING ELSE.
AND WRITING LYRICS AND SINGING THEM...IT ALWAYS FELT LIKE THE BEST WAY TO GET OUT ALL MY FEELINGS.
DID YOU KNOW YOU WERE THE FIRST PERSON TO HEAR ME SING, CHARLIE?
AND NOW I GUESS, ALL THESE OTHER PEOPLE ARE STARTING TO HEAR ME SING TOO. IT'S PRETTY AMAZING.

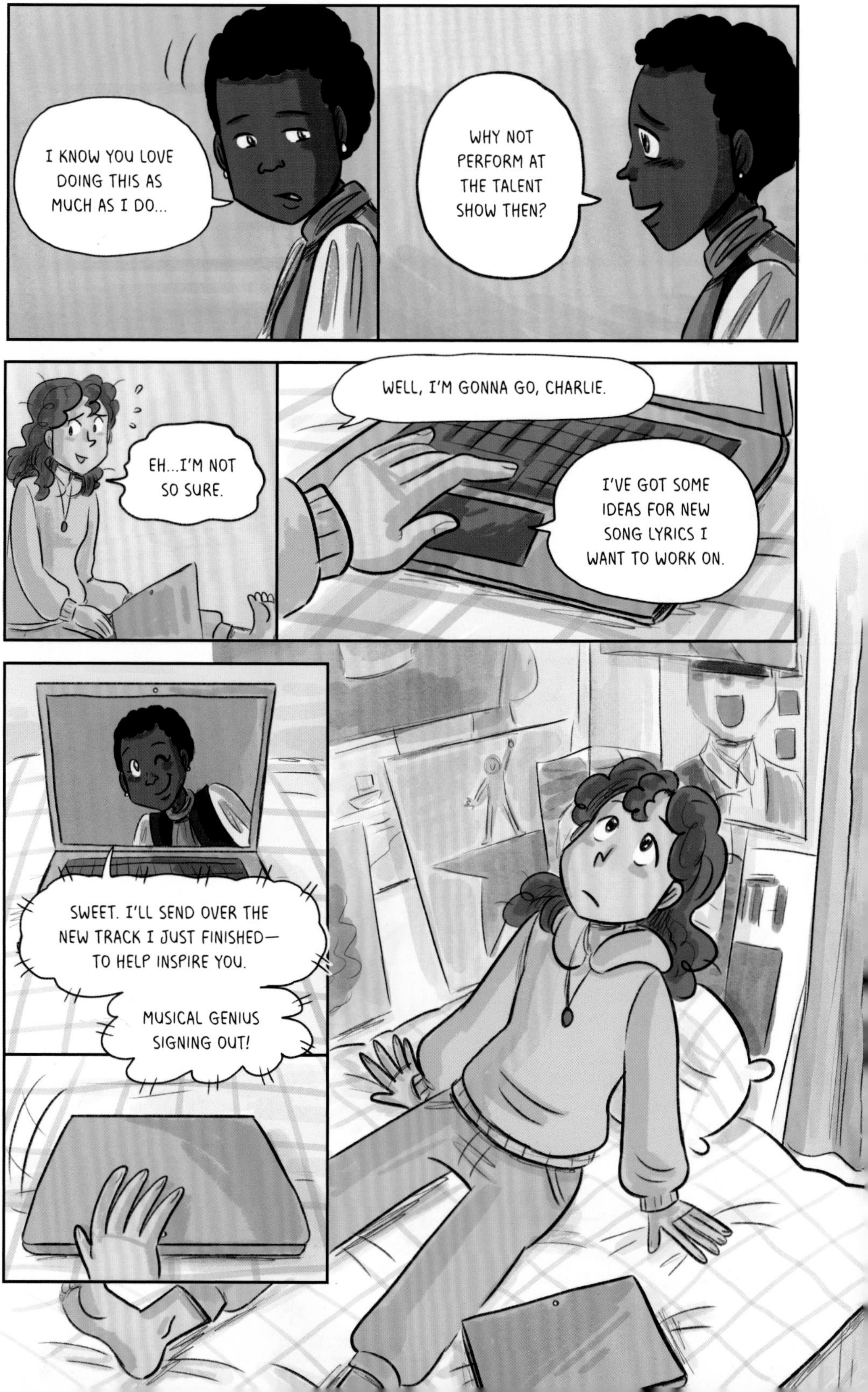
I KNOW YOU LOVE DOING THIS AS MUCH AS I DO...
WHY NOT PERFORM AT THE TALENT SHOW THEN?
EH...I'M NOT SO SURE.
WELL, I'M GONNA GO, CHARLIE.
I'VE GOT SOME IDEAS FOR NEW SONG LYRICS I WANT TO WORK ON.
SWEET. I'LL SEND OVER THE NEW TRACK I JUST FINISHED— TO HELP INSPIRE YOU.
MUSICAL GENIUS SIGNING OUT!

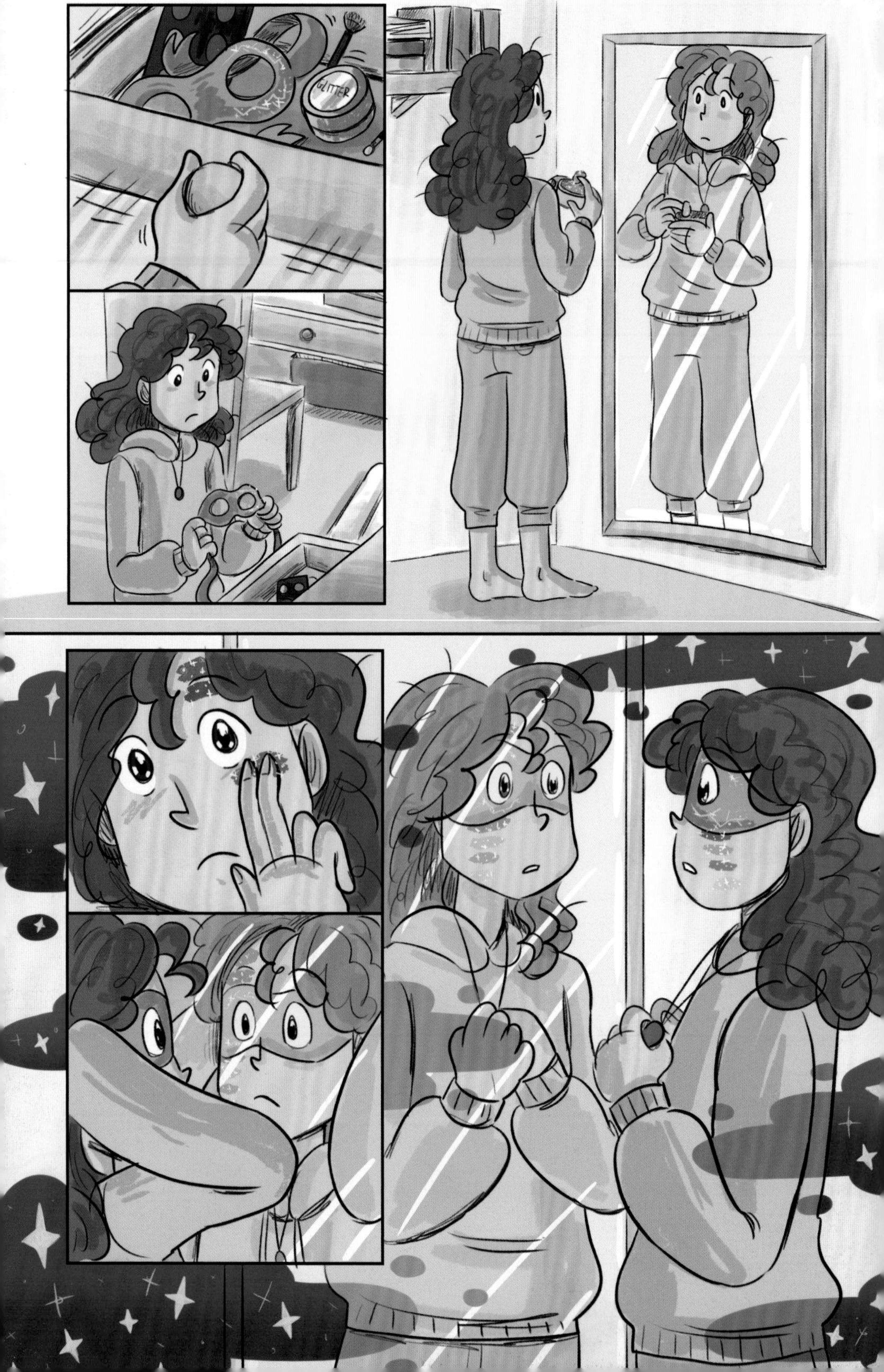
GLITTER

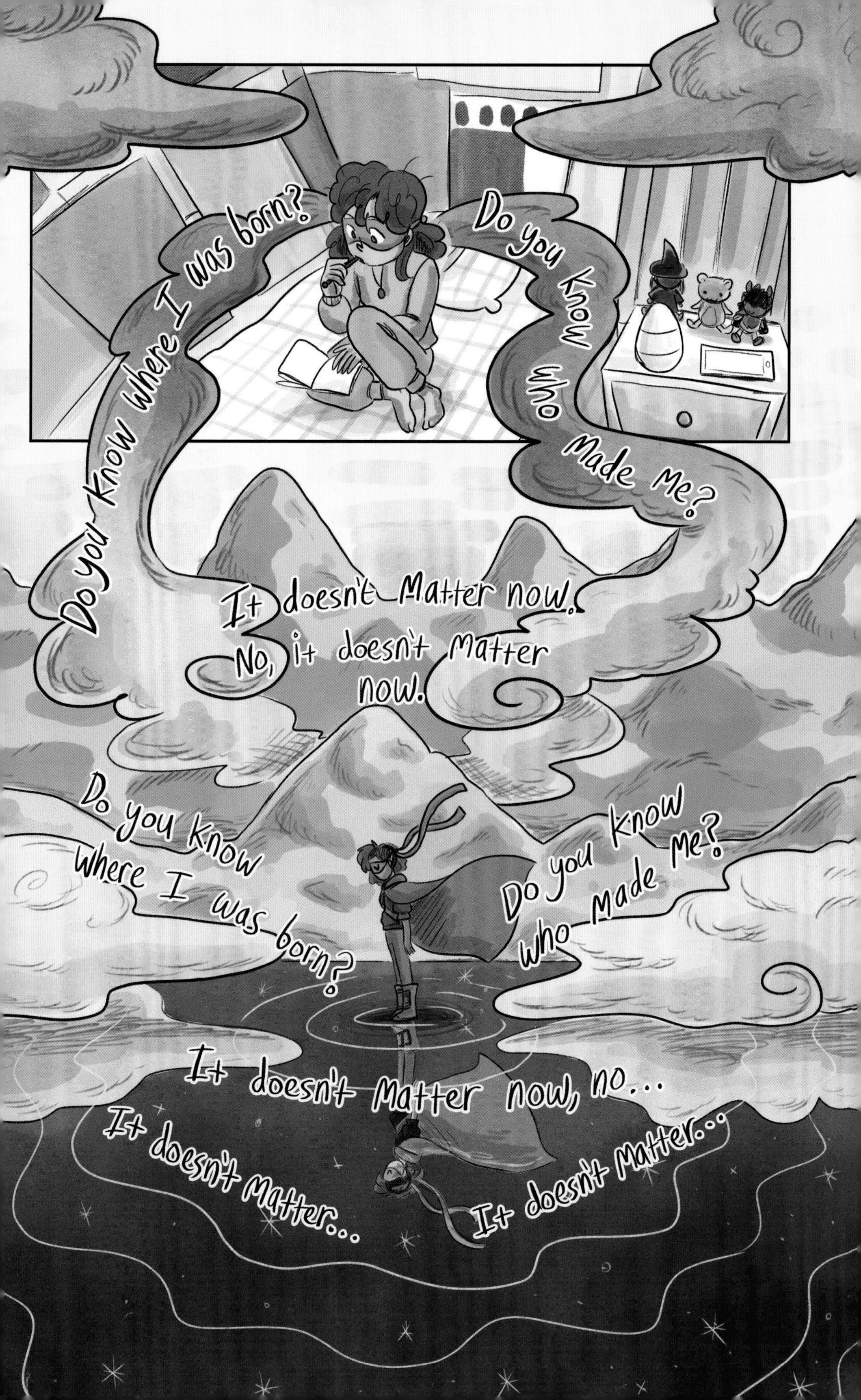
Do you know where I was born?
Do you know who made me?
It doesn't matter now.
No, it doesn't matter now.
Do you know where I was born?
Do you know who made me?
It doesn't matter now, no...
It doesn't matter...
It doesn't matter...

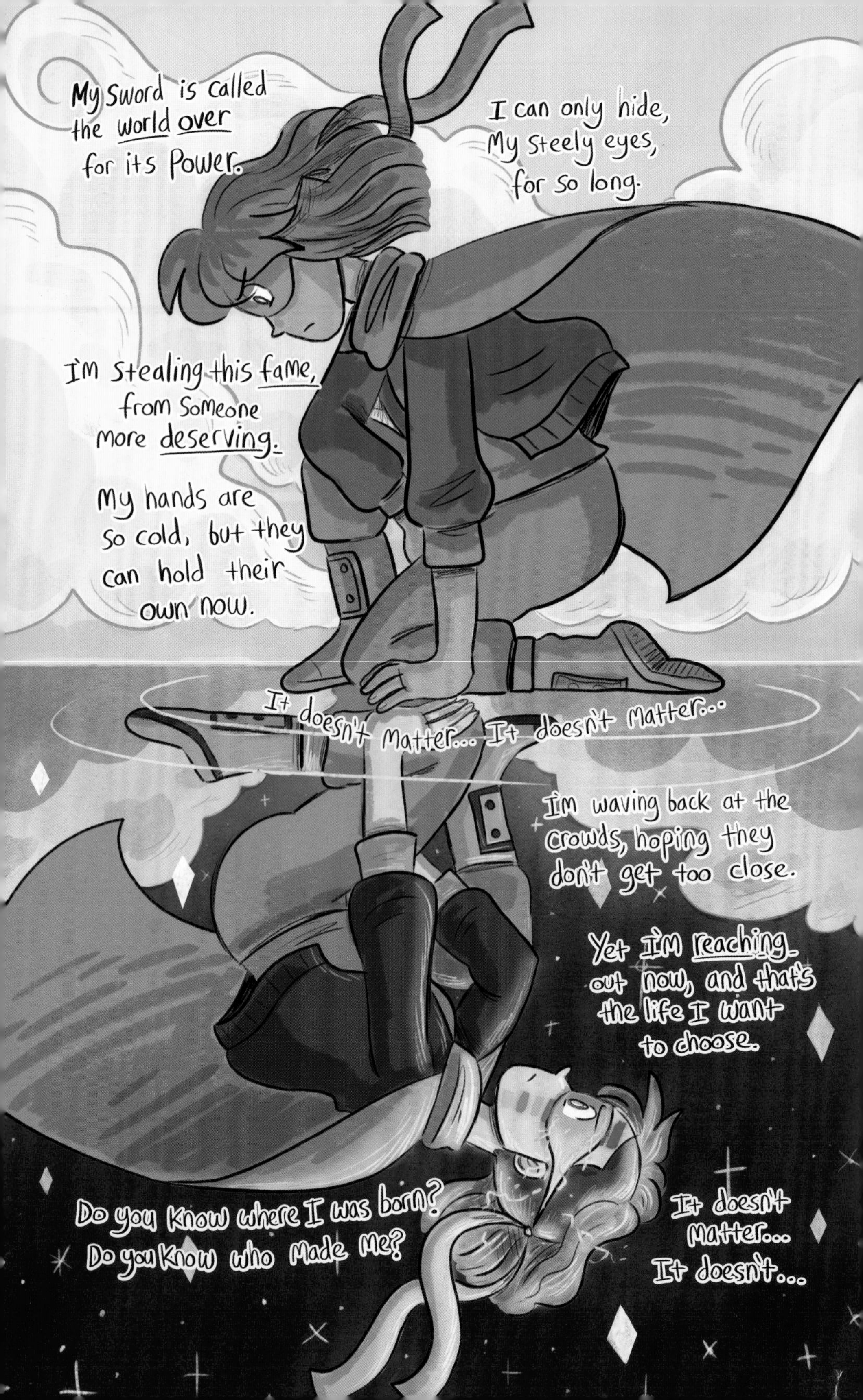

# CHAPTER THREE

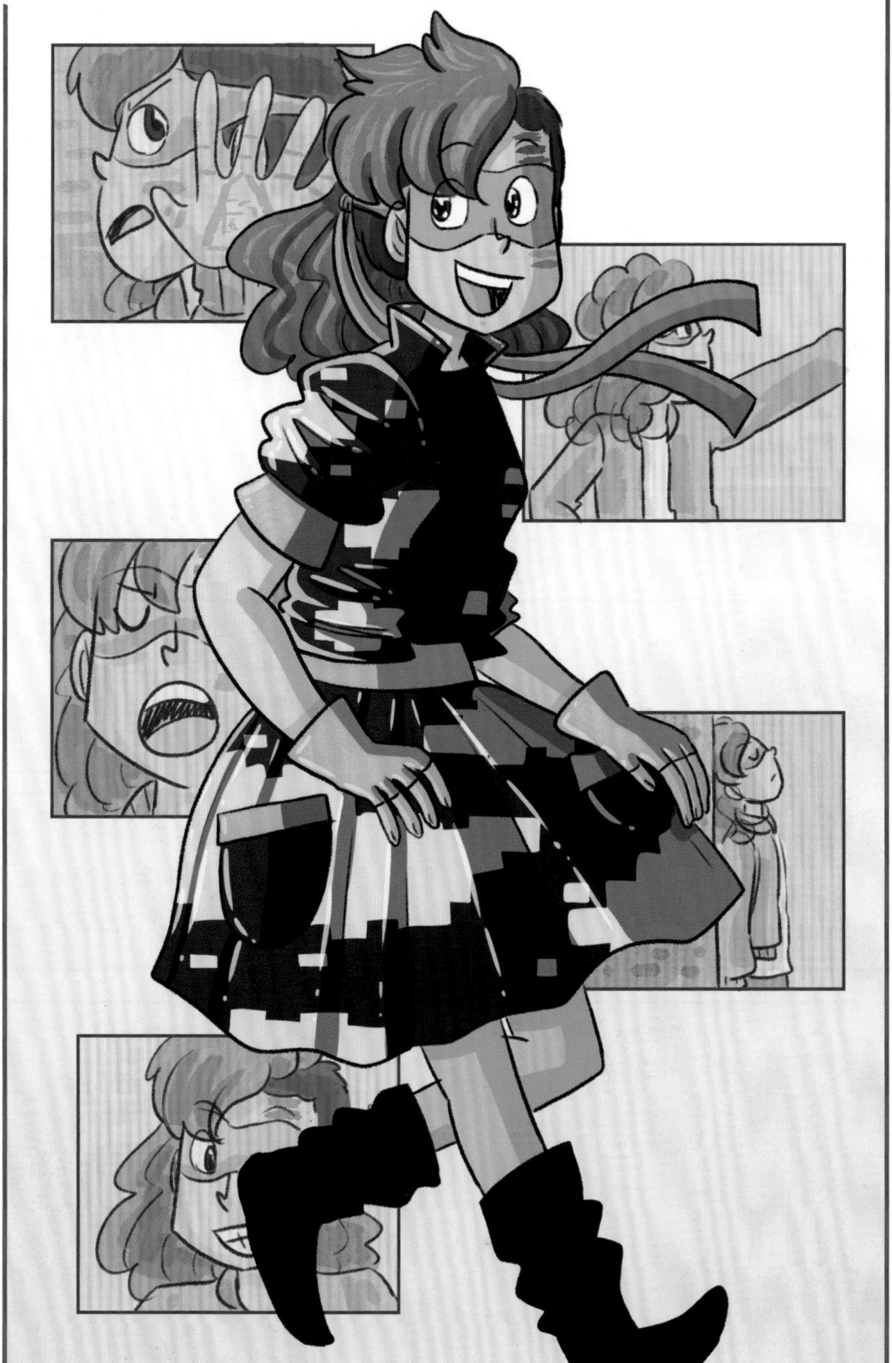

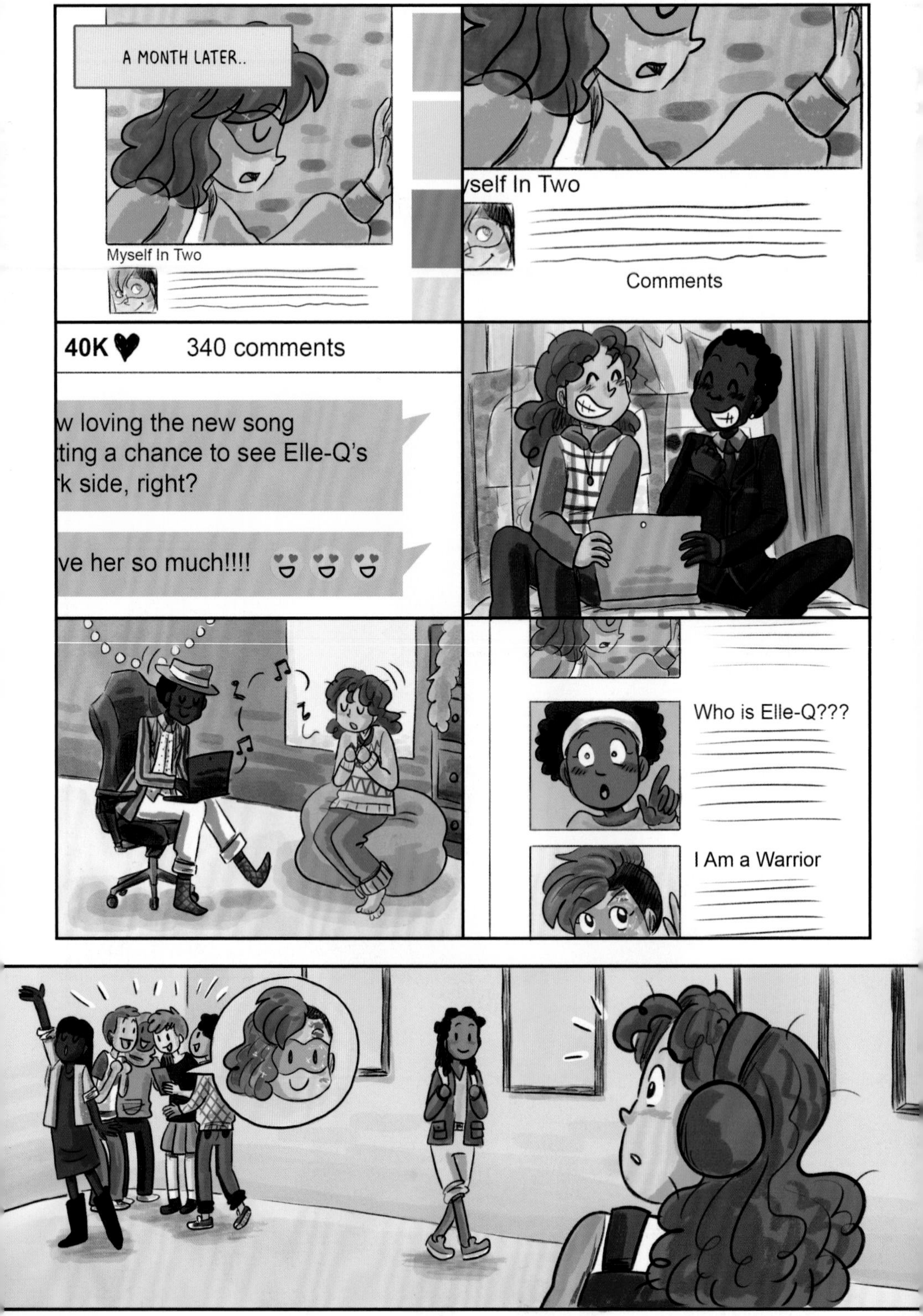
A MONTH LATER..
Myself In Two
yself In Two
Comments
40K
340 comments
w loving the new song
tting a chance to see Elle-Q's
rk side, right?
ve her so much!!!!
Who is Elle-Q???
I Am a Warrior

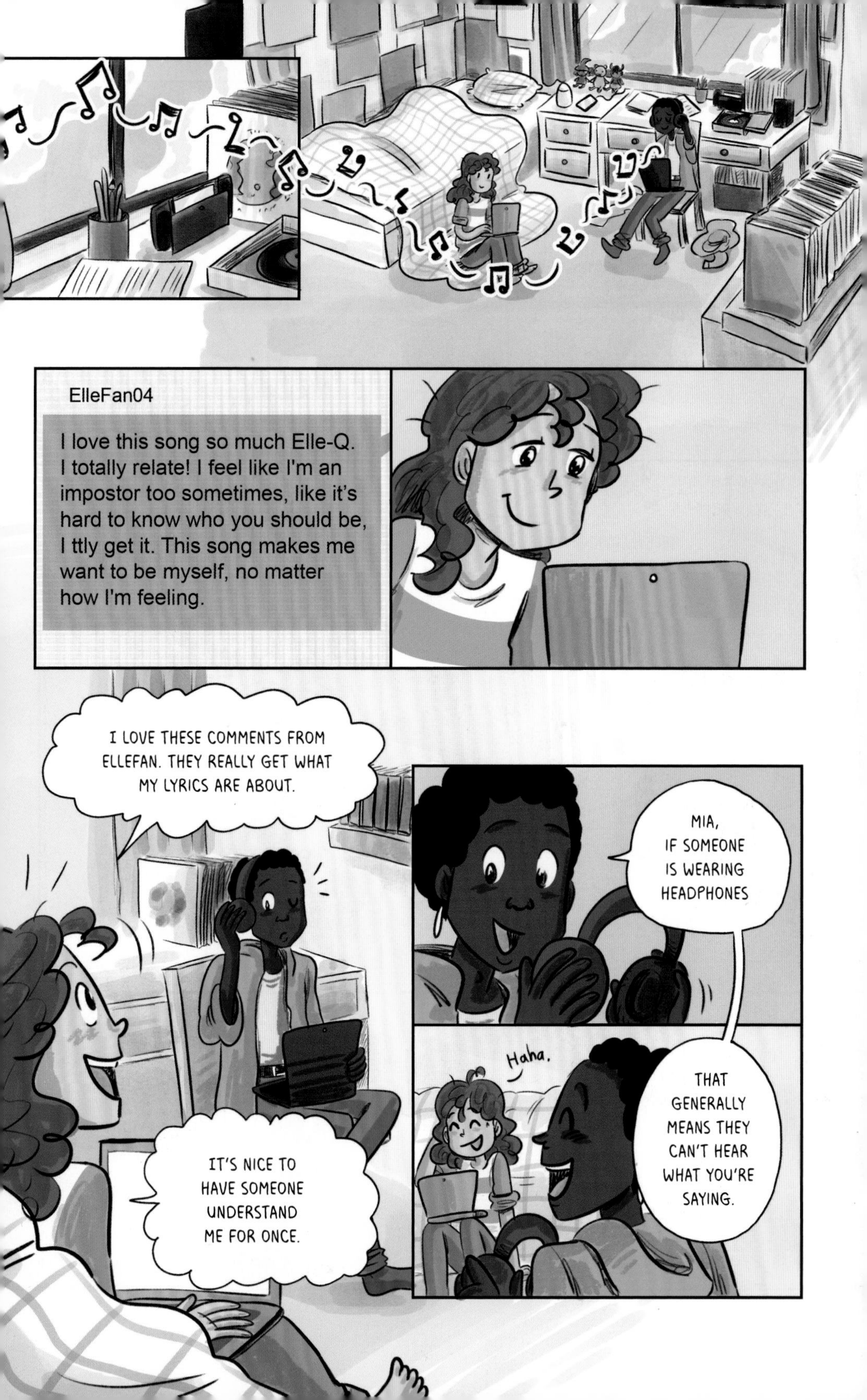
ElleFan04
I love this song so much Elle-Q. I totally relate! I feel like I'm an impostor too sometimes, like it's hard to know who you should be, I ttly get it. This song makes me want to be myself, no matter how I'm feeling.
I LOVE THESE COMMENTS FROM ELLEFAN. THEY REALLY GET WHAT MY LYRICS ARE ABOUT.
IT'S NICE TO HAVE SOMEONE UNDERSTAND ME FOR ONCE.
MIA, IF SOMEONE IS WEARING HEADPHONES
Haha.
THAT GENERALLY MEANS THEY CAN'T HEAR WHAT YOU'RE SAYING.

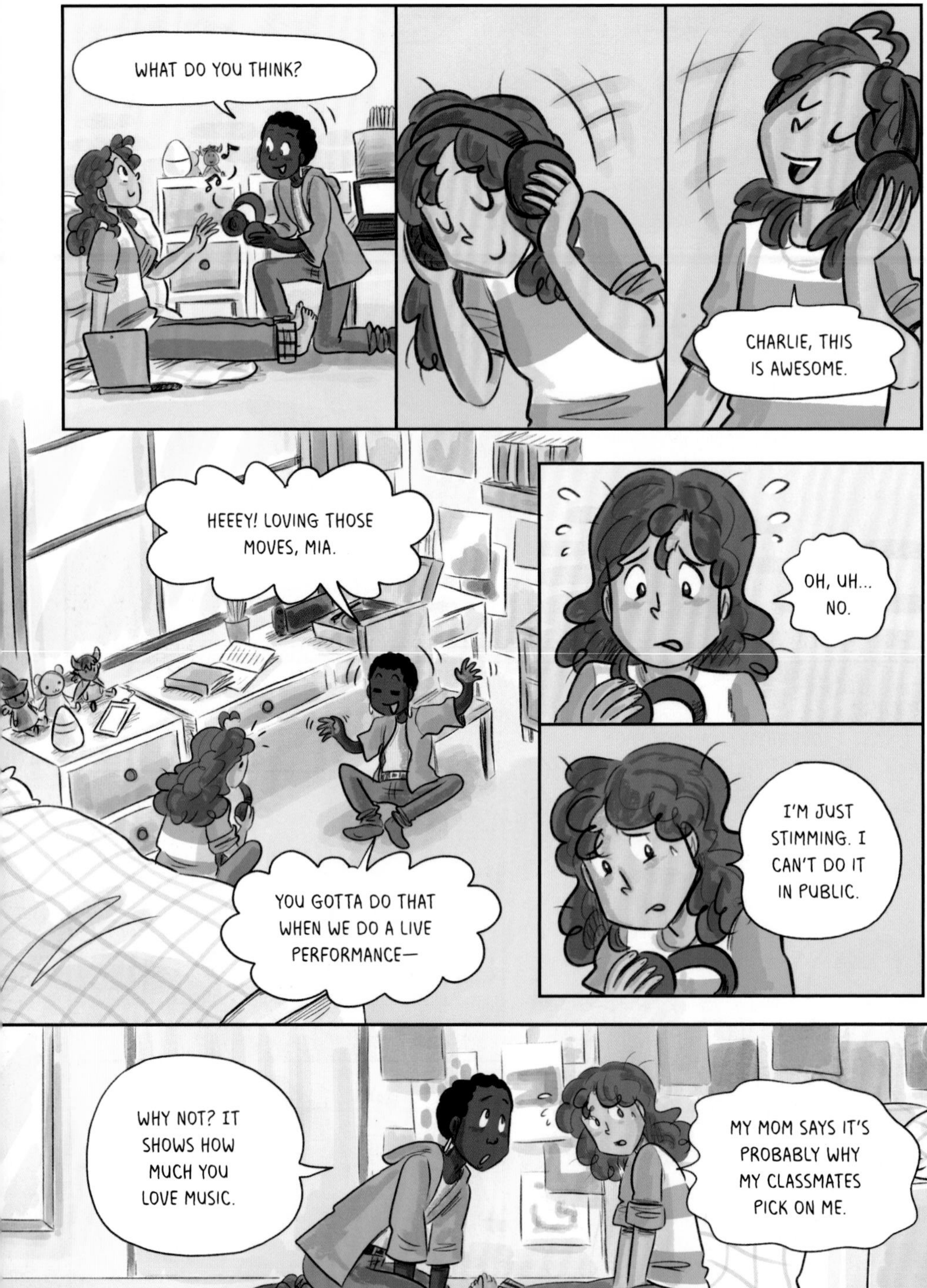
WHAT DO YOU THINK?
CHARLIE, THIS IS AWESOME.
HEEEY! LOVING THOSE MOVES, MIA.
YOU GOTTA DO THAT WHEN WE DO A LIVE PERFORMANCE—
OH, UH... NO.
I'M JUST STIMMING. I CAN'T DO IT IN PUBLIC.
WHY NOT? IT SHOWS HOW MUCH YOU LOVE MUSIC.
MY MOM SAYS IT'S PROBABLY WHY MY CLASSMATES PICK ON ME.

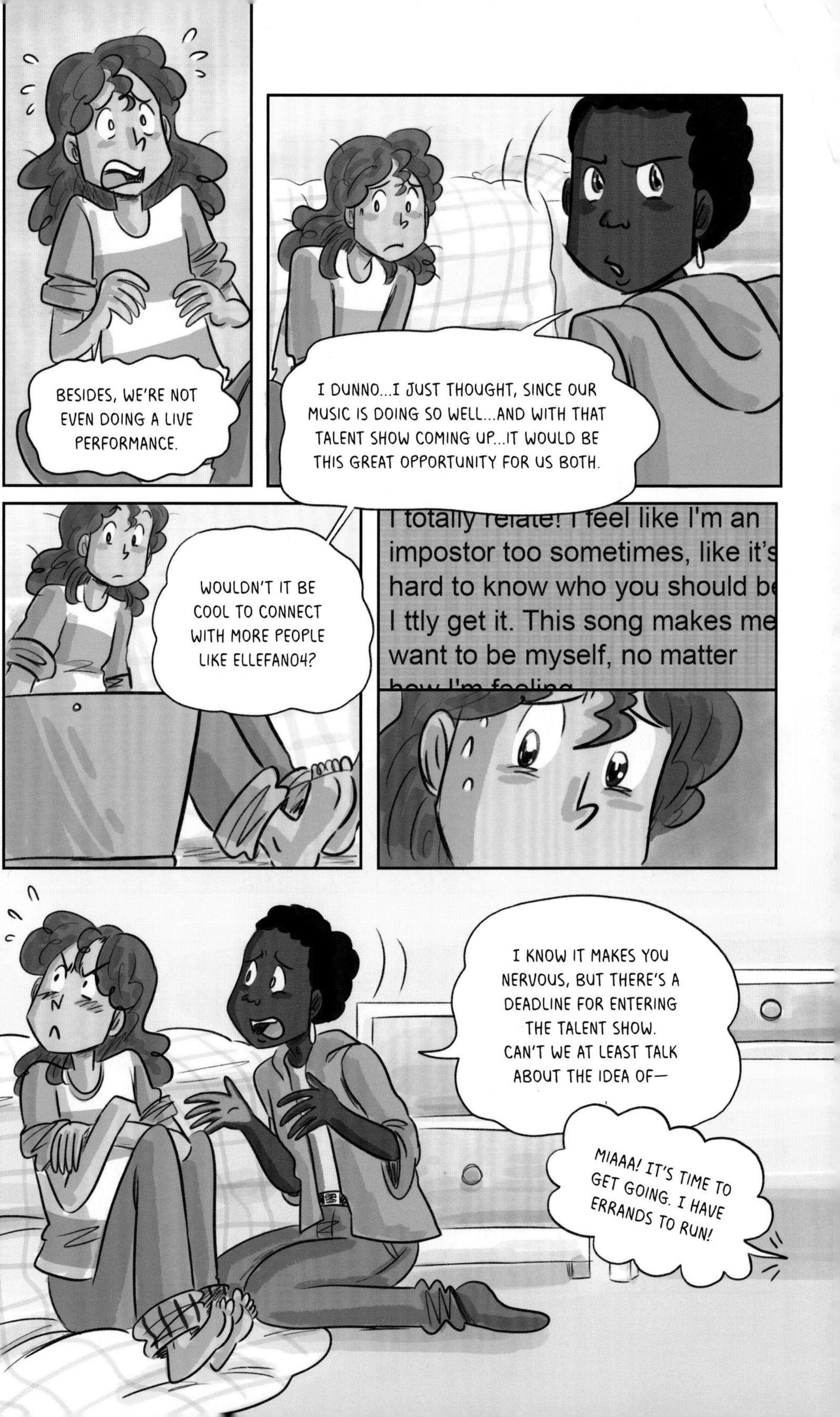

BESIDES, WE'RE NOT EVEN DOING A LIVE PERFORMANCE.
I DUNNO...I JUST THOUGHT, SINCE OUR MUSIC IS DOING SO WELL...AND WITH THAT TALENT SHOW COMING UP...IT WOULD BE THIS GREAT OPPORTUNITY FOR US BOTH.
WOULDN'T IT BE COOL TO CONNECT WITH MORE PEOPLE LIKE ELLEFAN04?
I totally relate! I feel like I'm an
impostor too sometimes, like it's
hard to know who you should b
I ttly get it. This song makes me
want to be myself, no matter
I KNOW IT MAKES YOU NERVOUS, BUT THERE'S A DEADLINE FOR ENTERING THE TALENT SHOW. CAN'T WE AT LEAST TALK ABOUT THE IDEA OF—
MIAAA! IT'S TIME TO GET GOING. I HAVE ERRANDS TO RUN!

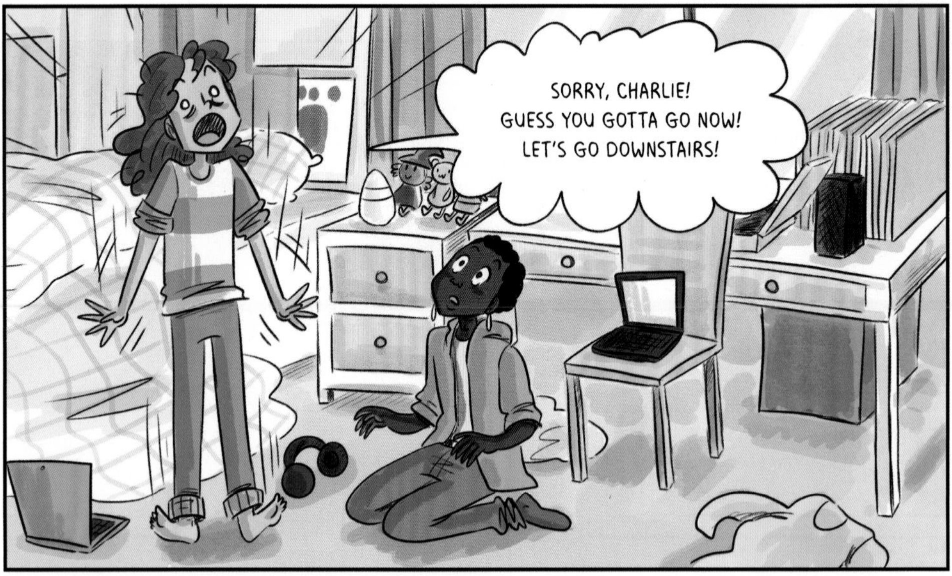
SORRY, CHARLIE!
GUESS YOU GOTTA GO NOW!
LET'S GO DOWNSTAIRS!

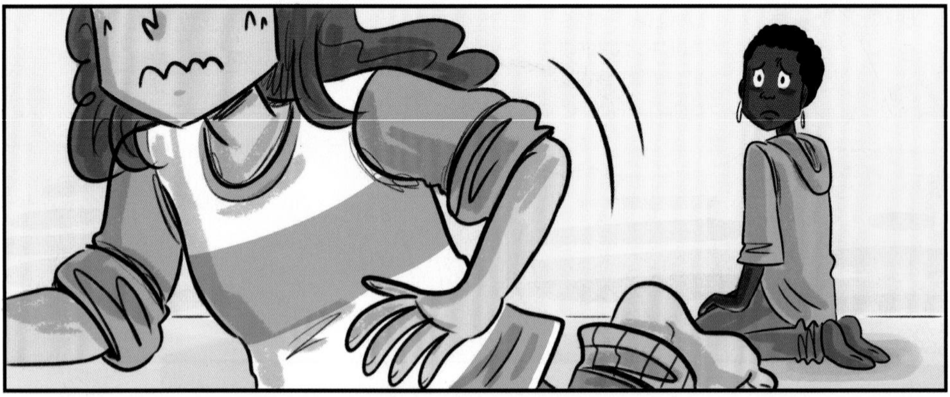

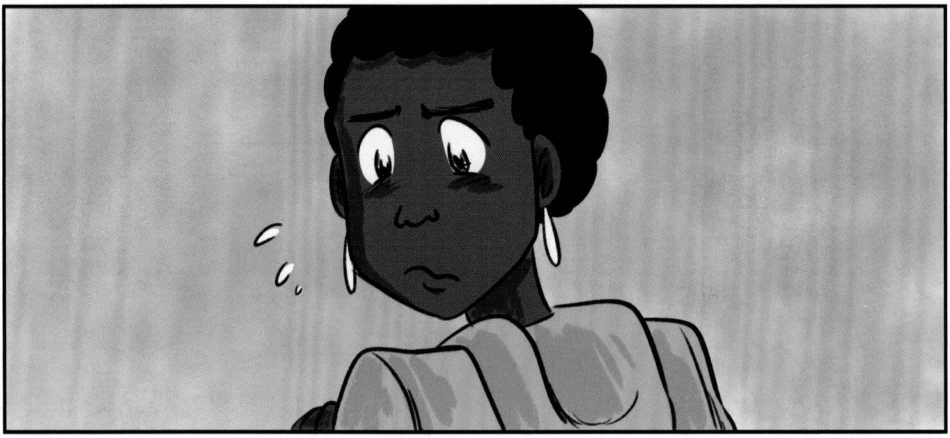

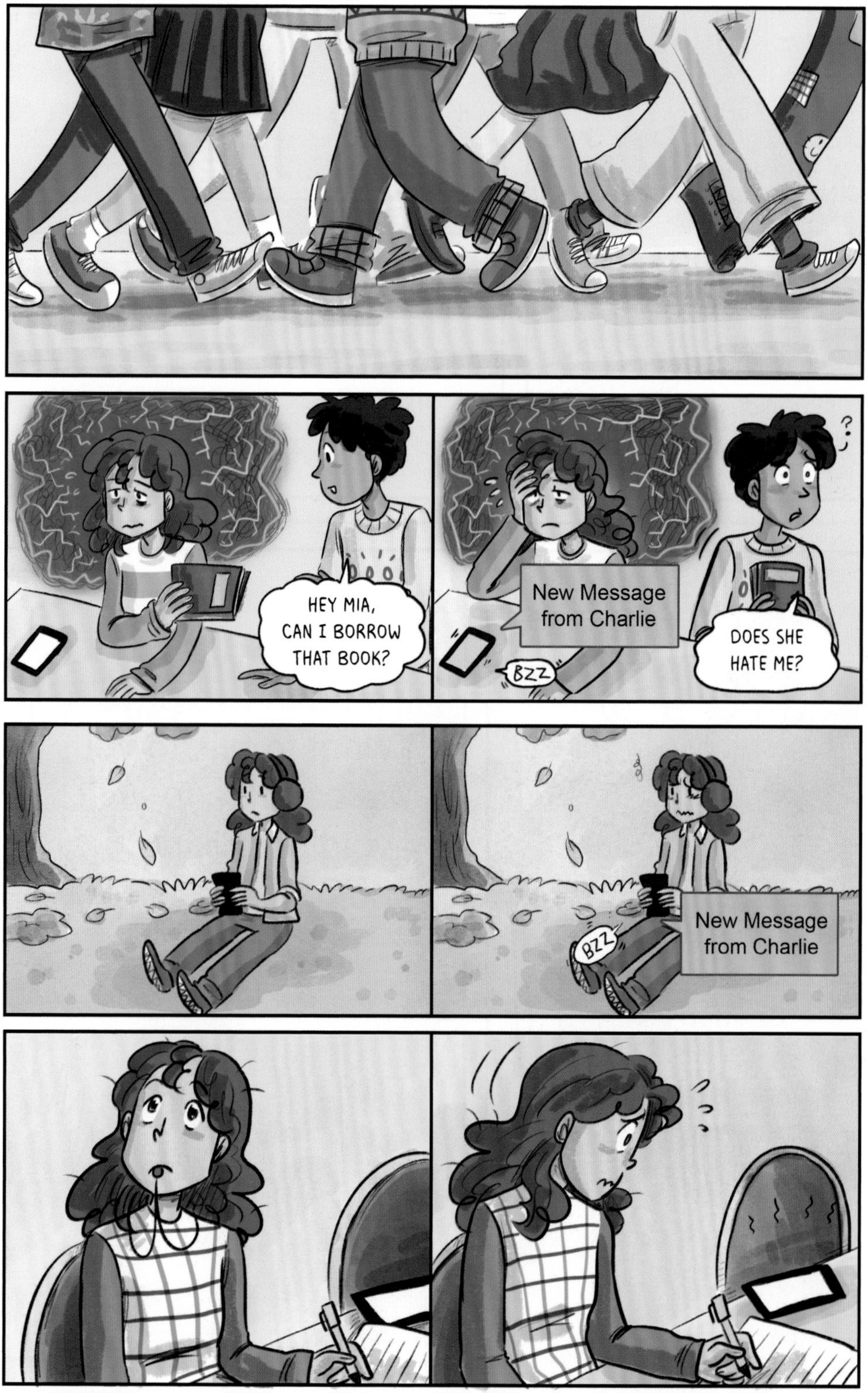
HEY MIA,
CAN I BORROW
THAT BOOK?
New Message
from Charlie
BZZ
DOES SHE
HATE ME?
BZZ
New Message
from Charlie

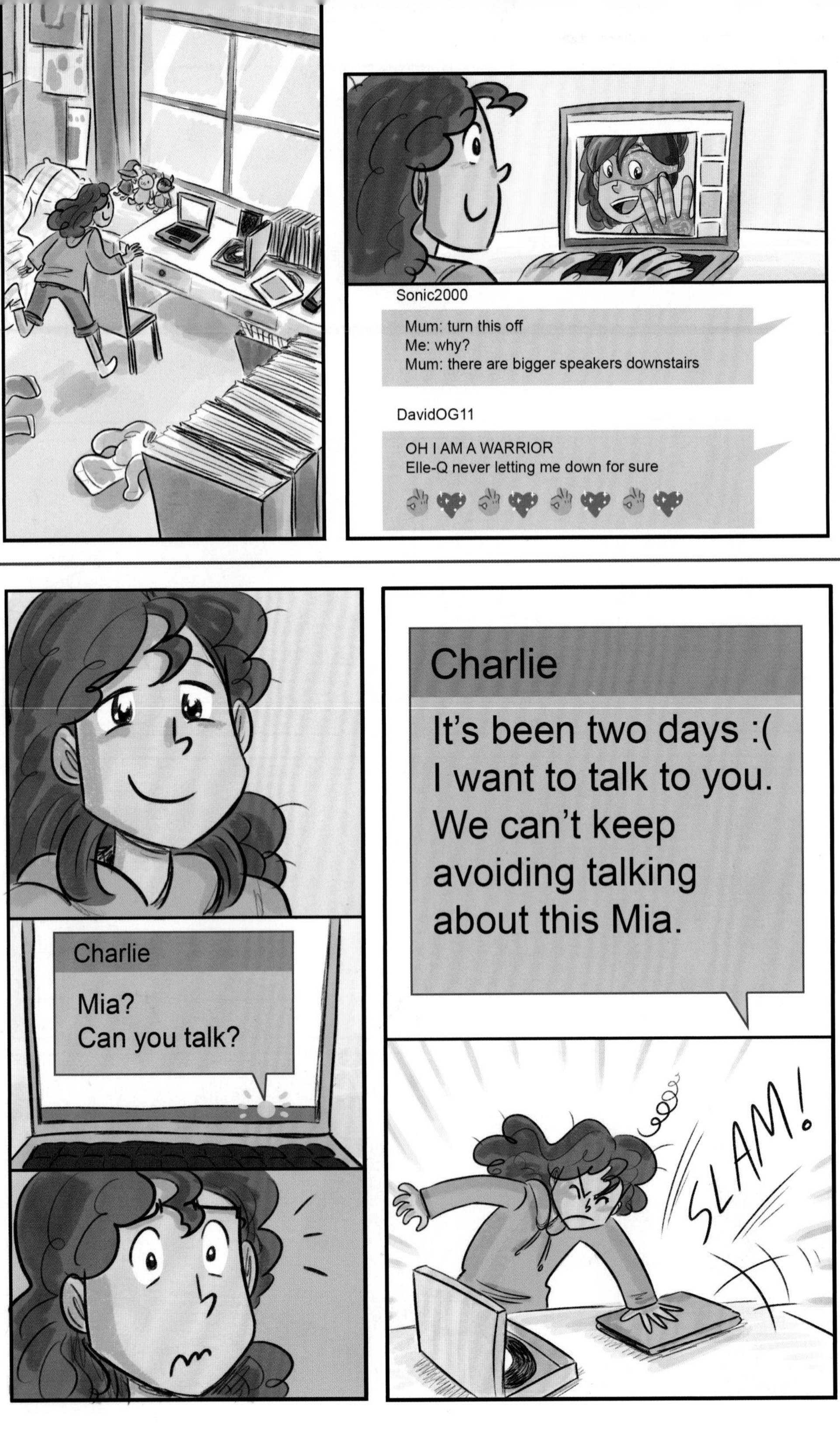
Sonic2000
Mum: turn this off
Me: why?
Mum: there are bigger speakers downstairs
DavidOG11
OH I AM A WARRIOR
Elle-Q never letting me down for sure
Charlie
It's been two days :(
I want to talk to you.
We can't keep avoiding talking about this Mia.
Charlie
Mia?
Can you talk?
SLAM!

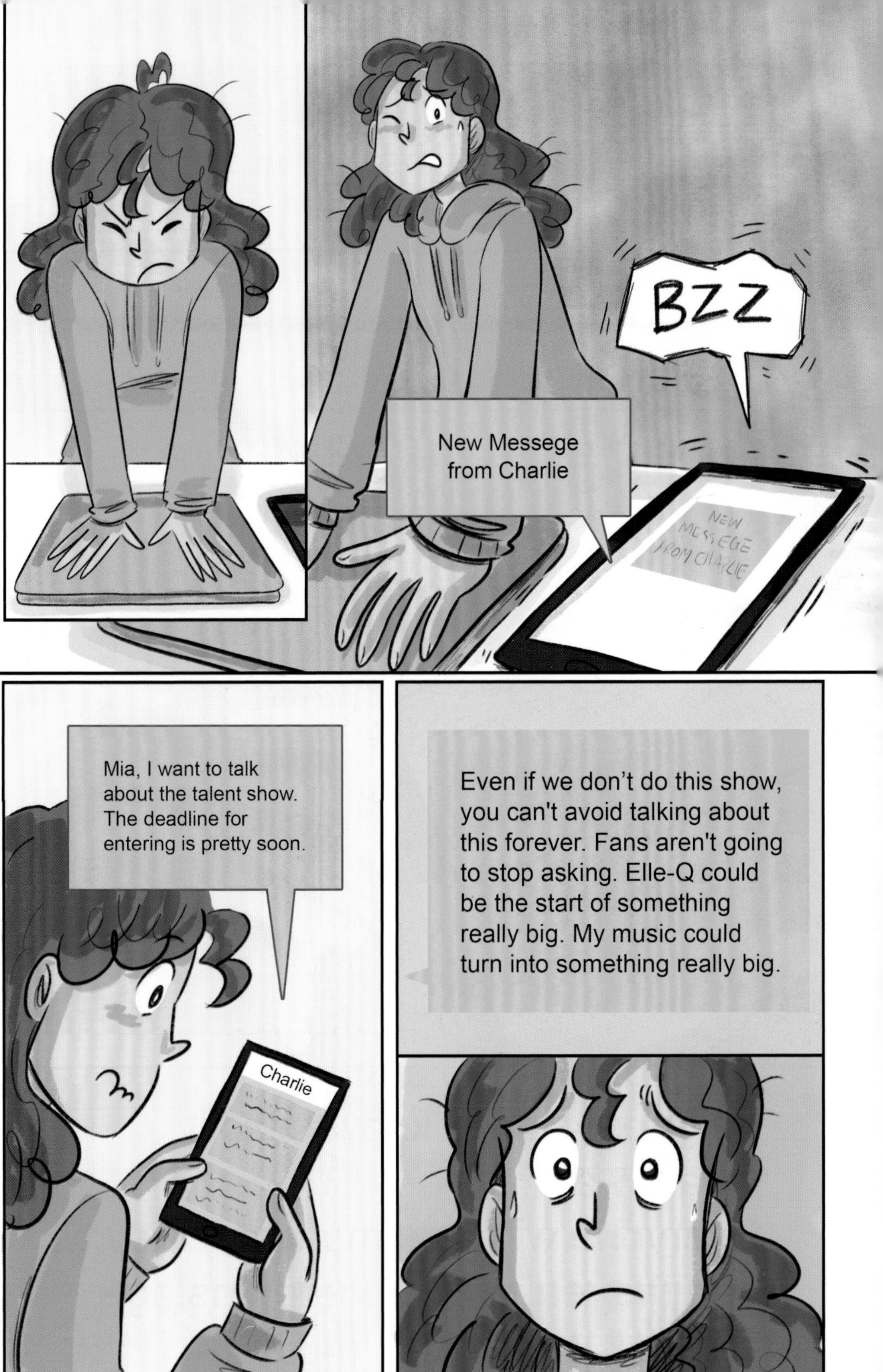
BZZ
New Messege from Charlie
NEW MESSEGE FROM CHARLIE
Mia, I want to talk about the talent show. The deadline for entering is pretty soon.
Charlie
Even if we don't do this show, you can't avoid talking about this forever. Fans aren't going to stop asking. Elle-Q could be the start of something really big. My music could turn into something really big.

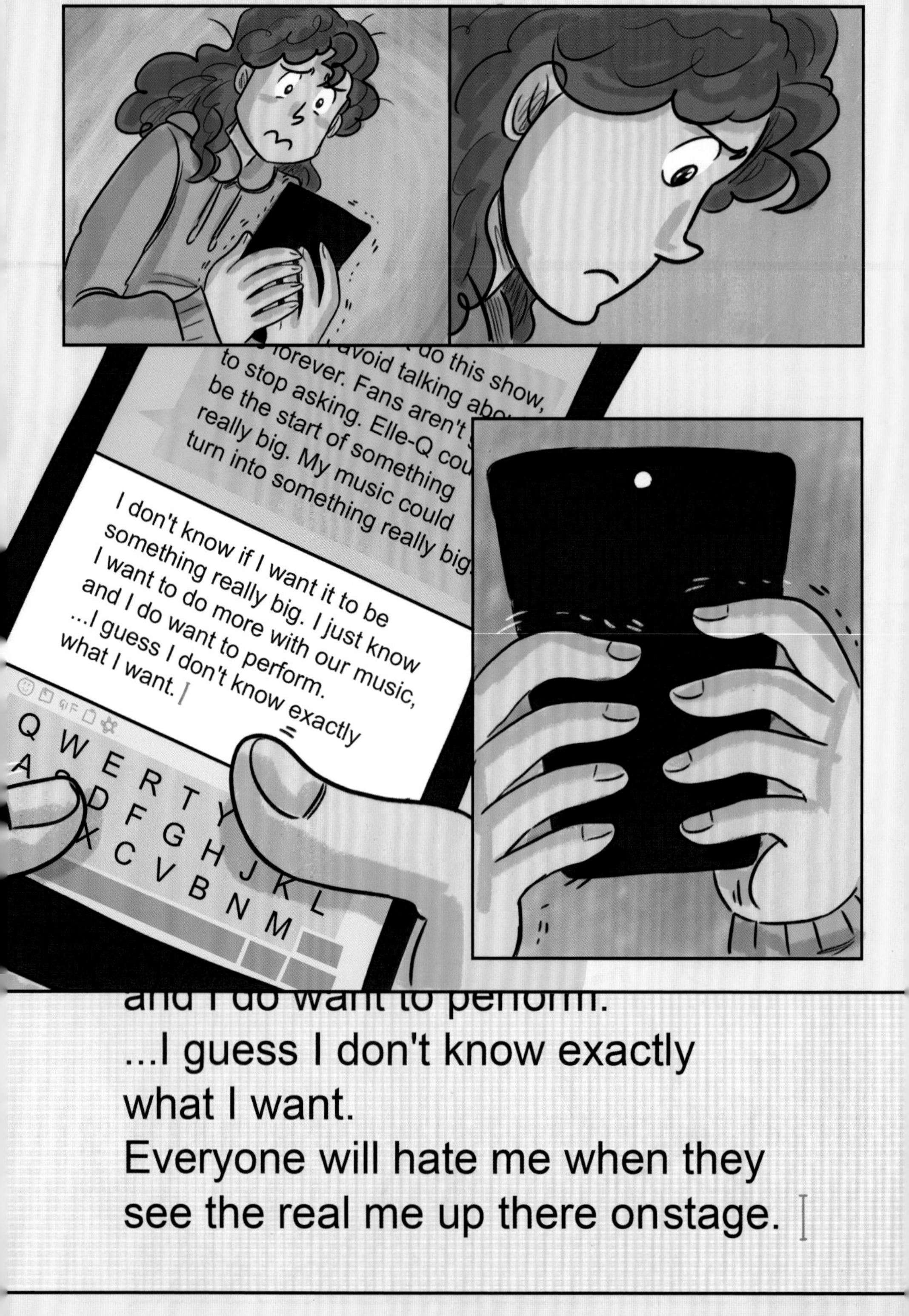
do this show,
avoid talking abo
forever. Fans aren't
to stop asking. Elle-Q cou
be the start of something
really big. My music could
turn into something really big.
I don't know if I want it to be something really big. I just know I want to do more with our music, and I do want to perform. ...I guess I don't know exactly what I want.
QWERTY
ASDFGHJKL
XCVBNM
...I guess I don't know exactly what I want.
Everyone will hate me when they see the real me up there onstage.

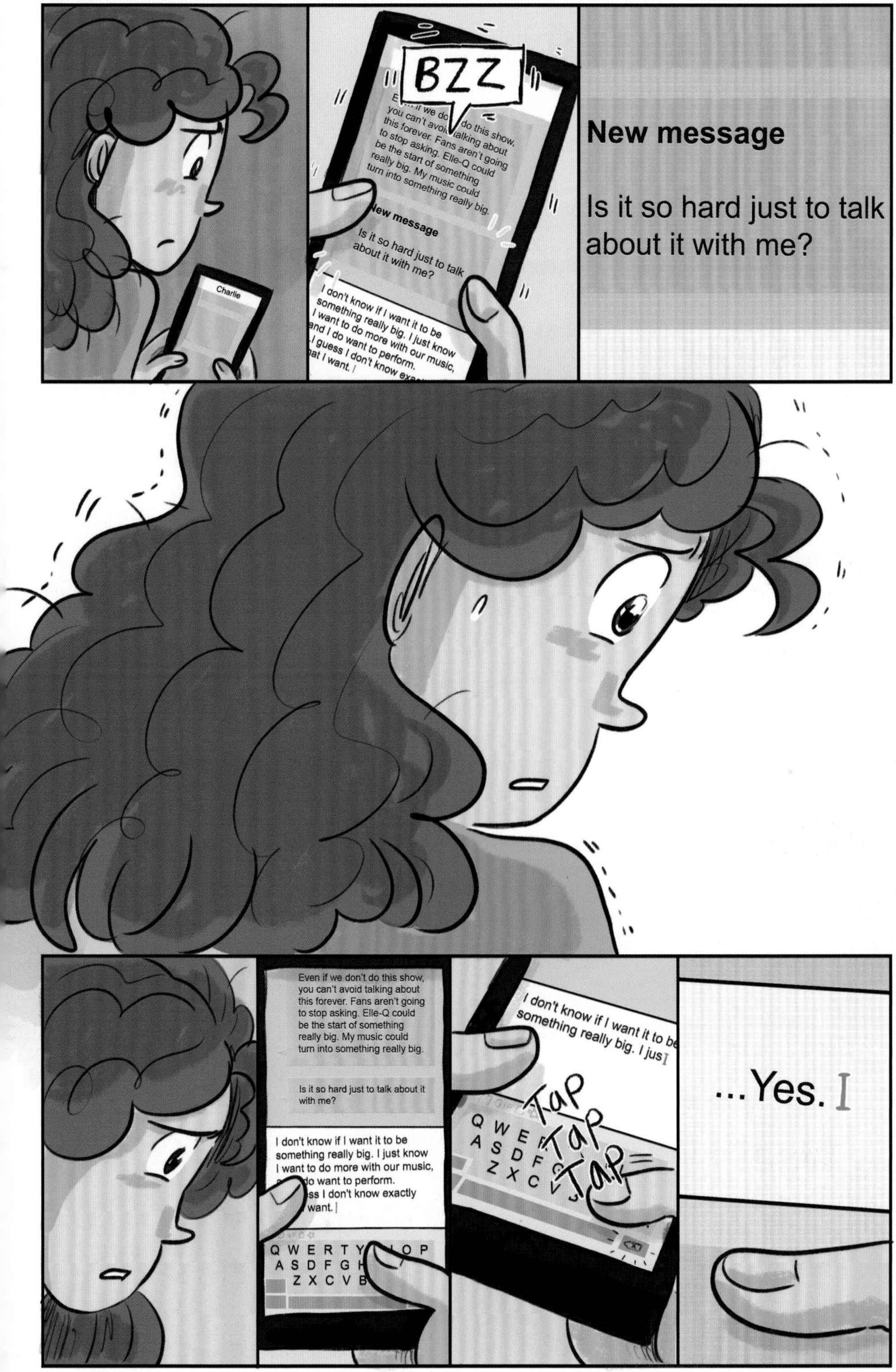
Charlie
BZZ
New message
Is it so hard just to talk about it with me?
Even if we don't do this show, you can't avoid talking about this forever. Fans aren't going to stop asking. Elle-Q could be the start of something really big. My music could turn into something really big.
Is it so hard just to talk about it with me?
I don't know if I want it to be something really big. I just know I want to do more with our music,
do want to perform.
ss I don't know exactly
want.
QWERTY OP
ASDFGH
ZXCVB
I don't know if I want it to be something really big. I jus
TAP
TAP
TAP
...Yes.

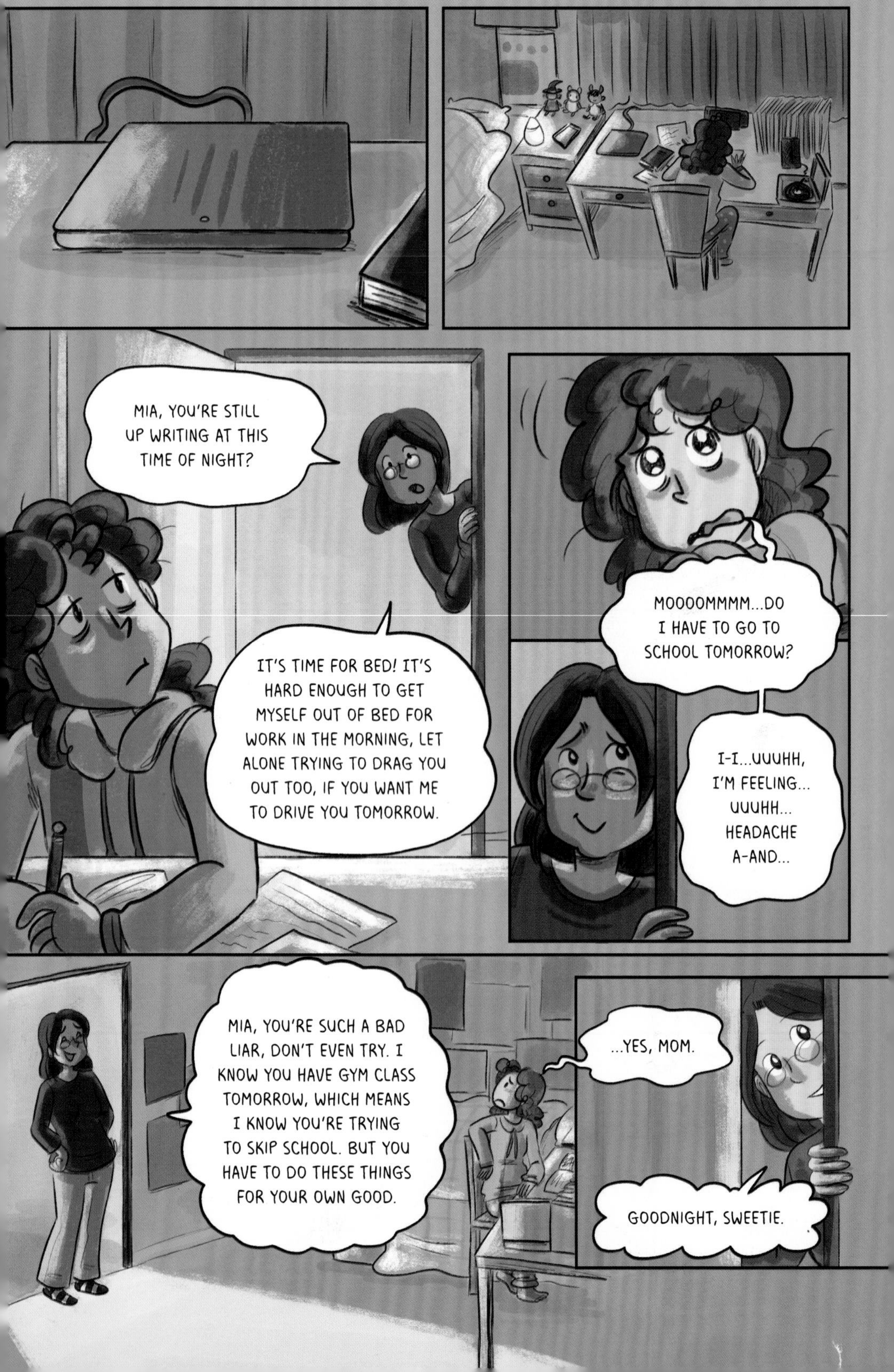
MIA, YOU'RE STILL UP WRITING AT THIS TIME OF NIGHT?
IT'S TIME FOR BED! IT'S HARD ENOUGH TO GET MYSELF OUT OF BED FOR WORK IN THE MORNING, LET ALONE TRYING TO DRAG YOU OUT TOO, IF YOU WANT ME TO DRIVE YOU TOMORROW.
MOOOOMMMM...DO I HAVE TO GO TO SCHOOL TOMORROW?
I-I...UUUHH, I'M FEELING... UUUHH... HEADACHE A-AND...
MIA, YOU'RE SUCH A BAD LIAR, DON'T EVEN TRY. I KNOW YOU HAVE GYM CLASS TOMORROW, WHICH MEANS I KNOW YOU'RE TRYING TO SKIP SCHOOL. BUT YOU HAVE TO DO THESE THINGS FOR YOUR OWN GOOD.
...YES, MOM.
GOODNIGHT, SWEETIE.

# CHAPTER FOUR

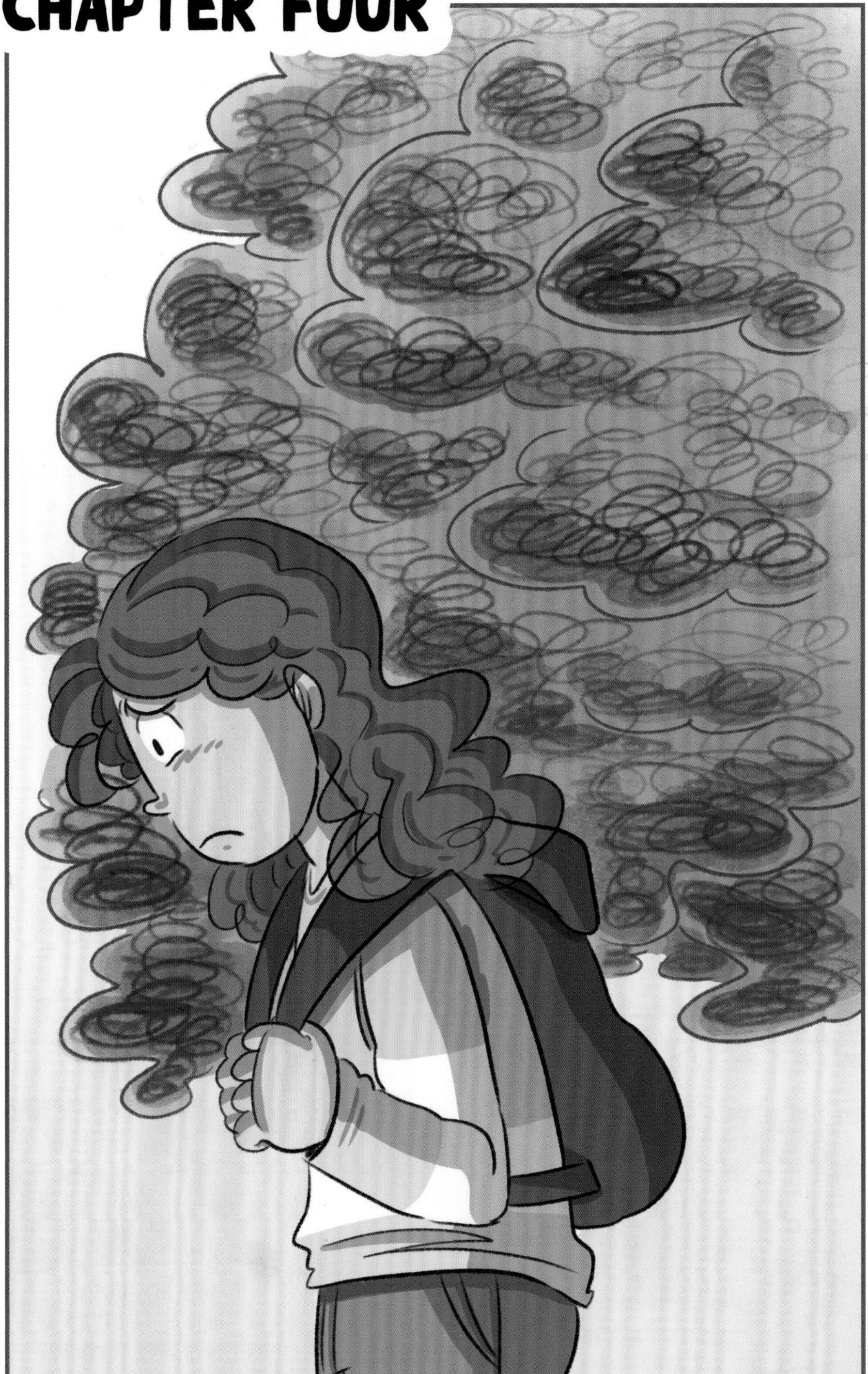

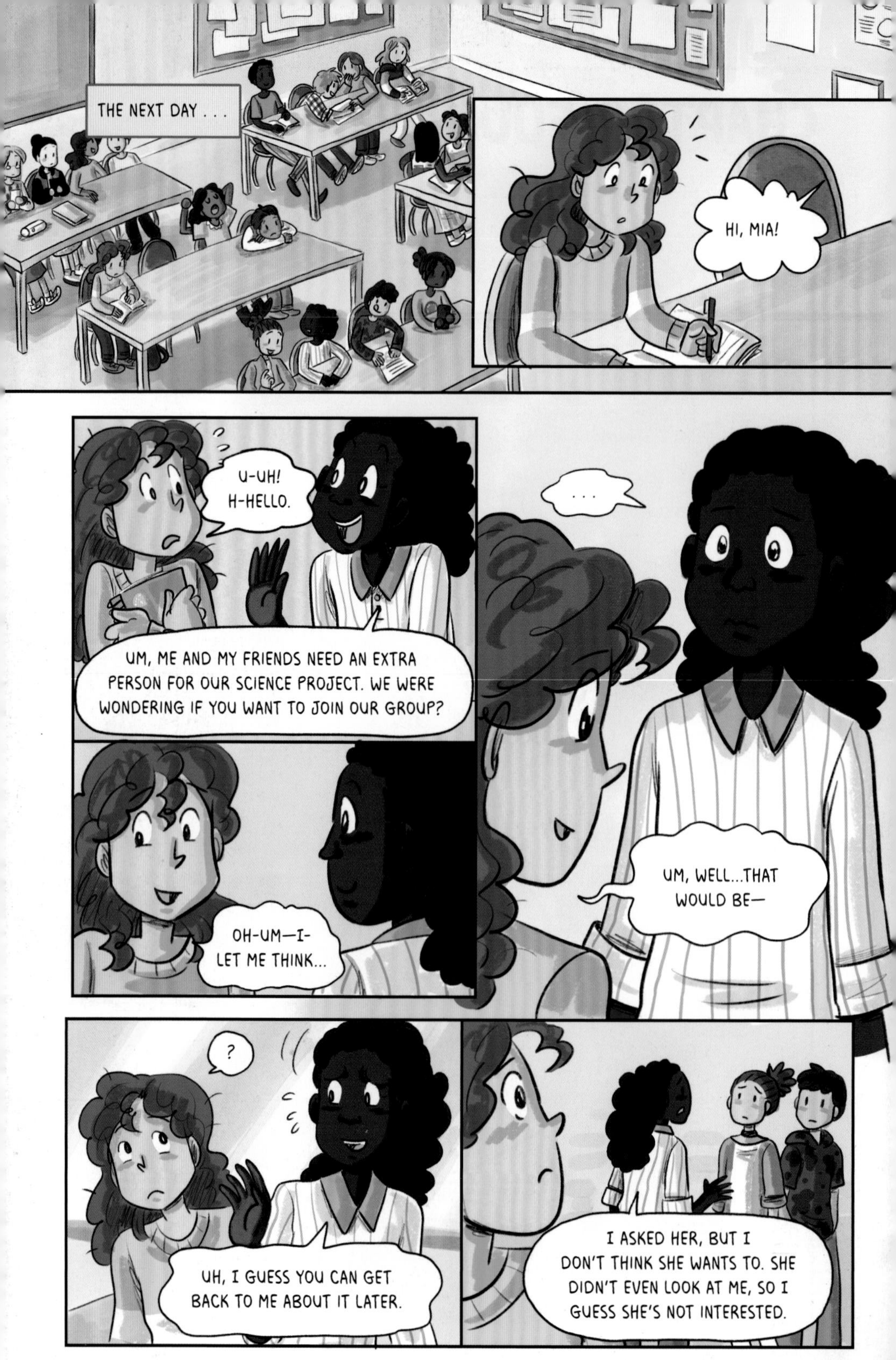
THE NEXT DAY . . .
HI, MIA!
U-UH! H-HELLO.
UM, ME AND MY FRIENDS NEED AN EXTRA PERSON FOR OUR SCIENCE PROJECT. WE WERE WONDERING IF YOU WANT TO JOIN OUR GROUP?
OH-UM—I- LET ME THINK...
. . .
UM, WELL...THAT WOULD BE—
?
UH, I GUESS YOU CAN GET BACK TO ME ABOUT IT LATER.
I ASKED HER, BUT I DON'T THINK SHE WANTS TO. SHE DIDN'T EVEN LOOK AT ME, SO I GUESS SHE'S NOT INTERESTED.

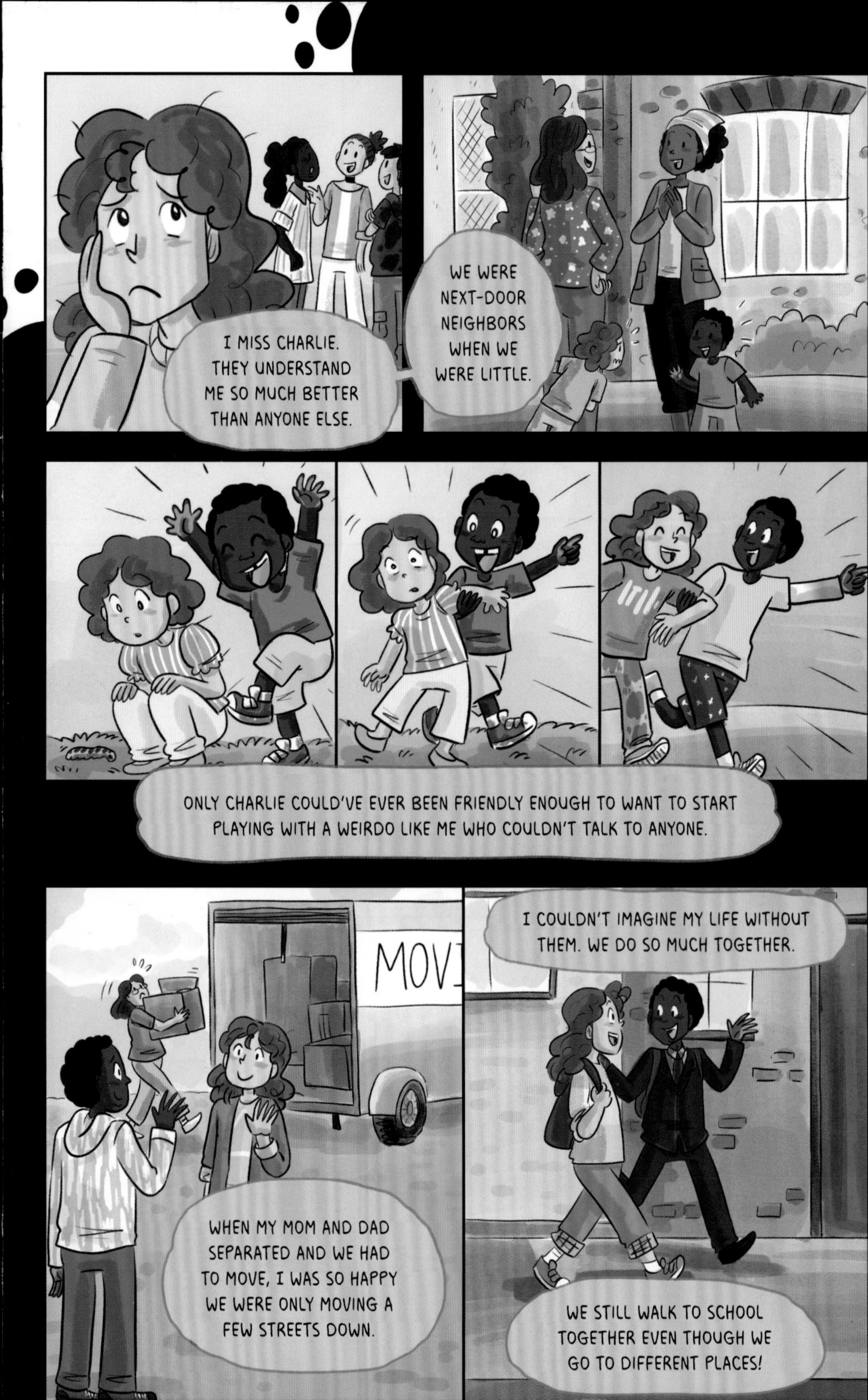
I MISS CHARLIE. THEY UNDERSTAND ME SO MUCH BETTER THAN ANYONE ELSE.
WE WERE NEXT-DOOR NEIGHBORS WHEN WE WERE LITTLE.
ONLY CHARLIE COULD'VE EVER BEEN FRIENDLY ENOUGH TO WANT TO START PLAYING WITH A WEIRDO LIKE ME WHO COULDN'T TALK TO ANYONE.
MOVI
WHEN MY MOM AND DAD SEPARATED AND WE HAD TO MOVE, I WAS SO HAPPY WE WERE ONLY MOVING A FEW STREETS DOWN.
I COULDN'T IMAGINE MY LIFE WITHOUT THEM. WE DO SO MUCH TOGETHER.
WE STILL WALK TO SCHOOL TOGETHER EVEN THOUGH WE GO TO DIFFERENT PLACES!

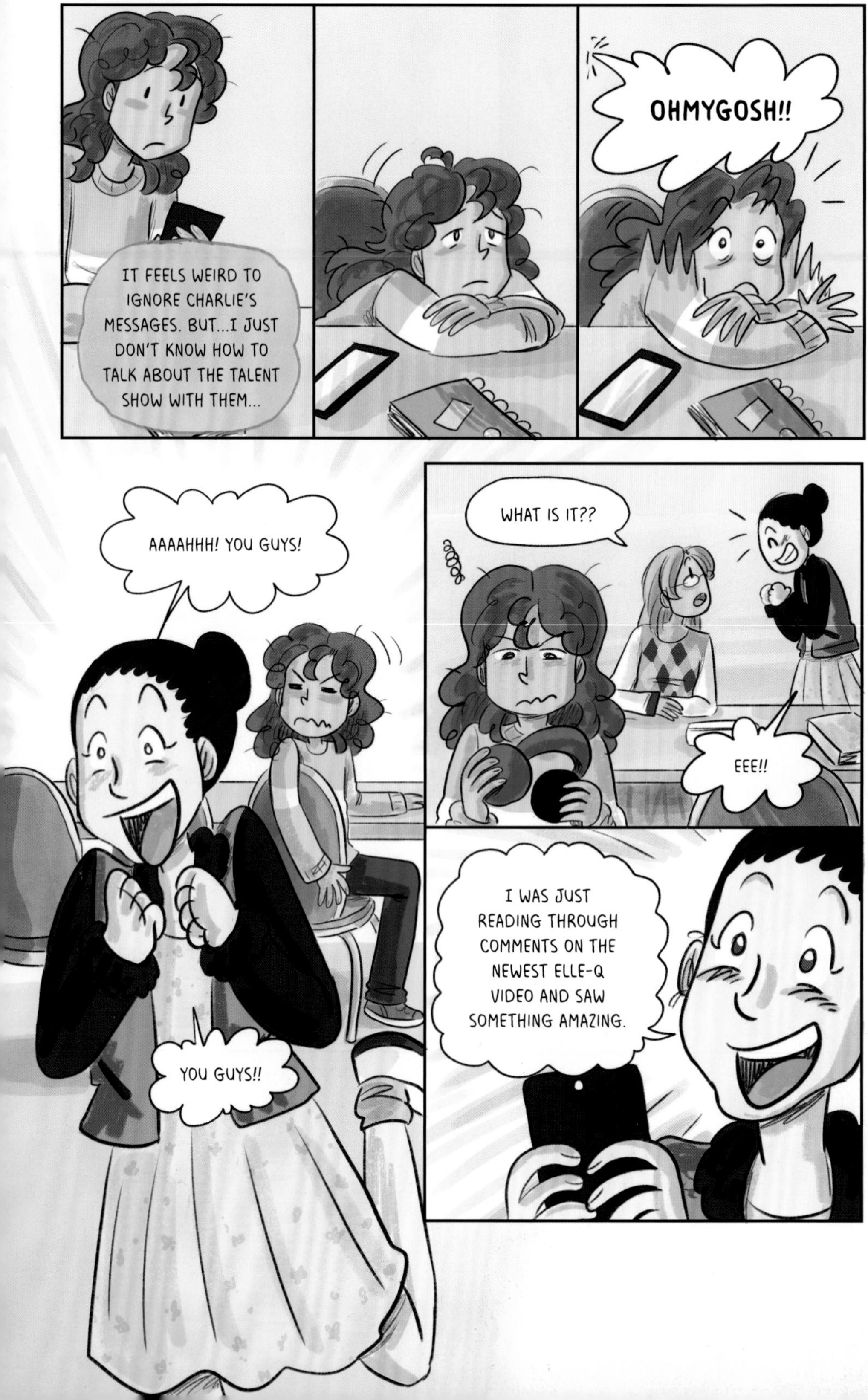
IT FEELS WEIRD TO IGNORE CHARLIE'S MESSAGES. BUT...I JUST DON'T KNOW HOW TO TALK ABOUT THE TALENT SHOW WITH THEM...
OHMYGOSH!!
AAAAHHH! YOU GUYS!
YOU GUYS!!
WHAT IS IT??
EEE!!
I WAS JUST READING THROUGH COMMENTS ON THE NEWEST ELLE-Q VIDEO AND SAW SOMETHING AMAZING.

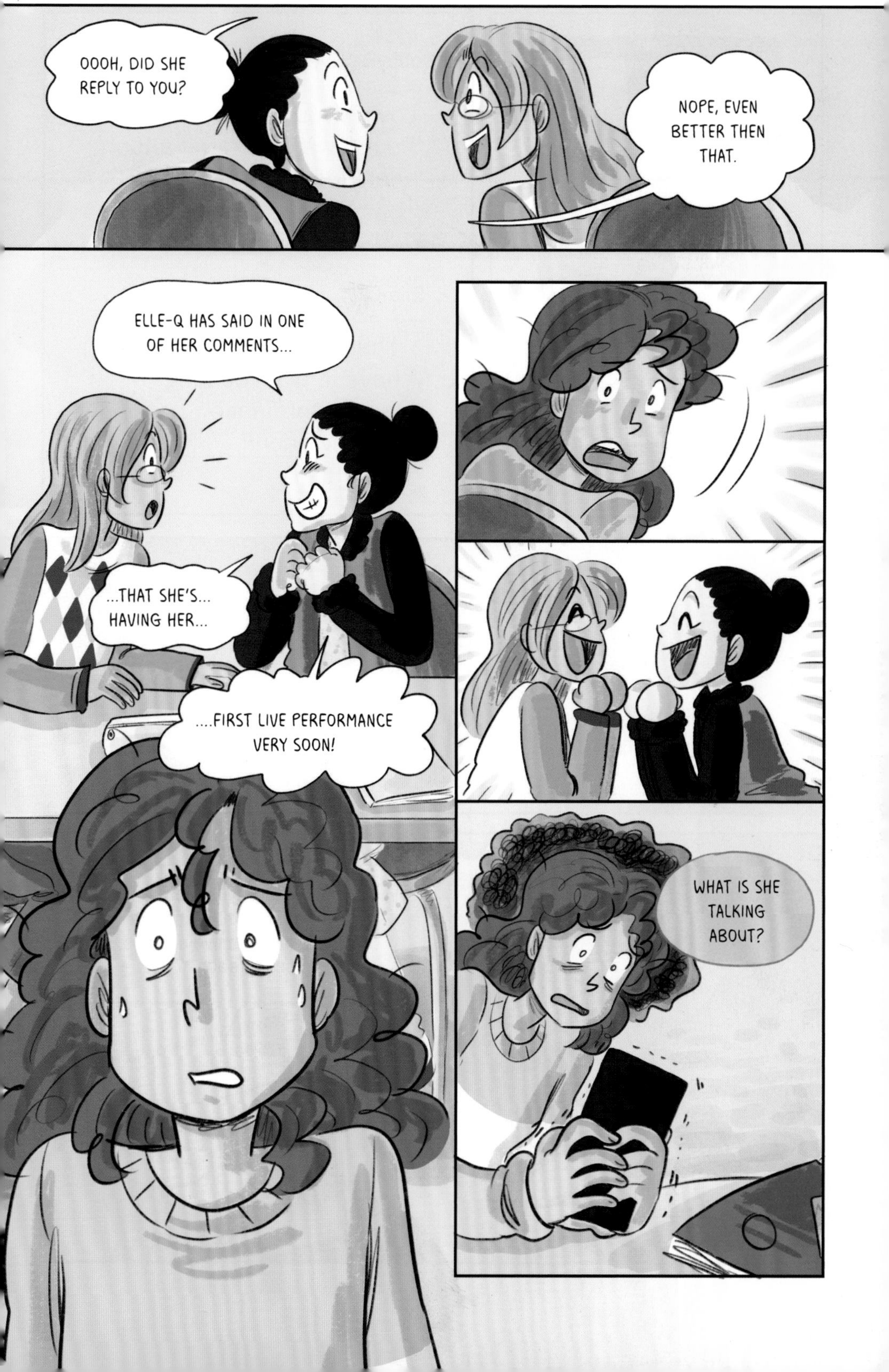
OOOH, DID SHE REPLY TO YOU?
NOPE, EVEN BETTER THEN THAT.
ELLE-Q HAS SAID IN ONE OF HER COMMENTS...
...THAT SHE'S... HAVING HER...
....FIRST LIVE PERFORMANCE VERY SOON!
WHAT IS SHE TALKING ABOUT?

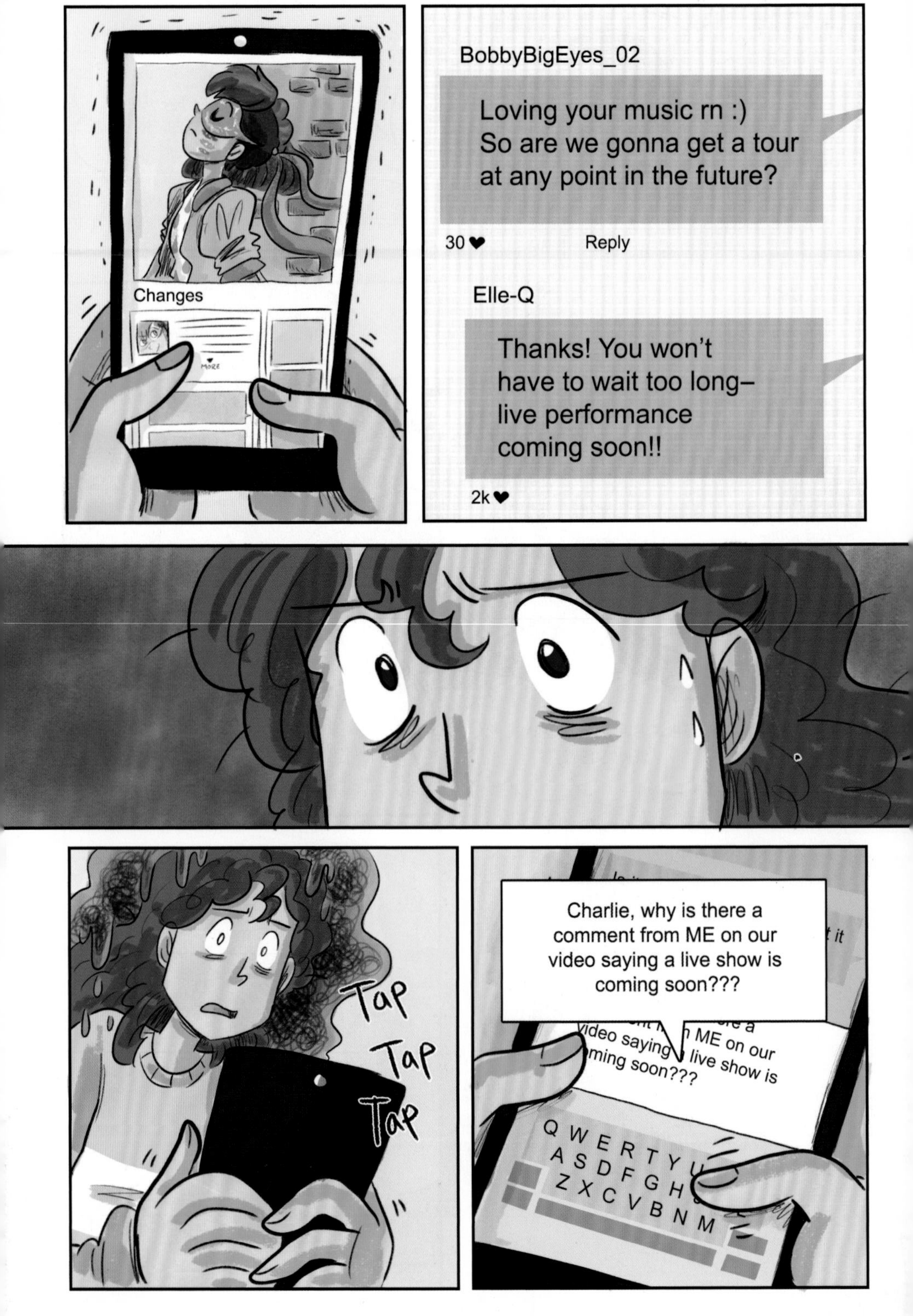
Changes
BobbyBigEyes_02
Loving your music rn :) So are we gonna get a tour at any point in the future?
30 ❤ Reply
Elle-Q
Thanks! You won't have to wait too long– live performance coming soon!!
2k ❤
Tap
Tap
Tap
Charlie, why is there a comment from ME on our video saying a live show is coming soon???

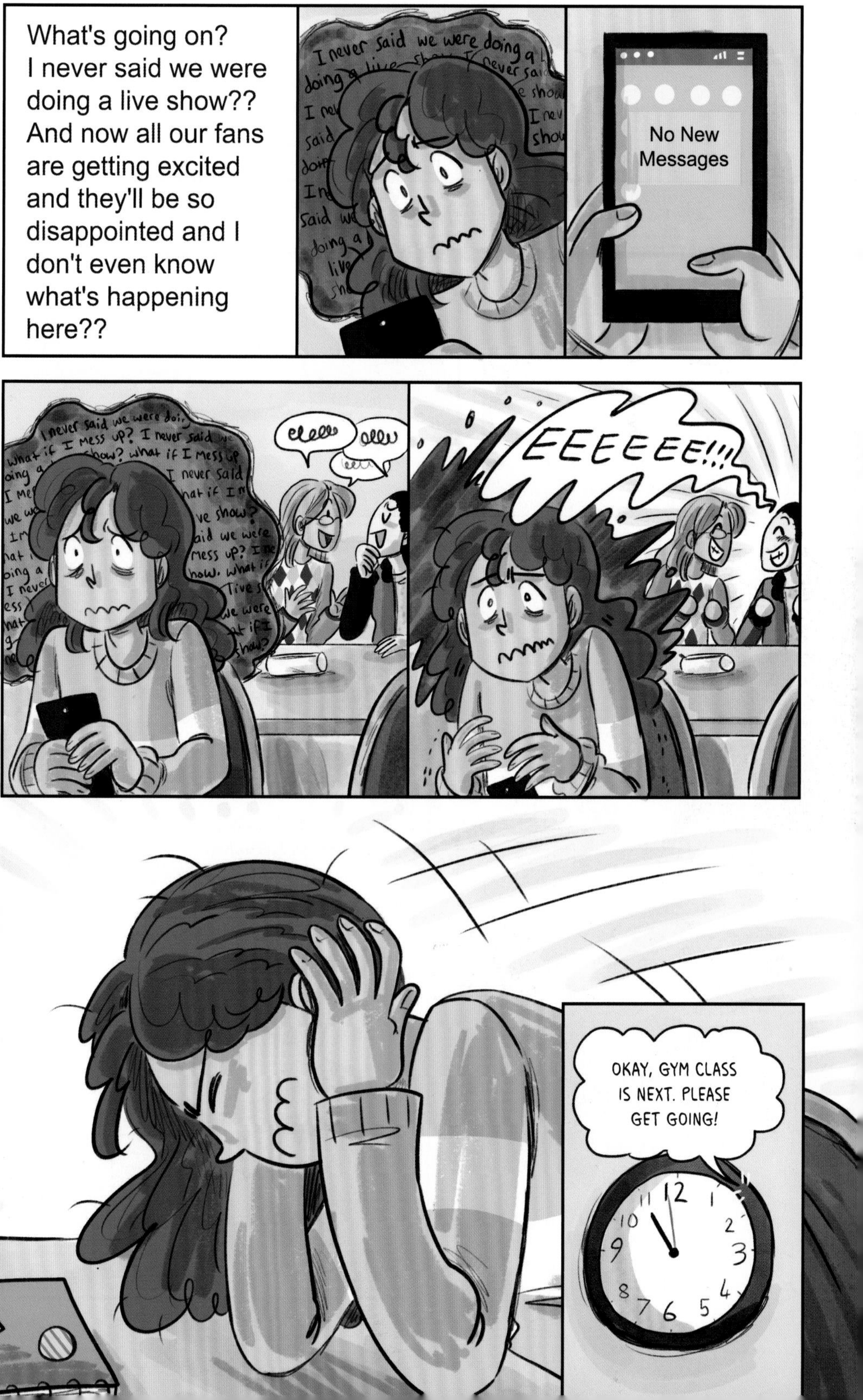
What's going on? I never said we were doing a live show?? And now all our fans are getting excited and they'll be so disappointed and I don't even know what's happening here??
I never said we were doing a live show
No New Messages
I never said we were doing a live show? what if I mess up?
EEEEEE!!!
OKAY, GYM CLASS IS NEXT. PLEASE GET GOING!

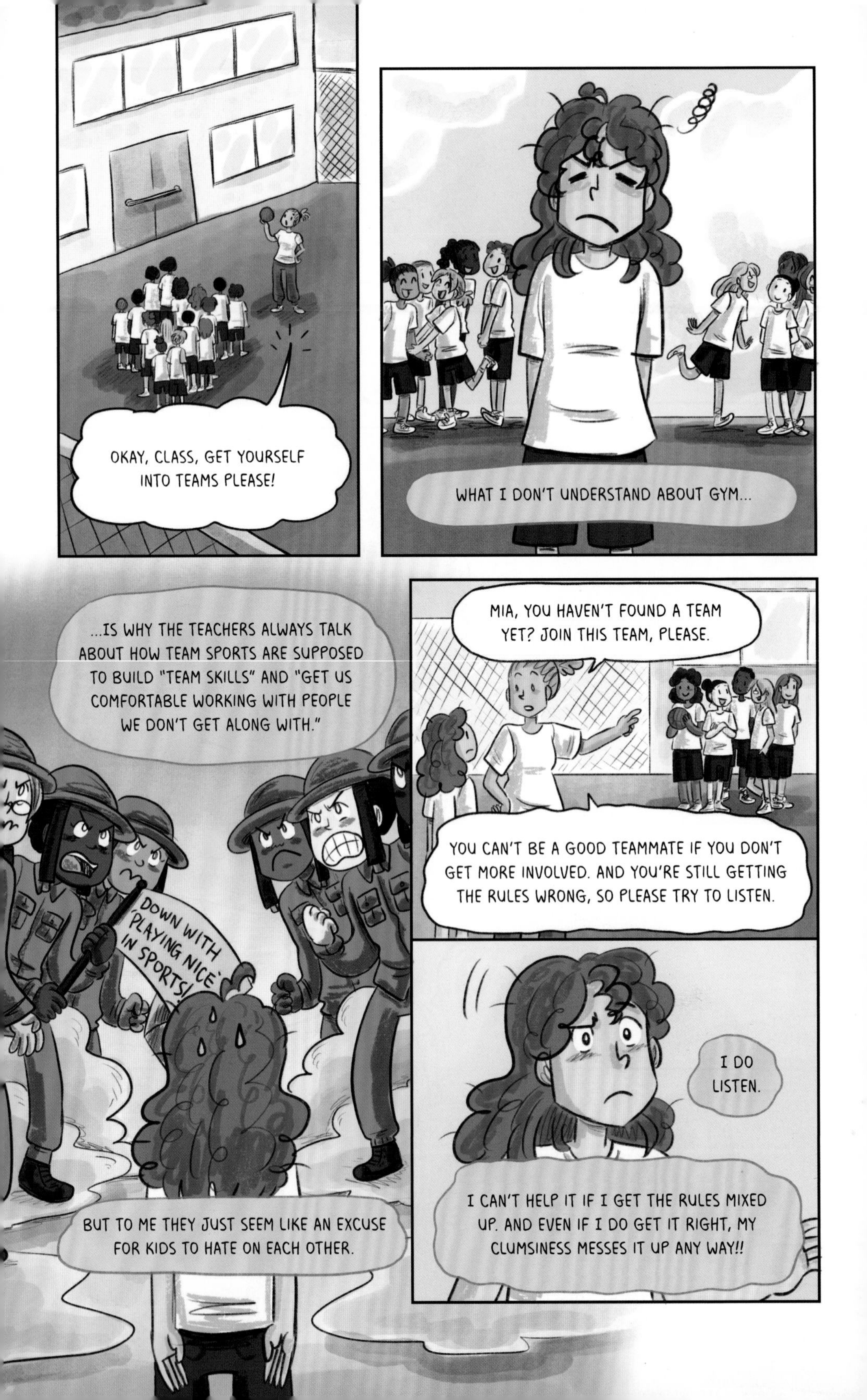
OKAY, CLASS, GET YOURSELF INTO TEAMS PLEASE!
WHAT I DON'T UNDERSTAND ABOUT GYM...
...IS WHY THE TEACHERS ALWAYS TALK ABOUT HOW TEAM SPORTS ARE SUPPOSED TO BUILD "TEAM SKILLS" AND "GET US COMFORTABLE WORKING WITH PEOPLE WE DON'T GET ALONG WITH."
DOWN WITH 'PLAYING NICE' IN SPORTS!
BUT TO ME THEY JUST SEEM LIKE AN EXCUSE FOR KIDS TO HATE ON EACH OTHER.
MIA, YOU HAVEN'T FOUND A TEAM YET? JOIN THIS TEAM, PLEASE.
YOU CAN'T BE A GOOD TEAMMATE IF YOU DON'T GET MORE INVOLVED. AND YOU'RE STILL GETTING THE RULES WRONG, SO PLEASE TRY TO LISTEN.
I DO LISTEN.
I CAN'T HELP IT IF I GET THE RULES MIXED UP. AND EVEN IF I DO GET IT RIGHT, MY CLUMSINESS MESSES IT UP ANY WAY!!

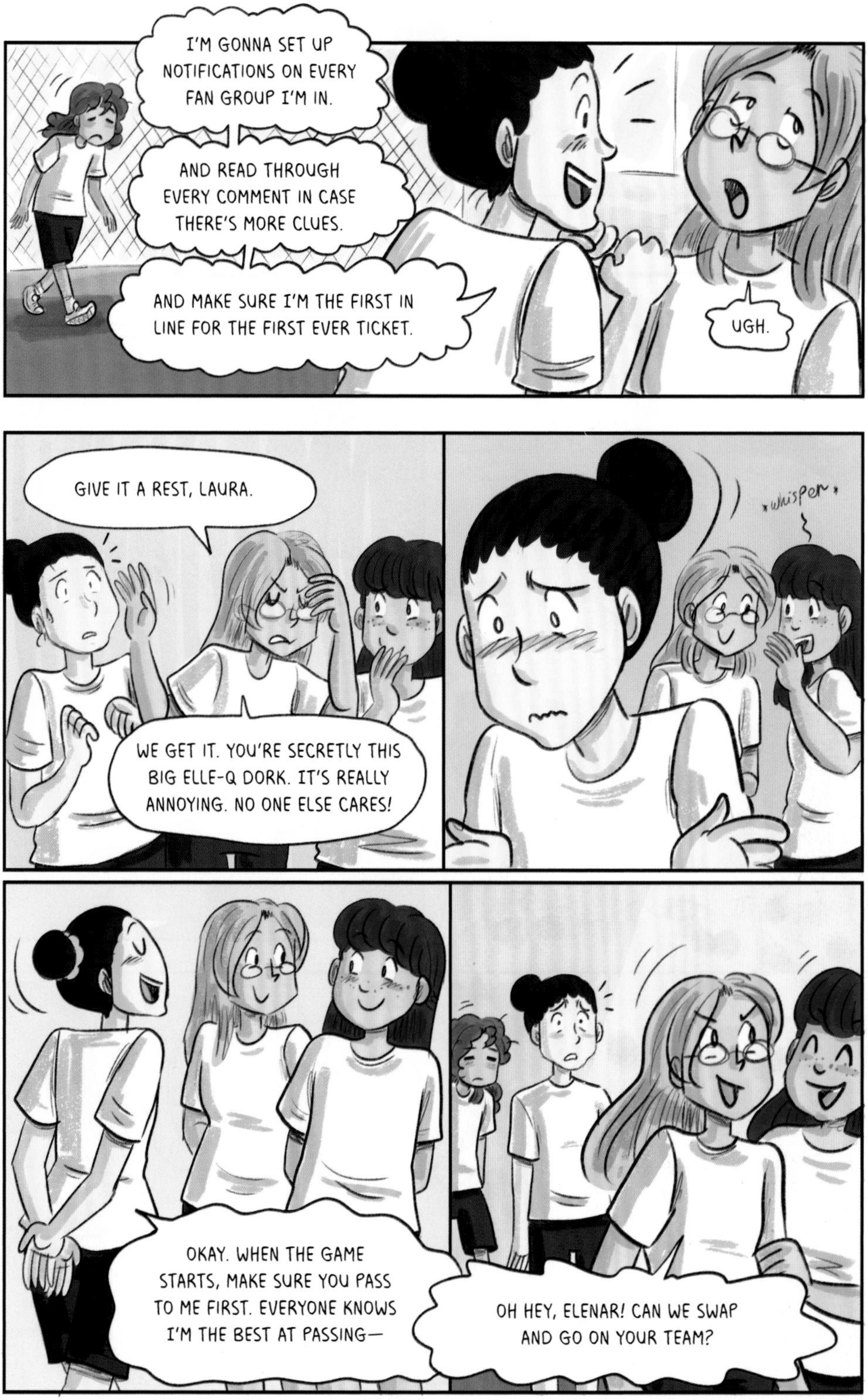
I'M GONNA SET UP NOTIFICATIONS ON EVERY FAN GROUP I'M IN.
AND READ THROUGH EVERY COMMENT IN CASE THERE'S MORE CLUES.
AND MAKE SURE I'M THE FIRST IN LINE FOR THE FIRST EVER TICKET.
UGH.
GIVE IT A REST, LAURA.
WE GET IT. YOU'RE SECRETLY THIS BIG ELLE-Q DORK. IT'S REALLY ANNOYING. NO ONE ELSE CARES!
*whisper*
OKAY. WHEN THE GAME STARTS, MAKE SURE YOU PASS TO ME FIRST. EVERYONE KNOWS I'M THE BEST AT PASSING—
OH HEY, ELENAR! CAN WE SWAP AND GO ON YOUR TEAM?

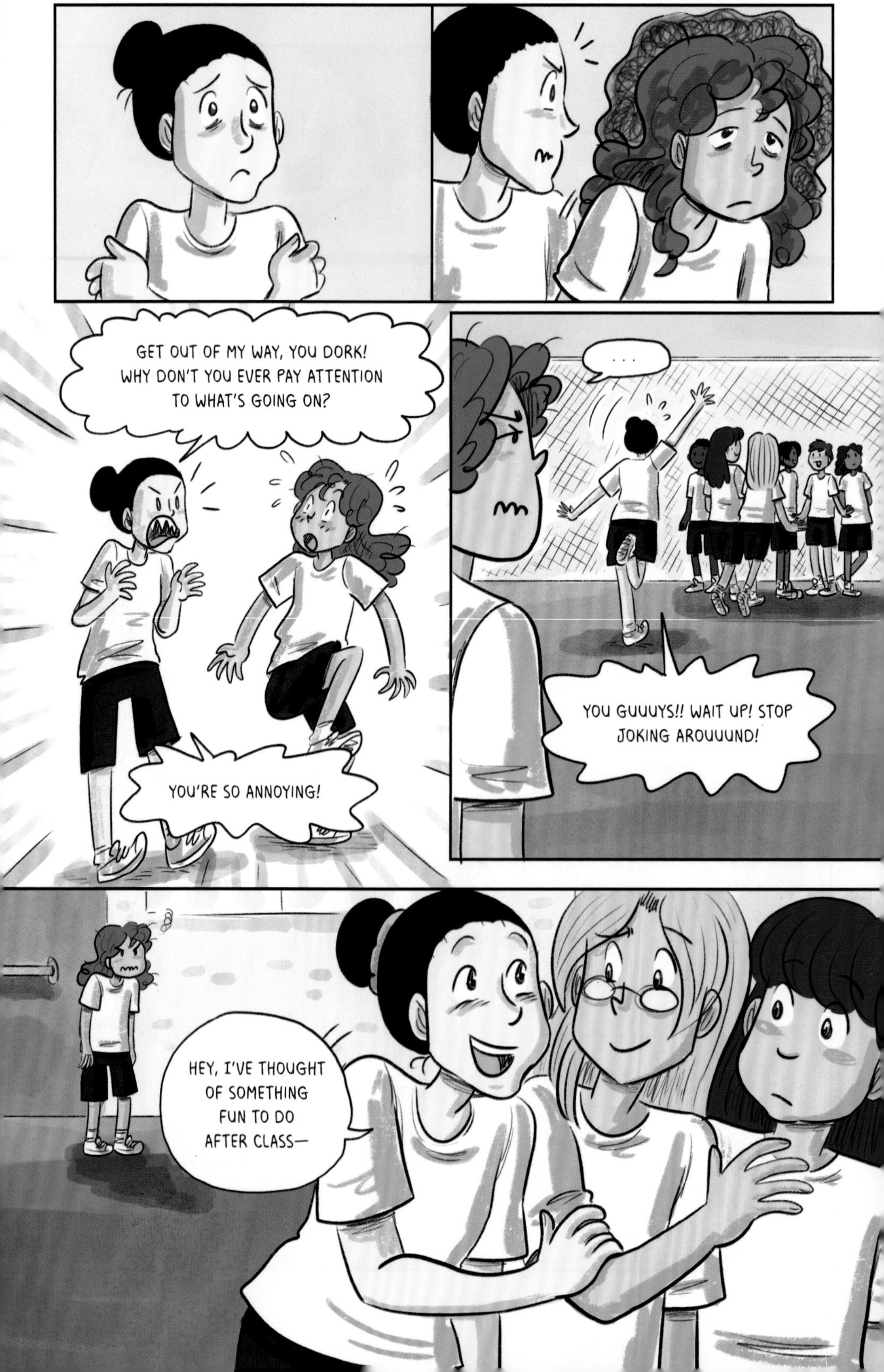
GET OUT OF MY WAY, YOU DORK! WHY DON'T YOU EVER PAY ATTENTION TO WHAT'S GOING ON?
YOU'RE SO ANNOYING!
. . .
YOU GUUUYS!! WAIT UP! STOP JOKING AROUUUND!
HEY, I'VE THOUGHT OF SOMETHING FUN TO DO AFTER CLASS—

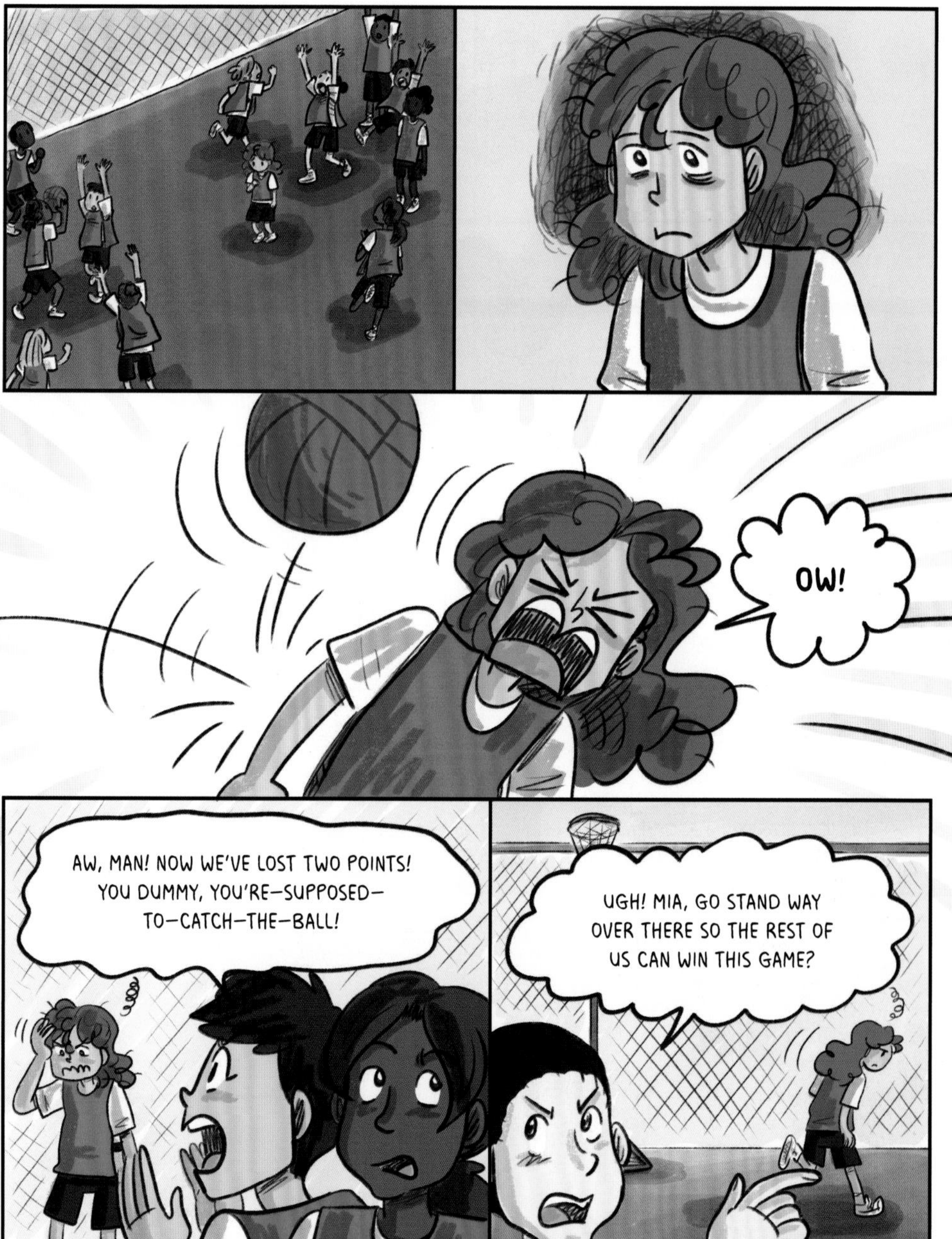
OW!
AW, MAN! NOW WE'VE LOST TWO POINTS! YOU DUMMY, YOU'RE—SUPPOSED—TO—CATCH—THE—BALL!
DON'T THROW TO HER. SHE ALWAYS STINKS AT SPORTS. SHE SAYS IT'S COS SHE'S AUTISTIC, BUT I THINK SHE'S JUST BEING LAZY.
UGH! MIA, GO STAND WAY OVER THERE SO THE REST OF US CAN WIN THIS GAME?

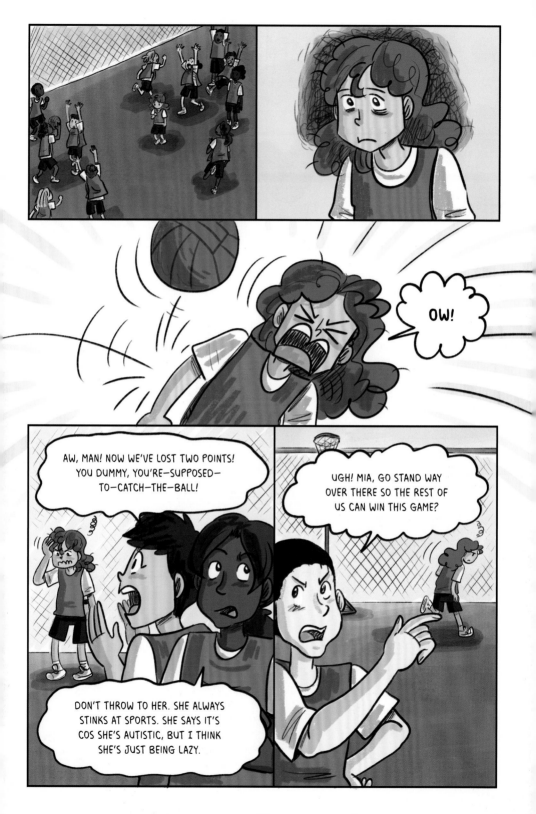

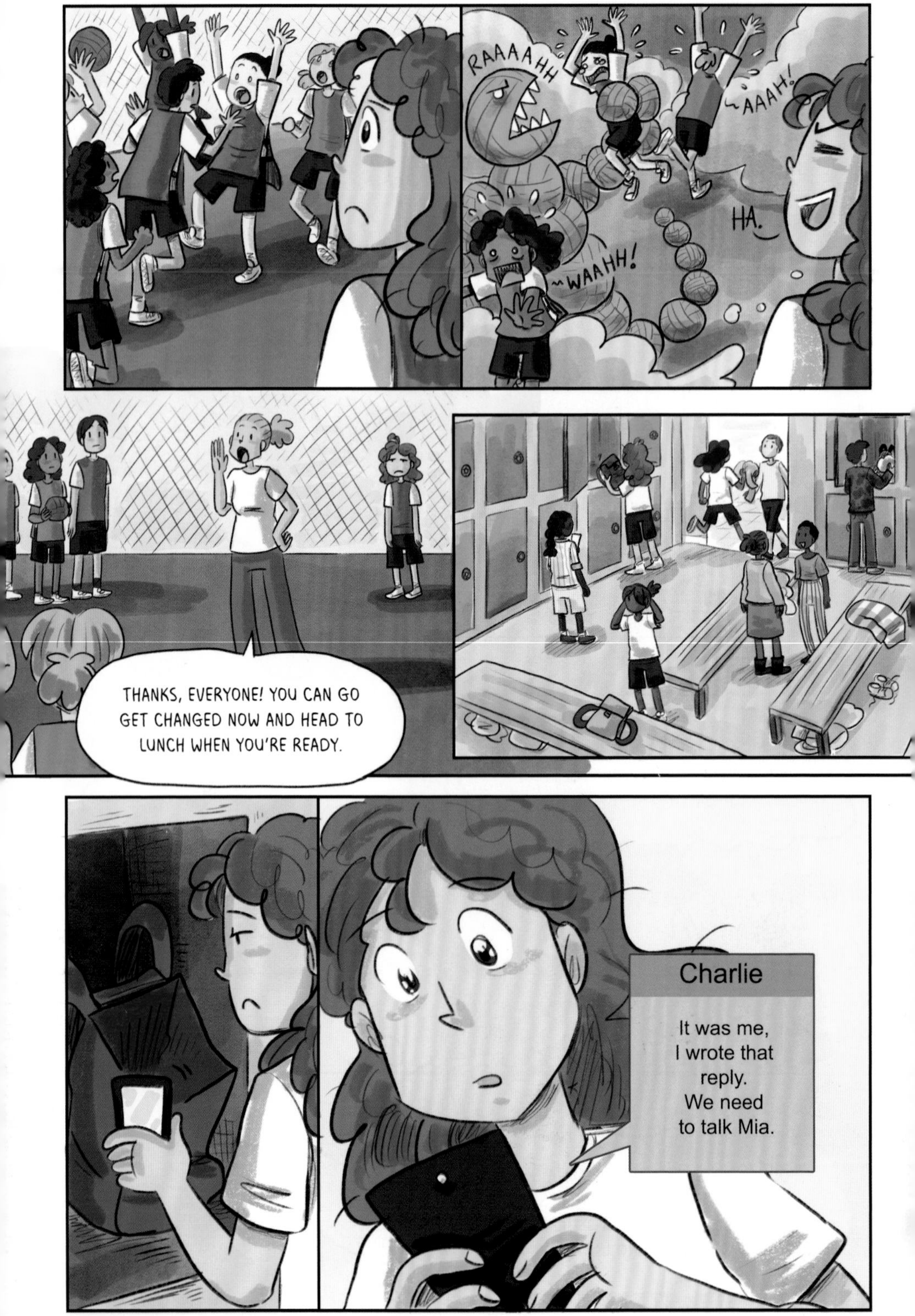
RAAAAHH
~AAAH!
HA.
~WAAHH!
THANKS, EVERYONE! YOU CAN GO GET CHANGED NOW AND HEAD TO LUNCH WHEN YOU'RE READY.
Charlie
It was me, I wrote that reply. We need to talk Mia.

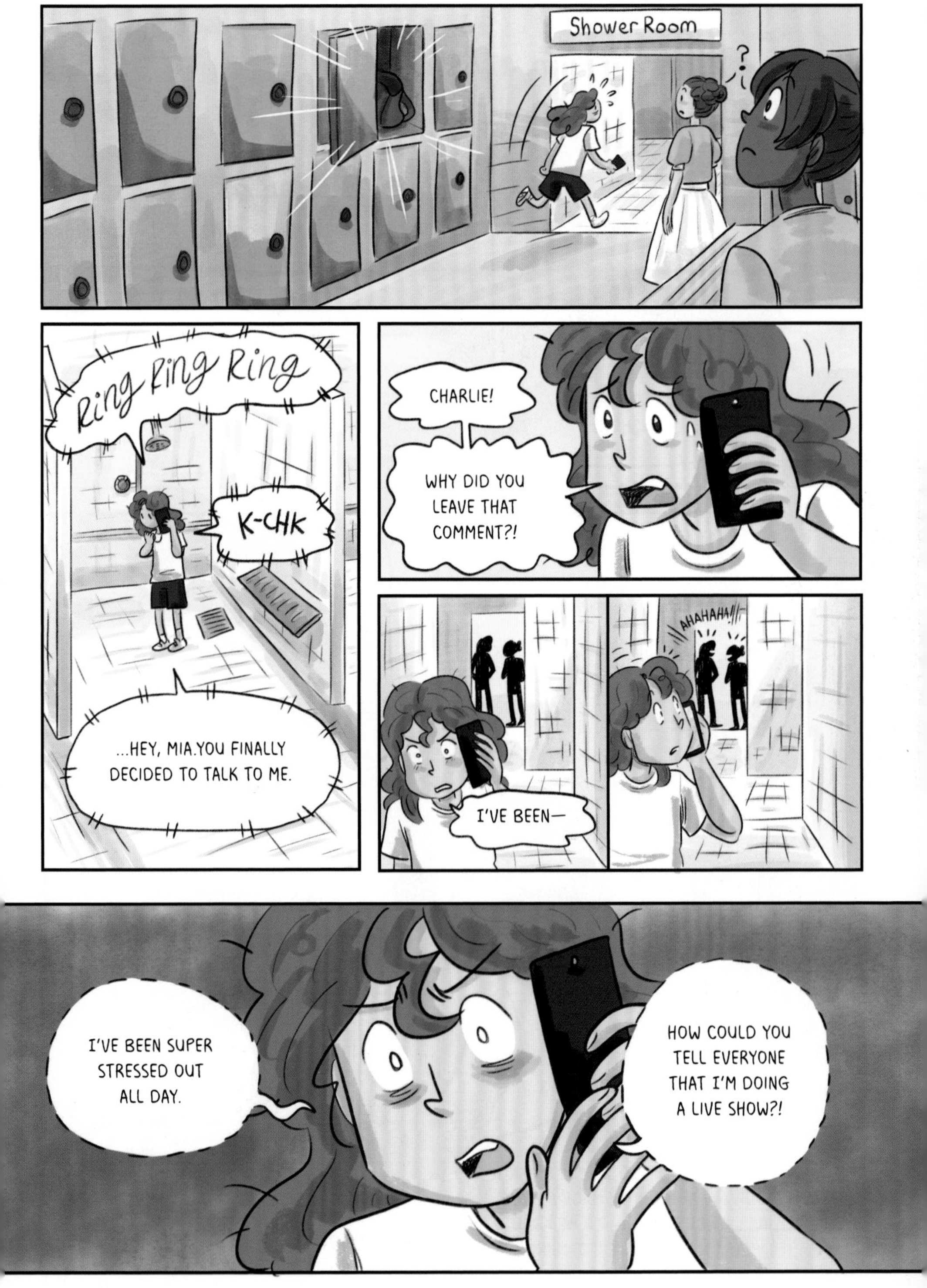
Shower Room
?
Ring Ring Ring
K-CHK
...HEY, MIA.YOU FINALLY DECIDED TO TALK TO ME.
CHARLIE!
WHY DID YOU LEAVE THAT COMMENT?!
I'VE BEEN—
AHAHAHA!!
I'VE BEEN SUPER STRESSED OUT ALL DAY.
HOW COULD YOU TELL EVERYONE THAT I'M DOING A LIVE SHOW?!

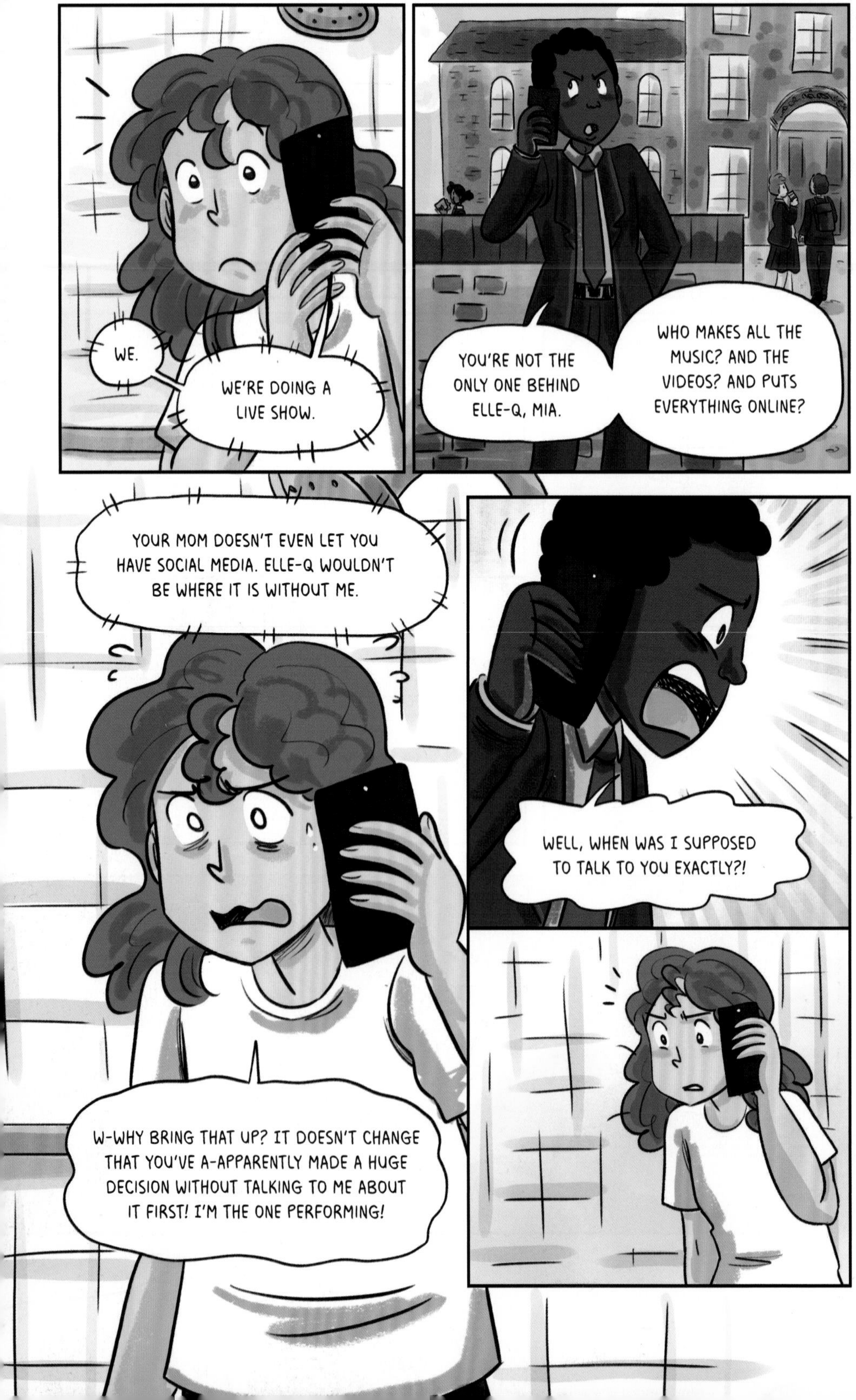
WE.
WE'RE DOING A LIVE SHOW.
YOU'RE NOT THE ONLY ONE BEHIND ELLE-Q, MIA.
WHO MAKES ALL THE MUSIC? AND THE VIDEOS? AND PUTS EVERYTHING ONLINE?
YOUR MOM DOESN'T EVEN LET YOU HAVE SOCIAL MEDIA. ELLE-Q WOULDN'T BE WHERE IT IS WITHOUT ME.
W-WHY BRING THAT UP? IT DOESN'T CHANGE THAT YOU'VE A-APPARENTLY MADE A HUGE DECISION WITHOUT TALKING TO ME ABOUT IT FIRST! I'M THE ONE PERFORMING!
WELL, WHEN WAS I SUPPOSED TO TALK TO YOU EXACTLY?!

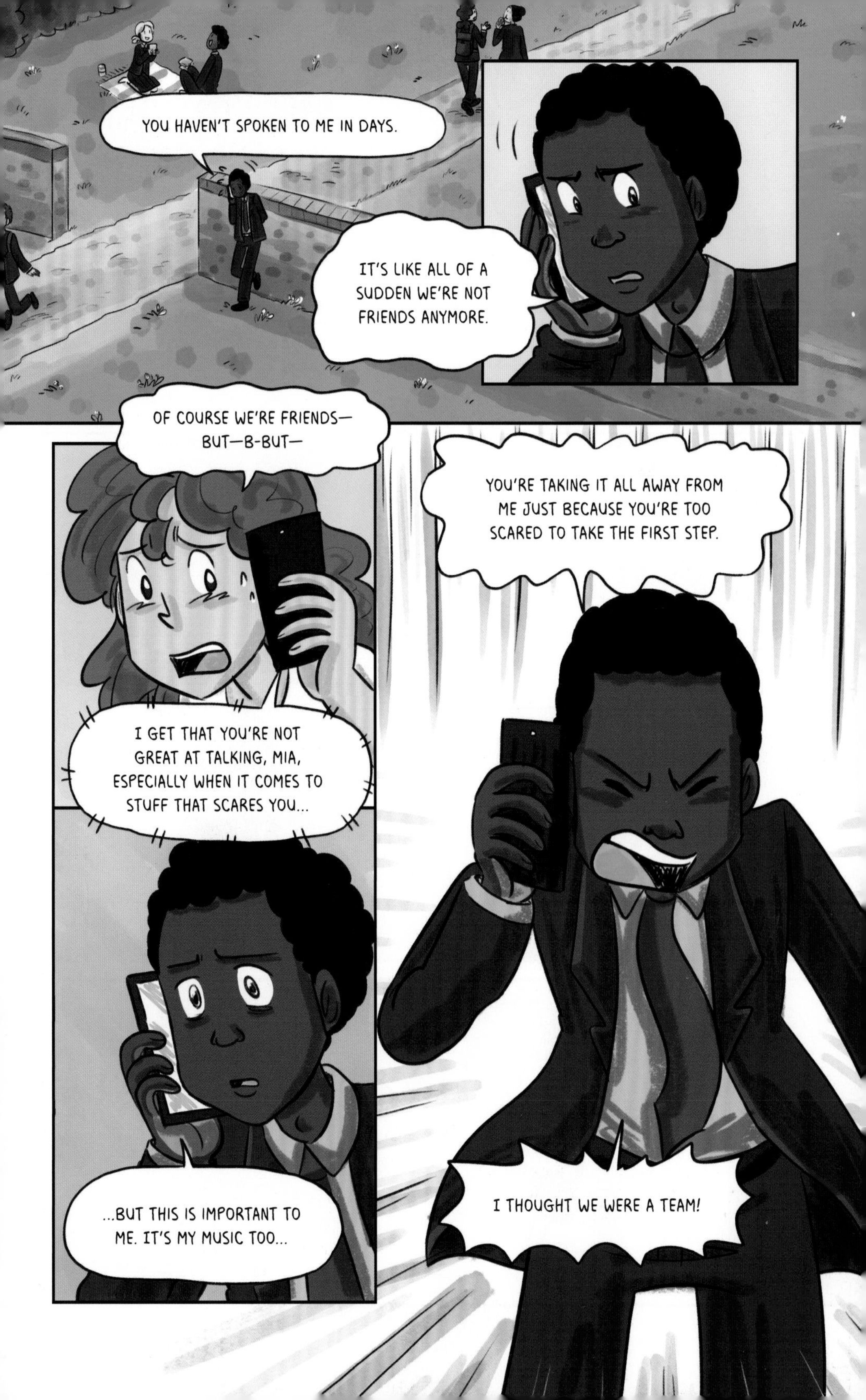
YOU HAVEN'T SPOKEN TO ME IN DAYS.
IT'S LIKE ALL OF A SUDDEN WE'RE NOT FRIENDS ANYMORE.
OF COURSE WE'RE FRIENDS— BUT—B-BUT—
I GET THAT YOU'RE NOT GREAT AT TALKING, MIA, ESPECIALLY WHEN IT COMES TO STUFF THAT SCARES YOU...
...BUT THIS IS IMPORTANT TO ME. IT'S MY MUSIC TOO...
YOU'RE TAKING IT ALL AWAY FROM ME JUST BECAUSE YOU'RE TOO SCARED TO TAKE THE FIRST STEP.
I THOUGHT WE WERE A TEAM!

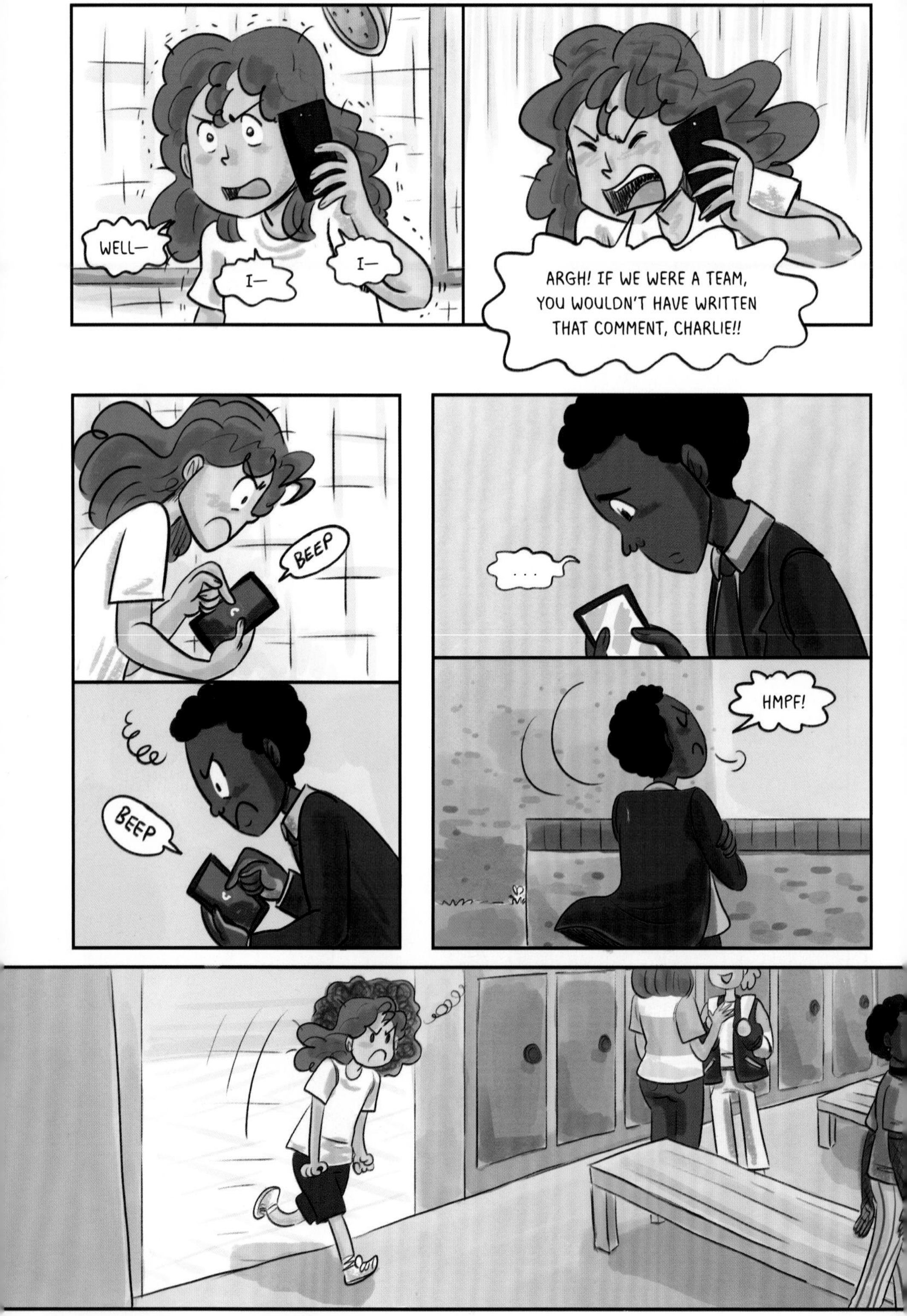
WELL—
I—
I—
ARGH! IF WE WERE A TEAM, YOU WOULDN'T HAVE WRITTEN THAT COMMENT, CHARLIE!!
BEEP
. . .
BEEP
HMPF!

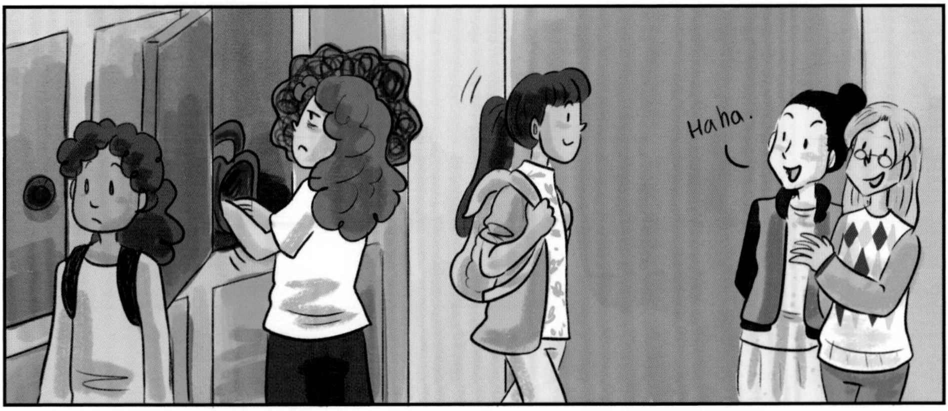
Haha.

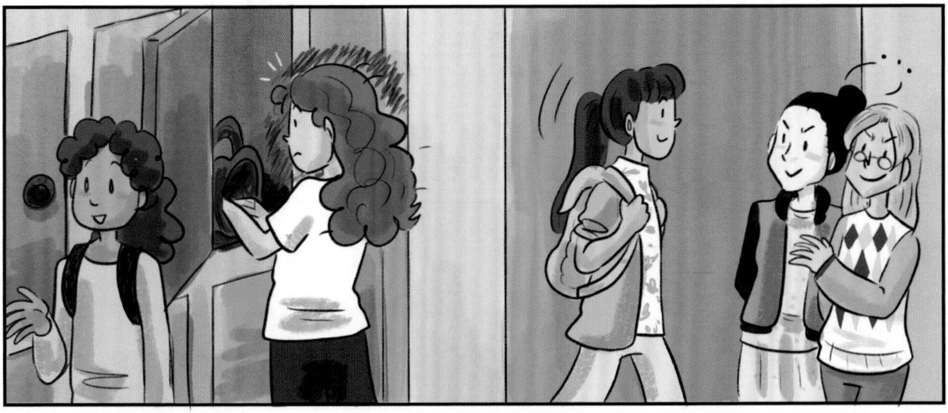

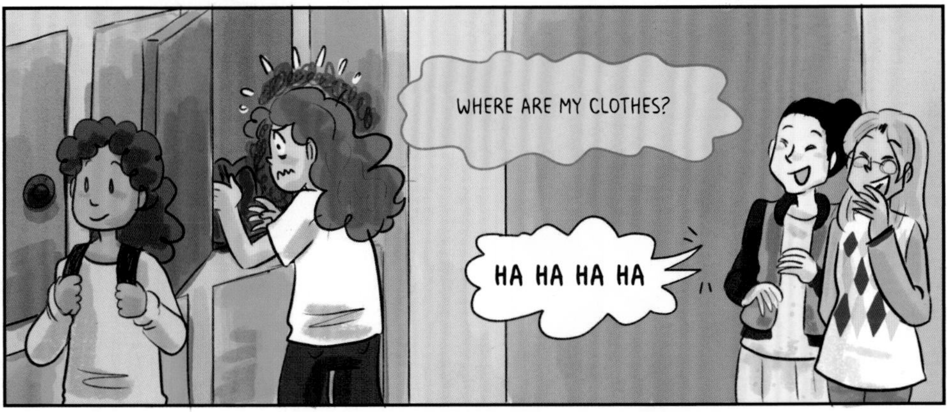
WHERE ARE MY CLOTHES?
HA HA HA HA

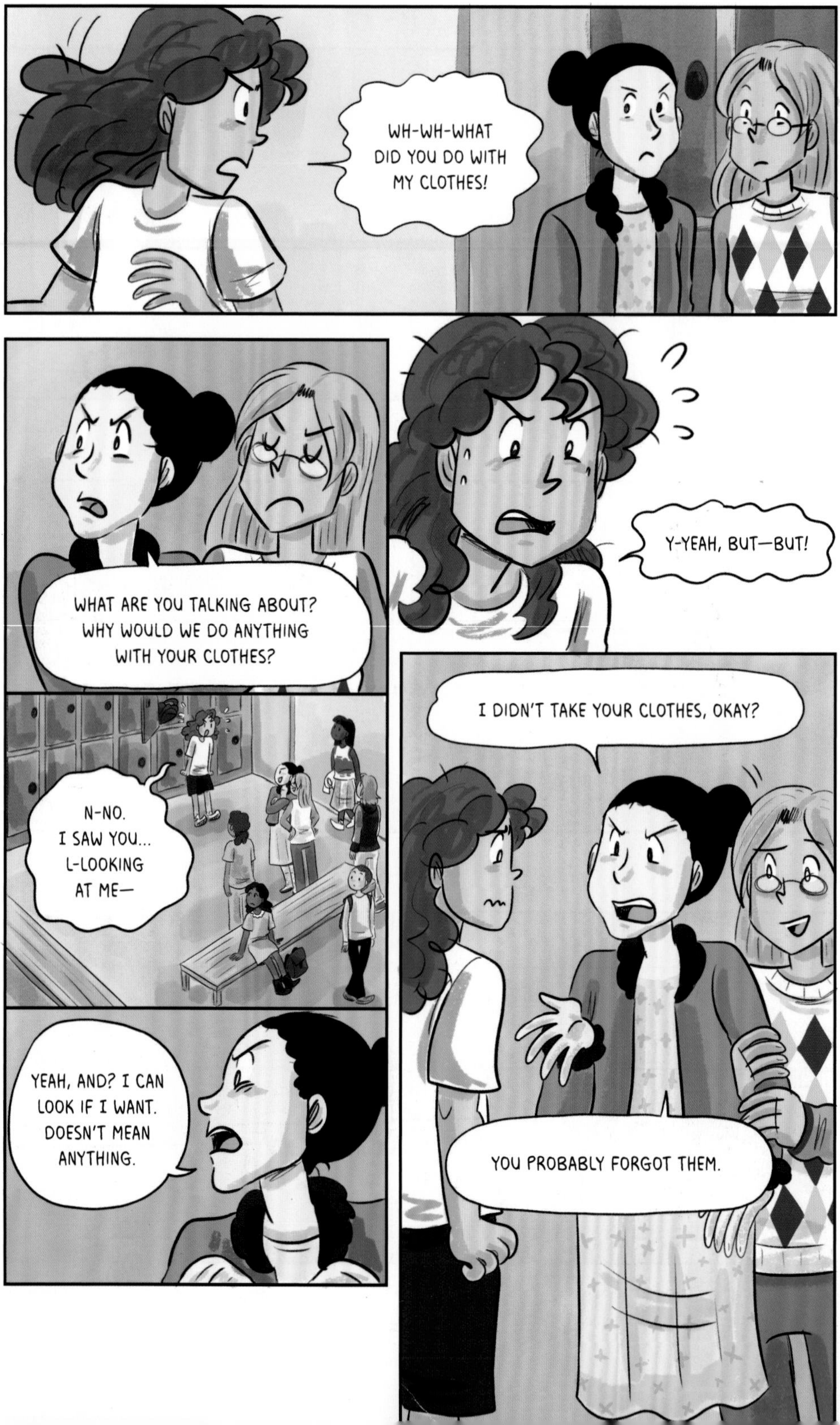
WH-WH-WHAT DID YOU DO WITH MY CLOTHES!
WHAT ARE YOU TALKING ABOUT? WHY WOULD WE DO ANYTHING WITH YOUR CLOTHES?
Y-YEAH, BUT—BUT!
N-NO. I SAW YOU... L-LOOKING AT ME—
YEAH, AND? I CAN LOOK IF I WANT. DOESN'T MEAN ANYTHING.
I DIDN'T TAKE YOUR CLOTHES, OKAY?
YOU PROBABLY FORGOT THEM.

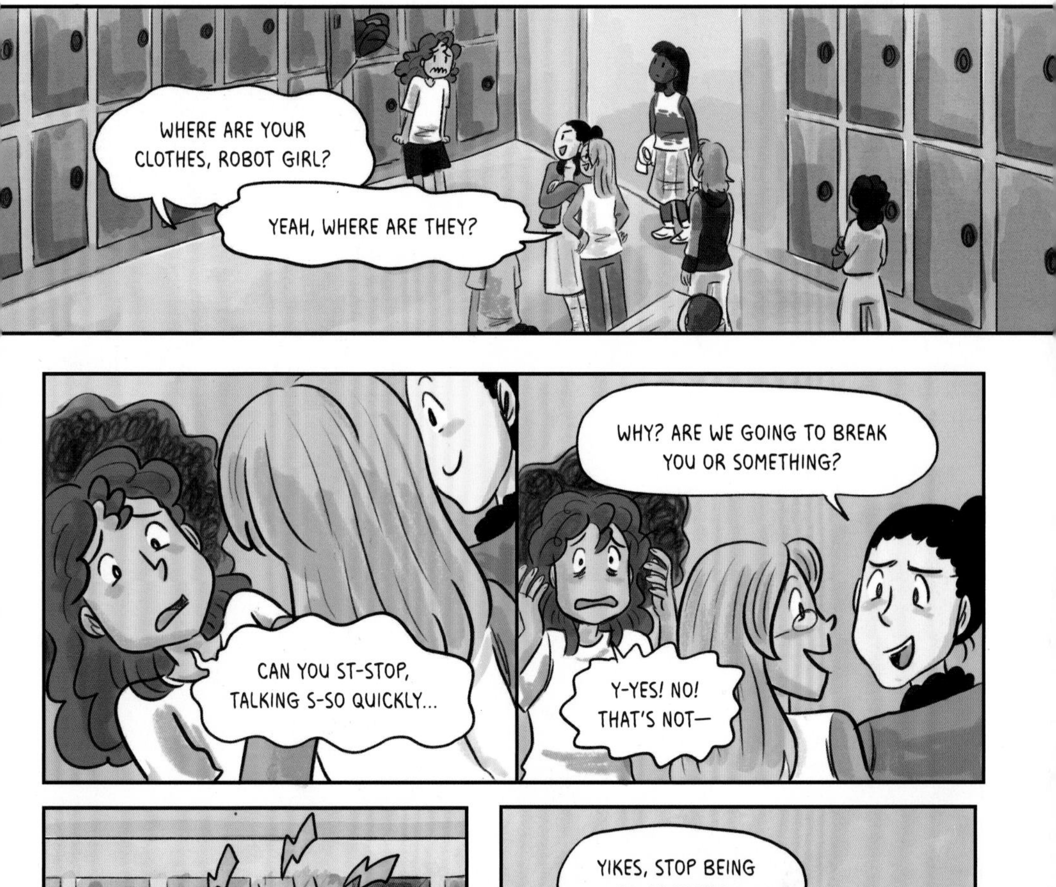
WHERE ARE YOUR CLOTHES, ROBOT GIRL?
YEAH, WHERE ARE THEY?
CAN YOU ST-STOP, TALKING S-SO QUICKLY...
WHY? ARE WE GOING TO BREAK YOU OR SOMETHING?
Y-YES! NO! THAT'S NOT—
DEO
Shhhhhhhh
AAAAH!
YIKES, STOP BEING SO DRAMATIC.
why are you making

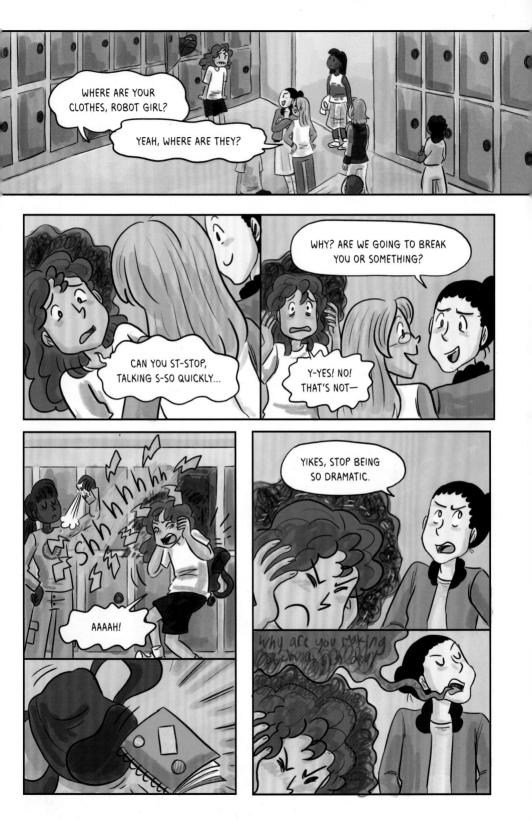

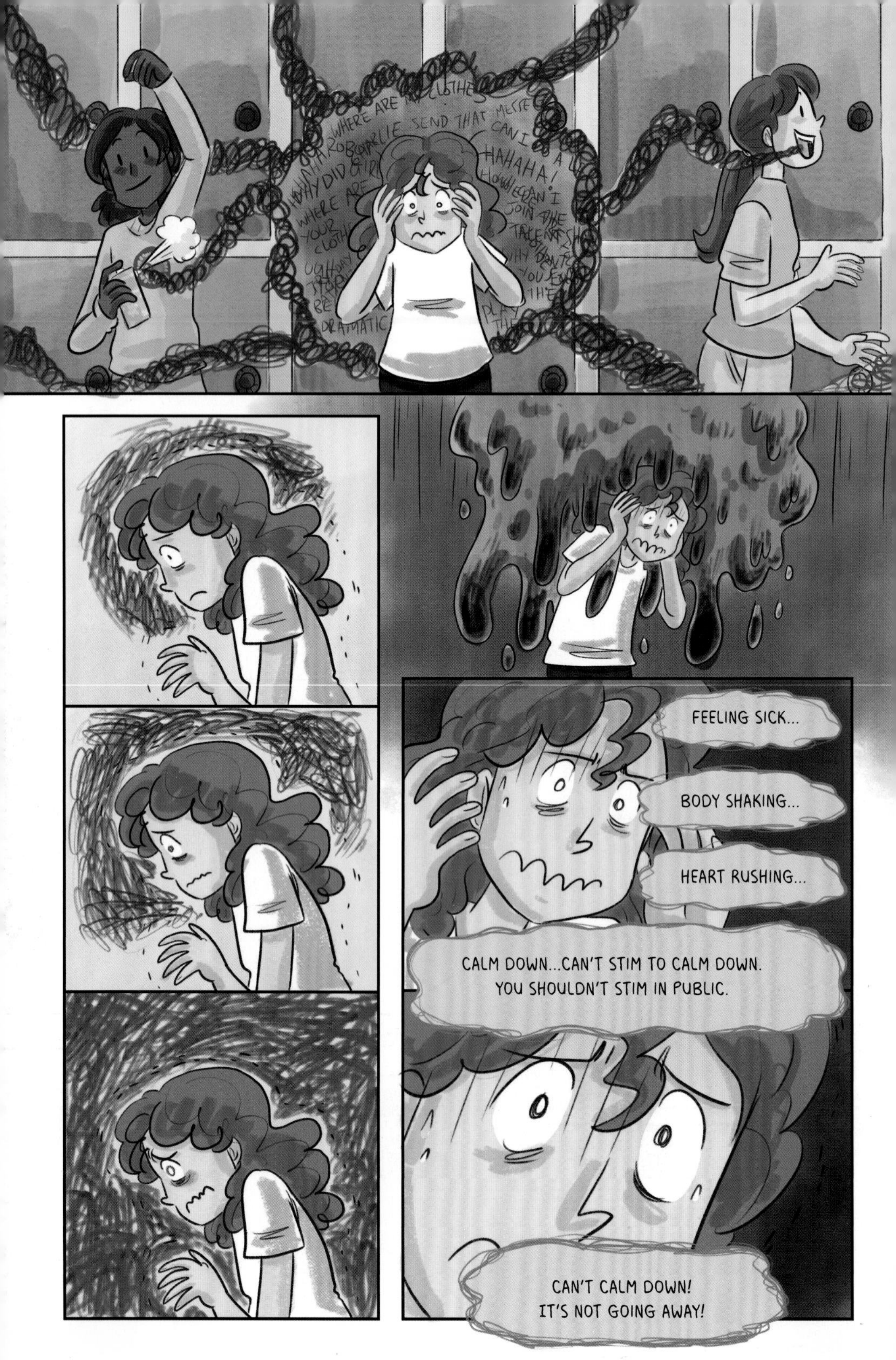
WHERE ARE MY CLOTHES
HAHAHA!
FEELING SICK...
BODY SHAKING...
HEART RUSHING...
CALM DOWN...CAN'T STIM TO CALM DOWN.
YOU SHOULDN'T STIM IN PUBLIC.
CAN'T CALM DOWN!
IT'S NOT GOING AWAY!

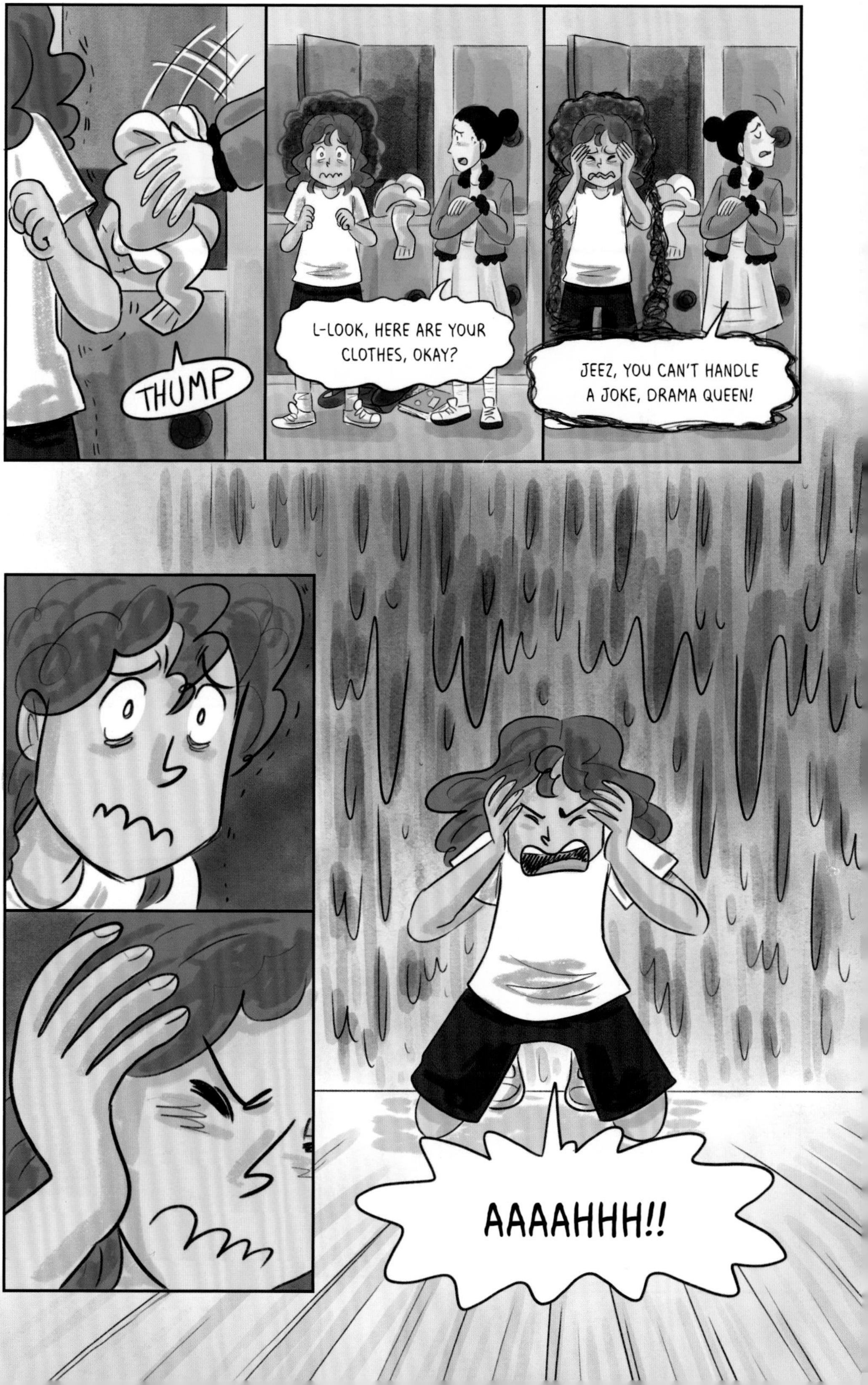
THUMP
L-LOOK, HERE ARE YOUR CLOTHES, OKAY?
JEEZ, YOU CAN'T HANDLE A JOKE, DRAMA QUEEN!
AAAAHHH!!

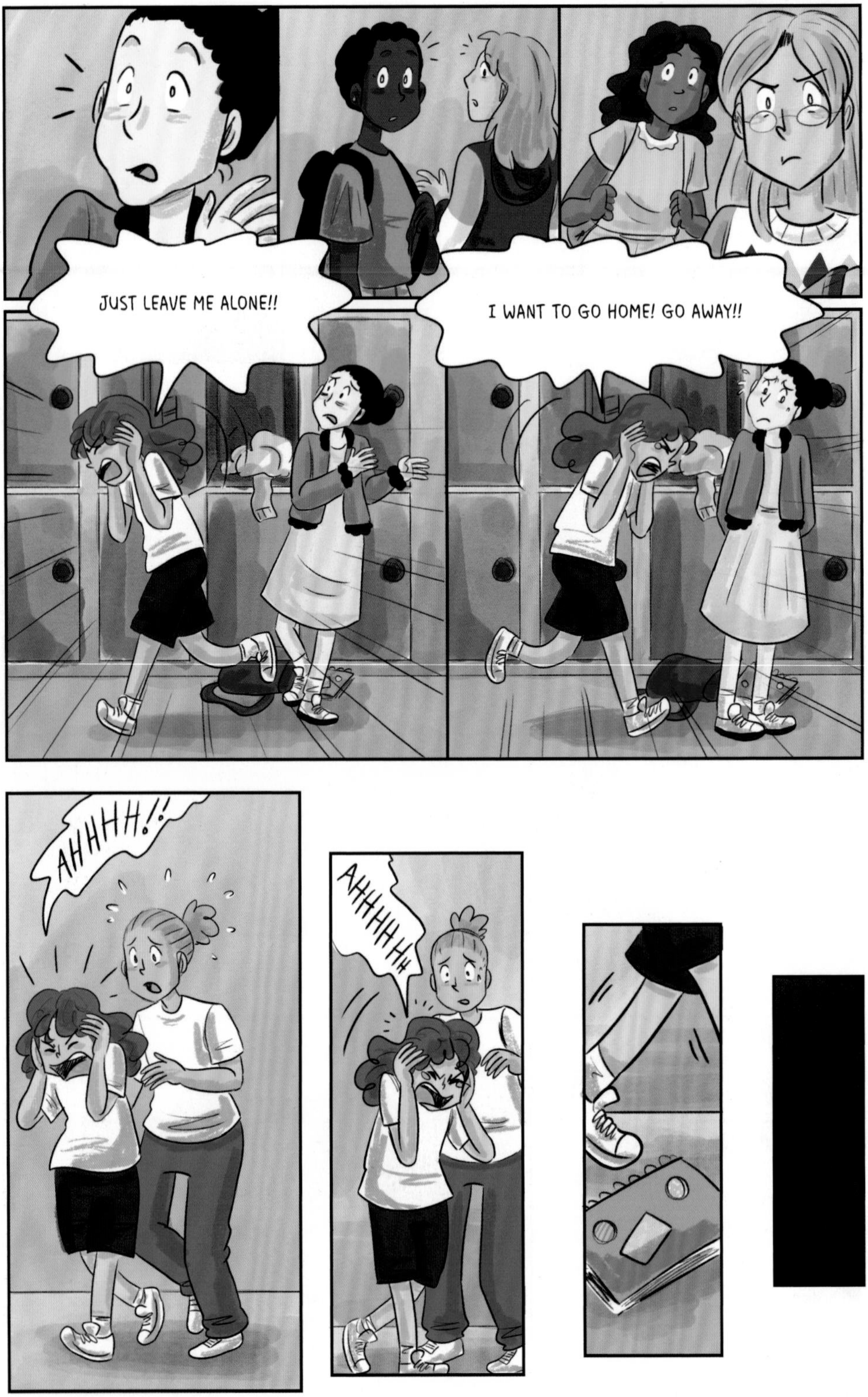
JUST LEAVE ME ALONE!!
I WANT TO GO HOME! GO AWAY!!
AHHHH!!
AHHHHH

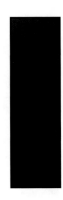

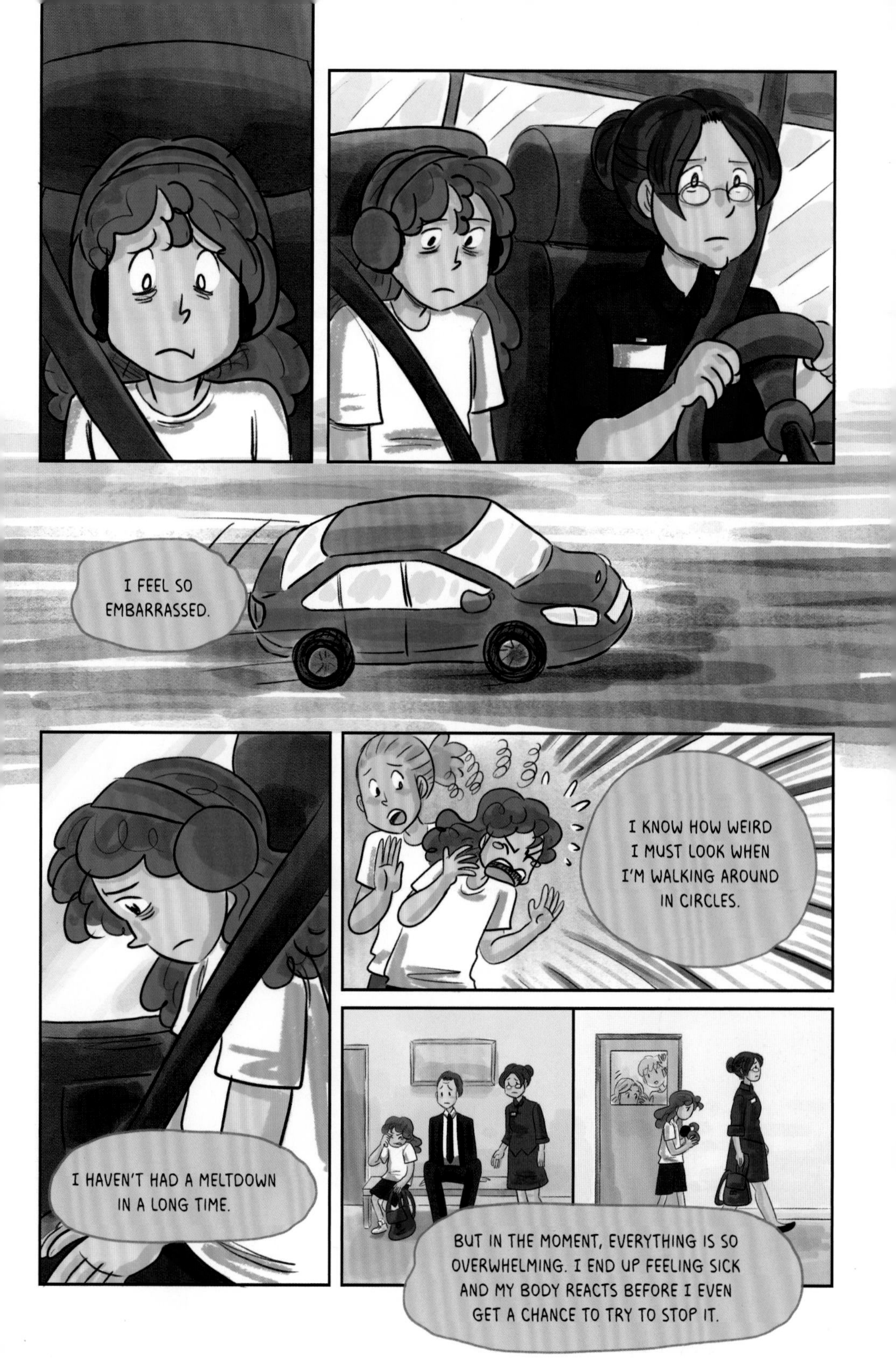
I FEEL SO EMBARRASSED.
I KNOW HOW WEIRD I MUST LOOK WHEN I'M WALKING AROUND IN CIRCLES.
I HAVEN'T HAD A MELTDOWN IN A LONG TIME.
BUT IN THE MOMENT, EVERYTHING IS SO OVERWHELMING. I END UP FEELING SICK AND MY BODY REACTS BEFORE I EVEN GET A CHANCE TO TRY TO STOP IT.

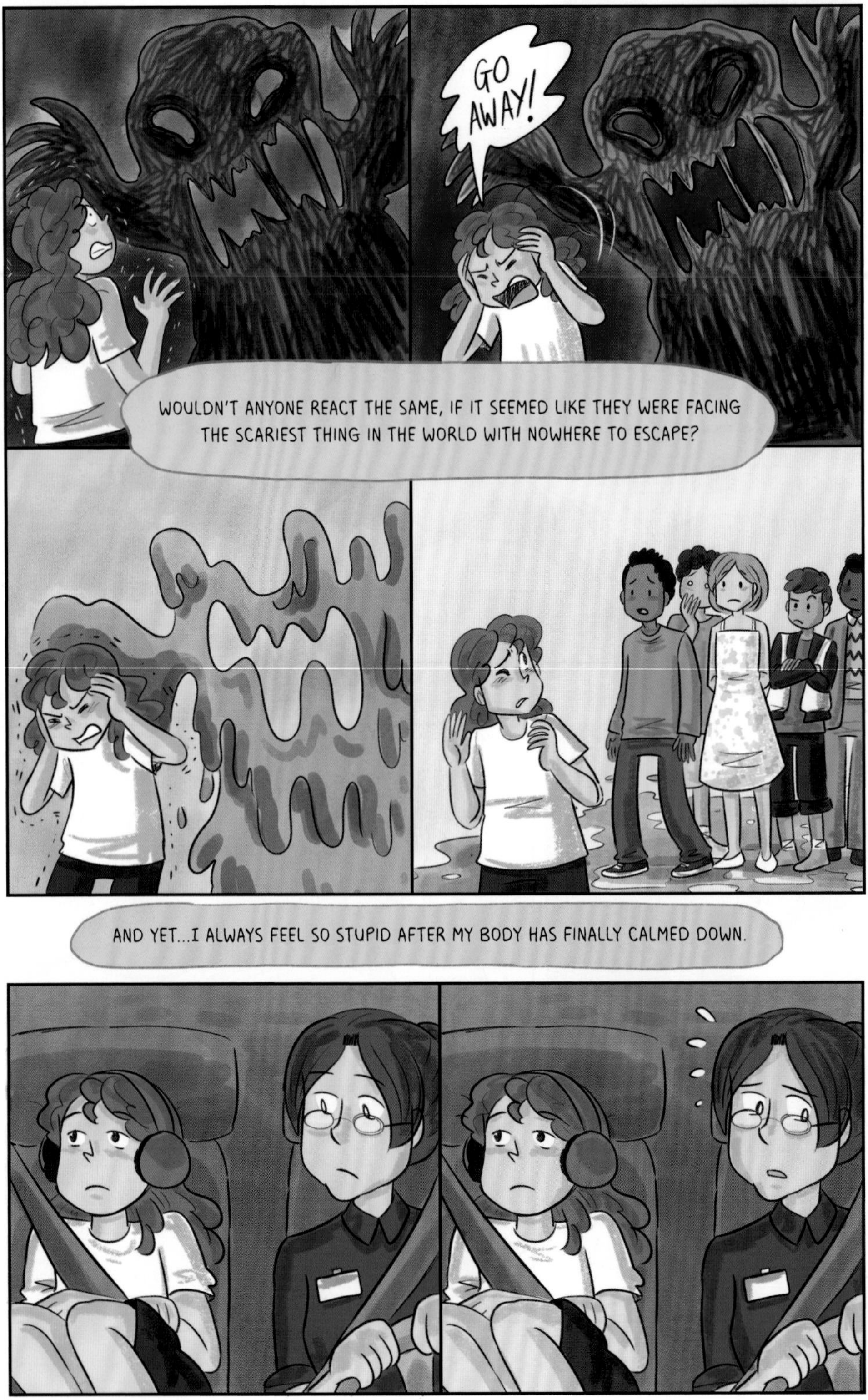
GO AWAY!
WOULDN'T ANYONE REACT THE SAME, IF IT SEEMED LIKE THEY WERE FACING THE SCARIEST THING IN THE WORLD WITH NOWHERE TO ESCAPE?
AND YET...I ALWAYS FEEL SO STUPID AFTER MY BODY HAS FINALLY CALMED DOWN.

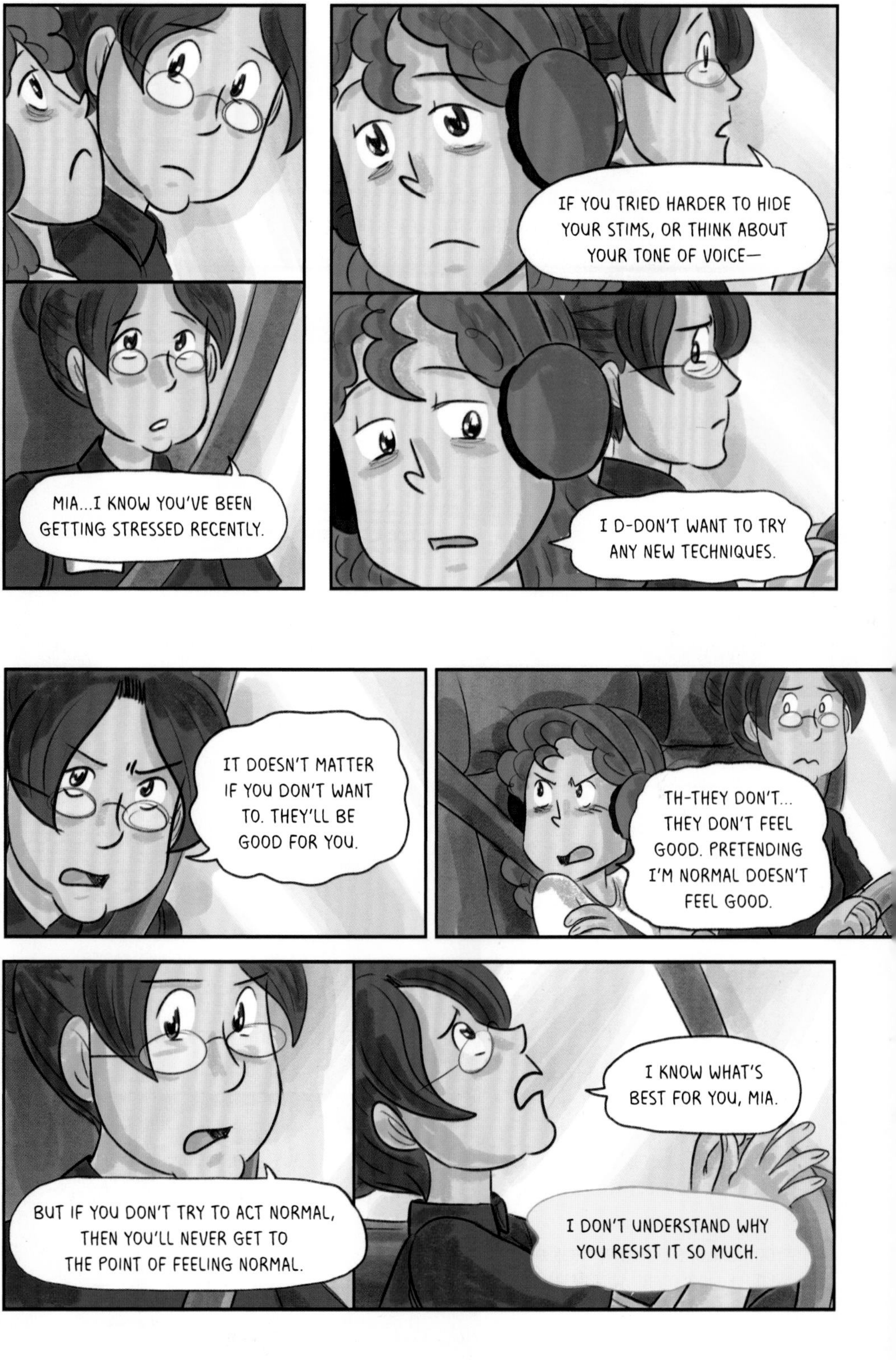
IF YOU TRIED HARDER TO HIDE YOUR STIMS, OR THINK ABOUT YOUR TONE OF VOICE—
MIA...I KNOW YOU'VE BEEN GETTING STRESSED RECENTLY.
I D-DON'T WANT TO TRY ANY NEW TECHNIQUES.
IT DOESN'T MATTER IF YOU DON'T WANT TO. THEY'LL BE GOOD FOR YOU.
TH-THEY DON'T... THEY DON'T FEEL GOOD. PRETENDING I'M NORMAL DOESN'T FEEL GOOD.
BUT IF YOU DON'T TRY TO ACT NORMAL, THEN YOU'LL NEVER GET TO THE POINT OF FEELING NORMAL.
I KNOW WHAT'S BEST FOR YOU, MIA.
I DON'T UNDERSTAND WHY YOU RESIST IT SO MUCH.

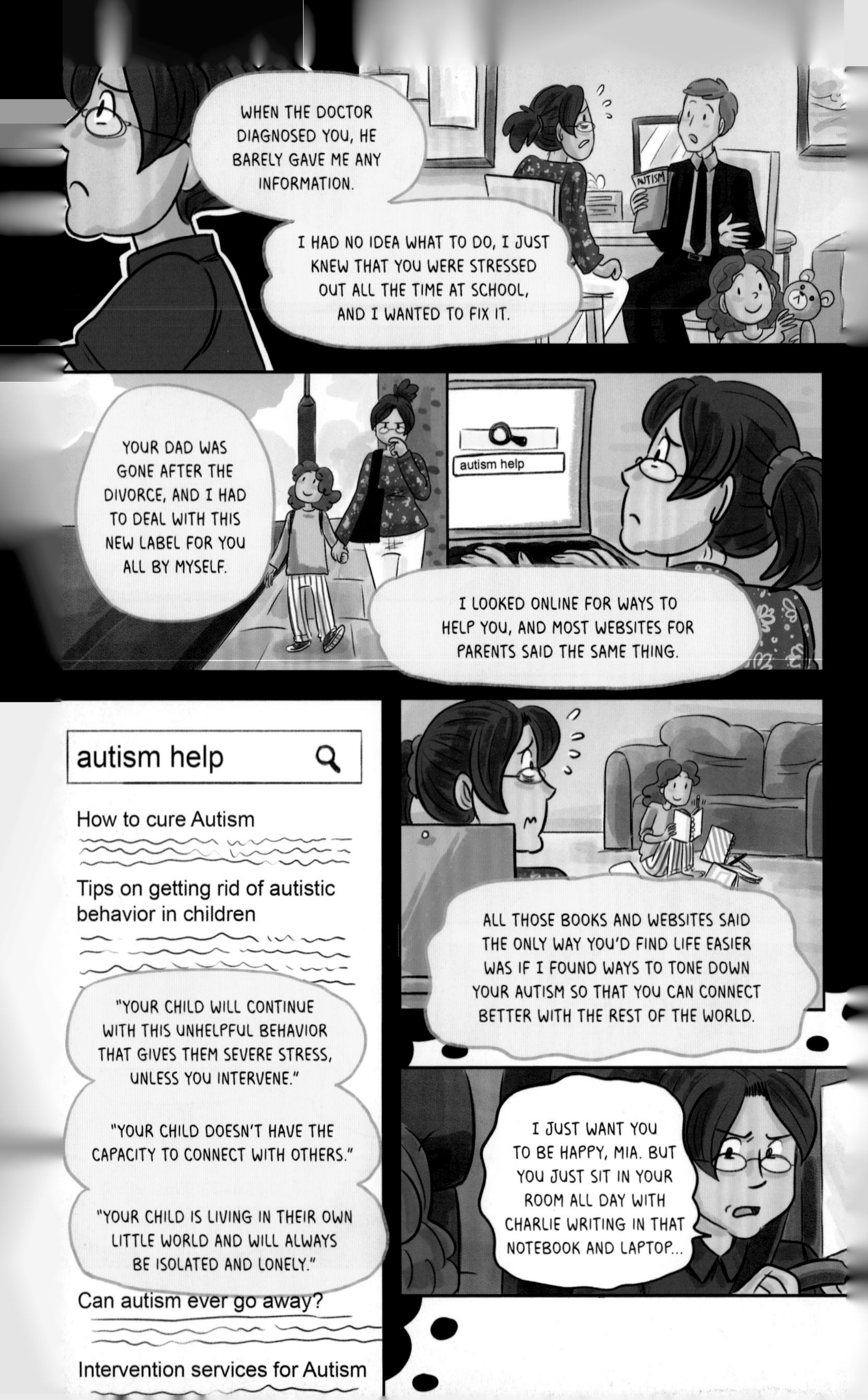
WHEN THE DOCTOR DIAGNOSED YOU, HE BARELY GAVE ME ANY INFORMATION.
I HAD NO IDEA WHAT TO DO, I JUST KNEW THAT YOU WERE STRESSED OUT ALL THE TIME AT SCHOOL, AND I WANTED TO FIX IT.
AUTISM
YOUR DAD WAS GONE AFTER THE DIVORCE, AND I HAD TO DEAL WITH THIS NEW LABEL FOR YOU ALL BY MYSELF.
autism help
I LOOKED ONLINE FOR WAYS TO HELP YOU, AND MOST WEBSITES FOR PARENTS SAID THE SAME THING.
autism help
How to cure Autism
Tips on getting rid of autistic behavior in children
"YOUR CHILD WILL CONTINUE WITH THIS UNHELPFUL BEHAVIOR THAT GIVES THEM SEVERE STRESS, UNLESS YOU INTERVENE."
"YOUR CHILD DOESN'T HAVE THE CAPACITY TO CONNECT WITH OTHERS."
"YOUR CHILD IS LIVING IN THEIR OWN LITTLE WORLD AND WILL ALWAYS BE ISOLATED AND LONELY."
Can autism ever go away?
Intervention services for Autism
ALL THOSE BOOKS AND WEBSITES SAID THE ONLY WAY YOU'D FIND LIFE EASIER WAS IF I FOUND WAYS TO TONE DOWN YOUR AUTISM SO THAT YOU CAN CONNECT BETTER WITH THE REST OF THE WORLD.
I JUST WANT YOU TO BE HAPPY, MIA. BUT YOU JUST SIT IN YOUR ROOM ALL DAY WITH CHARLIE WRITING IN THAT NOTEBOOK AND LAPTOP...

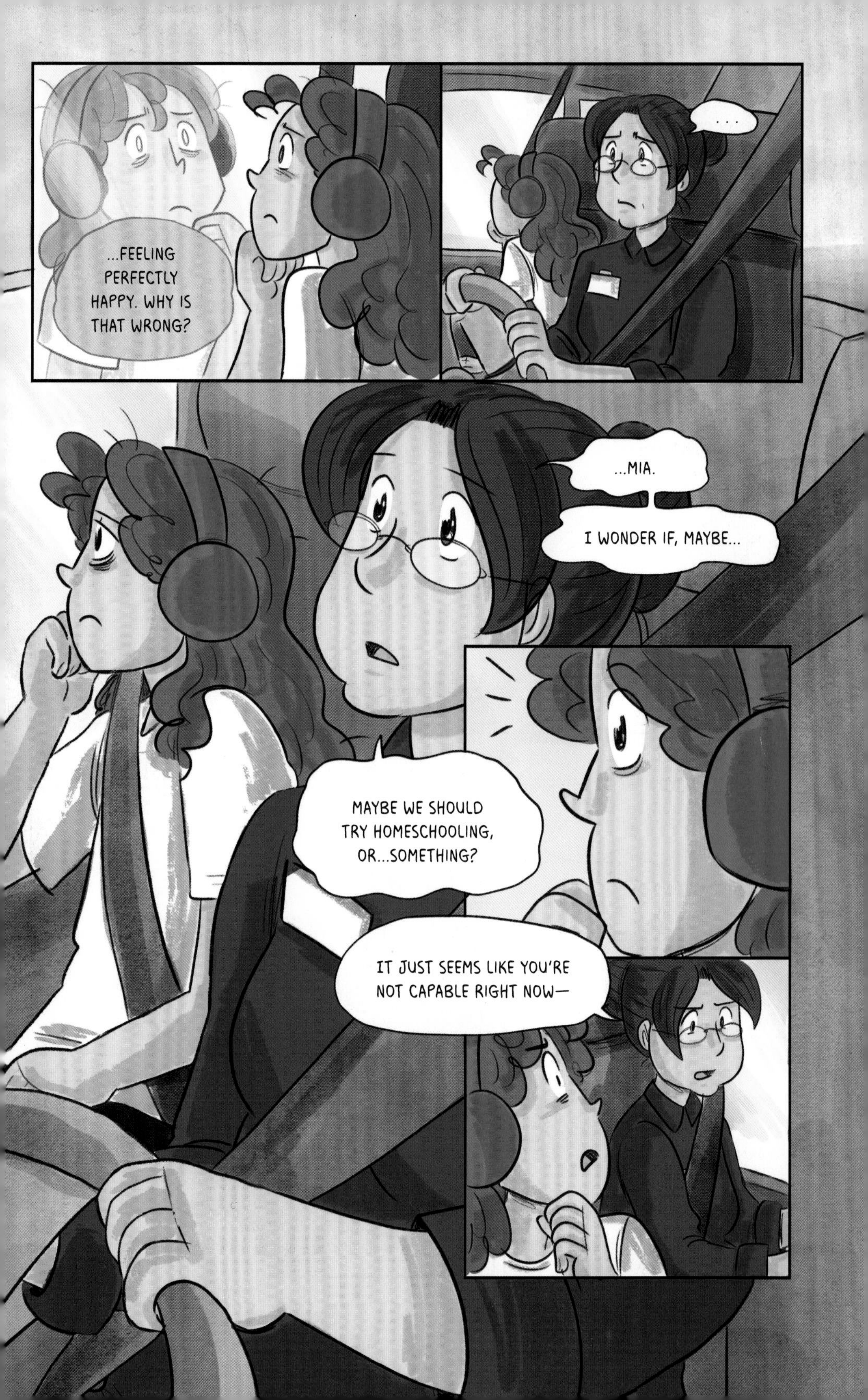
...FEELING PERFECTLY HAPPY. WHY IS THAT WRONG?
...
...MIA.
I WONDER IF, MAYBE...
MAYBE WE SHOULD TRY HOMESCHOOLING, OR...SOMETHING?
IT JUST SEEMS LIKE YOU'RE NOT CAPABLE RIGHT NOW—

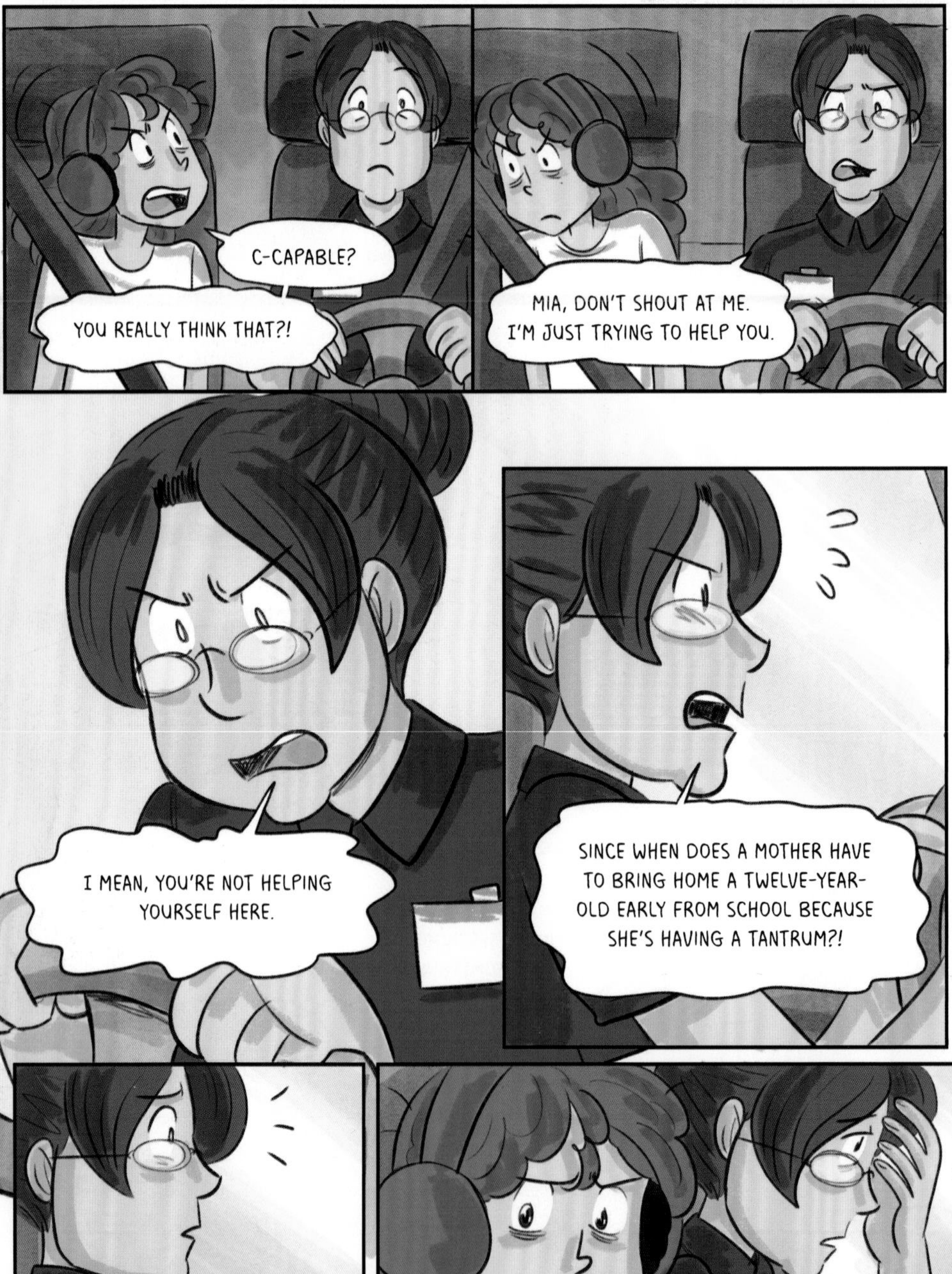
C-CAPABLE?
YOU REALLY THINK THAT?!
MIA, DON'T SHOUT AT ME. I'M JUST TRYING TO HELP YOU.
I MEAN, YOU'RE NOT HELPING YOURSELF HERE.
SINCE WHEN DOES A MOTHER HAVE TO BRING HOME A TWELVE-YEAR-OLD EARLY FROM SCHOOL BECAUSE SHE'S HAVING A TANTRUM?!
I-I DIDN'T MEAN THAT, SWEETIE. I'M SORRY.

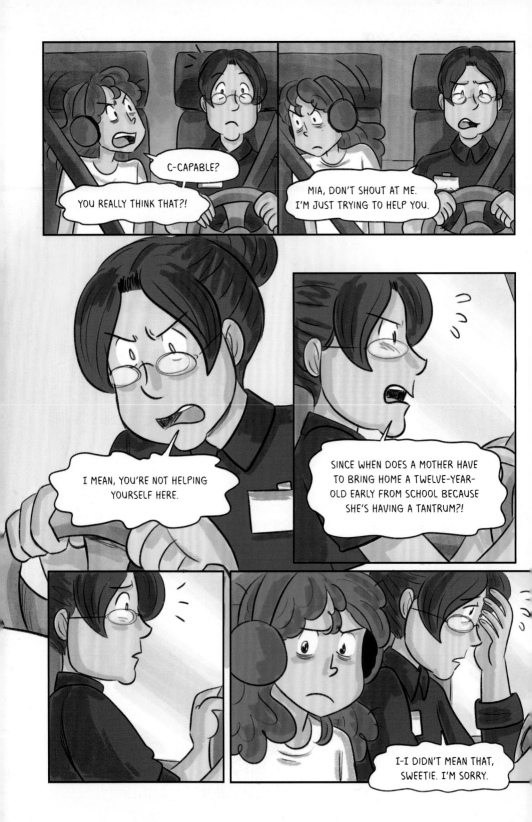

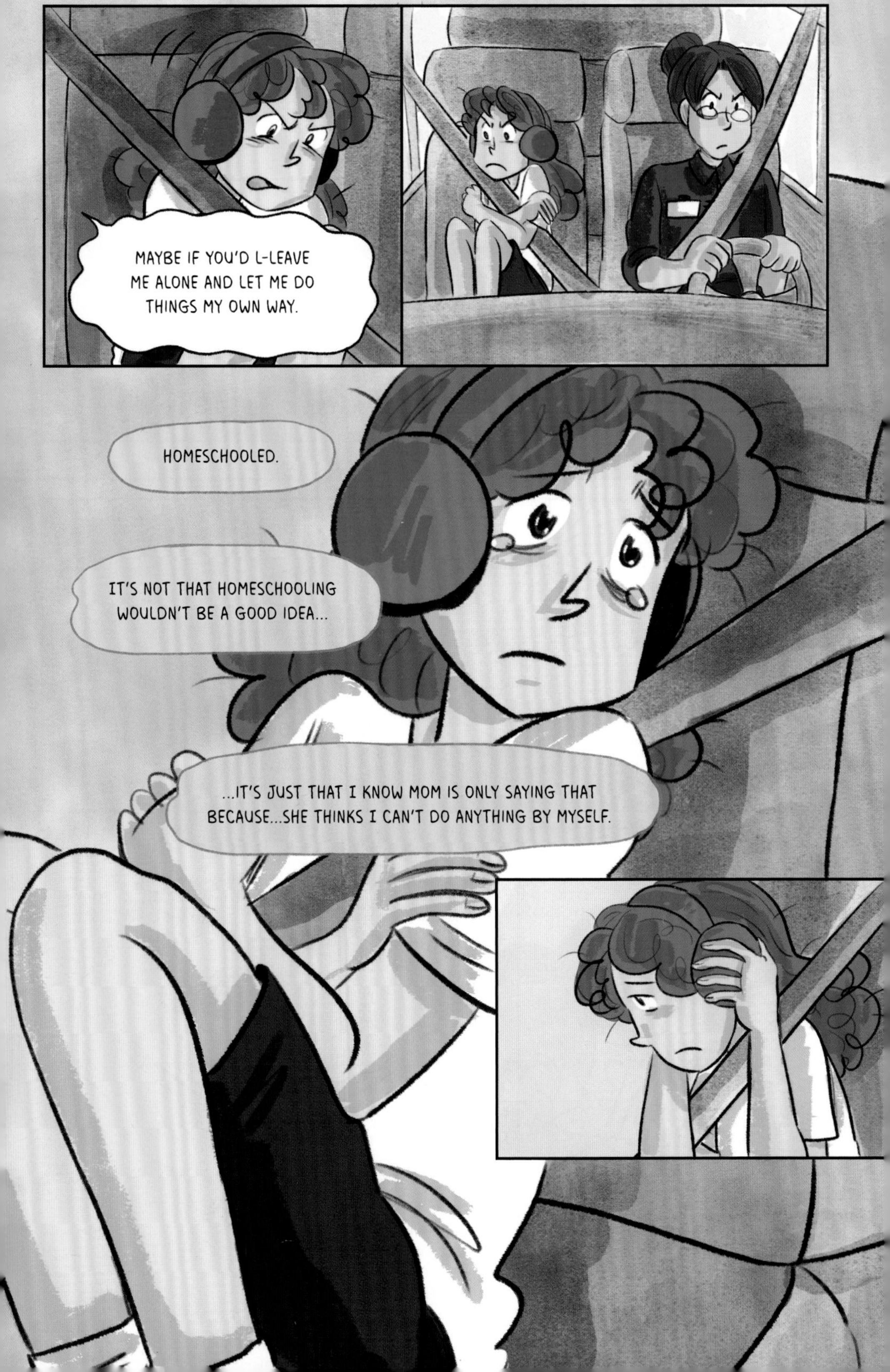
MAYBE IF YOU'D L-LEAVE ME ALONE AND LET ME DO THINGS MY OWN WAY.
HOMESCHOOLED.
IT'S NOT THAT HOMESCHOOLING WOULDN'T BE A GOOD IDEA...
...IT'S JUST THAT I KNOW MOM IS ONLY SAYING THAT BECAUSE...SHE THINKS I CAN'T DO ANYTHING BY MYSELF.

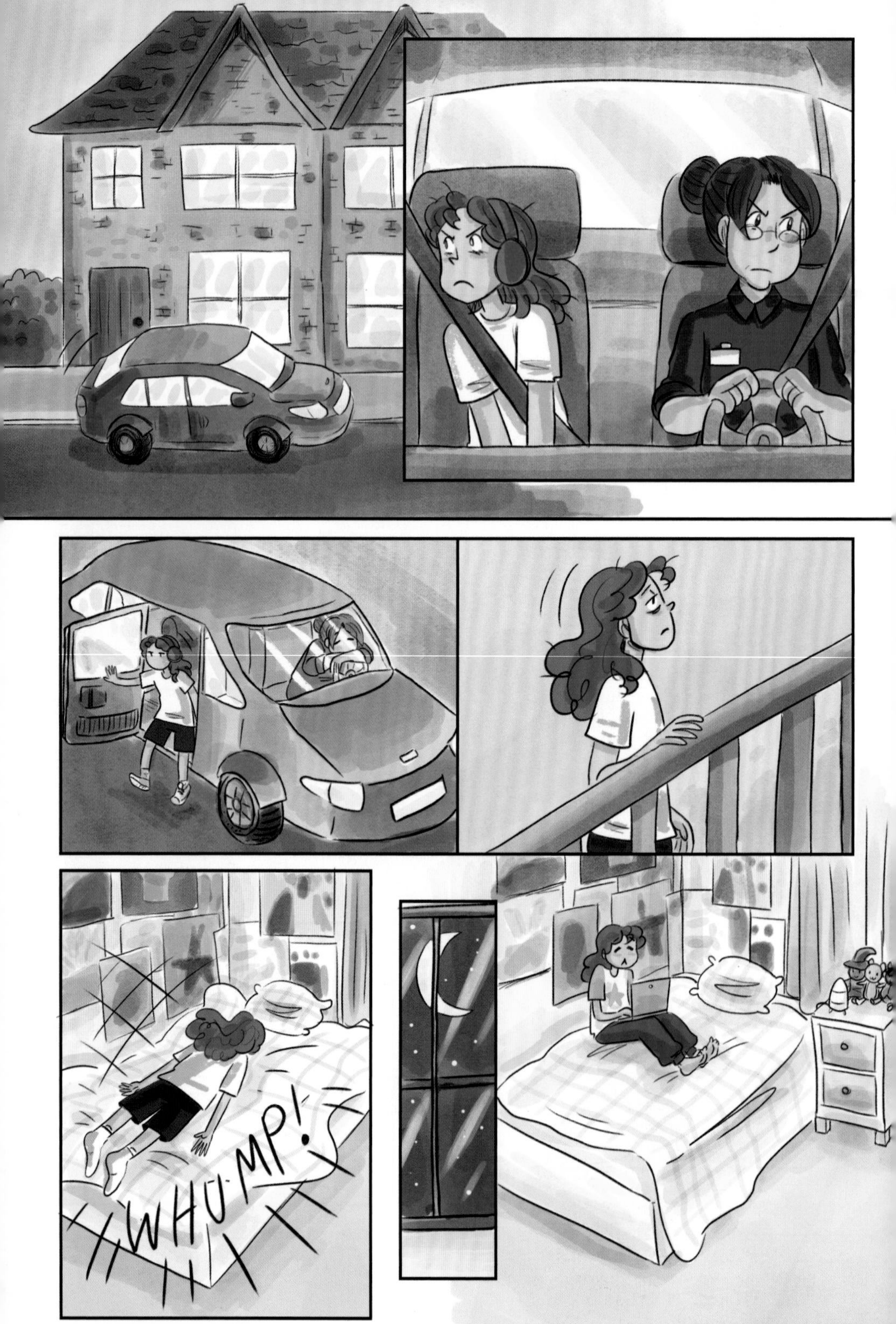
WHUMP!

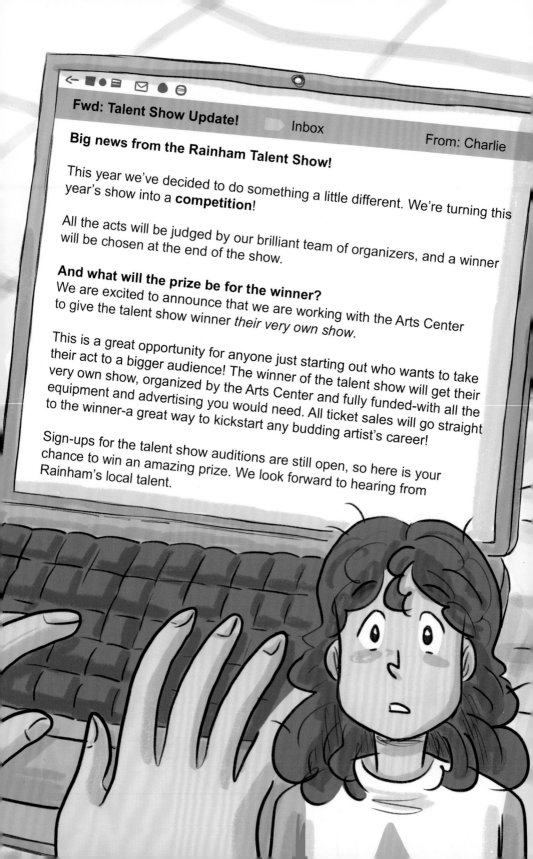

**Fwd: Talent Show Update!** ▶ Inbox

From: Charlie

# Big news from the Rainham Talent Show!

This year we've decided to do something a little different. We're turning this year's show into a **competition!**

All the acts will be judged by our brilliant team of organizers, and a winner will be chosen at the end of the show.

## And what will the prize be for the winner?
We are excited to announce that we are working with the Arts Center to give the talent show winner *their very own show.*

This is a great opportunity for anyone just starting out who wants to take their act to a bigger audience! The winner of the talent show will get their very own show, organized by the Arts Center and fully funded-with all the equipment and advertising you would need. All ticket sales will go straight to the winner-a great way to kickstart any budding artist's career!

Sign-ups for the talent show auditions are still open, so here is your chance to win an amazing prize. We look forward to hearing from Rainham's local talent.

# CHAPTER FIVE

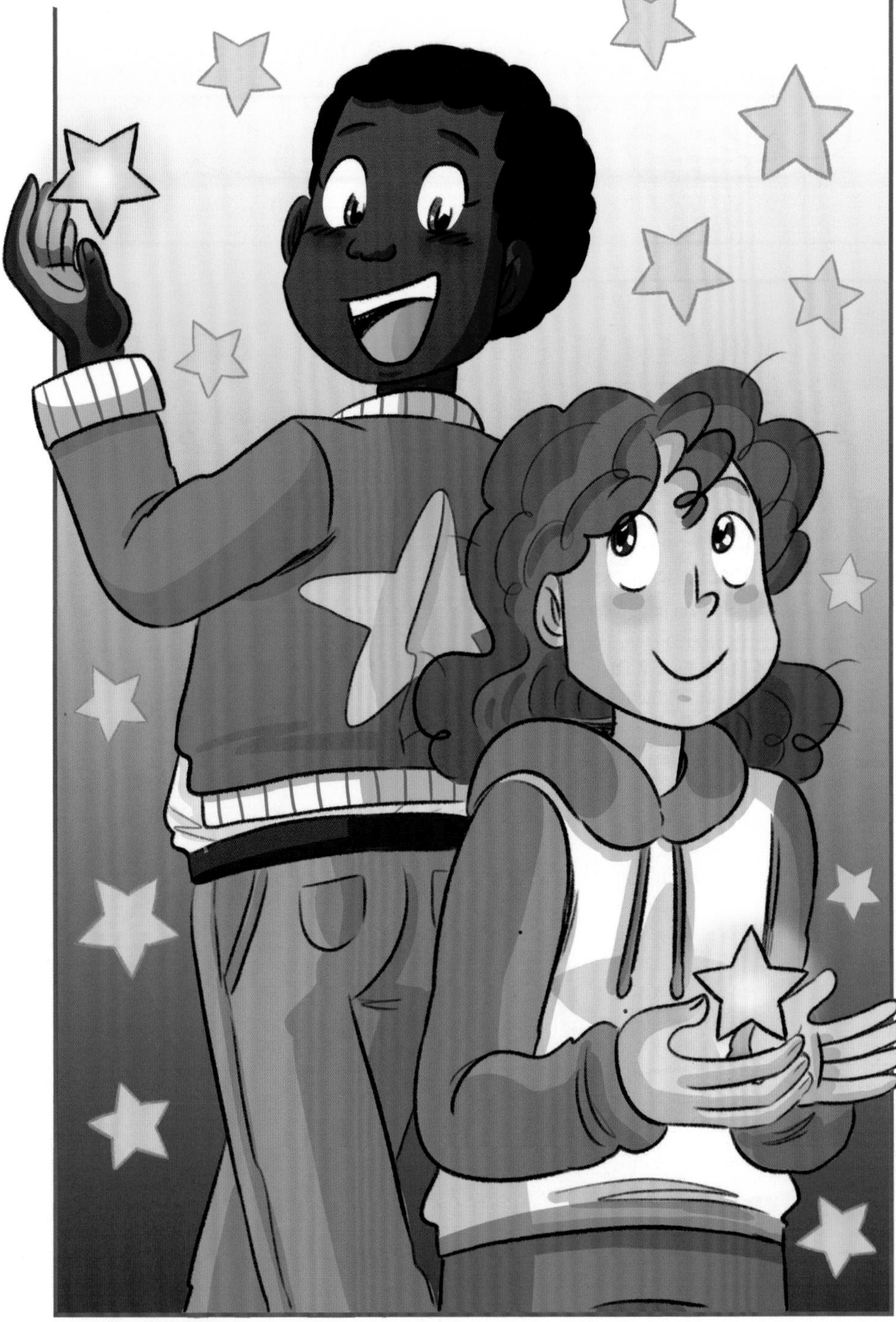

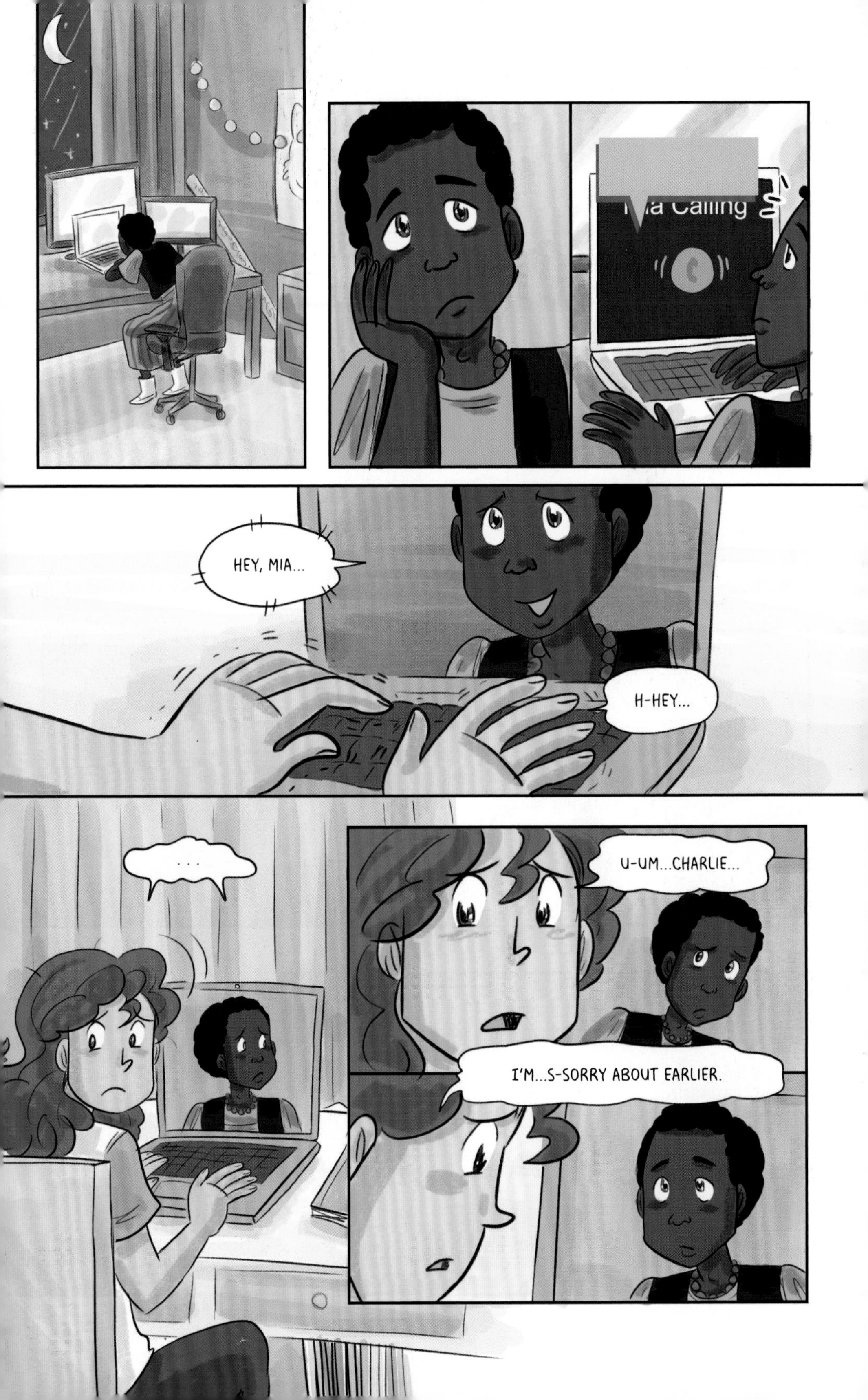
ia Calling
HEY, MIA...
H-HEY...
. . .
U-UM...CHARLIE...
I'M...S-SORRY ABOUT EARLIER.

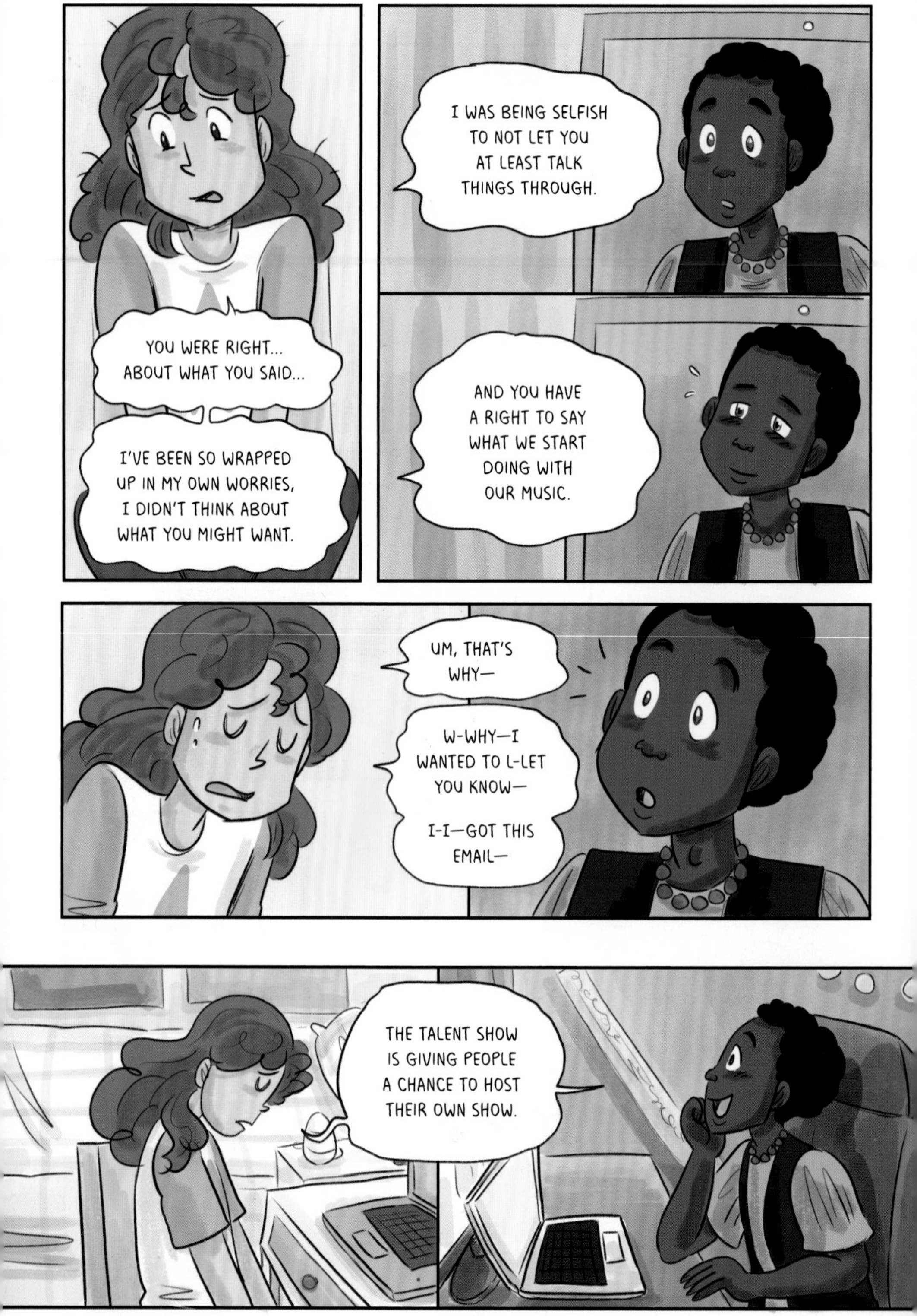
YOU WERE RIGHT... ABOUT WHAT YOU SAID...
I'VE BEEN SO WRAPPED UP IN MY OWN WORRIES, I DIDN'T THINK ABOUT WHAT YOU MIGHT WANT.
I WAS BEING SELFISH TO NOT LET YOU AT LEAST TALK THINGS THROUGH.
AND YOU HAVE A RIGHT TO SAY WHAT WE START DOING WITH OUR MUSIC.
UM, THAT'S WHY—
W-WHY—I WANTED TO L-LET YOU KNOW—
I-I—GOT THIS EMAIL—
THE TALENT SHOW IS GIVING PEOPLE A CHANCE TO HOST THEIR OWN SHOW.

?!

HOW DID YOU KNOW THAT?

HEH! I SAW THAT EMAIL A WHILE AGO, MIA...

...AND FINALLY DECIDED THAT YOU SHOULD SEE IT TOO.

From: Charlie

...t. We're turning this

UH! I WAS SO CAUGHT UP IN THE EMAIL I DIDN'T NOTICE WHO SENT IT!

SO I FORWARDED IT TO YOU! I'M SORRY I DIDN'T SAY ANYTHING WITH THE EMAIL. I THOUGHT YOU MIGHT IGNORE IT OTHERWISE.

WHEN THEY ANNOUNCED THAT PRIZE, SUDDENLY THIS WASN'T JUST SOMETHING WE COULD TRY OUT ANY YEAR. IT BECAME THIS BIG OPPORTUNITY THAT COULD BE AMAZING FOR US.

I KEPT TRYING TO BRING IT UP TO YOU—

BUT ANY TIME I MENTIONED PERFORMING AT THE TALENT SHOW, YOU CHANGED THE CONVERSATION OR TRIED TO AVOID ME!

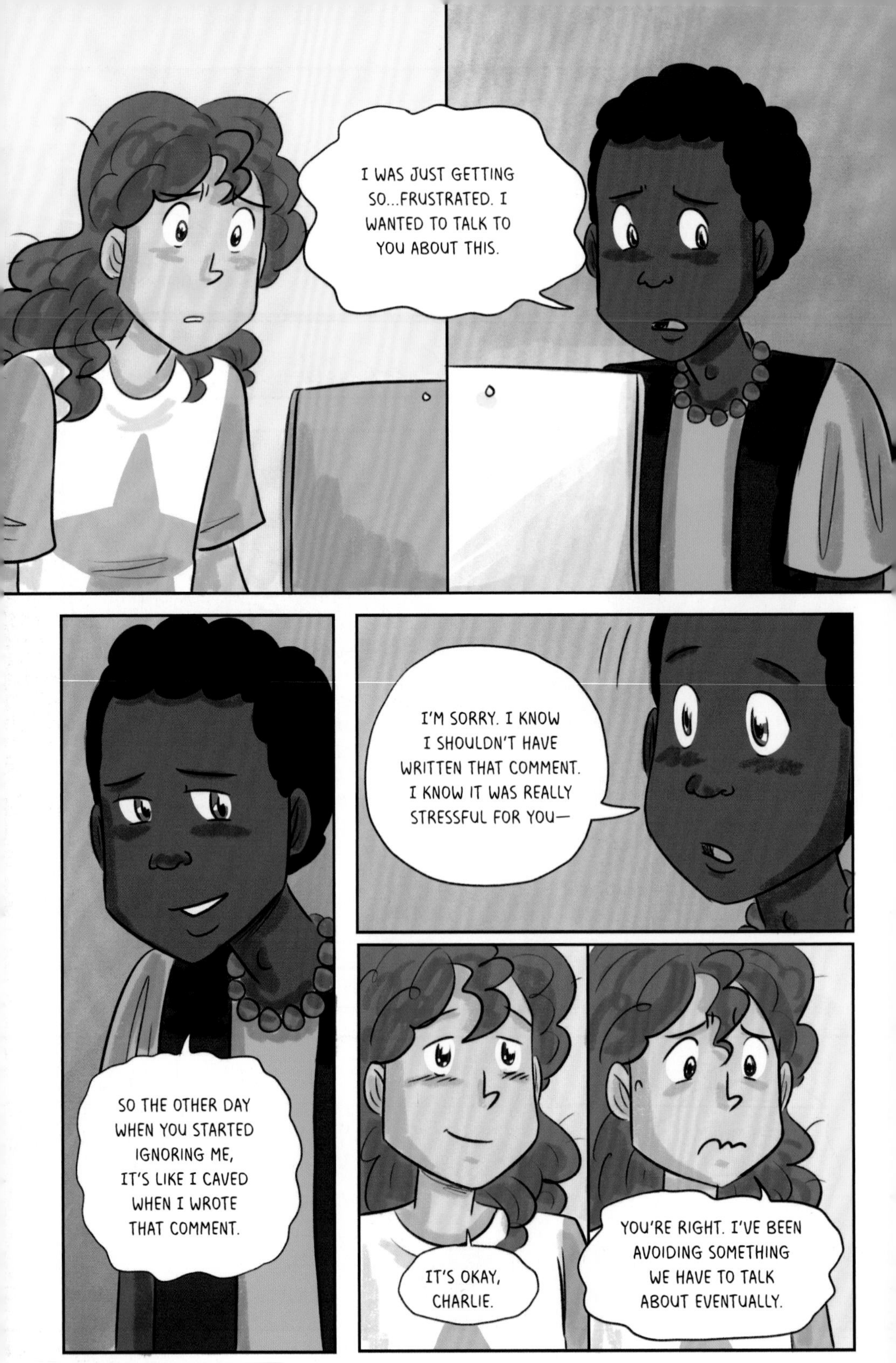
I WAS JUST GETTING SO...FRUSTRATED. I WANTED TO TALK TO YOU ABOUT THIS.
I'M SORRY. I KNOW I SHOULDN'T HAVE WRITTEN THAT COMMENT. I KNOW IT WAS REALLY STRESSFUL FOR YOU—
SO THE OTHER DAY WHEN YOU STARTED IGNORING ME, IT'S LIKE I CAVED WHEN I WROTE THAT COMMENT.
IT'S OKAY, CHARLIE.
YOU'RE RIGHT. I'VE BEEN AVOIDING SOMETHING WE HAVE TO TALK ABOUT EVENTUALLY.

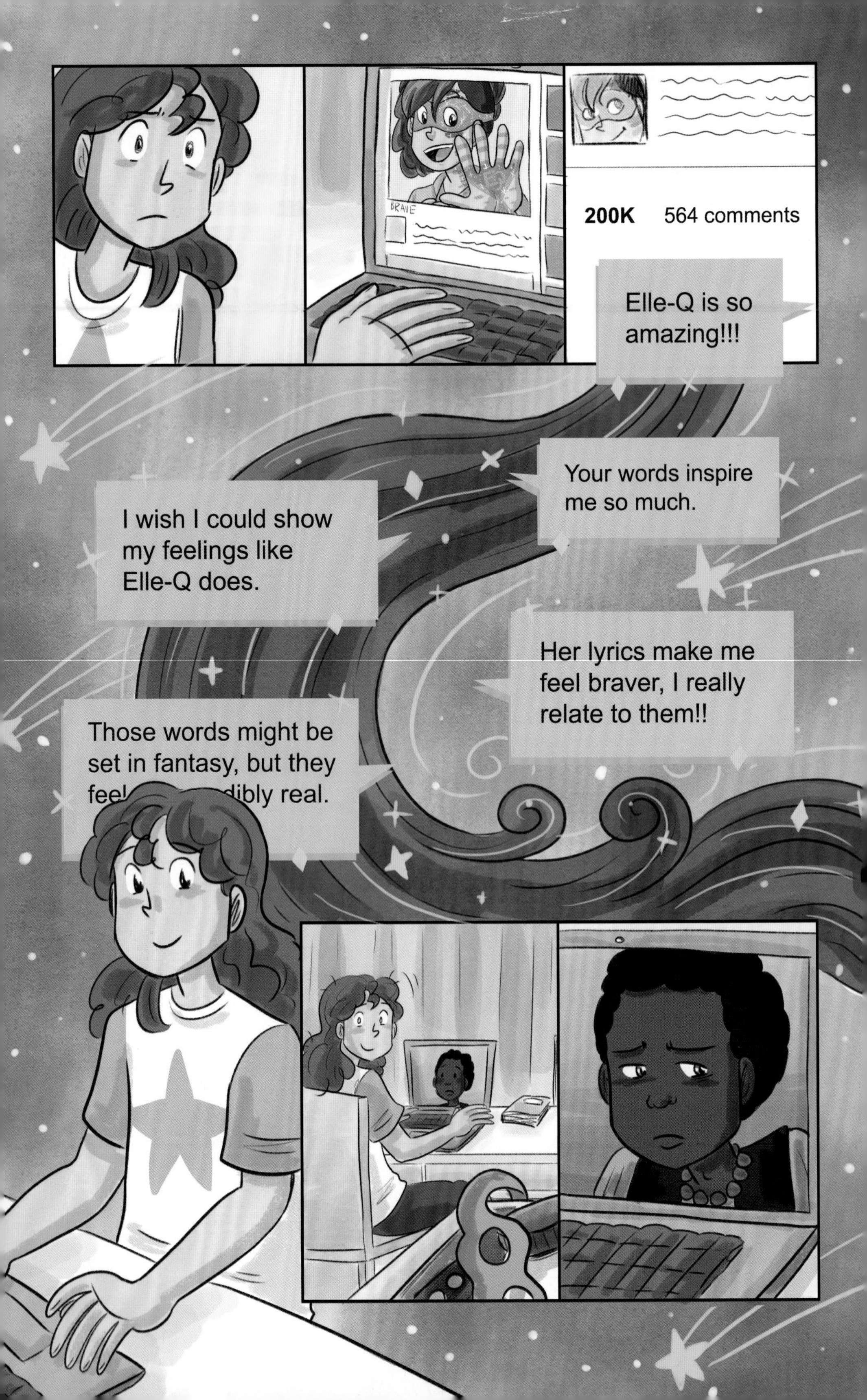

BRAVE
200K 564 comments
Elle-Q is so amazing!!!
Your words inspire me so much.
I wish I could show my feelings like Elle-Q does.
Her lyrics make me feel braver, I really relate to them!!
Those words might be set in fantasy, but they fee dibly real.

103

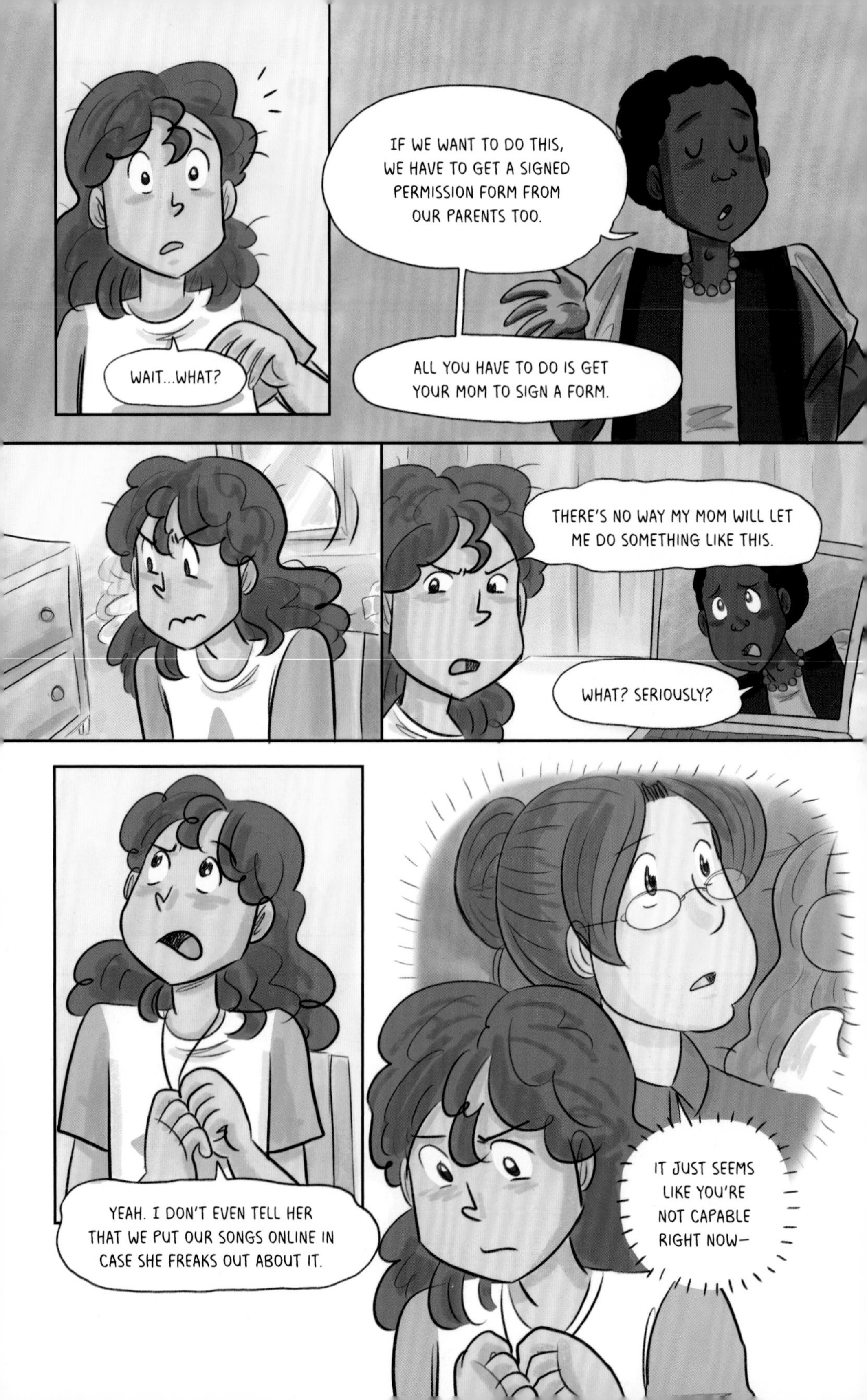
IF WE WANT TO DO THIS, WE HAVE TO GET A SIGNED PERMISSION FORM FROM OUR PARENTS TOO.
WAIT...WHAT?
ALL YOU HAVE TO DO IS GET YOUR MOM TO SIGN A FORM.
THERE'S NO WAY MY MOM WILL LET ME DO SOMETHING LIKE THIS.
WHAT? SERIOUSLY?
YEAH. I DON'T EVEN TELL HER THAT WE PUT OUR SONGS ONLINE IN CASE SHE FREAKS OUT ABOUT IT.
IT JUST SEEMS LIKE YOU'RE NOT CAPABLE RIGHT NOW—

SHE DOESN'T THINK I CAN DO THINGS BY MYSELF.

IT'S FINE. I'LL JUST SIGN THE FORM AND SAY MY MOM SAID YES.

WHOA, ARE YOU SURE ABOUT THAT?

DON'T WORRY, MY MOM WON'T FIND OUT.

SHE DOESN'T CARE ABOUT ALL THE WRITING AND MUSIC I DO ANYWAY.

SHE ONLY EVER TALKS ABOUT HOW SHE WANTS ME TO BE LIKE EVERYONE ELSE.

Rainham Talent Show Form

Parent Permission Sign:
Chloe Tab|

Tap
Tap
Tap

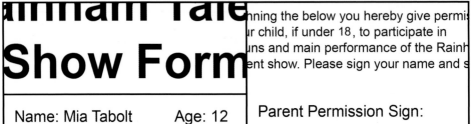

**ainham Tale**

# Show Form

nning the below you hereby give permis
ur child, if under 18, to participate in
uns and main performance of the Rainh
ent show. Please sign your name and s

Name: Mia Tabolt        Age: 12

Are you performing by yourself or
If participating in a group, name of

Parent Permission Sign:

Chloe Tabolt

Email Sent!

HEY, MAYBE WE COULD DEBUT A NEW SONG AT THE TALENT SHOW. WHAT DO YOU THINK?

OH COOL! DO YOU KNOW WHAT SONG YOU WANNA DO?

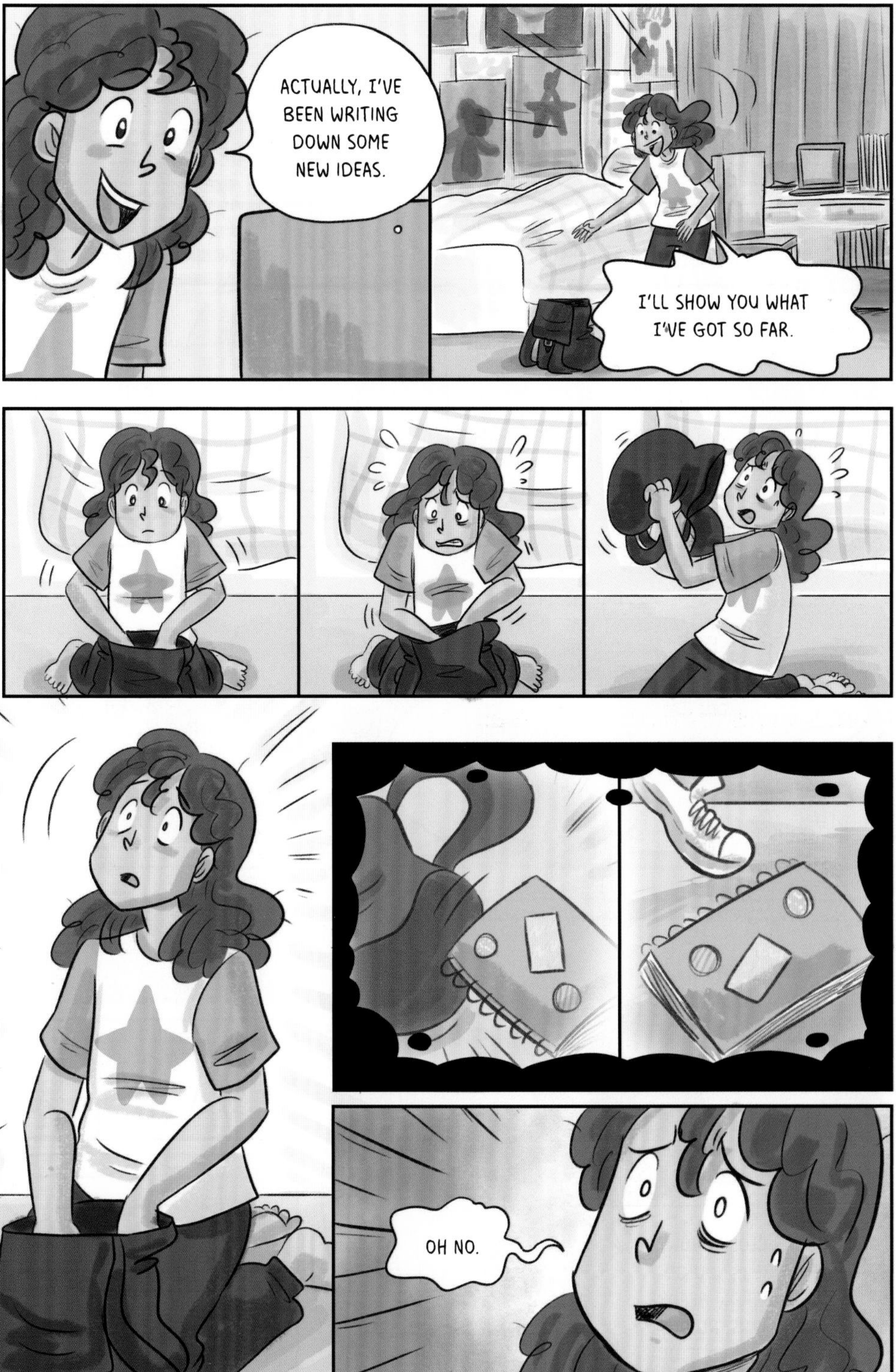
ACTUALLY, I'VE BEEN WRITING DOWN SOME NEW IDEAS.
I'LL SHOW YOU WHAT I'VE GOT SO FAR.
OH NO.

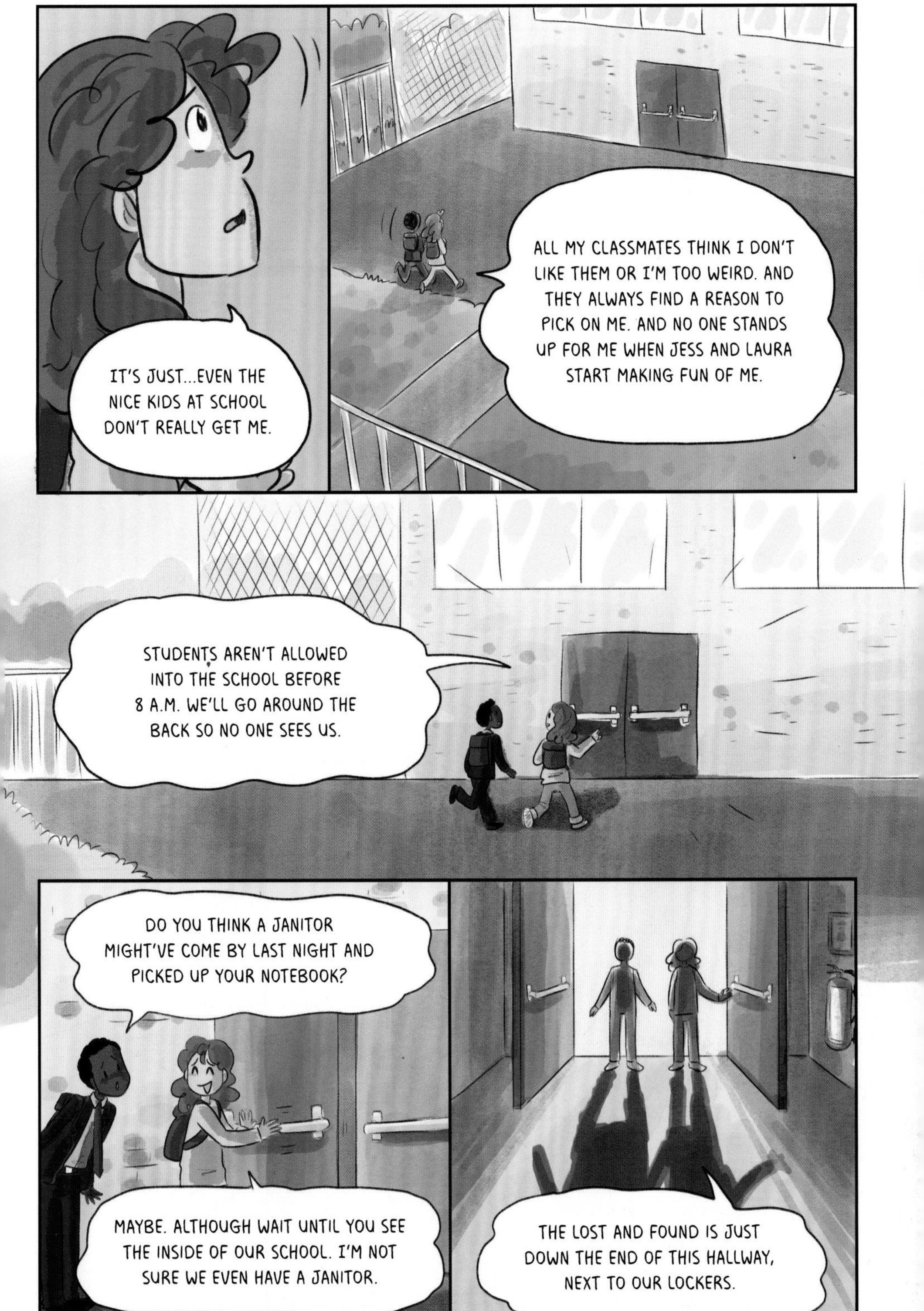
IT'S JUST...EVEN THE NICE KIDS AT SCHOOL DON'T REALLY GET ME.
ALL MY CLASSMATES THINK I DON'T LIKE THEM OR I'M TOO WEIRD. AND THEY ALWAYS FIND A REASON TO PICK ON ME. AND NO ONE STANDS UP FOR ME WHEN JESS AND LAURA START MAKING FUN OF ME.
STUDENTS AREN'T ALLOWED INTO THE SCHOOL BEFORE 8 A.M. WE'LL GO AROUND THE BACK SO NO ONE SEES US.
DO YOU THINK A JANITOR MIGHT'VE COME BY LAST NIGHT AND PICKED UP YOUR NOTEBOOK?
MAYBE. ALTHOUGH WAIT UNTIL YOU SEE THE INSIDE OF OUR SCHOOL. I'M NOT SURE WE EVEN HAVE A JANITOR.
THE LOST AND FOUND IS JUST DOWN THE END OF THIS HALLWAY, NEXT TO OUR LOCKERS.

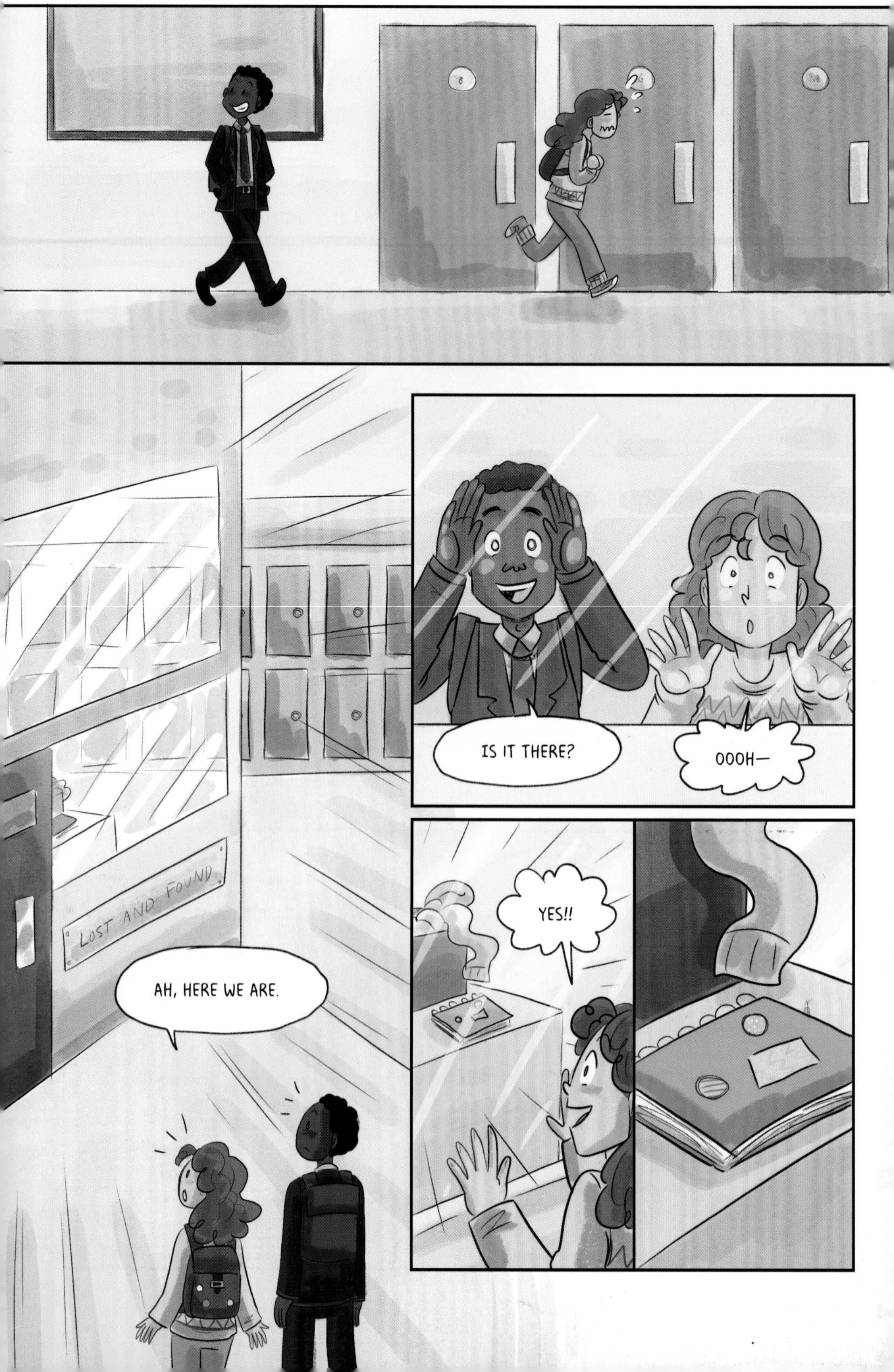
LOST AND FOUND
AH, HERE WE ARE.
IS IT THERE?
OOOH—
YES!!

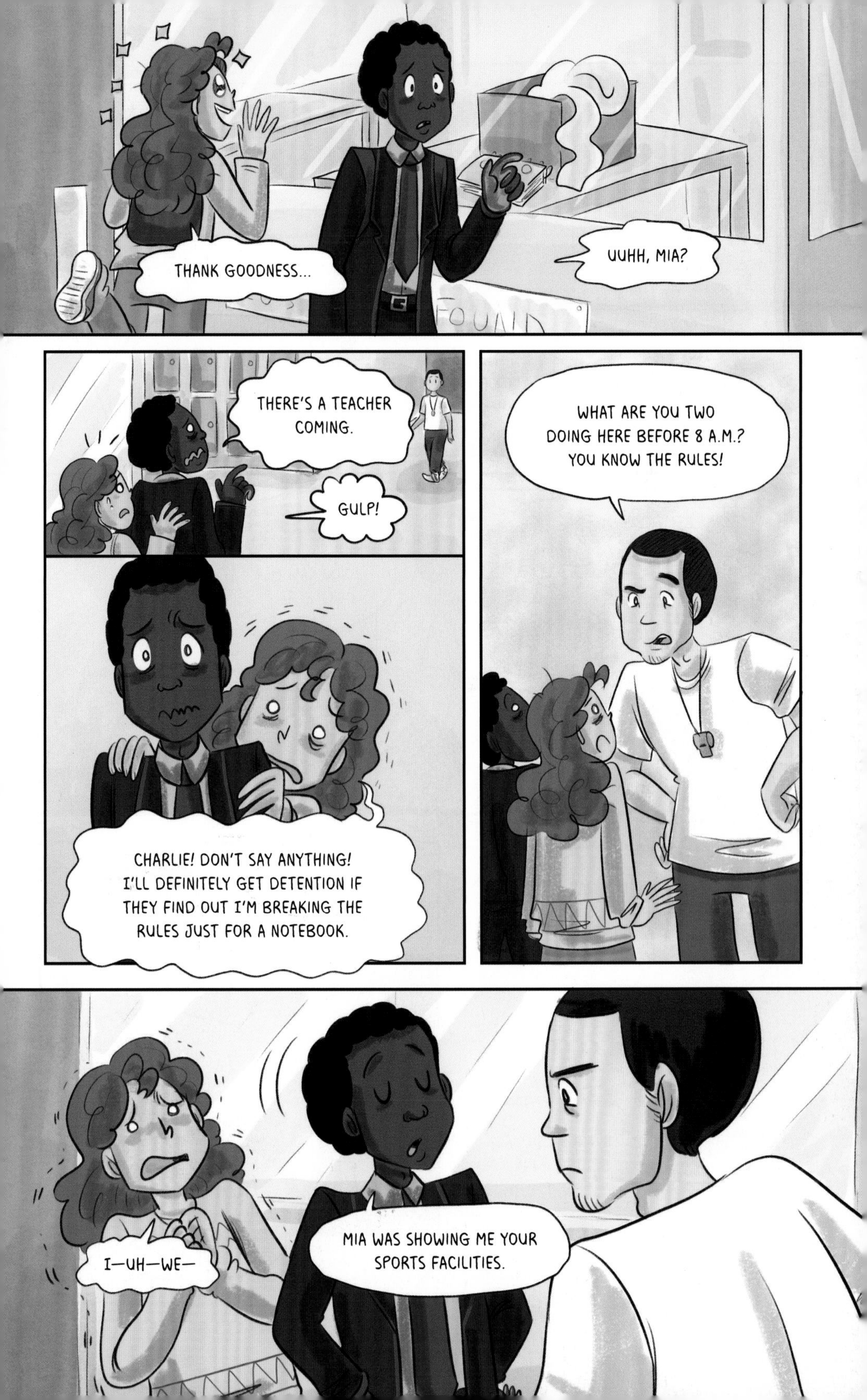
THANK GOODNESS...
UUHH, MIA?
THERE'S A TEACHER COMING.
GULP!
CHARLIE! DON'T SAY ANYTHING! I'LL DEFINITELY GET DETENTION IF THEY FIND OUT I'M BREAKING THE RULES JUST FOR A NOTEBOOK.
WHAT ARE YOU TWO DOING HERE BEFORE 8 A.M.? YOU KNOW THE RULES!
I—UH—WE—
MIA WAS SHOWING ME YOUR SPORTS FACILITIES.

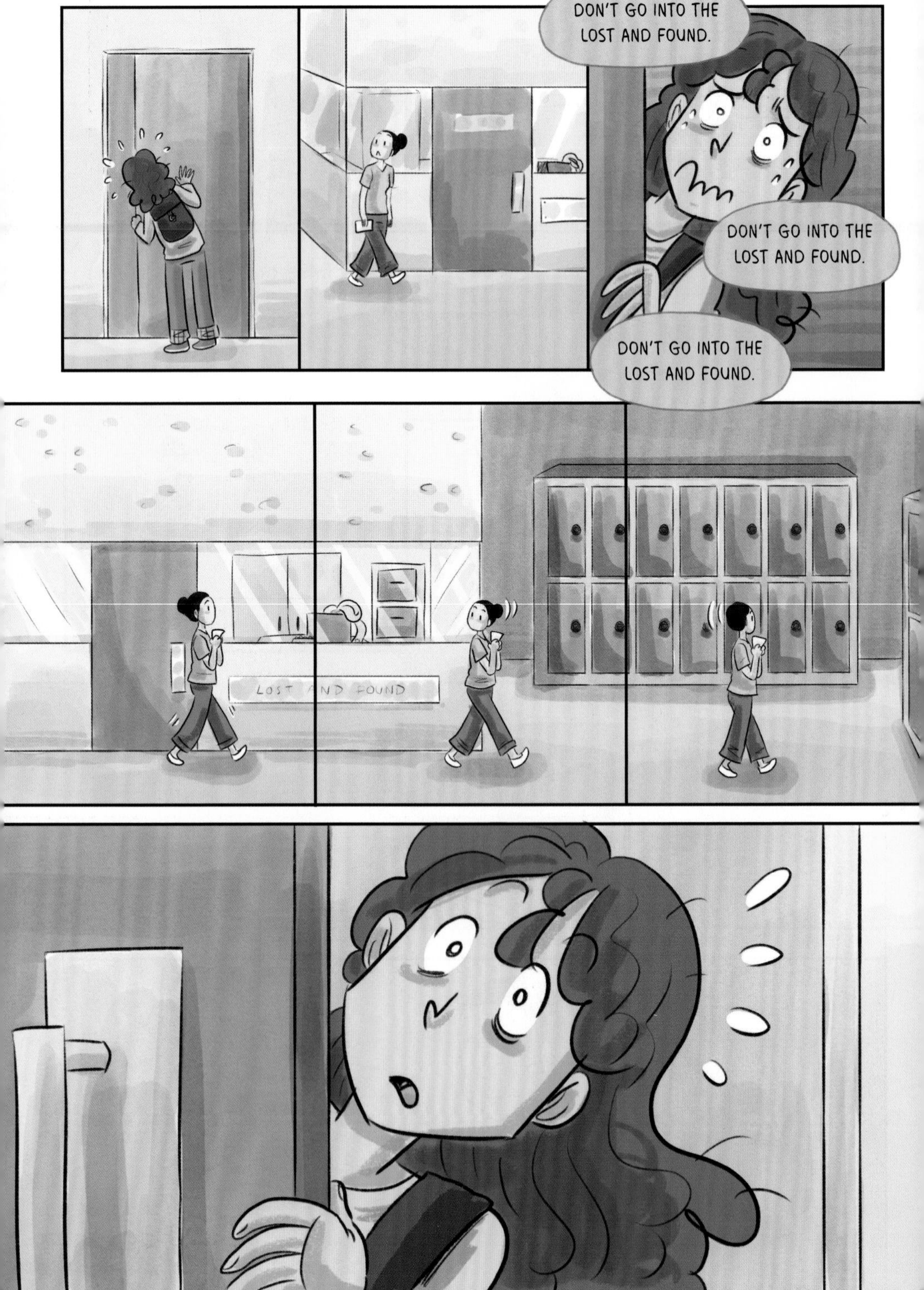
DON'T GO INTO THE LOST AND FOUND.
DON'T GO INTO THE LOST AND FOUND.
DON'T GO INTO THE LOST AND FOUND.
LOST AND FOUND

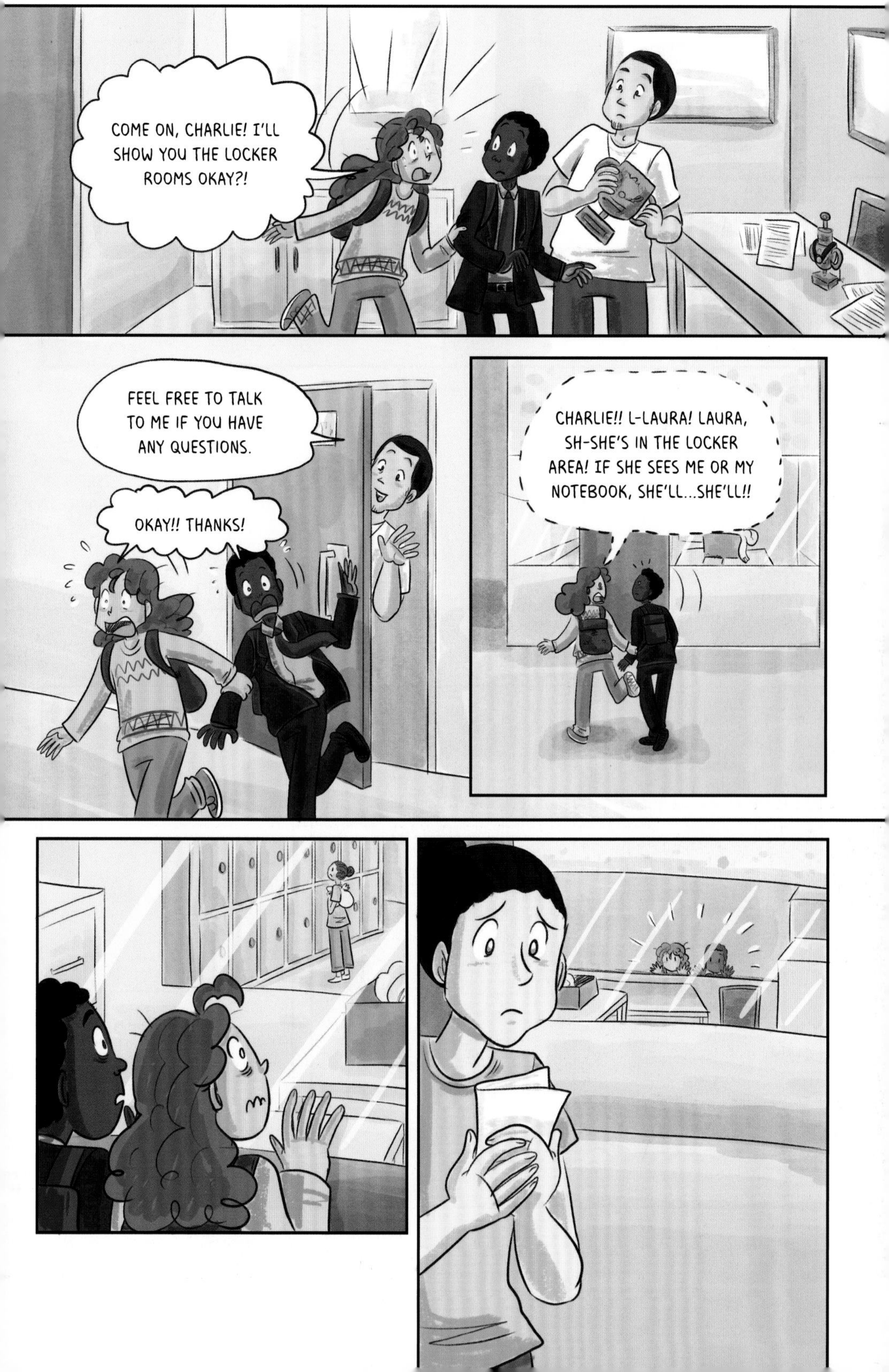

COME ON, CHARLIE! I'LL SHOW YOU THE LOCKER ROOMS OKAY?!
FEEL FREE TO TALK TO ME IF YOU HAVE ANY QUESTIONS.
OKAY!! THANKS!
CHARLIE!! L-LAURA! LAURA, SH-SHE'S IN THE LOCKER AREA! IF SHE SEES ME OR MY NOTEBOOK, SHE'LL...SHE'LL!!

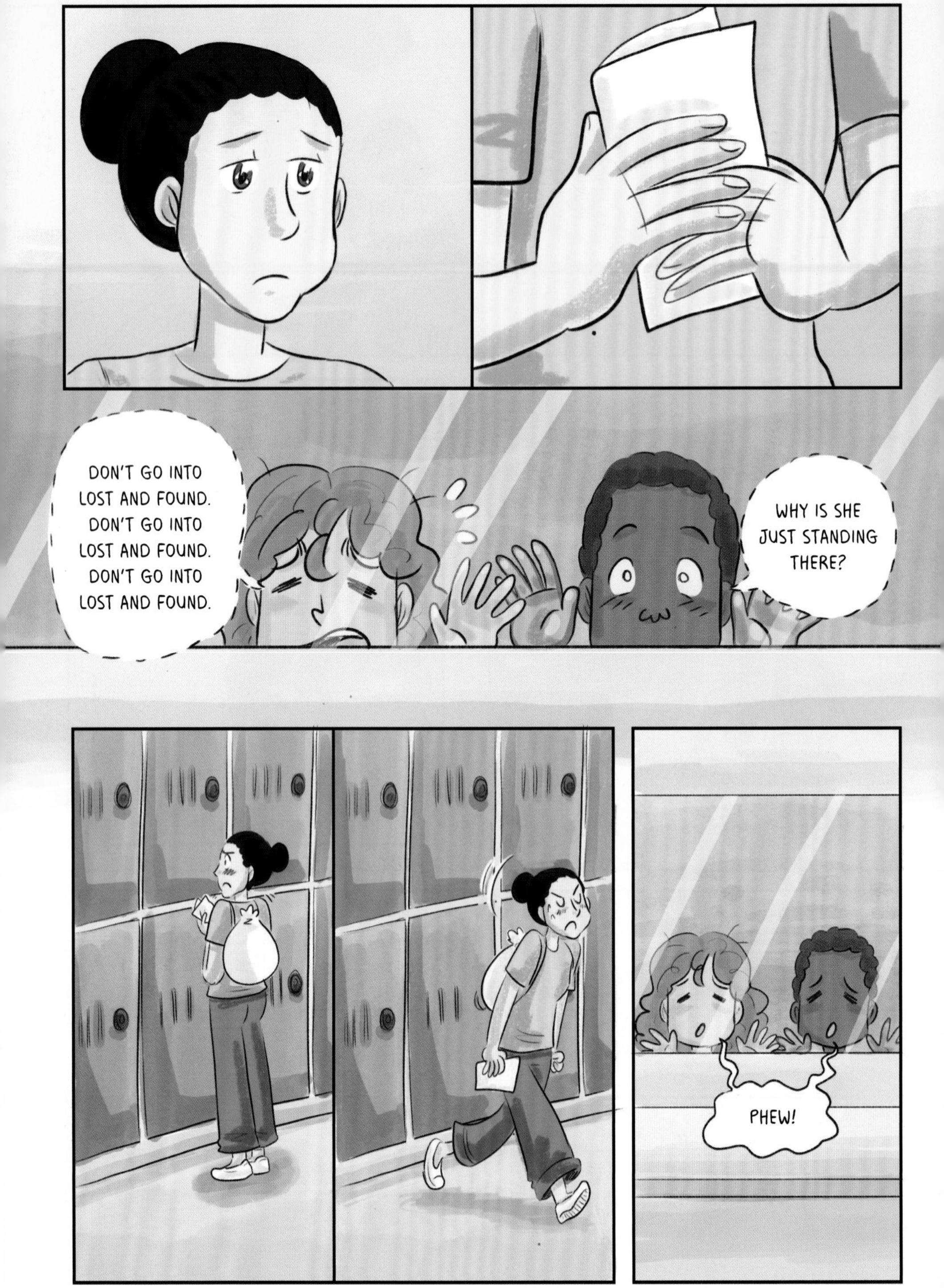
DON'T GO INTO LOST AND FOUND. DON'T GO INTO LOST AND FOUND. DON'T GO INTO LOST AND FOUND.
WHY IS SHE JUST STANDING THERE?
PHEW!

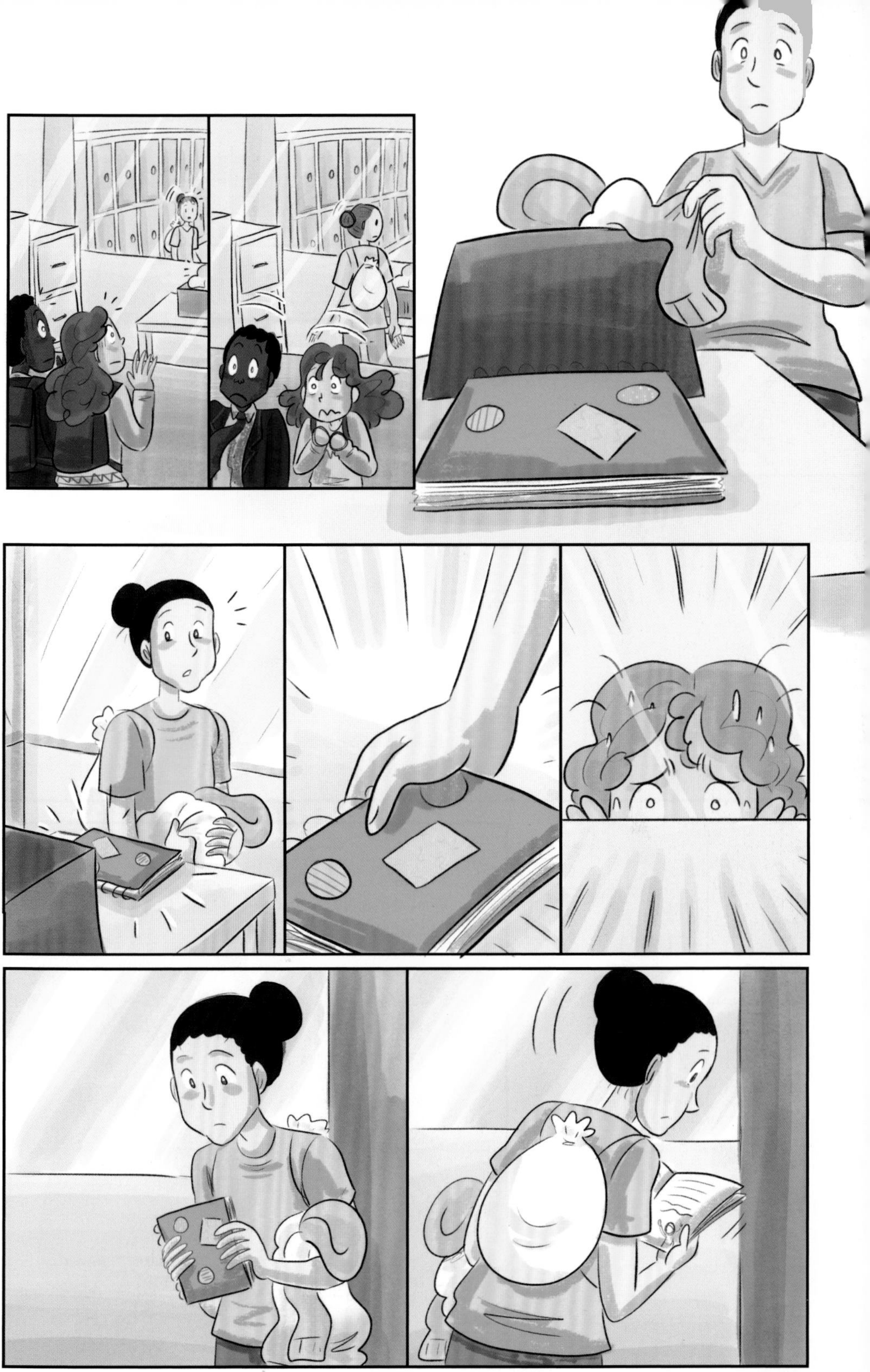

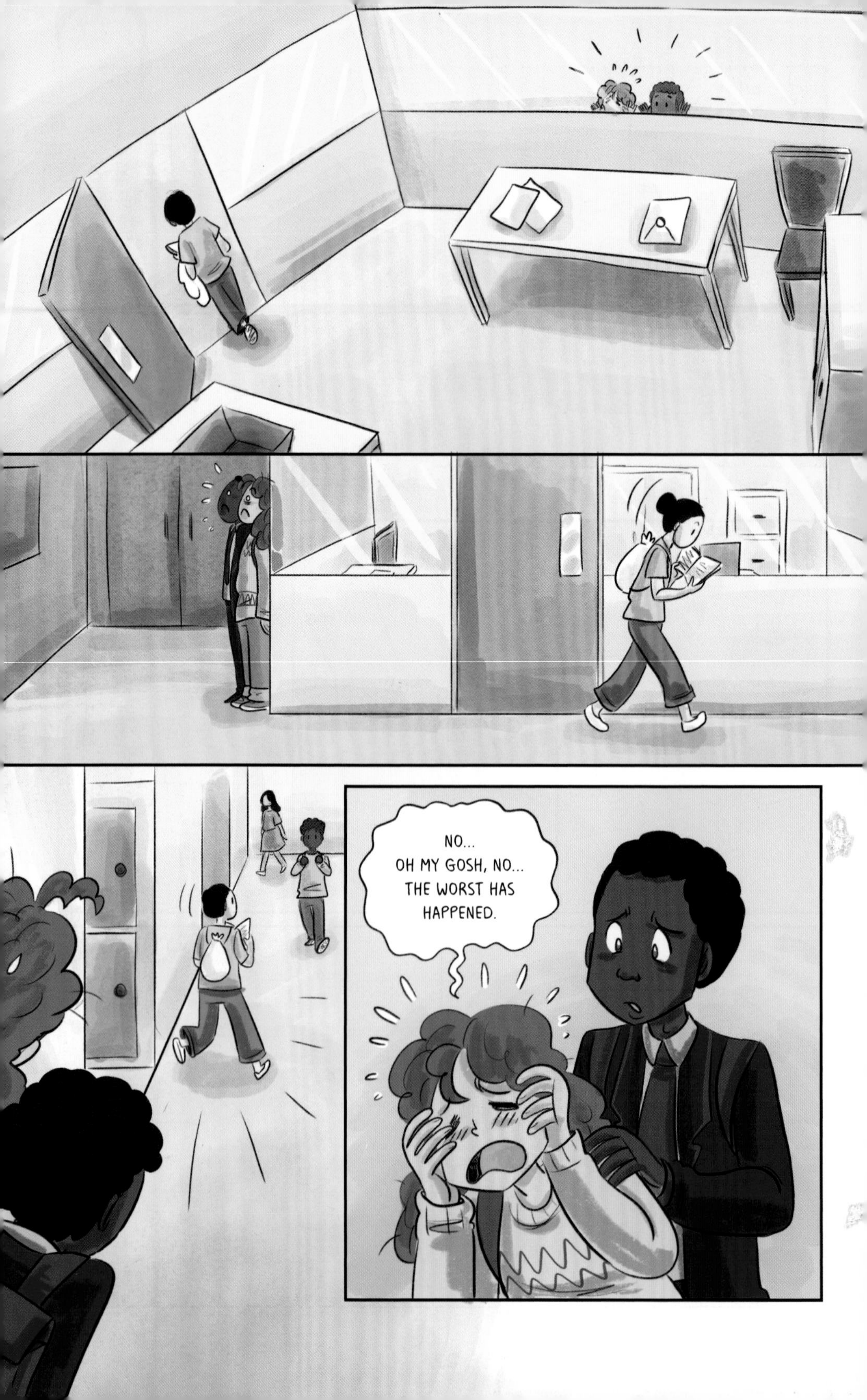
NO...
OH MY GOSH, NO...
THE WORST HAS
HAPPENED.

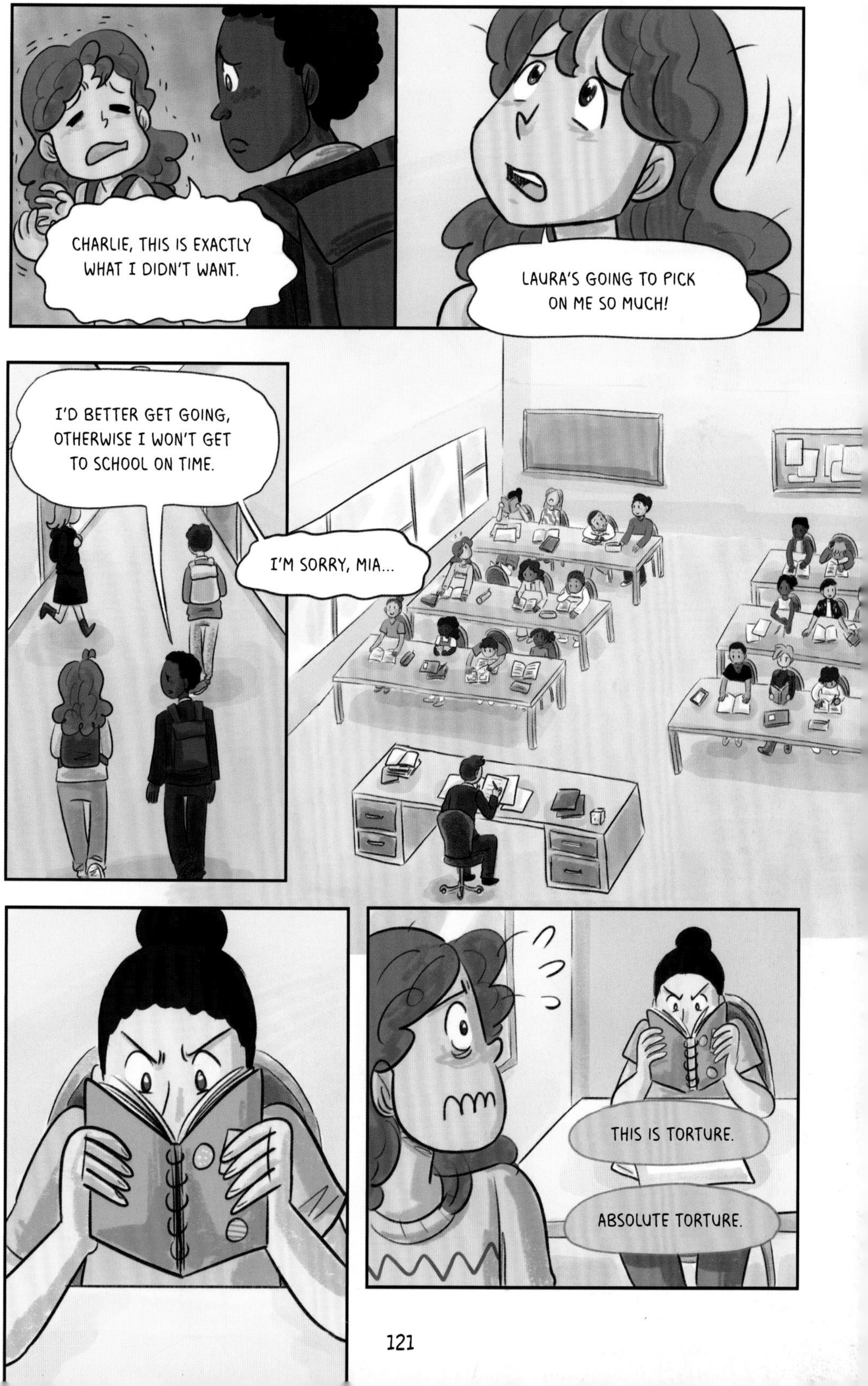
CHARLIE, THIS IS EXACTLY WHAT I DIDN'T WANT.
LAURA'S GOING TO PICK ON ME SO MUCH!
I'D BETTER GET GOING, OTHERWISE I WON'T GET TO SCHOOL ON TIME.
I'M SORRY, MIA...
THIS IS TORTURE.
ABSOLUTE TORTURE.

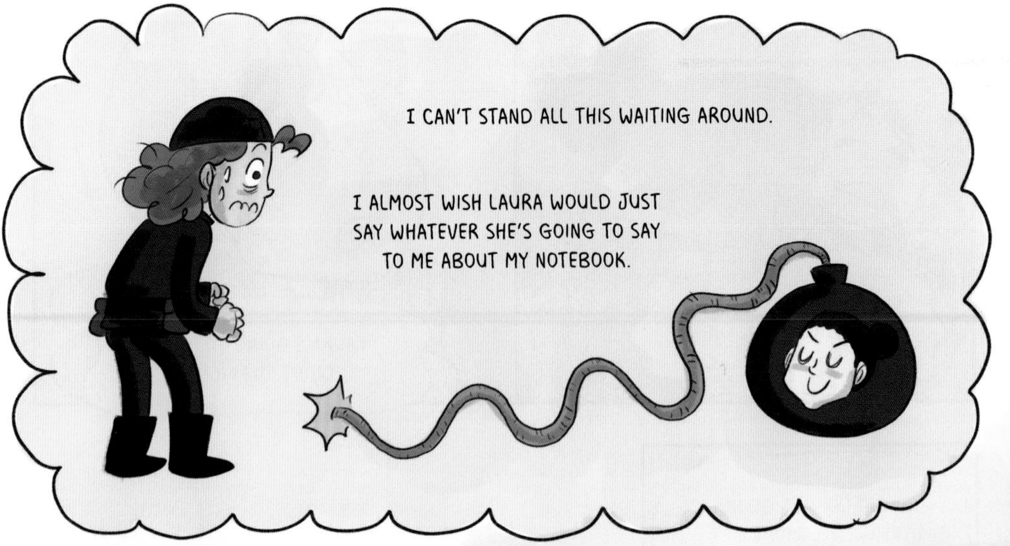
I CAN'T STAND ALL THIS WAITING AROUND.
I ALMOST WISH LAURA WOULD JUST SAY WHATEVER SHE'S GOING TO SAY TO ME ABOUT MY NOTEBOOK.

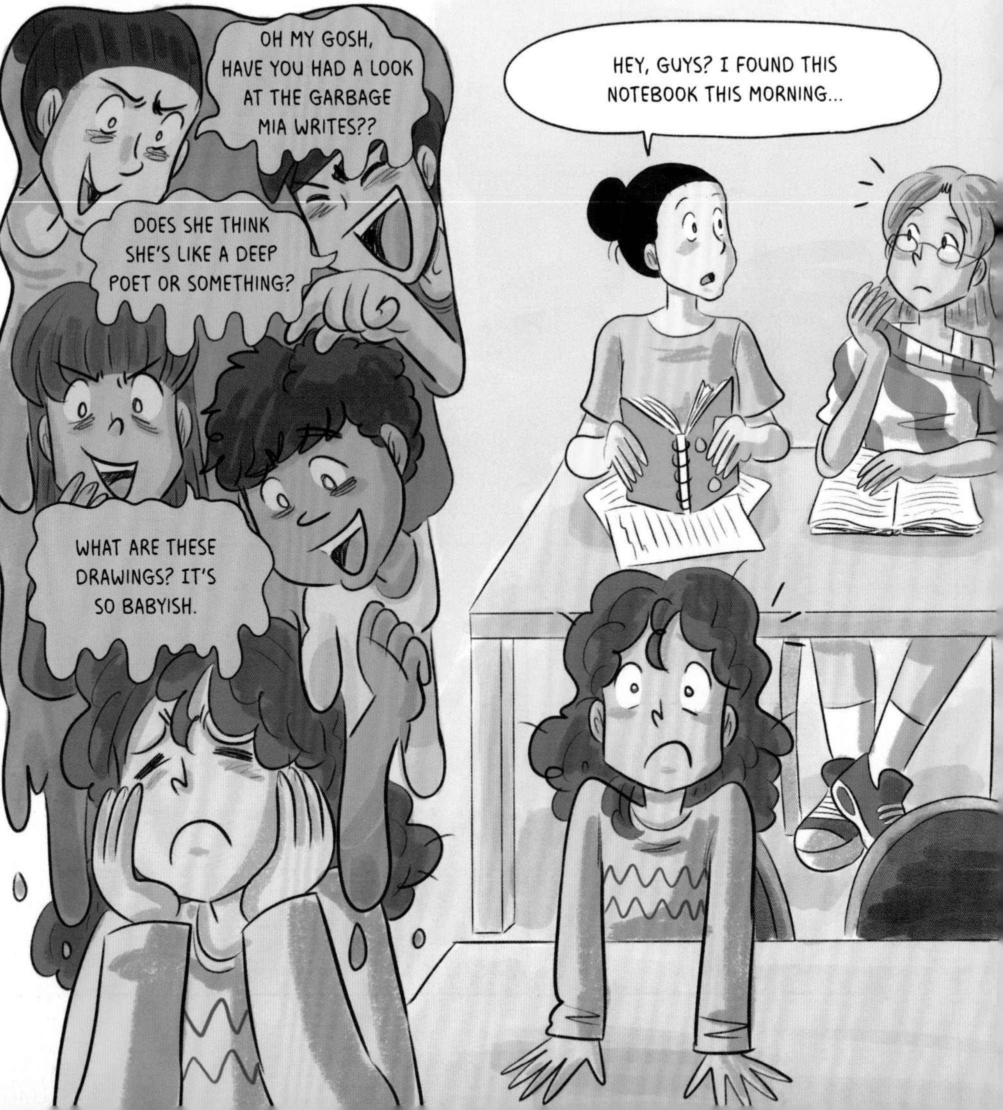
OH MY GOSH, HAVE YOU HAD A LOOK AT THE GARBAGE MIA WRITES??
DOES SHE THINK SHE'S LIKE A DEEP POET OR SOMETHING?
WHAT ARE THESE DRAWINGS? IT'S SO BABYISH.
HEY, GUYS? I FOUND THIS NOTEBOOK THIS MORNING...

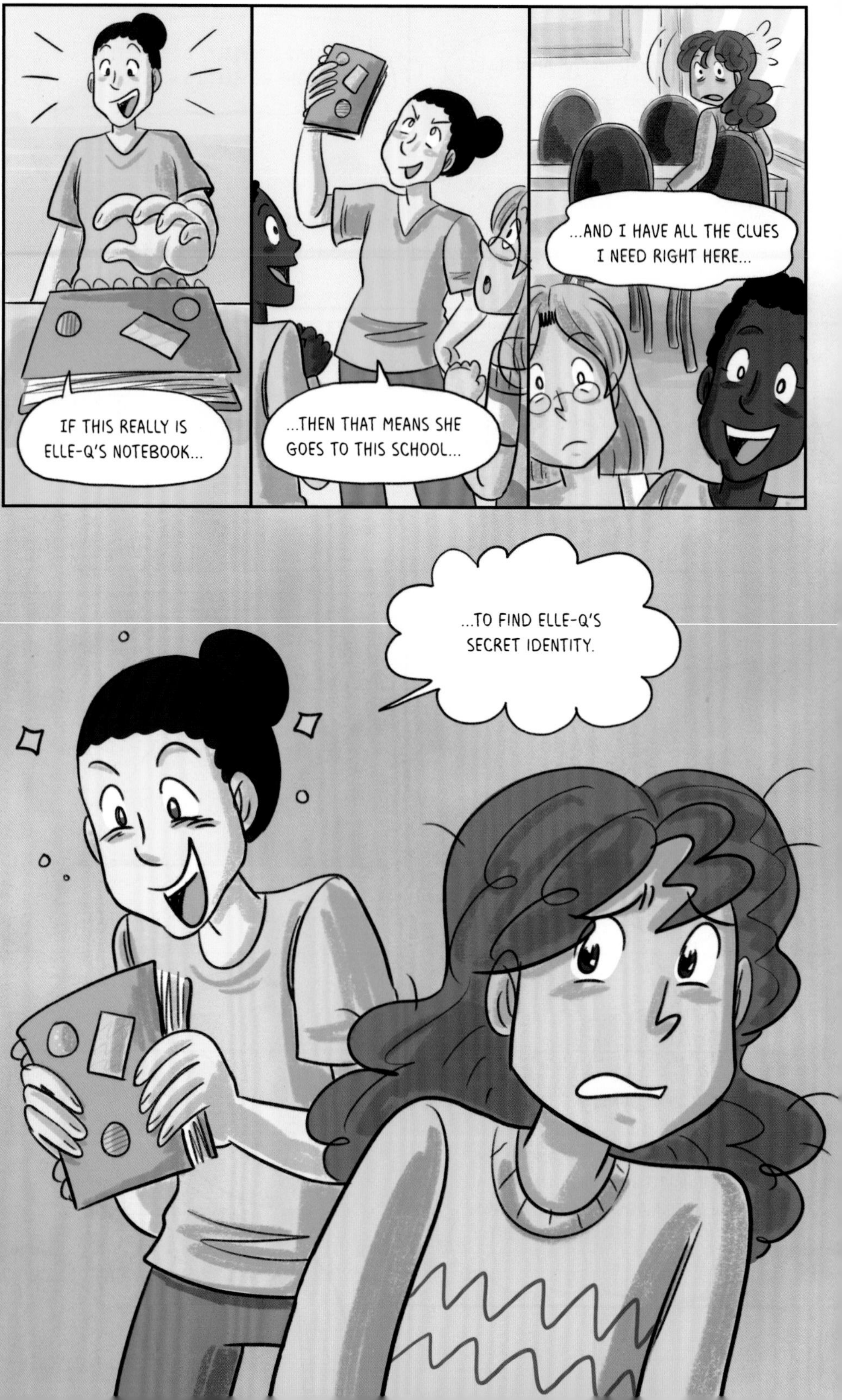
IF THIS REALLY IS ELLE-Q'S NOTEBOOK...
...THEN THAT MEANS SHE GOES TO THIS SCHOOL...
...AND I HAVE ALL THE CLUES I NEED RIGHT HERE...
...TO FIND ELLE-Q'S SECRET IDENTITY.

# CHAPTER SIX

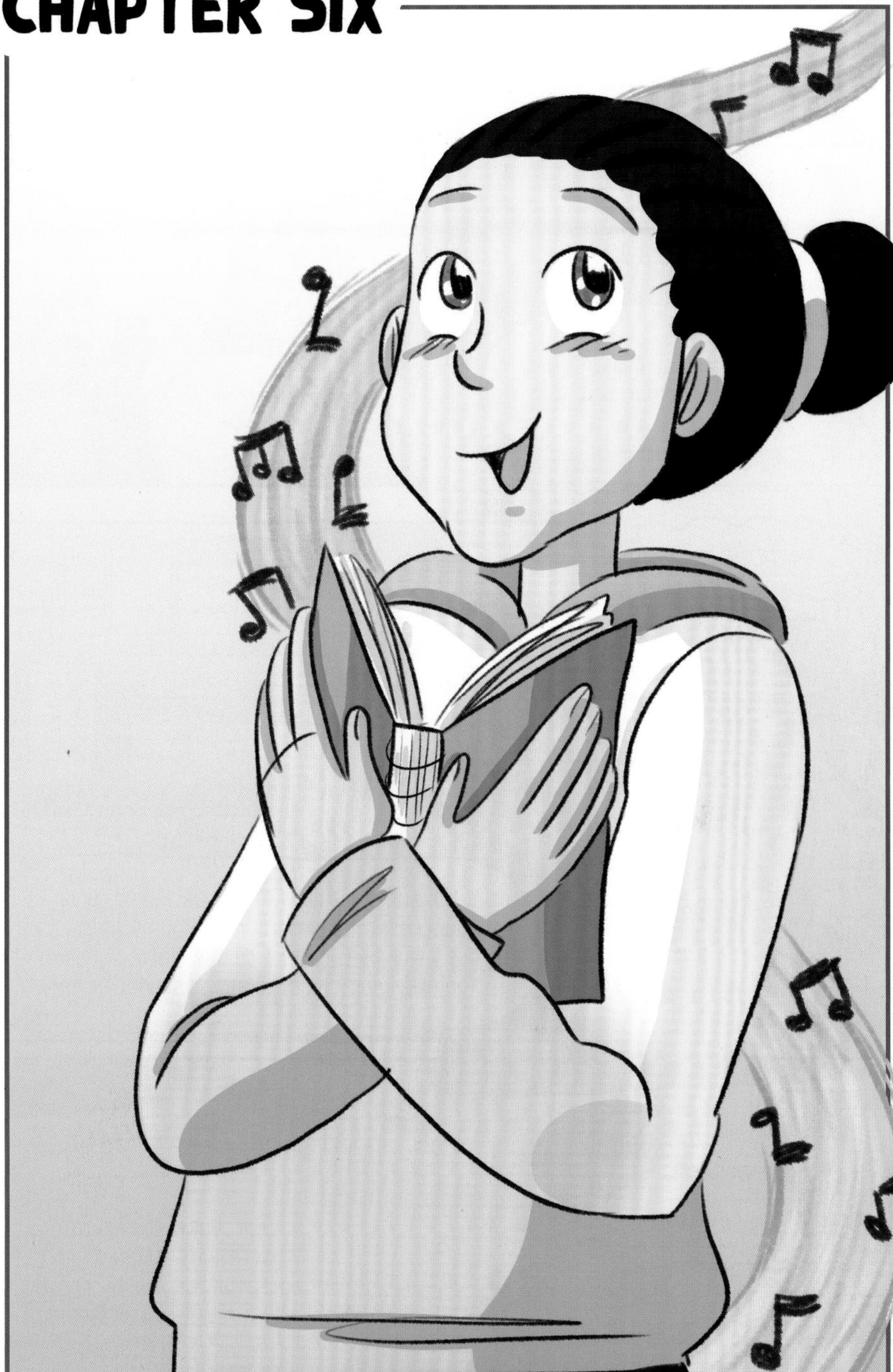

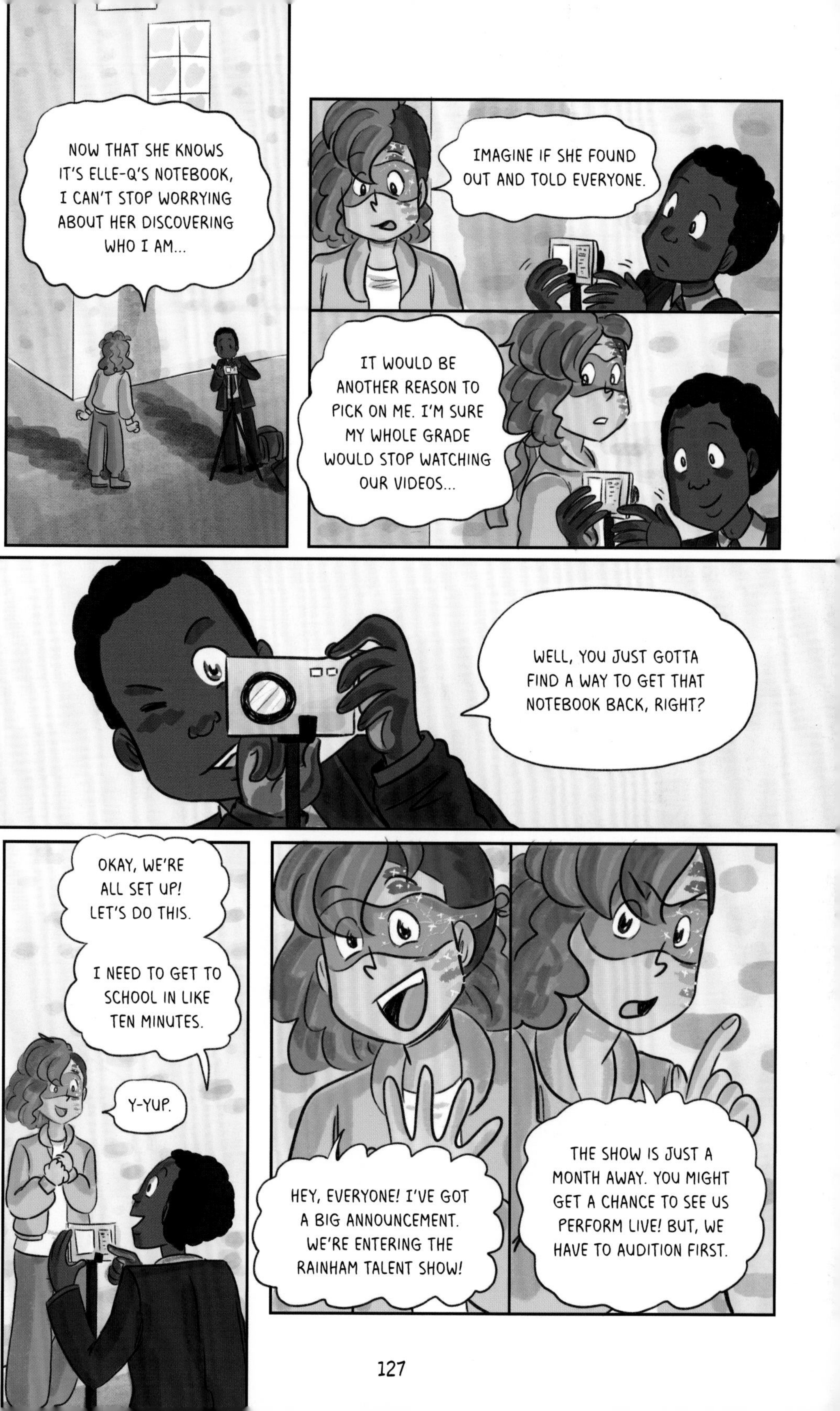
NOW THAT SHE KNOWS IT'S ELLE-Q'S NOTEBOOK, I CAN'T STOP WORRYING ABOUT HER DISCOVERING WHO I AM...
IMAGINE IF SHE FOUND OUT AND TOLD EVERYONE.
IT WOULD BE ANOTHER REASON TO PICK ON ME. I'M SURE MY WHOLE GRADE WOULD STOP WATCHING OUR VIDEOS...
WELL, YOU JUST GOTTA FIND A WAY TO GET THAT NOTEBOOK BACK, RIGHT?
OKAY, WE'RE ALL SET UP! LET'S DO THIS.
I NEED TO GET TO SCHOOL IN LIKE TEN MINUTES.
Y-YUP.
HEY, EVERYONE! I'VE GOT A BIG ANNOUNCEMENT. WE'RE ENTERING THE RAINHAM TALENT SHOW!
THE SHOW IS JUST A MONTH AWAY. YOU MIGHT GET A CHANCE TO SEE US PERFORM LIVE! BUT, WE HAVE TO AUDITION FIRST.

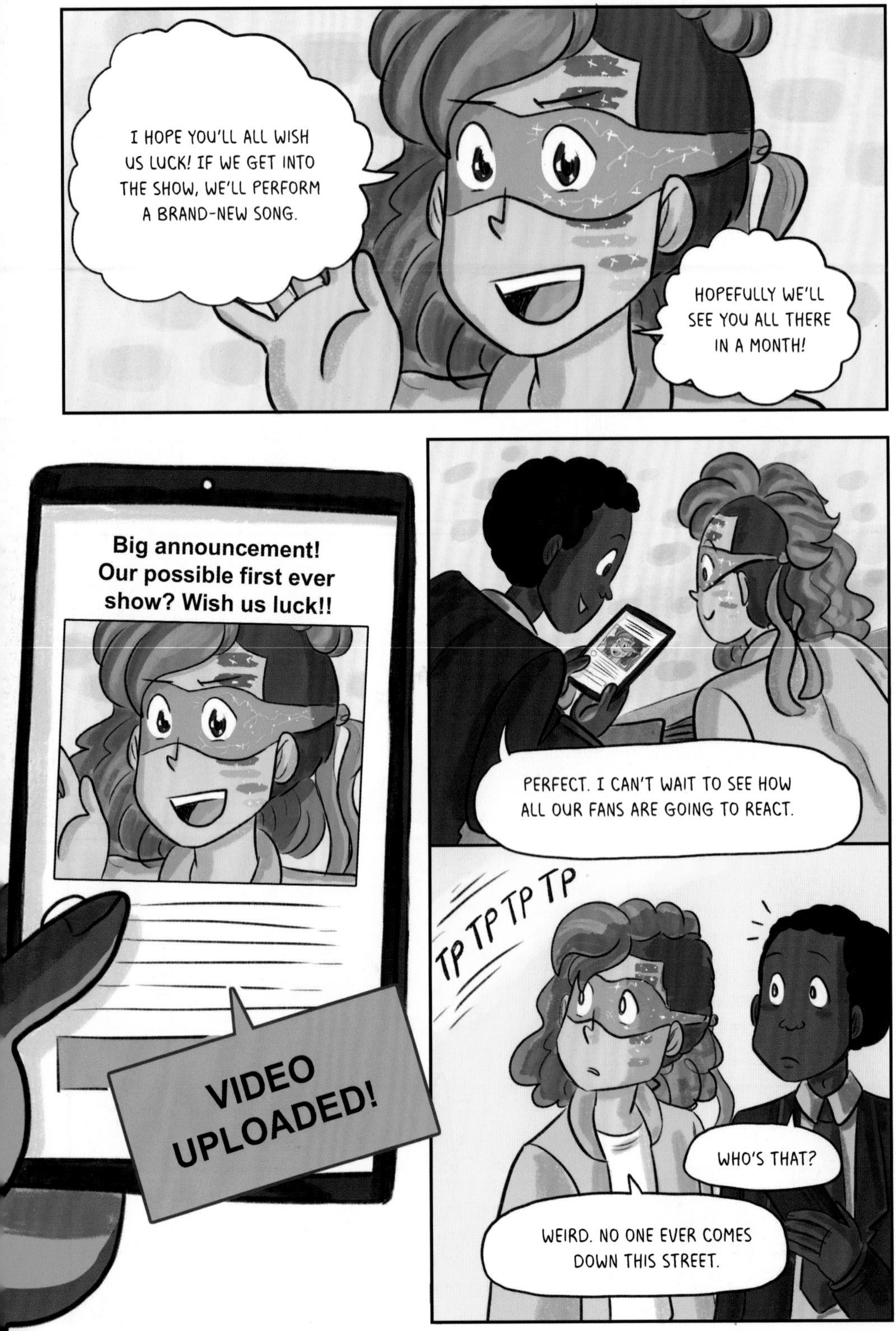
I HOPE YOU'LL ALL WISH US LUCK! IF WE GET INTO THE SHOW, WE'LL PERFORM A BRAND-NEW SONG.
HOPEFULLY WE'LL SEE YOU ALL THERE IN A MONTH!
Big announcement! Our possible first ever show? Wish us luck!!
VIDEO UPLOADED!
PERFECT. I CAN'T WAIT TO SEE HOW ALL OUR FANS ARE GOING TO REACT.
TP TP TP TP
WHO'S THAT?
WEIRD. NO ONE EVER COMES DOWN THIS STREET.

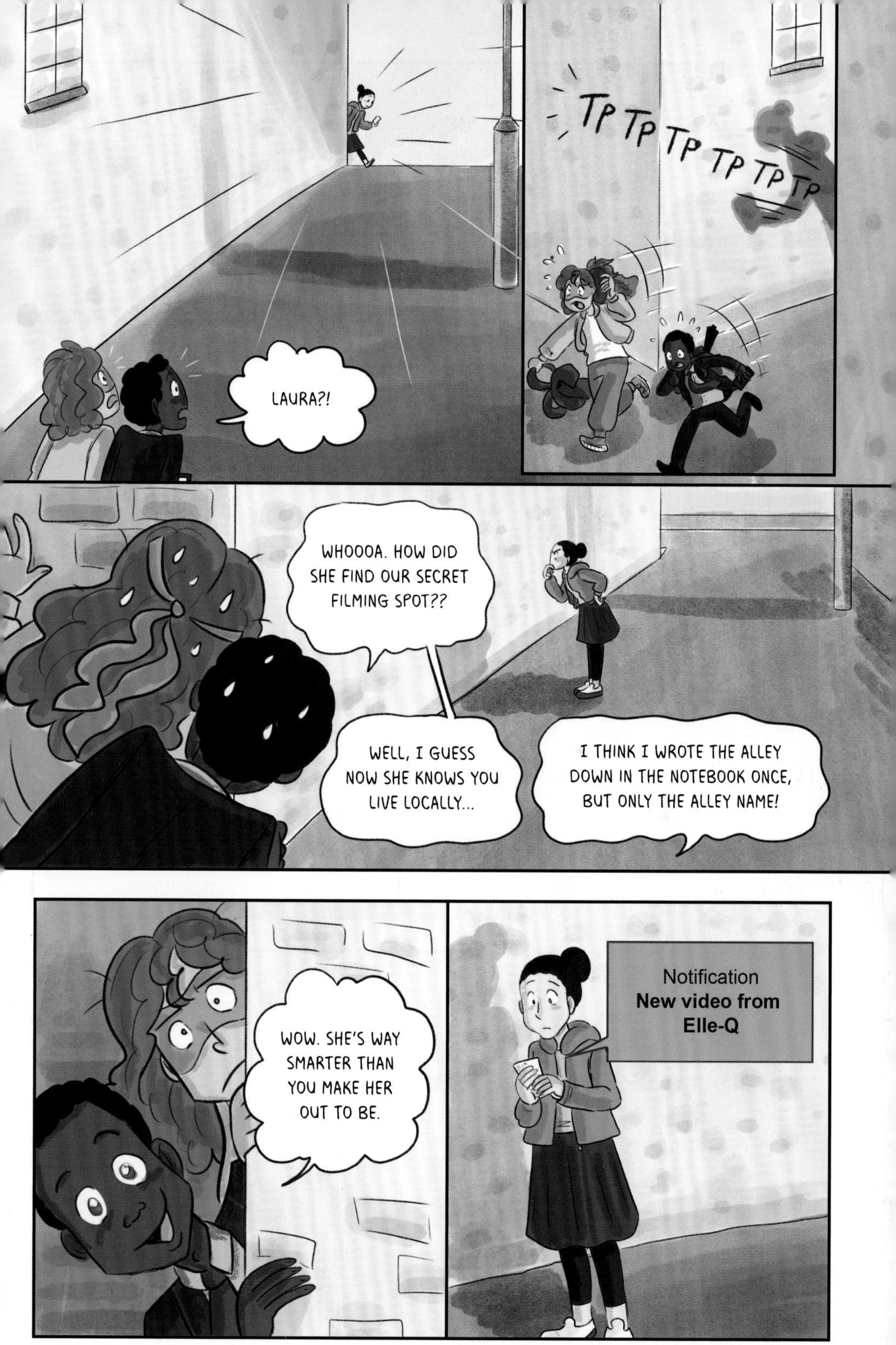

TP TP TP TP TP TP TP
LAURA?!
WHOOOA. HOW DID SHE FIND OUR SECRET FILMING SPOT??
WELL, I GUESS NOW SHE KNOWS YOU LIVE LOCALLY...
I THINK I WROTE THE ALLEY DOWN IN THE NOTEBOOK ONCE, BUT ONLY THE ALLEY NAME!
WOW. SHE'S WAY SMARTER THAN YOU MAKE HER OUT TO BE.
Notification
New video from Elle-Q

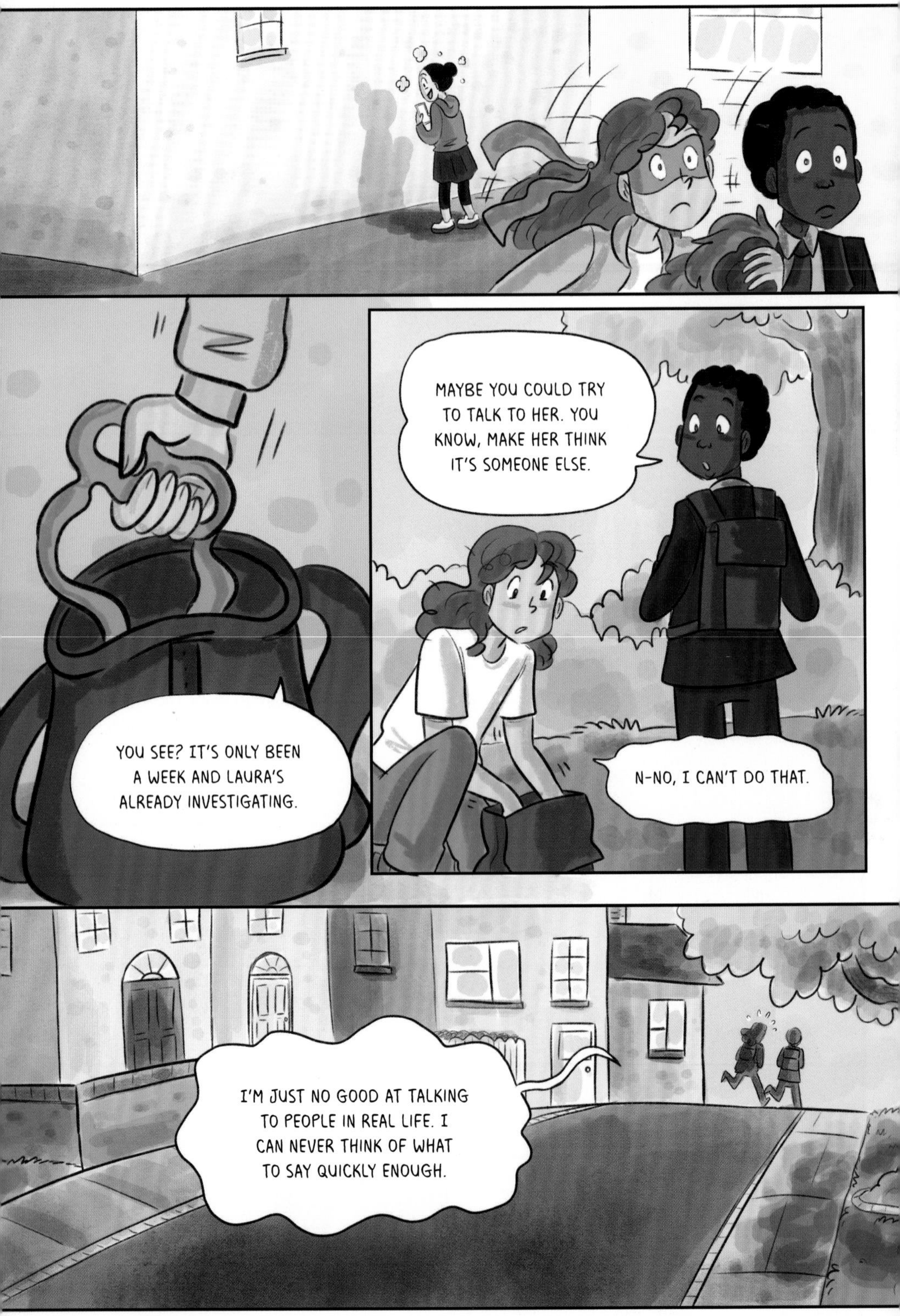
YOU SEE? IT'S ONLY BEEN A WEEK AND LAURA'S ALREADY INVESTIGATING.
MAYBE YOU COULD TRY TO TALK TO HER. YOU KNOW, MAKE HER THINK IT'S SOMEONE ELSE.
N-NO, I CAN'T DO THAT.
I'M JUST NO GOOD AT TALKING TO PEOPLE IN REAL LIFE. I CAN NEVER THINK OF WHAT TO SAY QUICKLY ENOUGH.

131

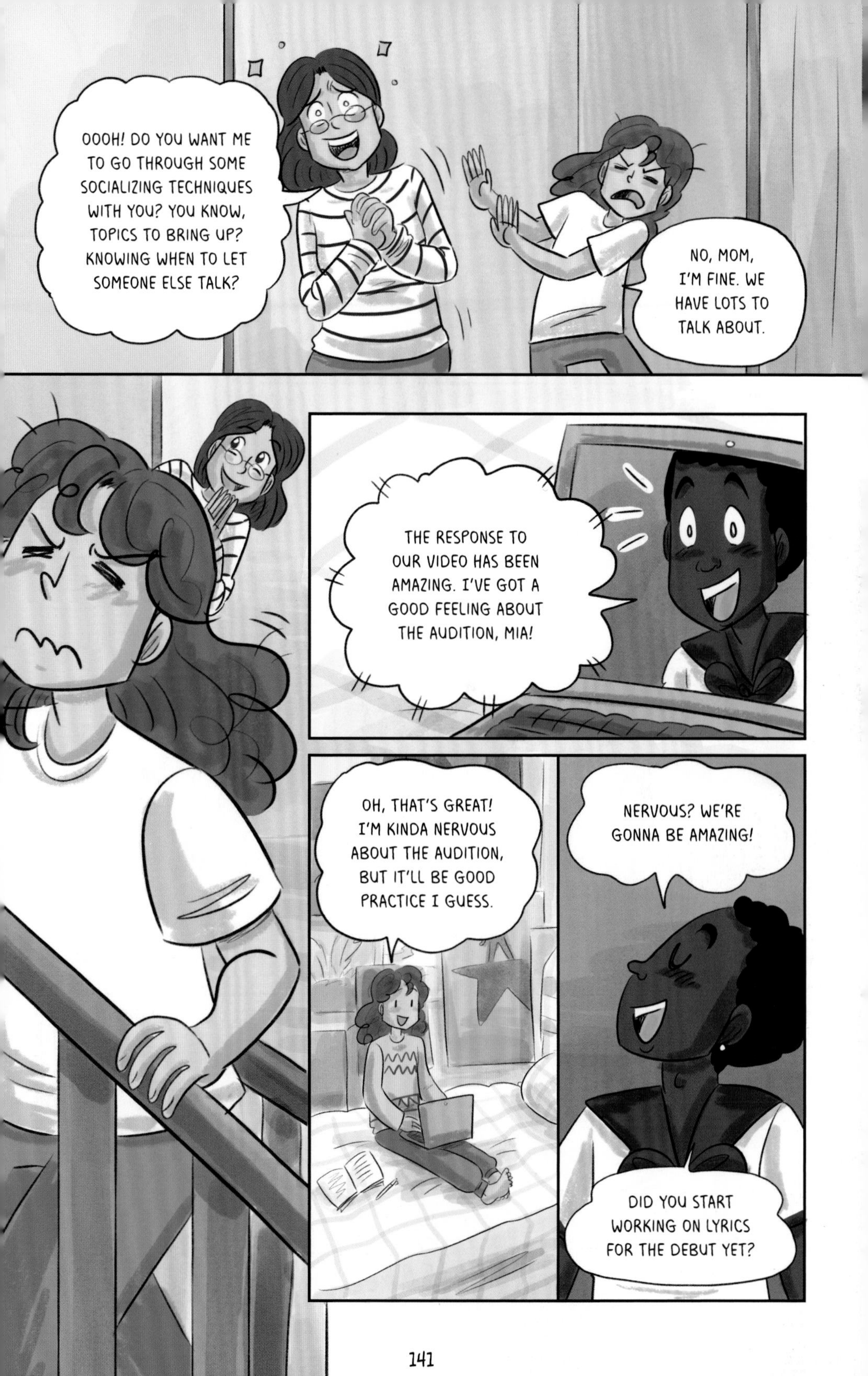
OOOH! DO YOU WANT ME TO GO THROUGH SOME SOCIALIZING TECHNIQUES WITH YOU? YOU KNOW, TOPICS TO BRING UP? KNOWING WHEN TO LET SOMEONE ELSE TALK?
NO, MOM, I'M FINE. WE HAVE LOTS TO TALK ABOUT.
THE RESPONSE TO OUR VIDEO HAS BEEN AMAZING. I'VE GOT A GOOD FEELING ABOUT THE AUDITION, MIA!
OH, THAT'S GREAT! I'M KINDA NERVOUS ABOUT THE AUDITION, BUT IT'LL BE GOOD PRACTICE I GUESS.
NERVOUS? WE'RE GONNA BE AMAZING!
DID YOU START WORKING ON LYRICS FOR THE DEBUT YET?

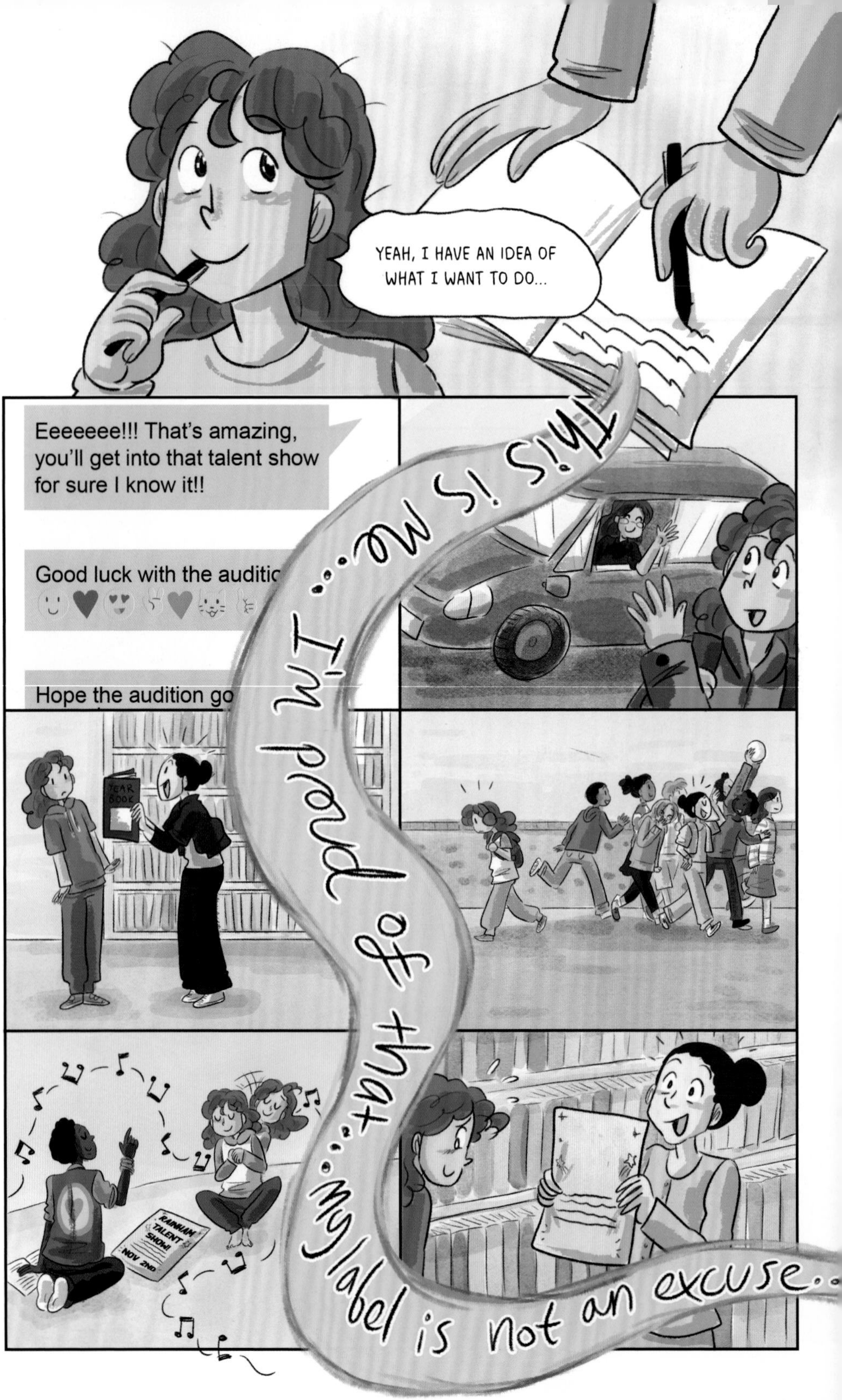

YEAH, I HAVE AN IDEA OF WHAT I WANT TO DO...
Eeeeeee!!! That's amazing, you'll get into that talent show for sure I know it!!
Good luck with the auditic
Hope the audition go
YEAR BOOK
RAINHAM TALENT SHOW! NOV 2ND
This is me... I'm proud of that... My label is not an excuse...

161

HEE.

YES!

WE'RE IN! WHOOO!

WHILE WE'RE HERE, DO YOU HAVE ANY QUESTIONS ABOUT THE SHOW?

...UH, I'M AUTISTIC. AND I TEND TO GET OVERLOADED BY BRIGHT LIGHTS AND TOO MUCH NOISE.

OH—UH—

A-ACTUALLY...

SO...I-I WAS WONDERING IF I COULD HAVE THE LIGHTS TURNED DOWN WHEN I'M ONSTAGE TO FEEL MORE COMFORTABLE, AND BE ALLOWED TO WEAR HEADPHONES AND SOME COMFY CLOTHES, AND GO BAREFOOT TOO...?

# CHAPTER SEVEN

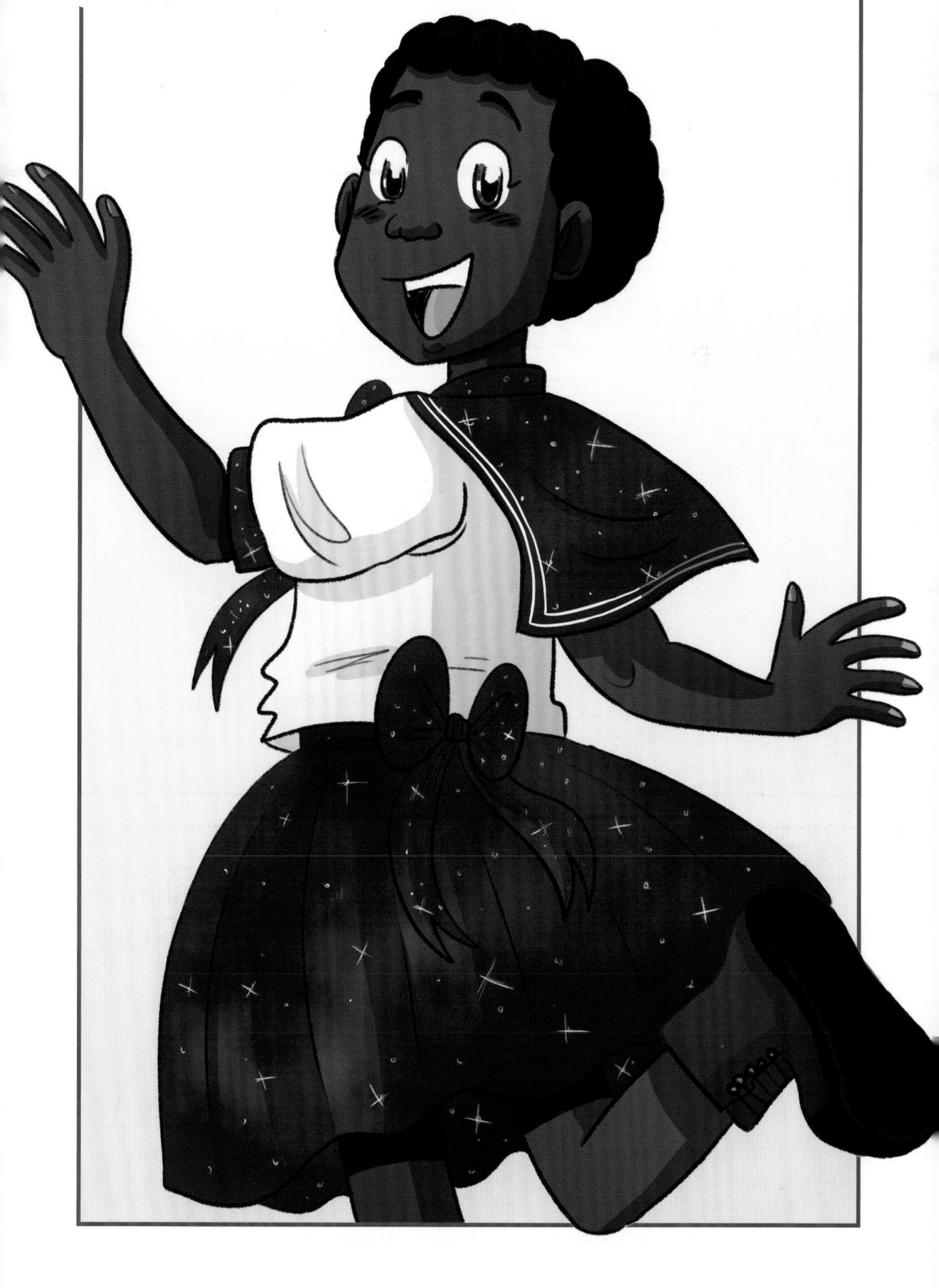

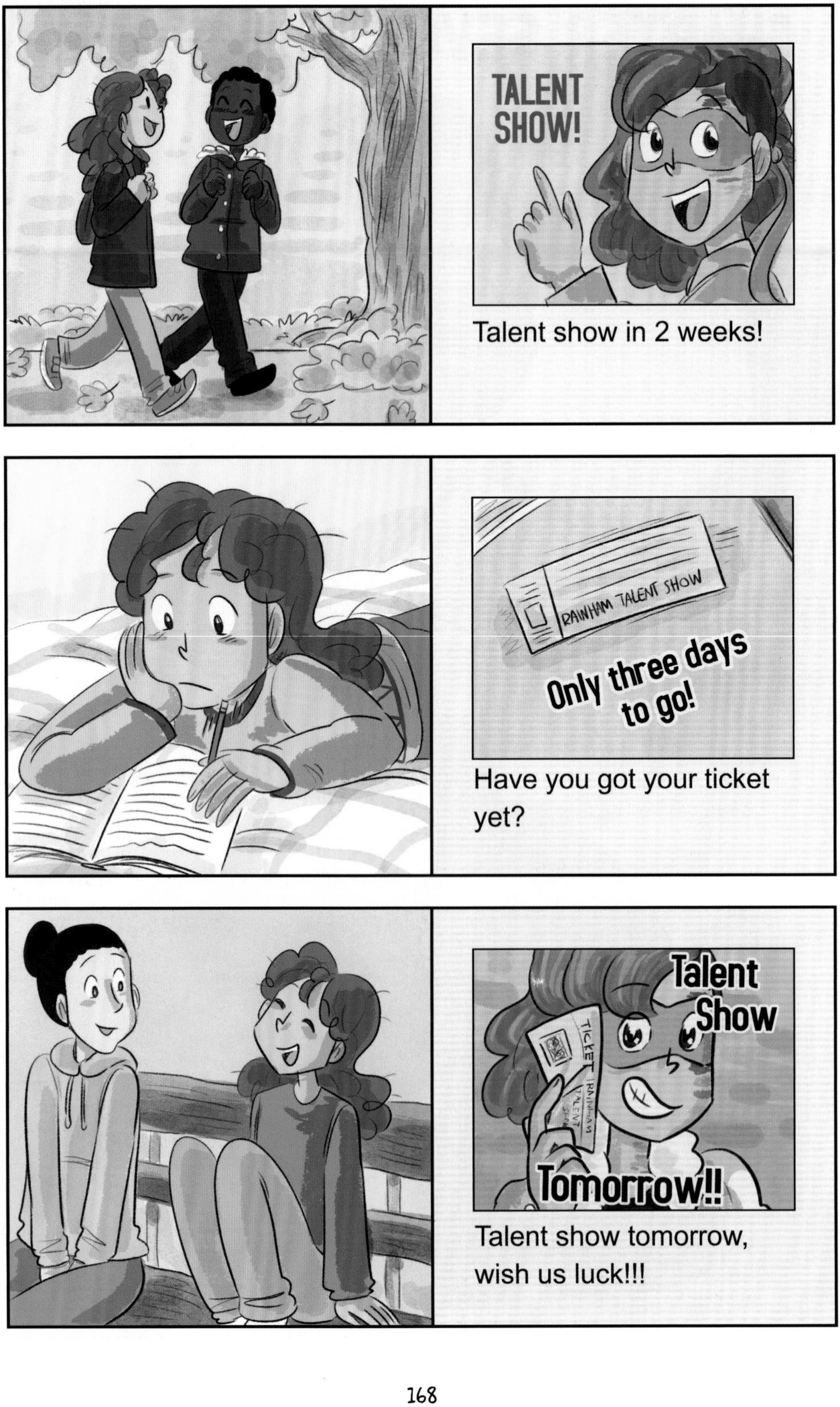
TALENT SHOW!
Talent show in 2 weeks!
RAINHAM TALENT SHOW
Only three days to go!
Have you got your ticket yet?
Talent Show
TICKET
Tomorrow!!
Talent show tomorrow, wish us luck!!!

WELL, MY MOM SAID SHE'D DRIVE ME TO SCHOOL TODAY, SO YOU'D BETTER GET GOING.

ANYWAY, I'D BETTER HEAD TO SCHOOL. SEE YOU TOMORROW AT THE TALENT SH—

SHHHHOOO...SHAUL? SCHOOL? SCHOOL! SEE YOU OUTSIDE YOUR...VERY...TALENTED... SCHOOL! UH, BYE!

IT'S TIME FOR US TO HEAD OUT TOO, MIA.

ARE YOU MAKING SOME MORE FRIENDS AT YOUR WRITING CLUB? I'M SURPRISED YOU HAVEN'T INVITED ANYONE OVER TO OUR HOUSE YET.

ARE YOU TRYING TO TALK WITH THE OTHER KIDS MORE ABOUT THEIR INTERESTS? OR MAYBE YOU'RE MAKING MORE EYE CONTACT?

IT'S GREAT TO SEE YOU DOING SO WELL RECENTLY, MIA.

175

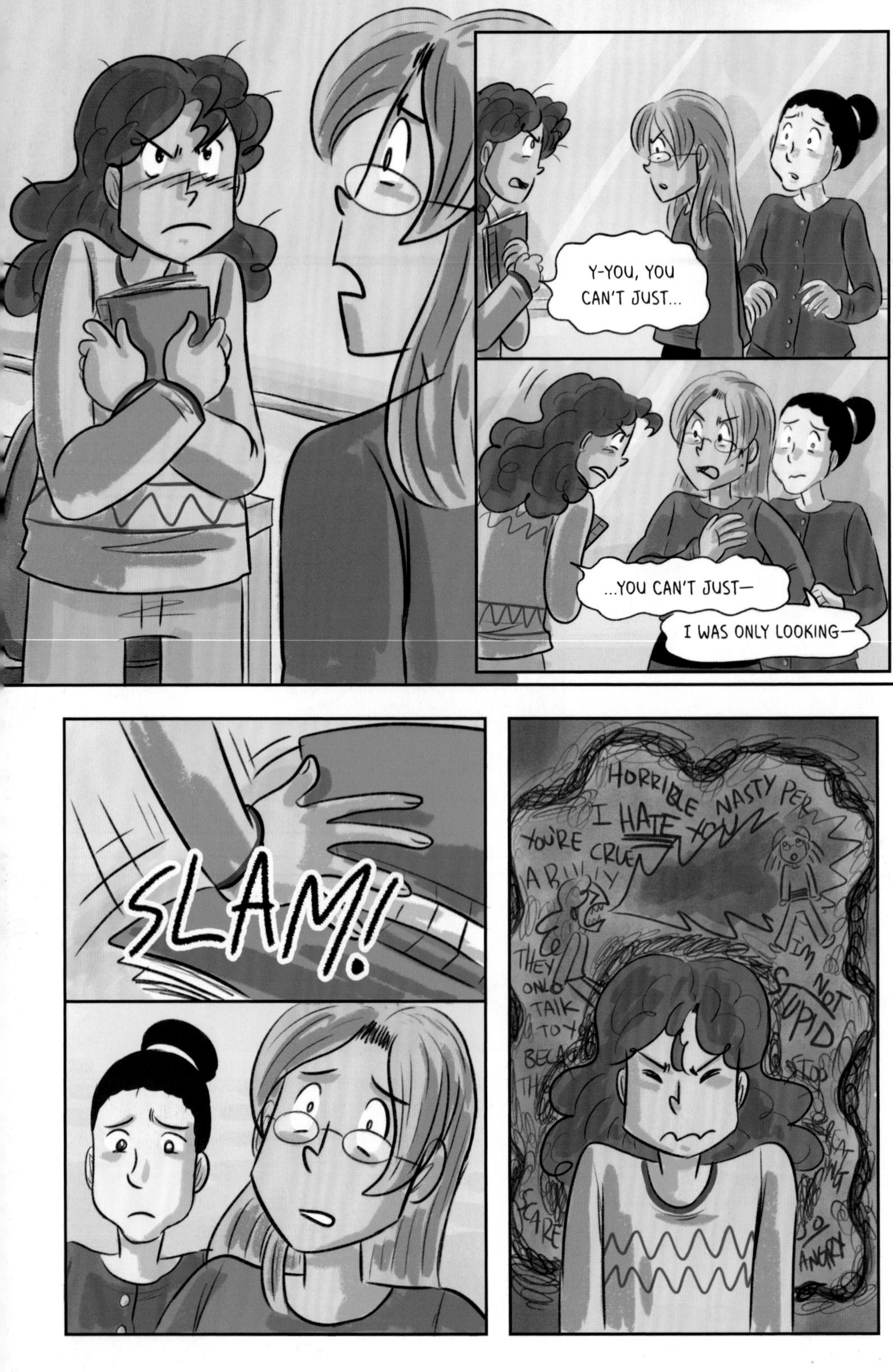
Y-YOU, YOU CAN'T JUST...
...YOU CAN'T JUST—
I WAS ONLY LOOKING—
SLAM!
HORRIBLE NASTY PER
I HATE YOU
YOU'RE CRUEL
I'M NOT STUPID
ANGRY

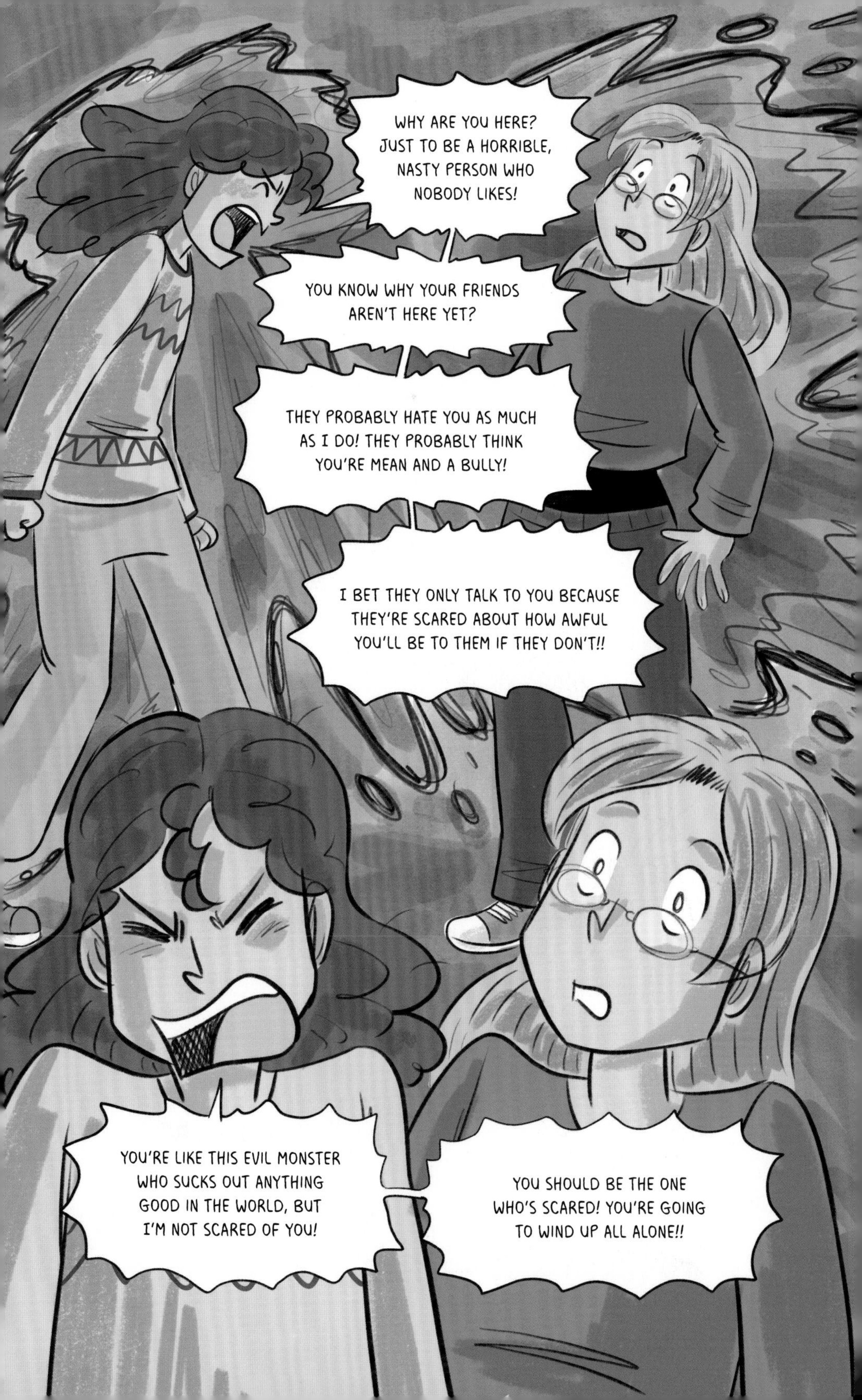
WHY ARE YOU HERE? JUST TO BE A HORRIBLE, NASTY PERSON WHO NOBODY LIKES!
YOU KNOW WHY YOUR FRIENDS AREN'T HERE YET?
THEY PROBABLY HATE YOU AS MUCH AS I DO! THEY PROBABLY THINK YOU'RE MEAN AND A BULLY!
I BET THEY ONLY TALK TO YOU BECAUSE THEY'RE SCARED ABOUT HOW AWFUL YOU'LL BE TO THEM IF THEY DON'T!!
YOU'RE LIKE THIS EVIL MONSTER WHO SUCKS OUT ANYTHING GOOD IN THE WORLD, BUT I'M NOT SCARED OF YOU!
YOU SHOULD BE THE ONE WHO'S SCARED! YOU'RE GOING TO WIND UP ALL ALONE!!

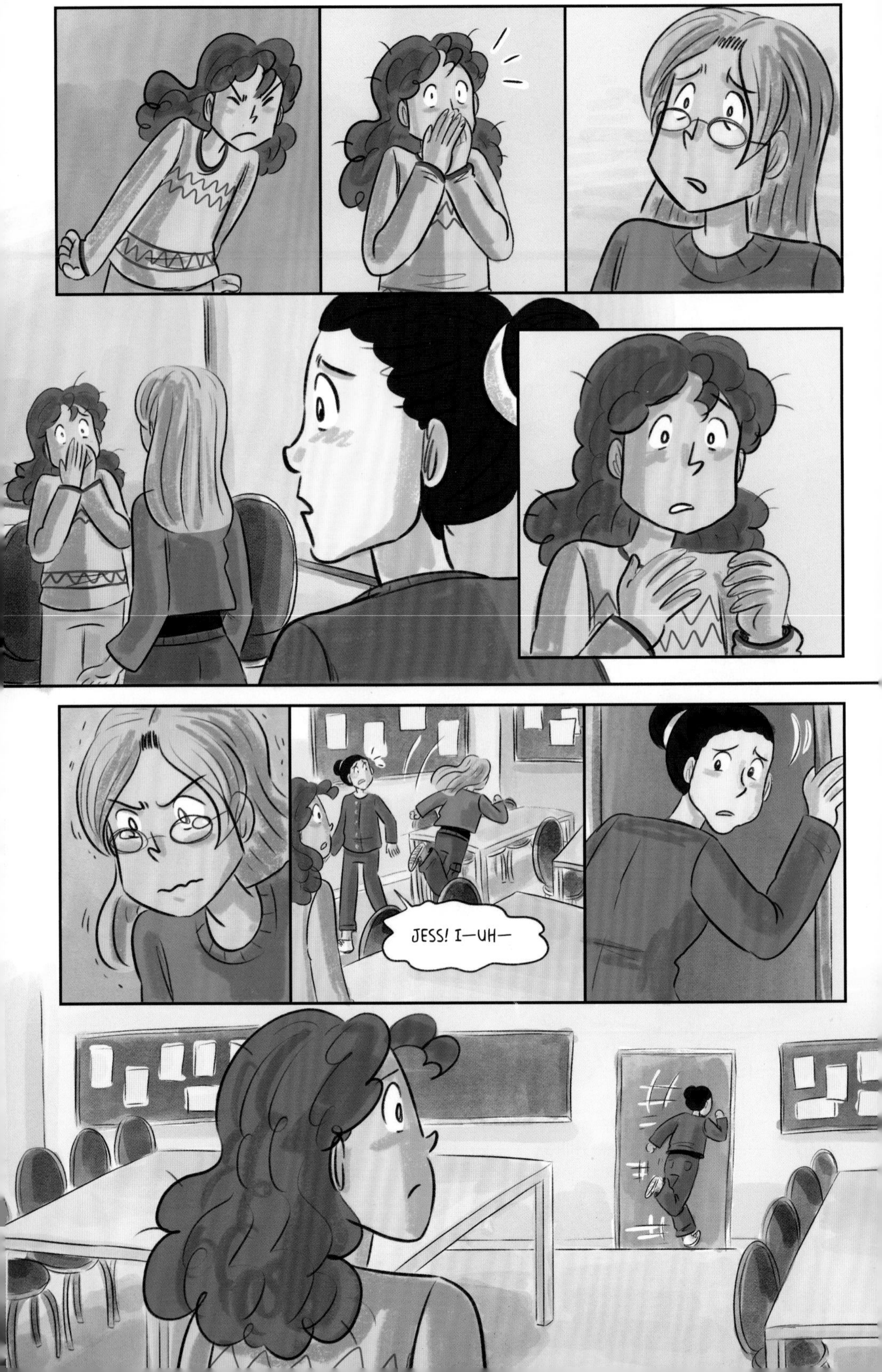
JESS! I—UH—

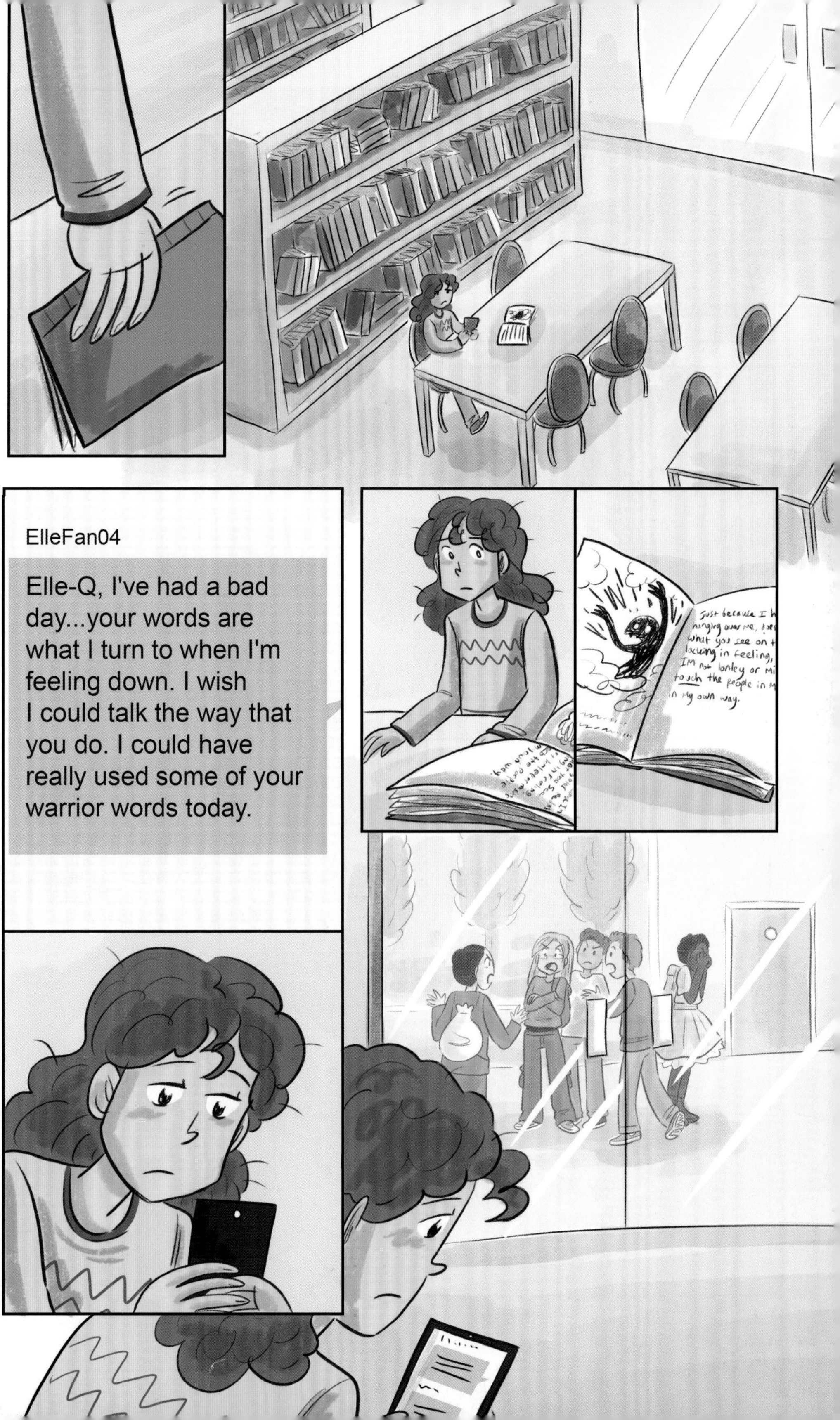
ElleFan04
Elle-Q, I've had a bad day...your words are what I turn to when I'm feeling down. I wish I could talk the way that you do. I could have really used some of your warrior words today.
Just because I
hanging over me,
what you see on
lacking in feeling,
IM not lonley or
touch the people in
in my own way.

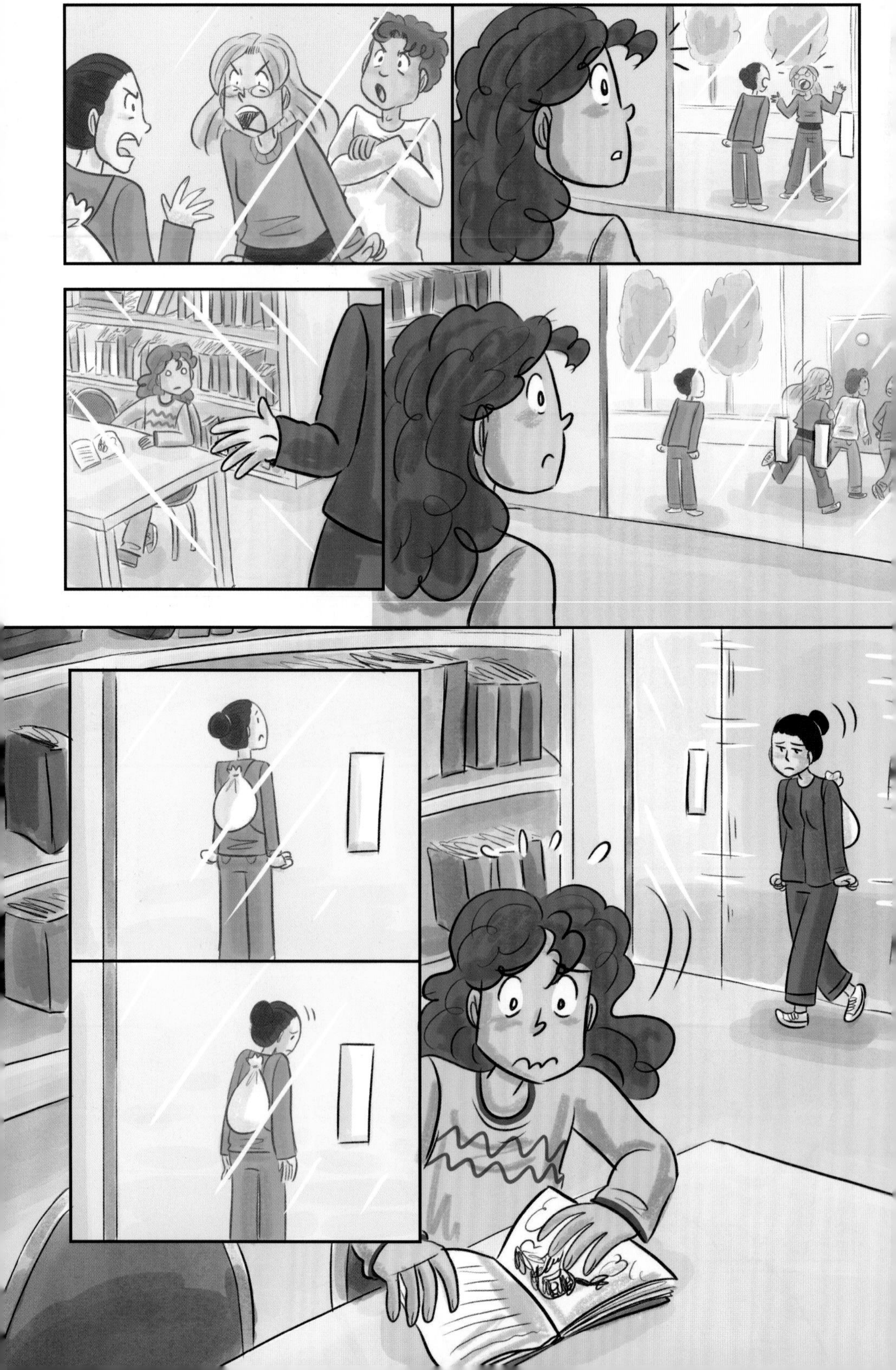

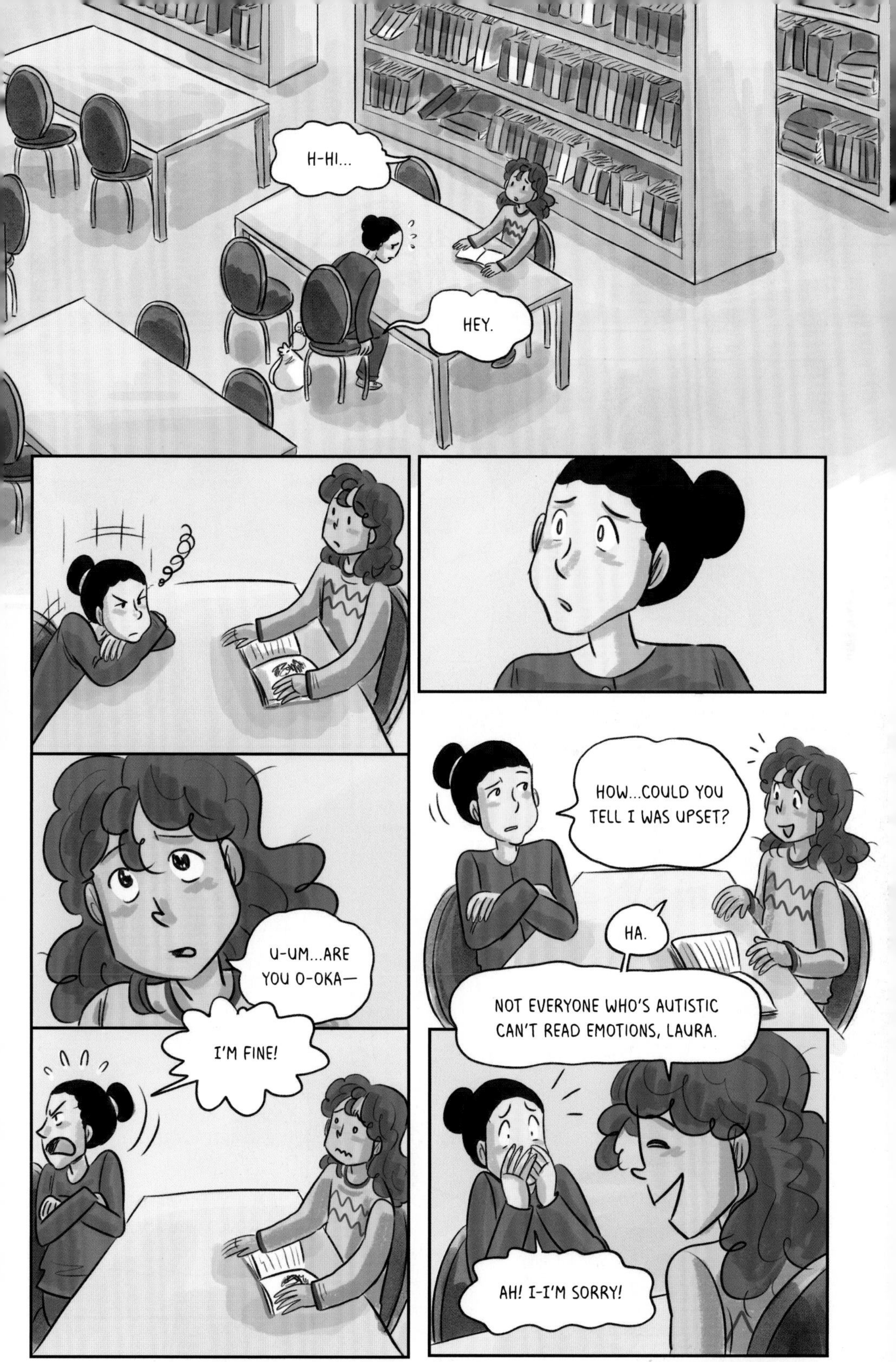
H-HI...
HEY.
U-UM...ARE YOU O-OKA—
I'M FINE!
HOW...COULD YOU TELL I WAS UPSET?
HA.
NOT EVERYONE WHO'S AUTISTIC CAN'T READ EMOTIONS, LAURA.
AH! I-I'M SORRY!

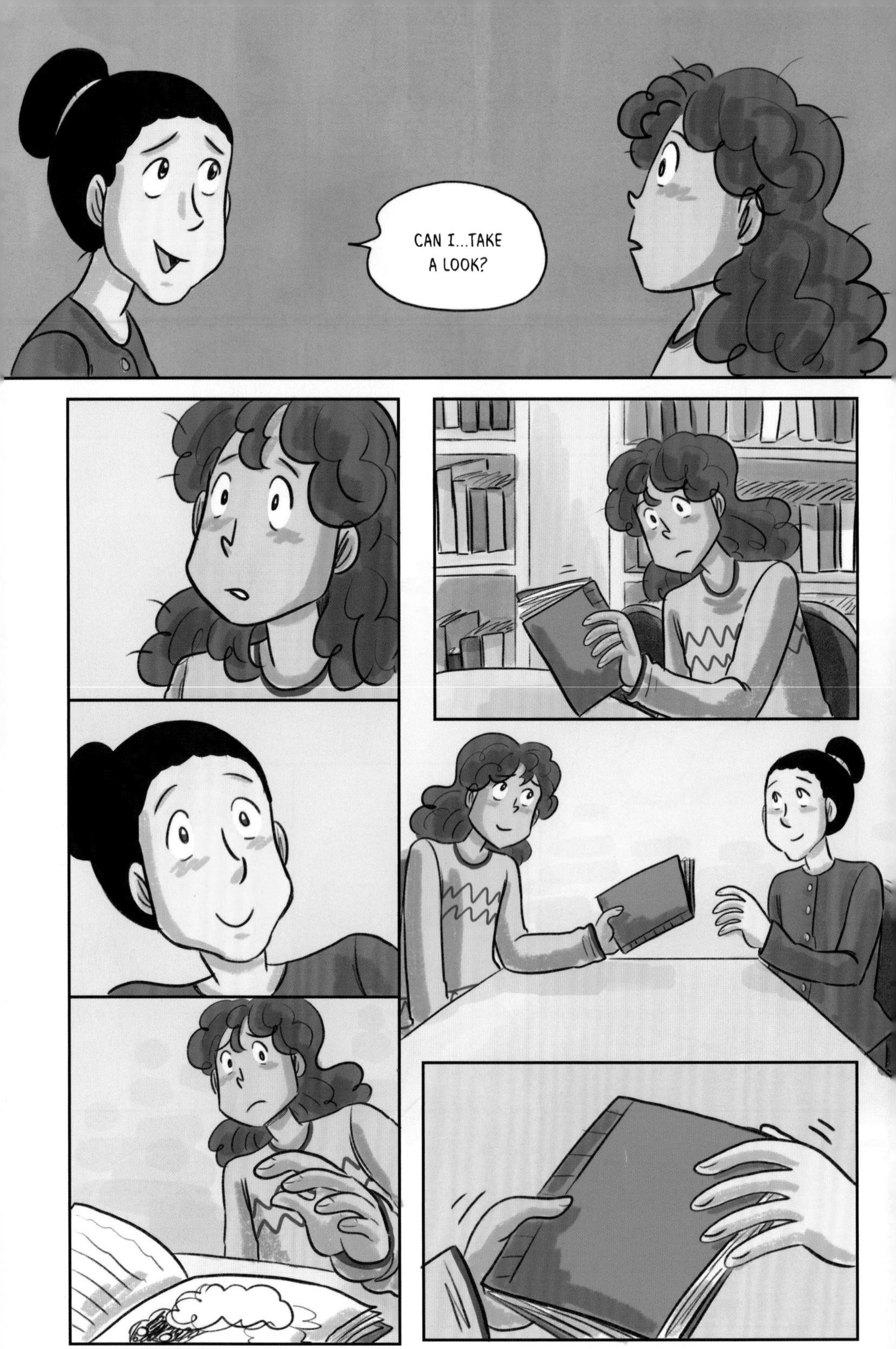
CAN I...TAKE
A LOOK?

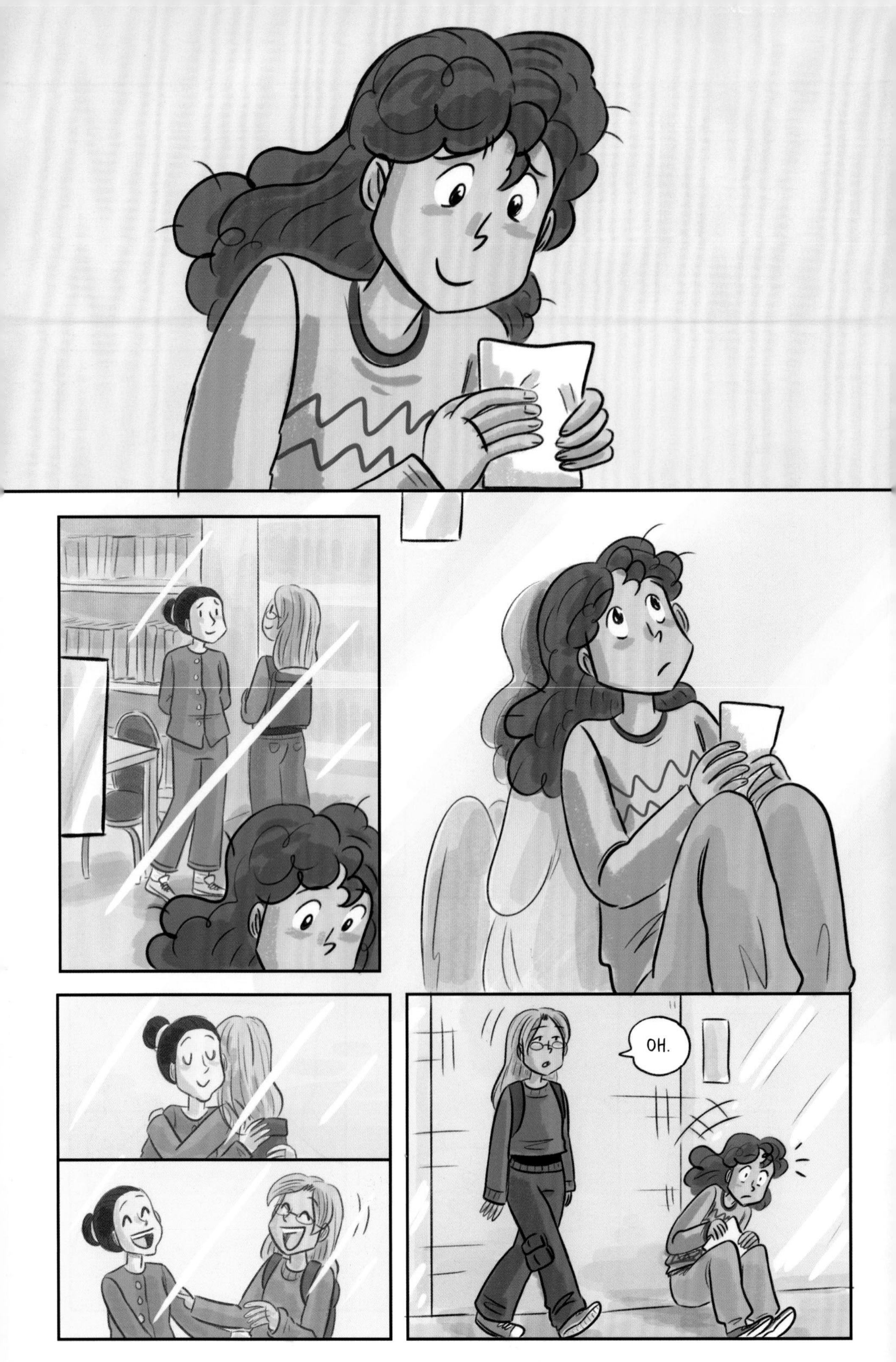
OH.

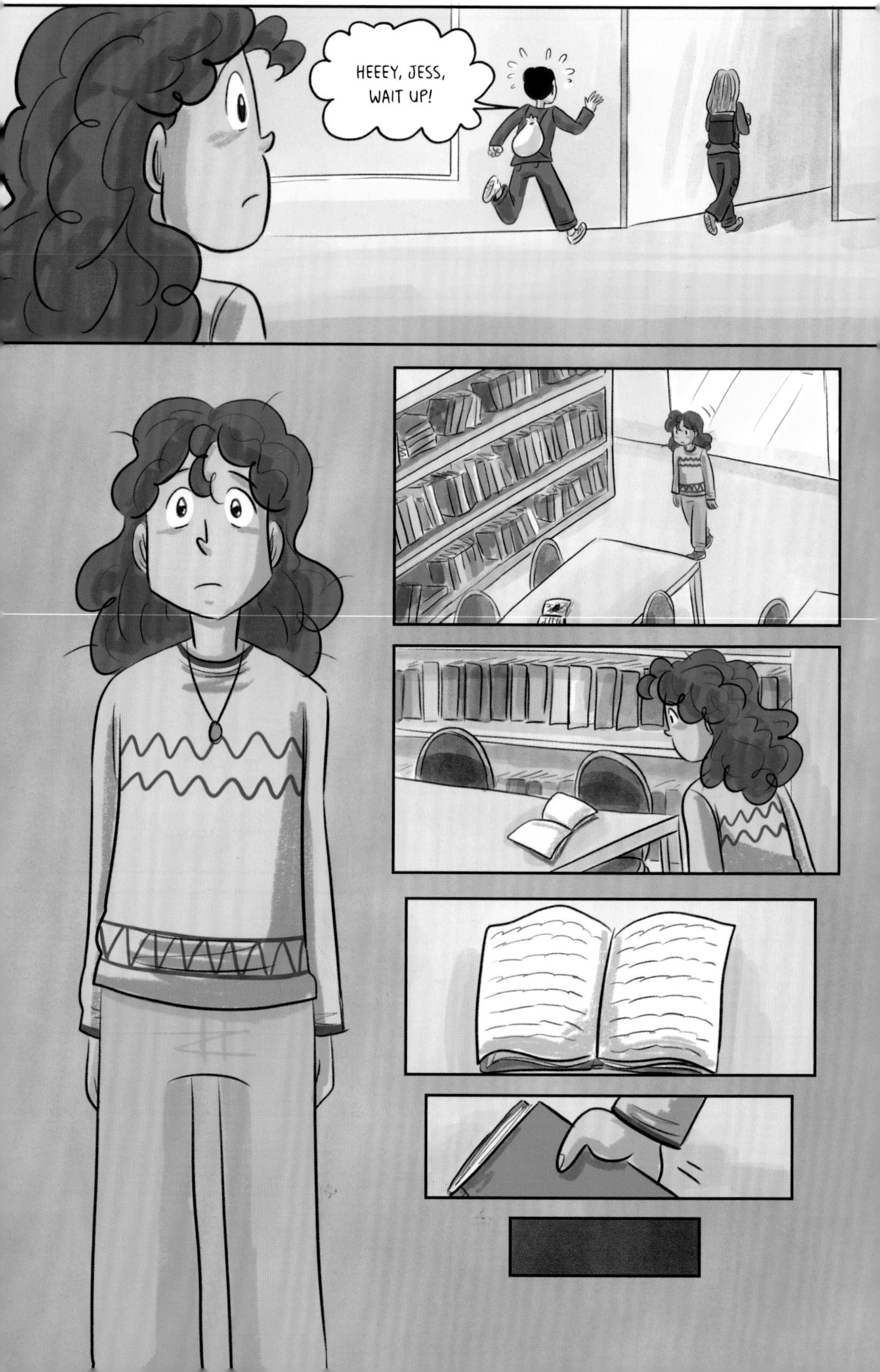
HEEEY, JESS, WAIT UP!

# CHAPTER EIGHT

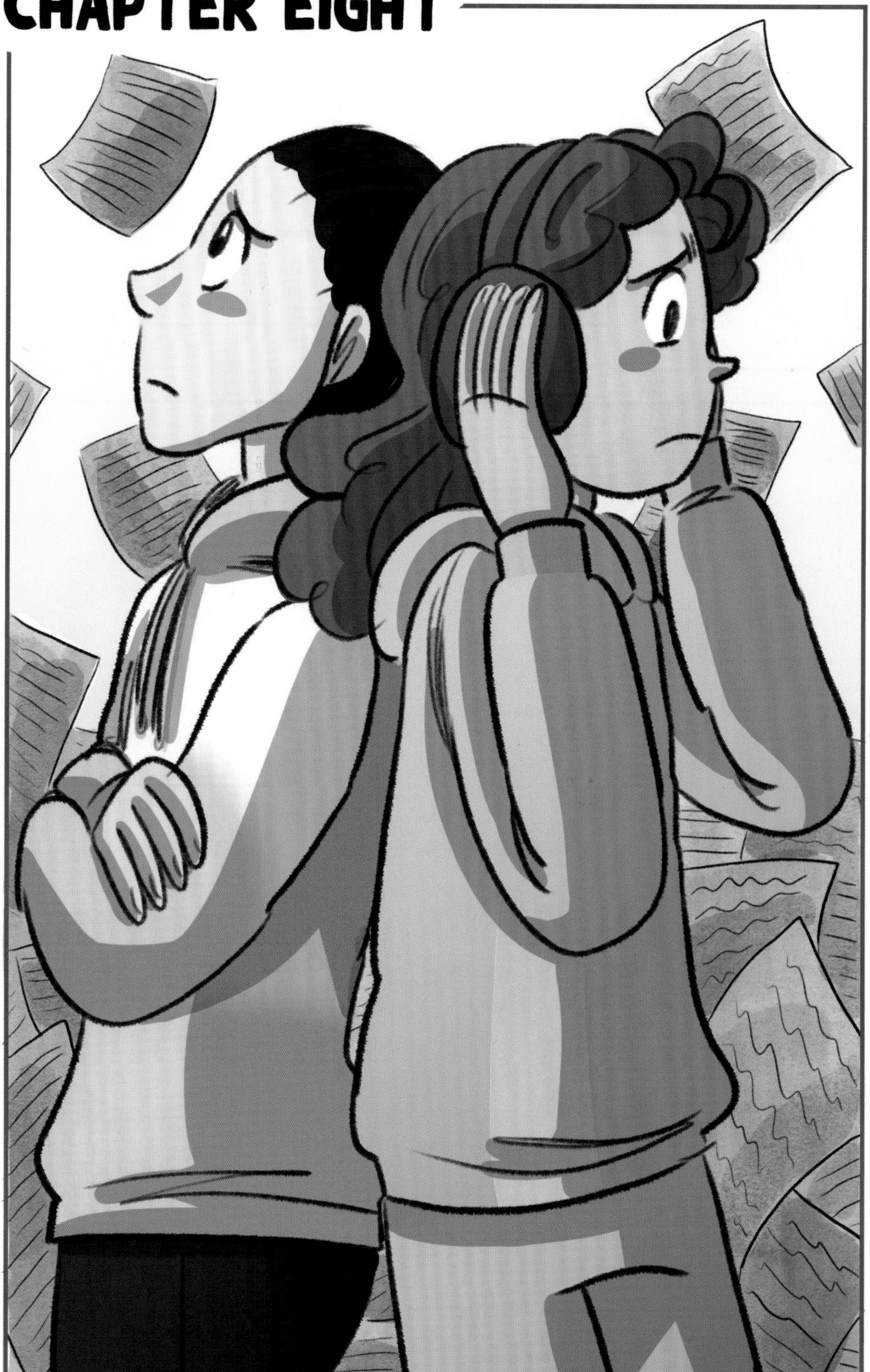

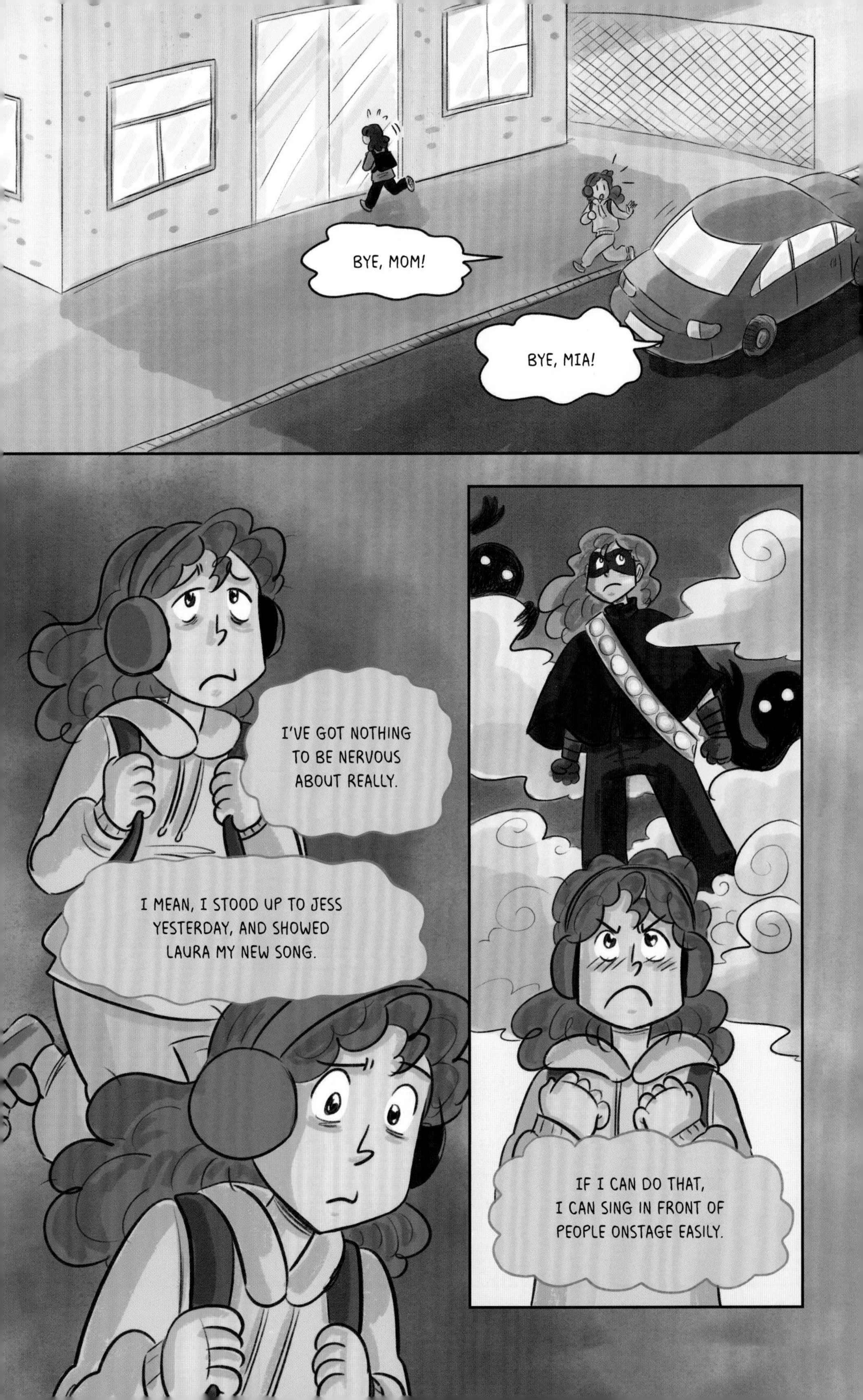
BYE, MOM!
BYE, MIA!
I'VE GOT NOTHING TO BE NERVOUS ABOUT REALLY.
I MEAN, I STOOD UP TO JESS YESTERDAY, AND SHOWED LAURA MY NEW SONG.
IF I CAN DO THAT, I CAN SING IN FRONT OF PEOPLE ONSTAGE EASILY.

I ALWAYS IMAGINED MYSELF AS A WARRIOR SLAYING ANY MONSTERS THAT DID HARM TO ME.

BUT NOW ALL I CAN IMAGINE...

...IS HOW ANGRY MY MOM IS GONNA BE AT ME FOR FIGHTING ONE OF THOSE MONSTERS. AND HOW BAD I FEEL.

...

205

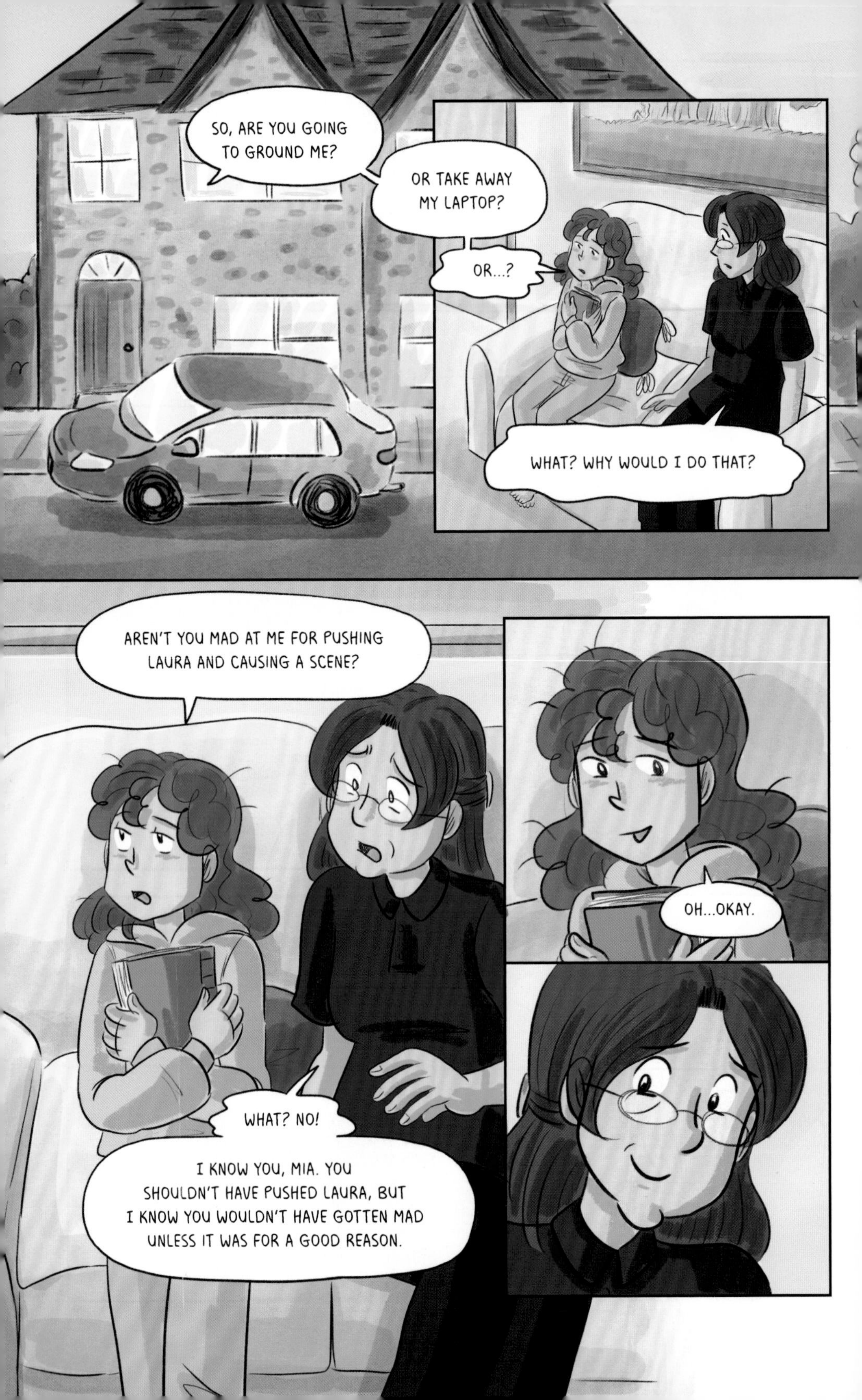
SO, ARE YOU GOING TO GROUND ME?
OR TAKE AWAY MY LAPTOP?
OR...?
WHAT? WHY WOULD I DO THAT?
AREN'T YOU MAD AT ME FOR PUSHING LAURA AND CAUSING A SCENE?
WHAT? NO!
I KNOW YOU, MIA. YOU SHOULDN'T HAVE PUSHED LAURA, BUT I KNOW YOU WOULDN'T HAVE GOTTEN MAD UNLESS IT WAS FOR A GOOD REASON.
OH...OKAY.

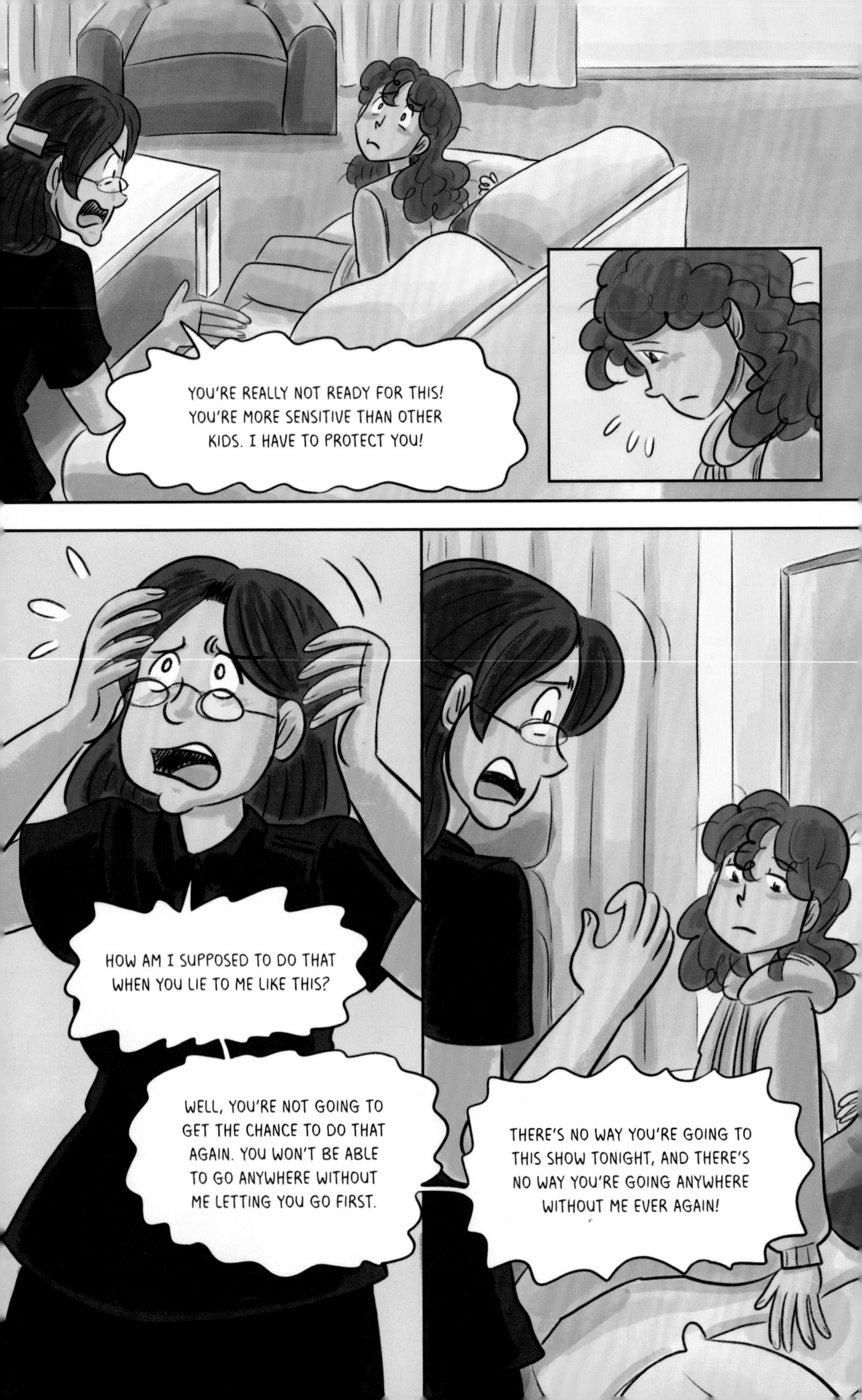
YOU'RE REALLY NOT READY FOR THIS! YOU'RE MORE SENSITIVE THAN OTHER KIDS. I HAVE TO PROTECT YOU!
HOW AM I SUPPOSED TO DO THAT WHEN YOU LIE TO ME LIKE THIS?
WELL, YOU'RE NOT GOING TO GET THE CHANCE TO DO THAT AGAIN. YOU WON'T BE ABLE TO GO ANYWHERE WITHOUT ME LETTING YOU GO FIRST.
THERE'S NO WAY YOU'RE GOING TO THIS SHOW TONIGHT, AND THERE'S NO WAY YOU'RE GOING ANYWHERE WITHOUT ME EVER AGAIN!

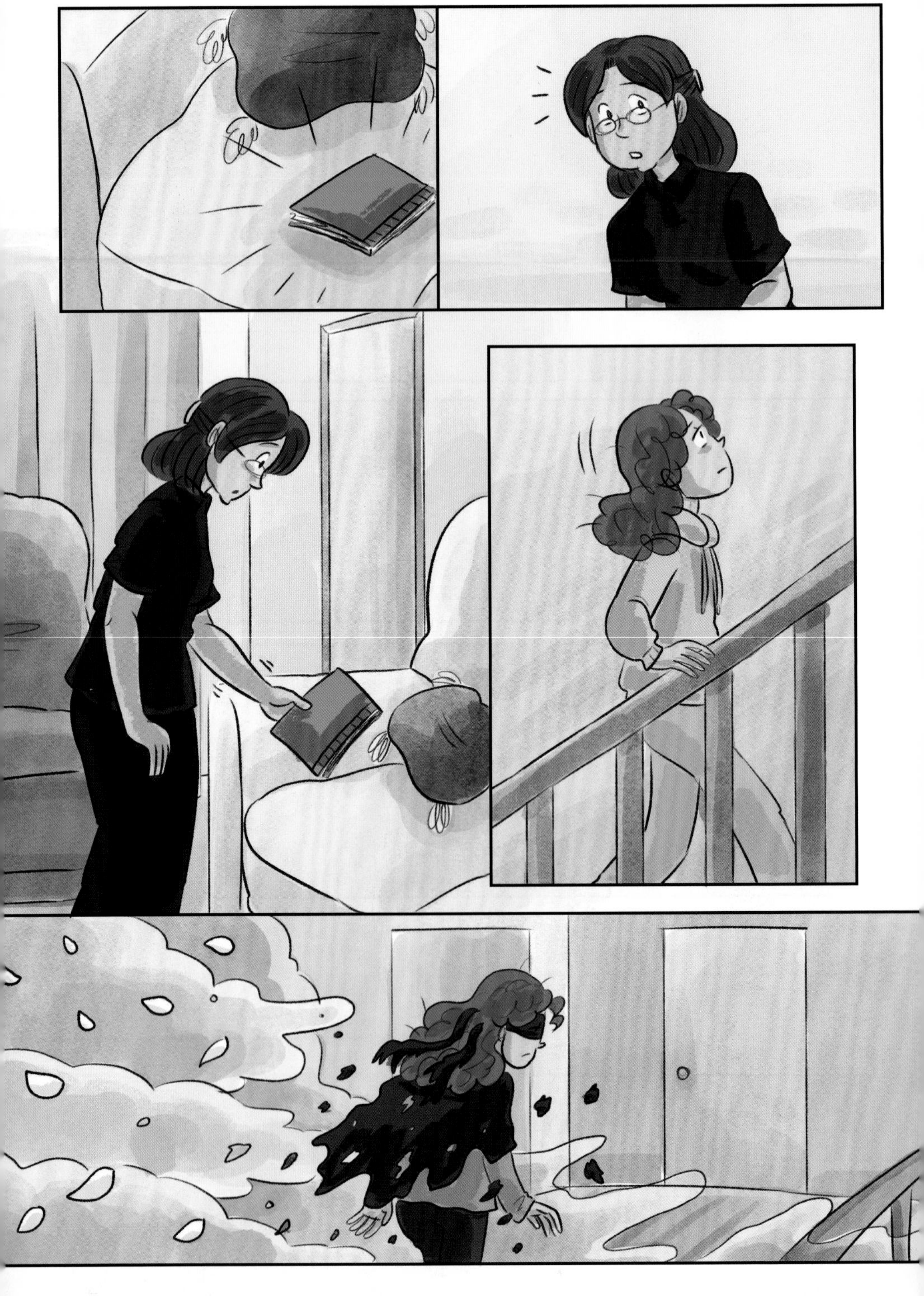

# CHAPTER NINE

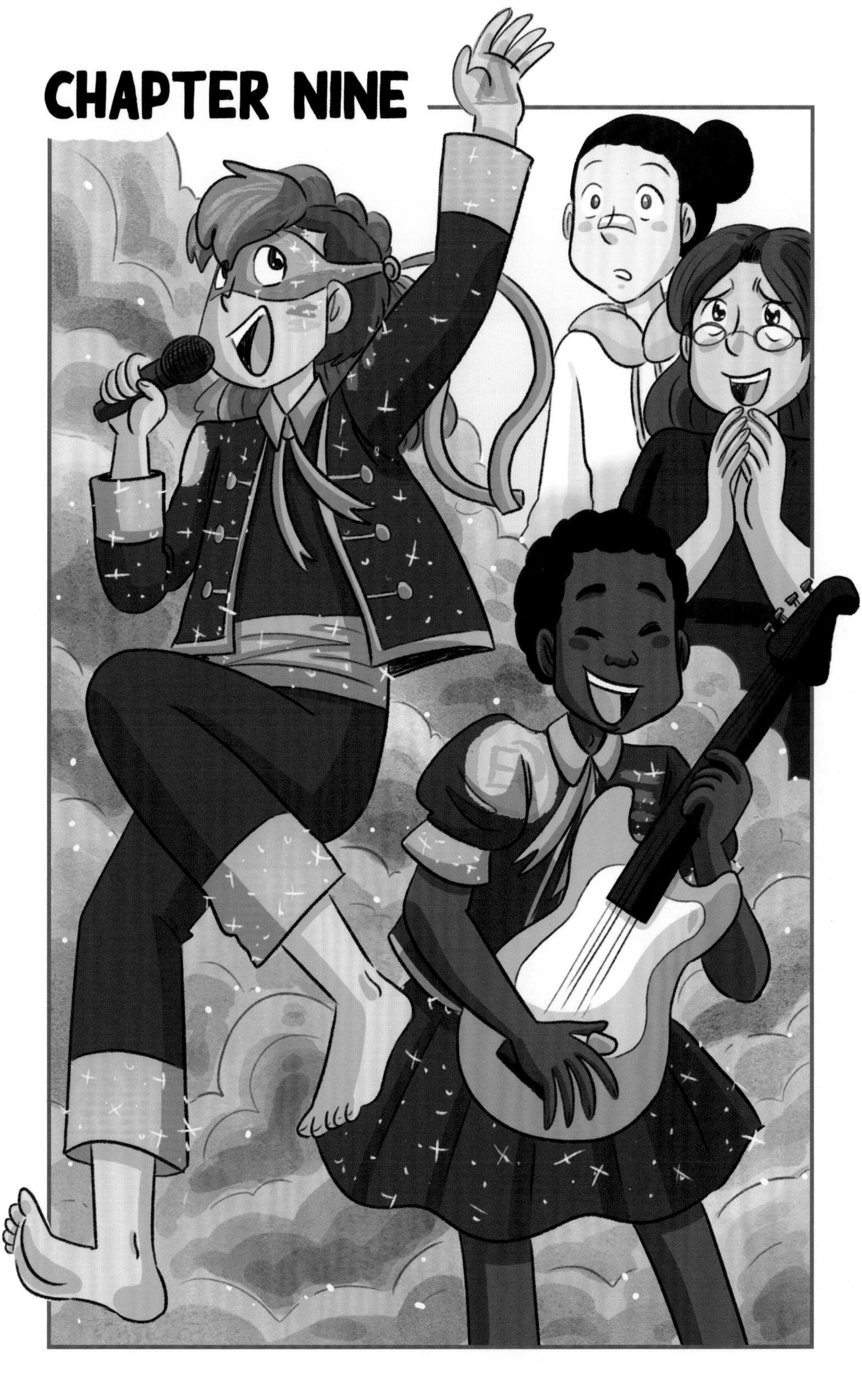

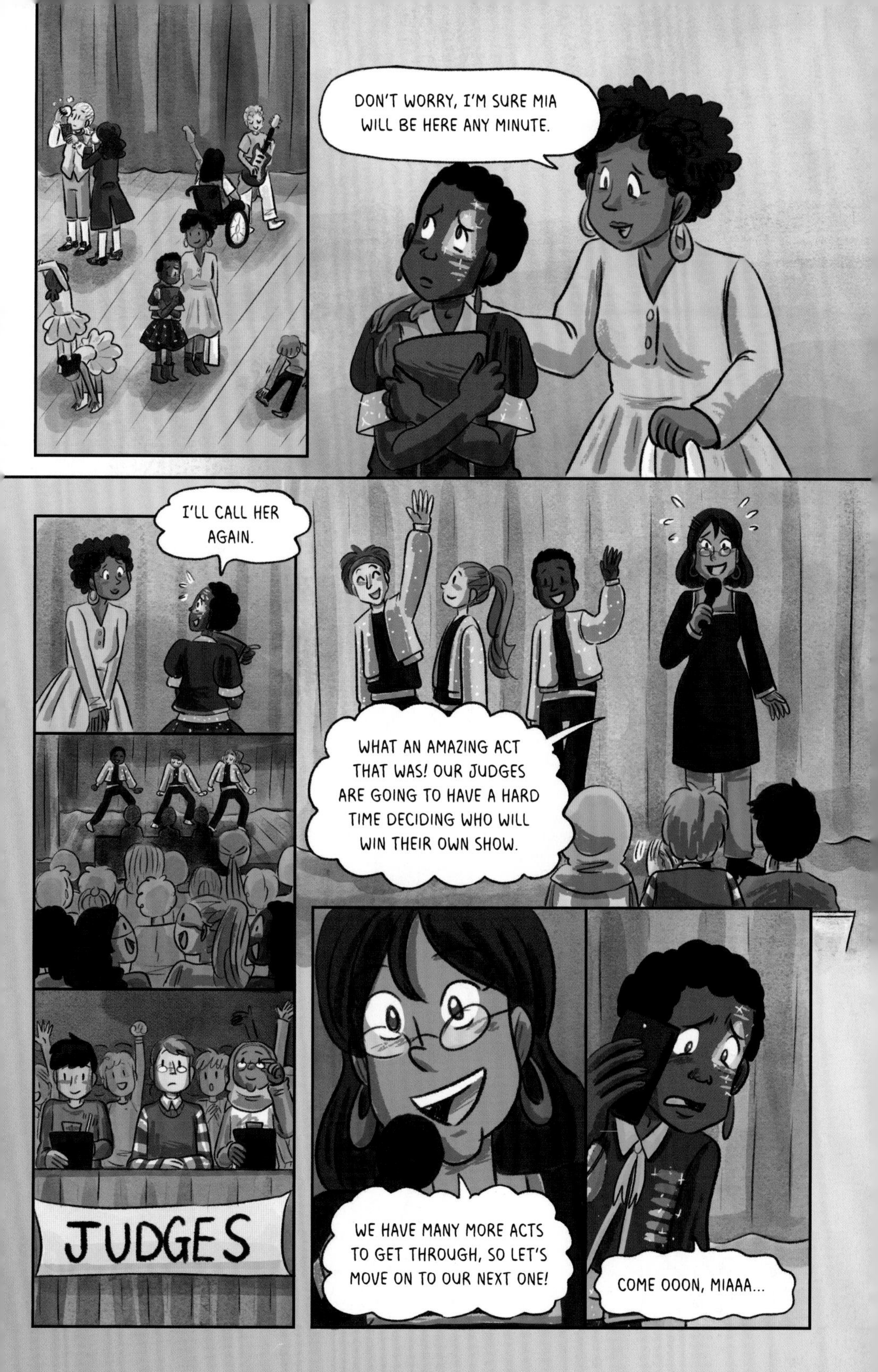
DON'T WORRY, I'M SURE MIA WILL BE HERE ANY MINUTE.
I'LL CALL HER AGAIN.
WHAT AN AMAZING ACT THAT WAS! OUR JUDGES ARE GOING TO HAVE A HARD TIME DECIDING WHO WILL WIN THEIR OWN SHOW.
JUDGES
WE HAVE MANY MORE ACTS TO GET THROUGH, SO LET'S MOVE ON TO OUR NEXT ONE!
COME OOON, MIAAA...

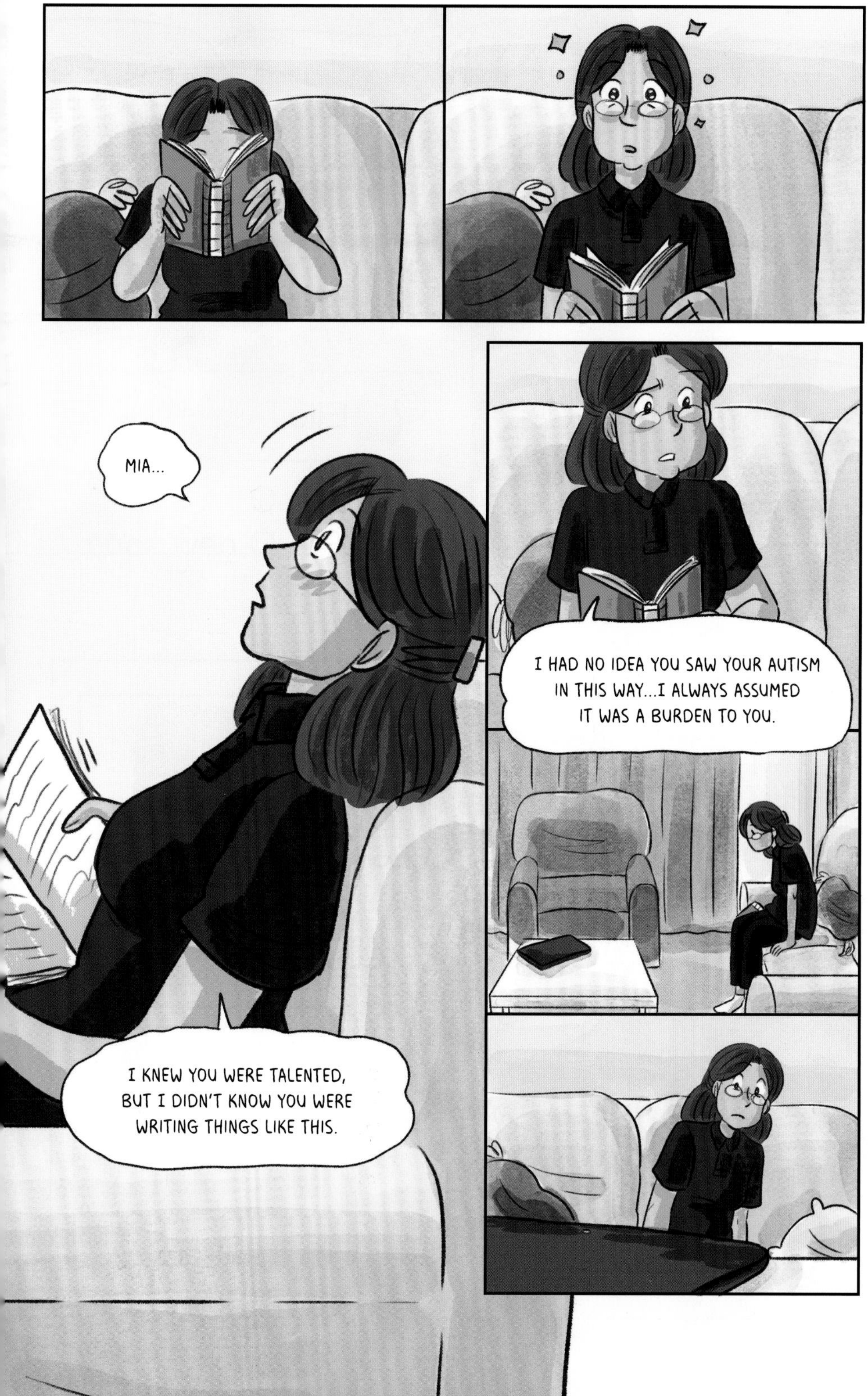
MIA...
I HAD NO IDEA YOU SAW YOUR AUTISM IN THIS WAY...I ALWAYS ASSUMED IT WAS A BURDEN TO YOU.
I KNEW YOU WERE TALENTED, BUT I DIDN'T KNOW YOU WERE WRITING THINGS LIKE THIS.

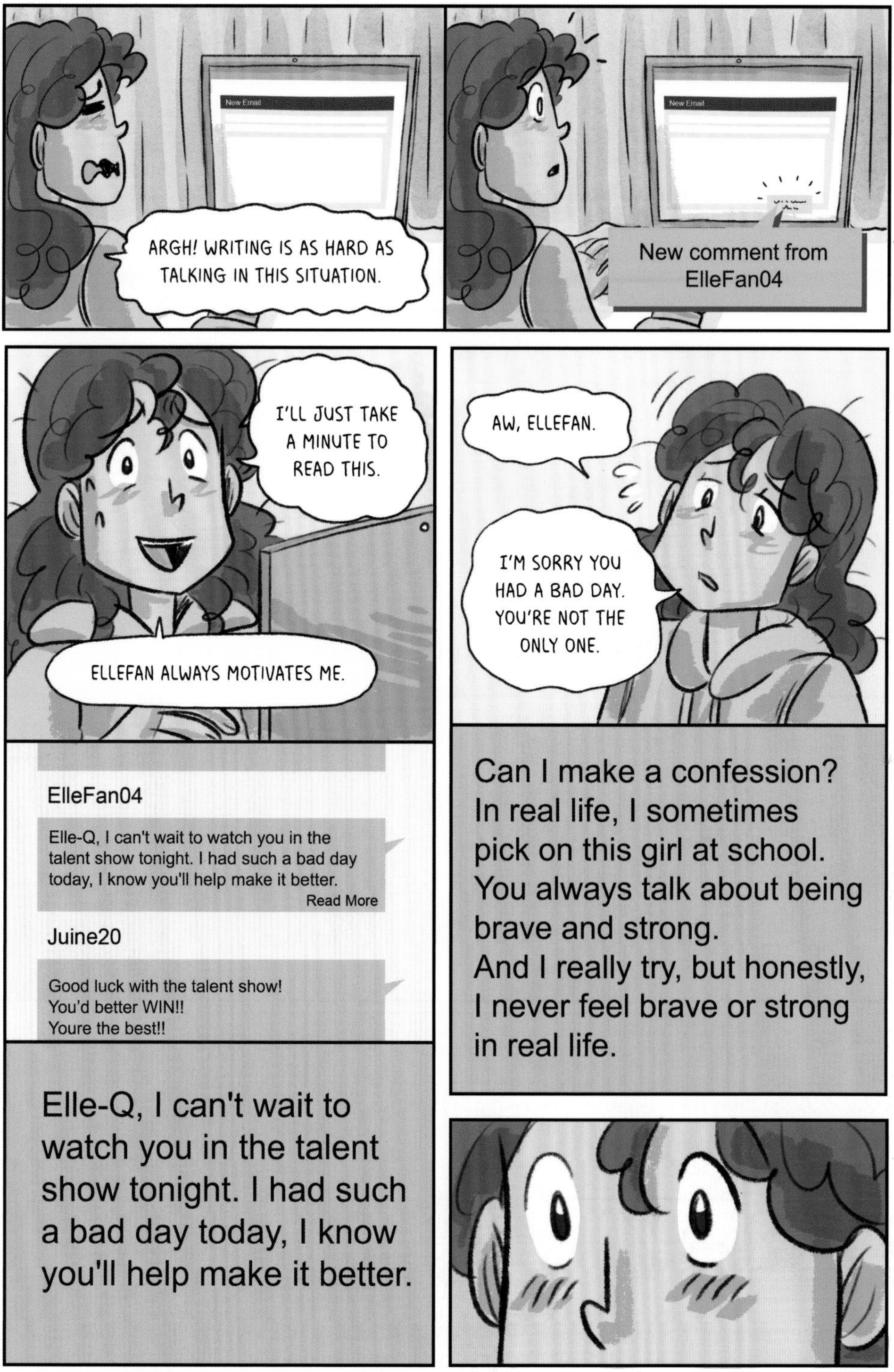
New Email
ARGH! WRITING IS AS HARD AS TALKING IN THIS SITUATION.
New Email
New comment from ElleFan04
I'LL JUST TAKE A MINUTE TO READ THIS.
ELLEFAN ALWAYS MOTIVATES ME.
AW, ELLEFAN.
I'M SORRY YOU HAD A BAD DAY. YOU'RE NOT THE ONLY ONE.
ElleFan04
Elle-Q, I can't wait to watch you in the talent show tonight. I had such a bad day today, I know you'll help make it better.
Read More
Juine20
Good luck with the talent show! You'd better WIN!! Youre the best!!
Elle-Q, I can't wait to watch you in the talent show tonight. I had such a bad day today, I know you'll help make it better.
Can I make a confession? In real life, I sometimes pick on this girl at school. You always talk about being brave and strong. And I really try, but honestly, I never feel brave or strong in real life.

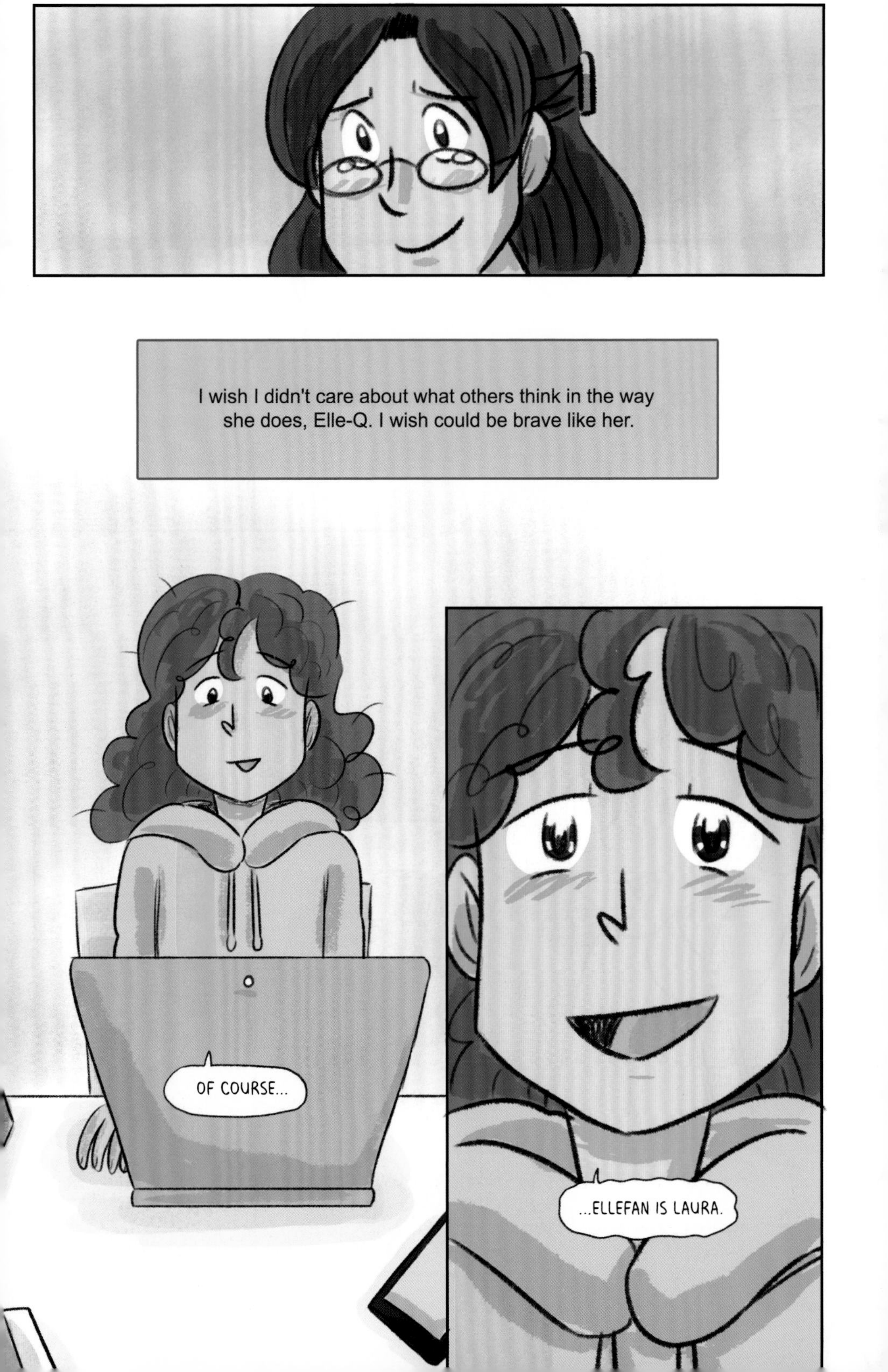
I wish I didn't care about what others think in the way she does, Elle-Q. I wish could be brave like her.
OF COURSE...
...ELLEFAN IS LAURA.

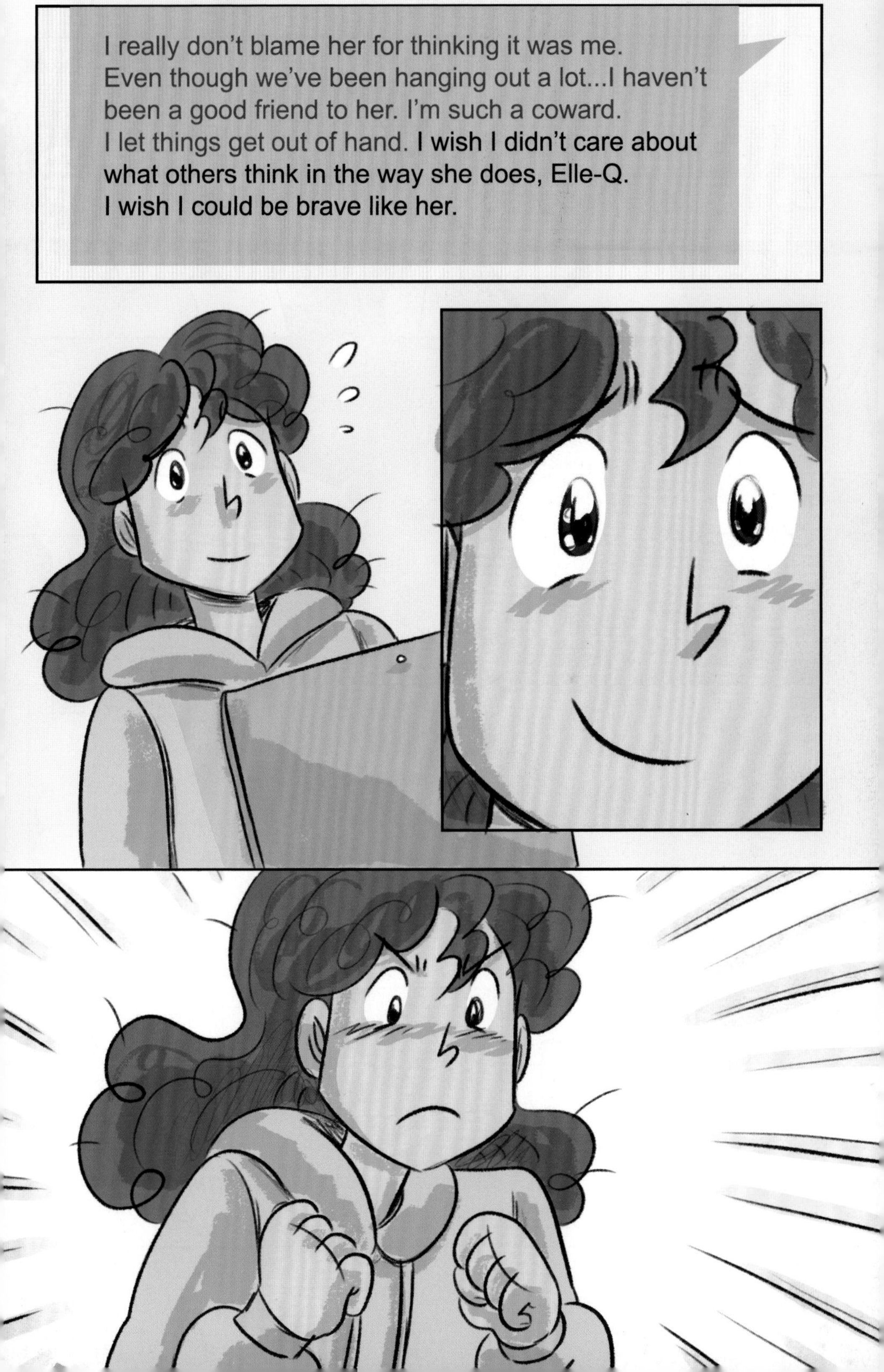
I really don't blame her for thinking it was me. Even though we've been hanging out a lot...I haven't been a good friend to her. I'm such a coward. I let things get out of hand. I wish I didn't care about what others think in the way she does, Elle-Q. I wish I could be brave like her.

229

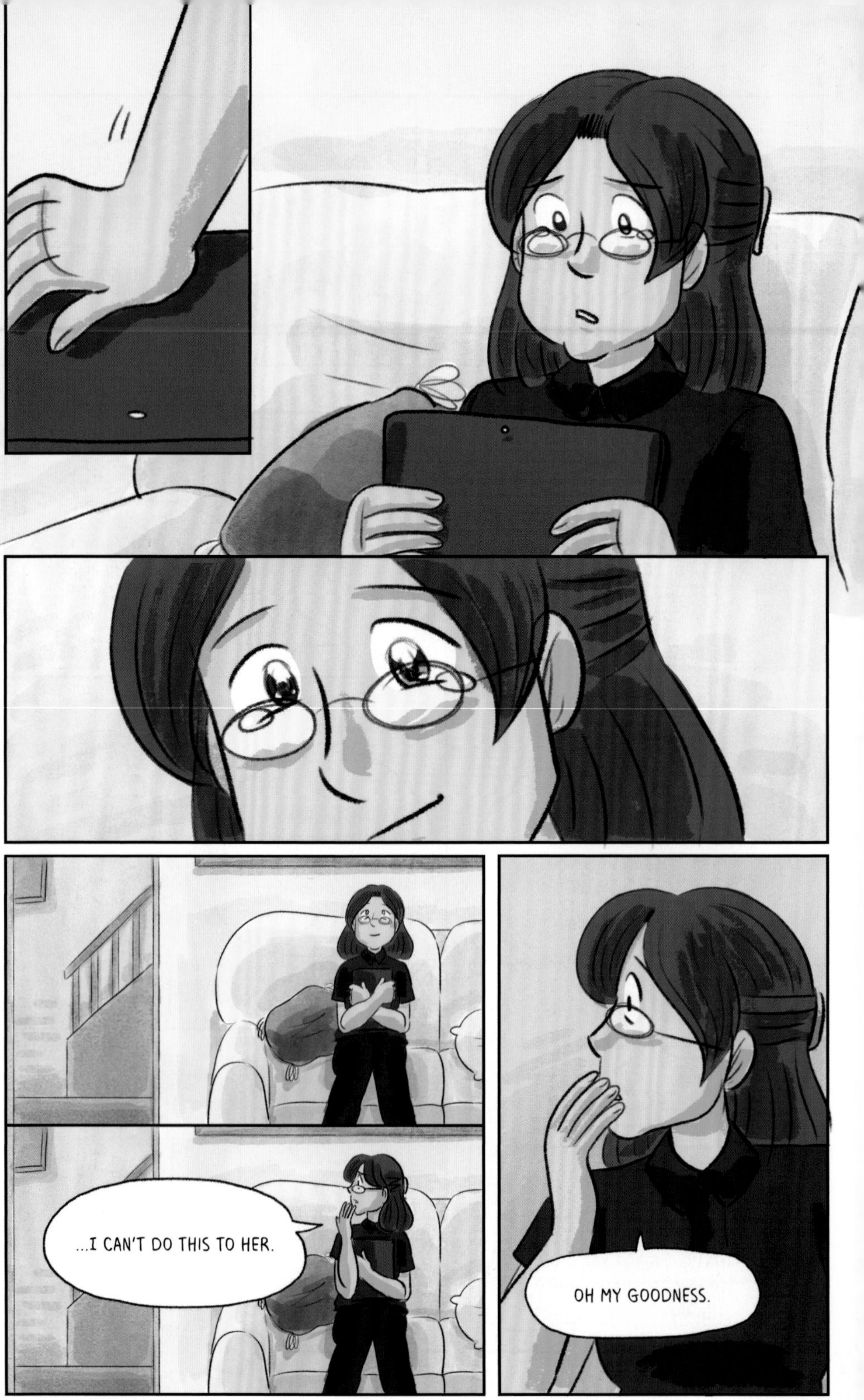
...I CAN'T DO THIS TO HER.
OH MY GOODNESS.

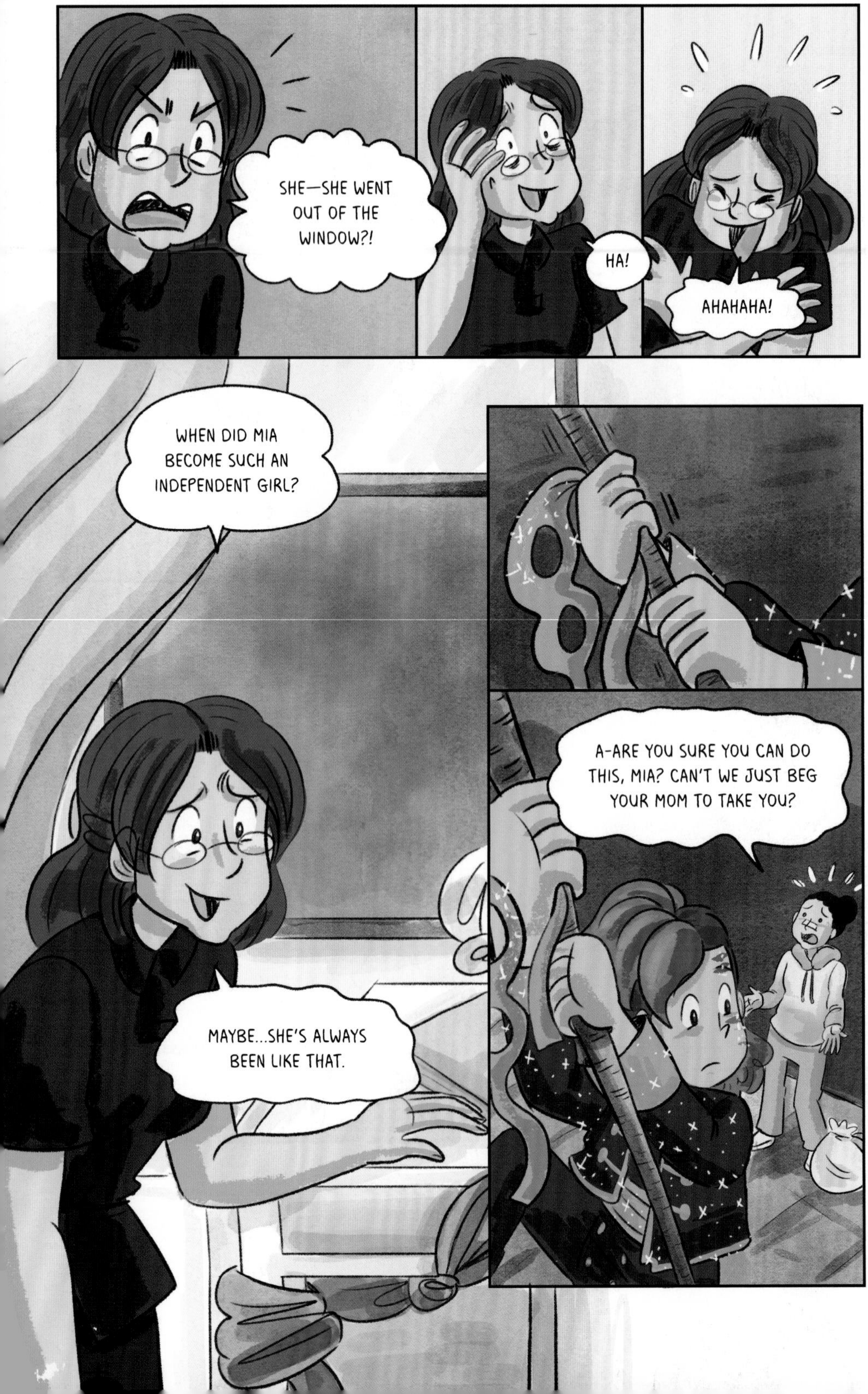
SHE—SHE WENT OUT OF THE WINDOW?!
HA!
AHAHAHA!
WHEN DID MIA BECOME SUCH AN INDEPENDENT GIRL?
MAYBE...SHE'S ALWAYS BEEN LIKE THAT.
A-ARE YOU SURE YOU CAN DO THIS, MIA? CAN'T WE JUST BEG YOUR MOM TO TAKE YOU?

HA! THIS IS SO AMAZING.

ROOAAARRR

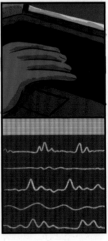

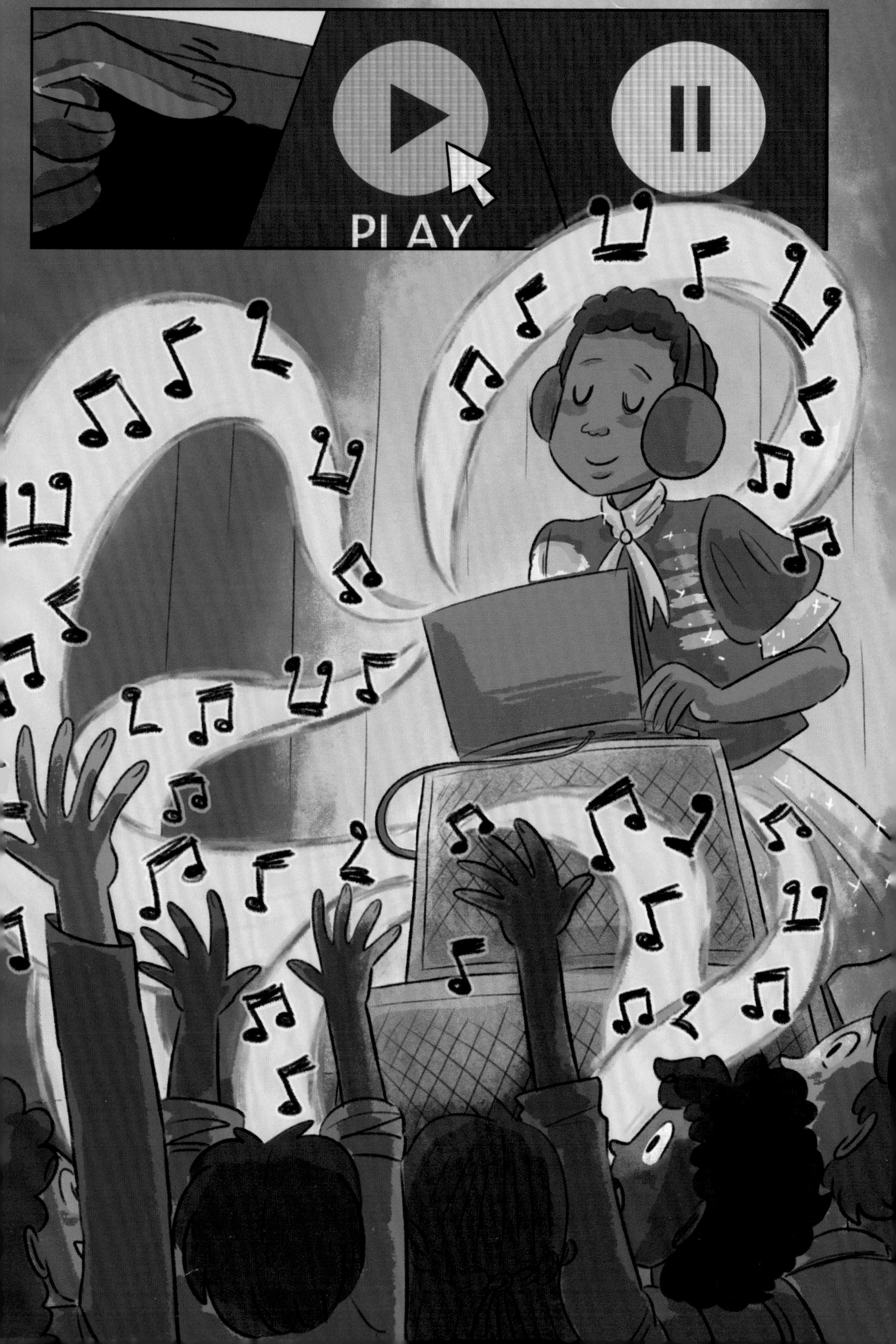
PLAY

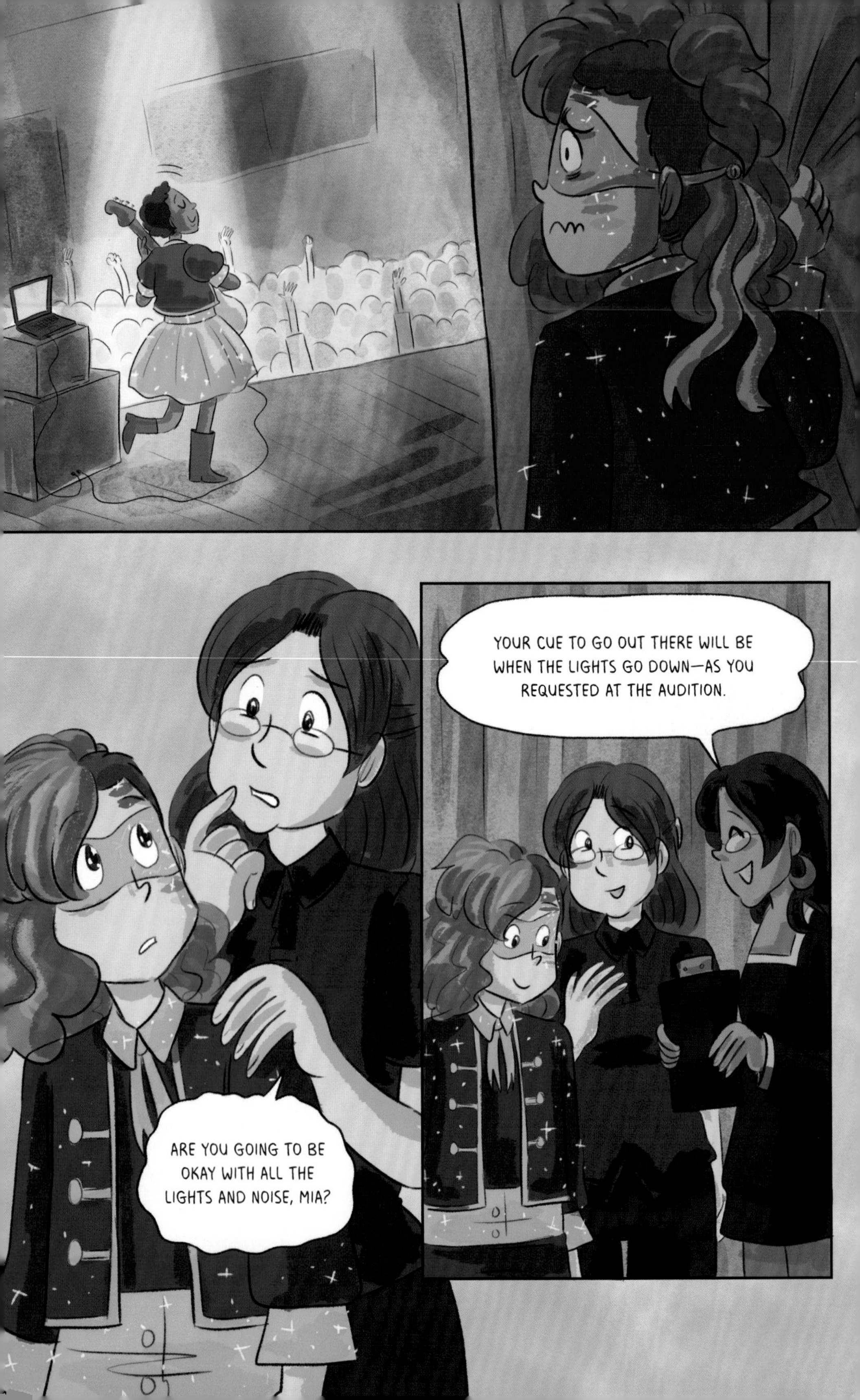
YOUR CUE TO GO OUT THERE WILL BE WHEN THE LIGHTS GO DOWN—AS YOU REQUESTED AT THE AUDITION.
ARE YOU GOING TO BE OKAY WITH ALL THE LIGHTS AND NOISE, MIA?

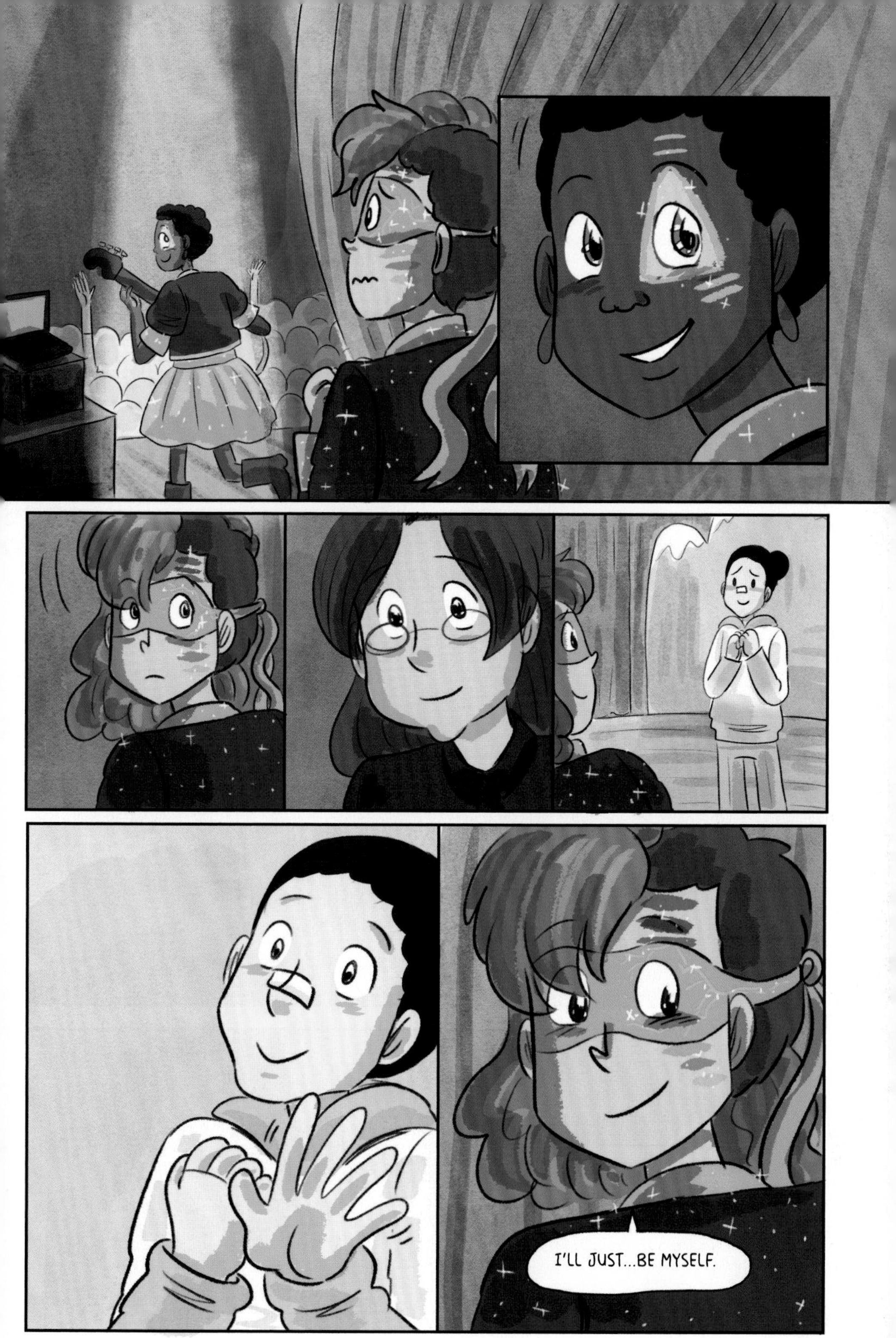
I'LL JUST...BE MYSELF.

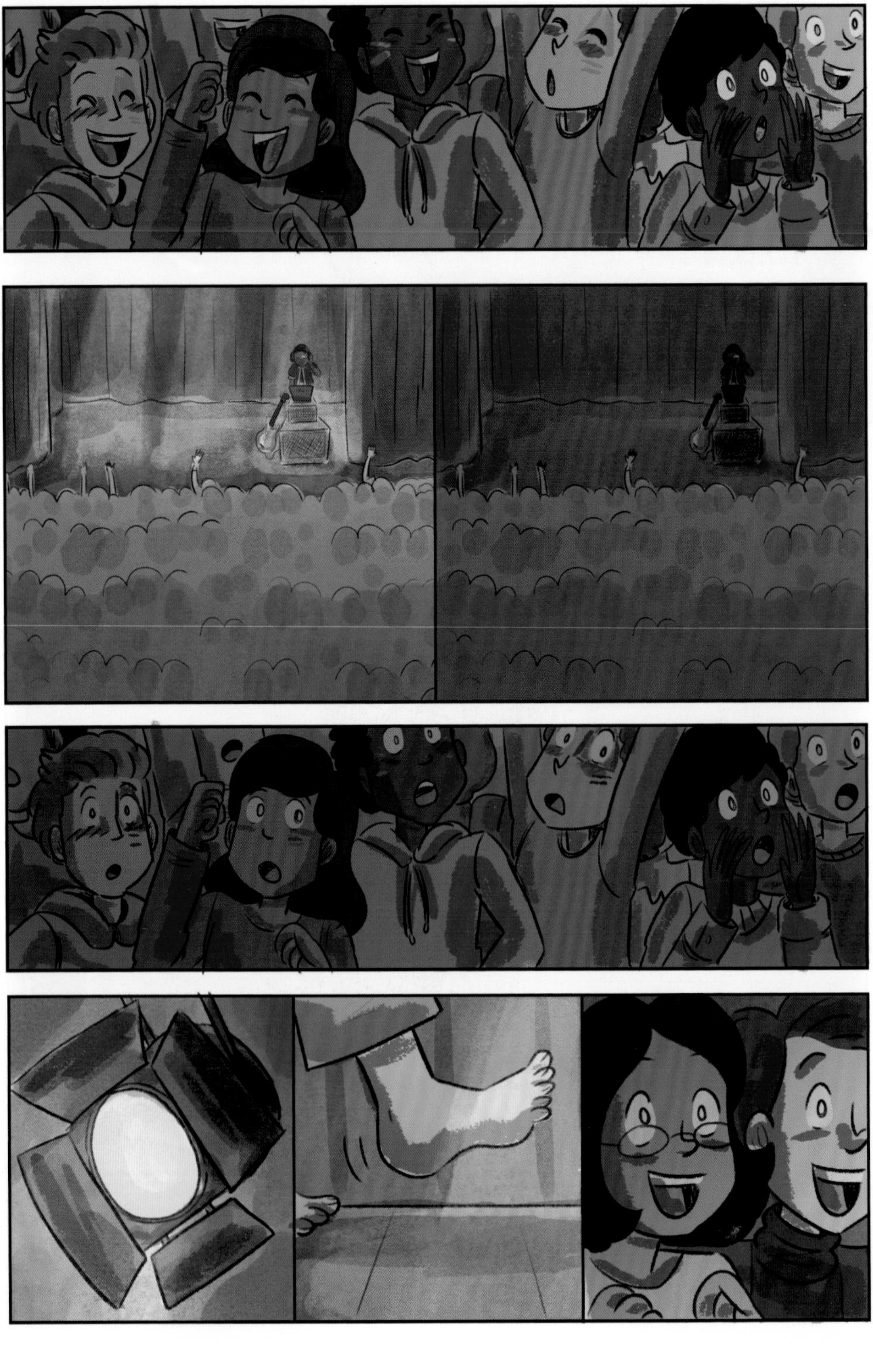

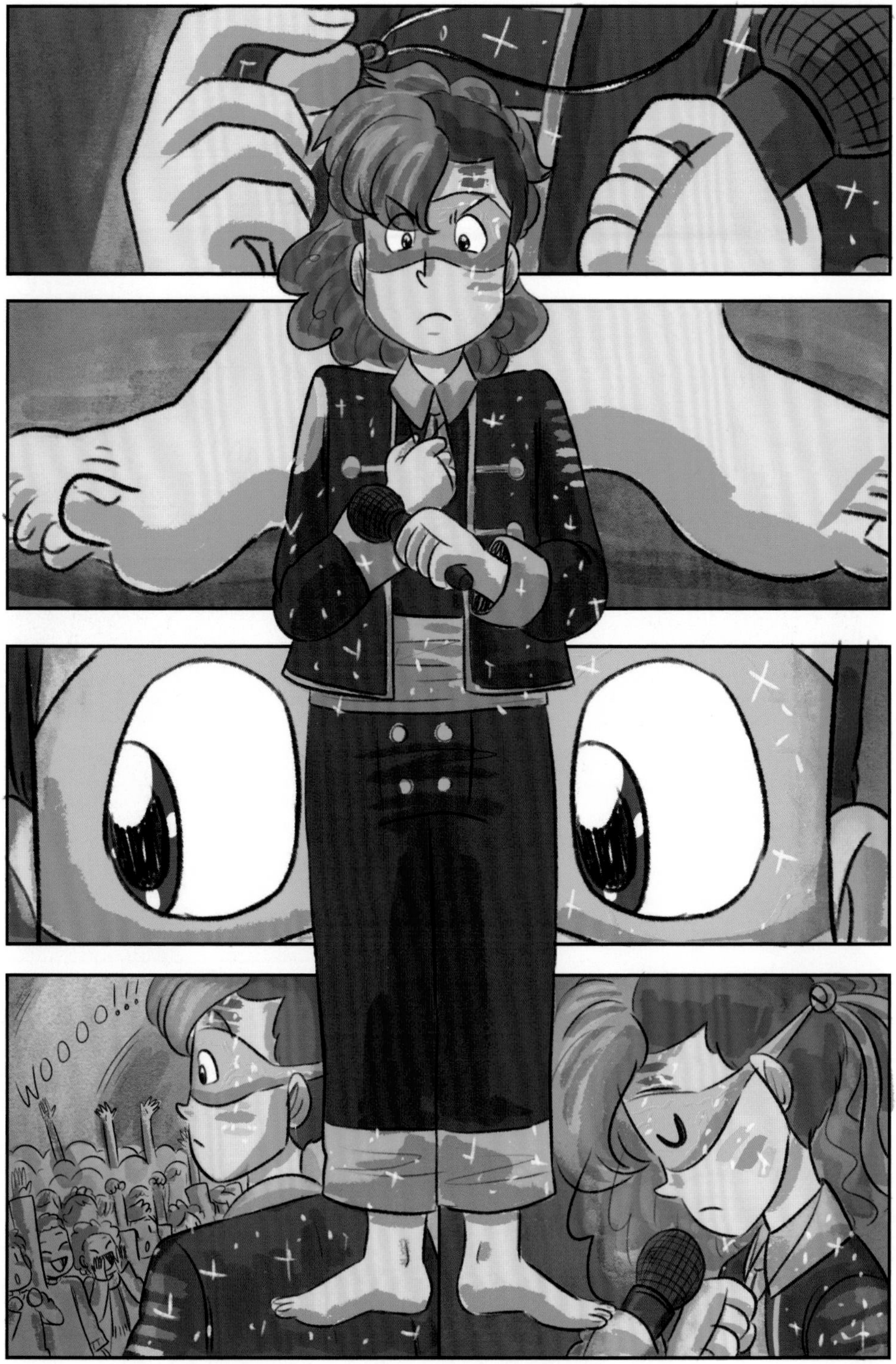
WOOOO!!!

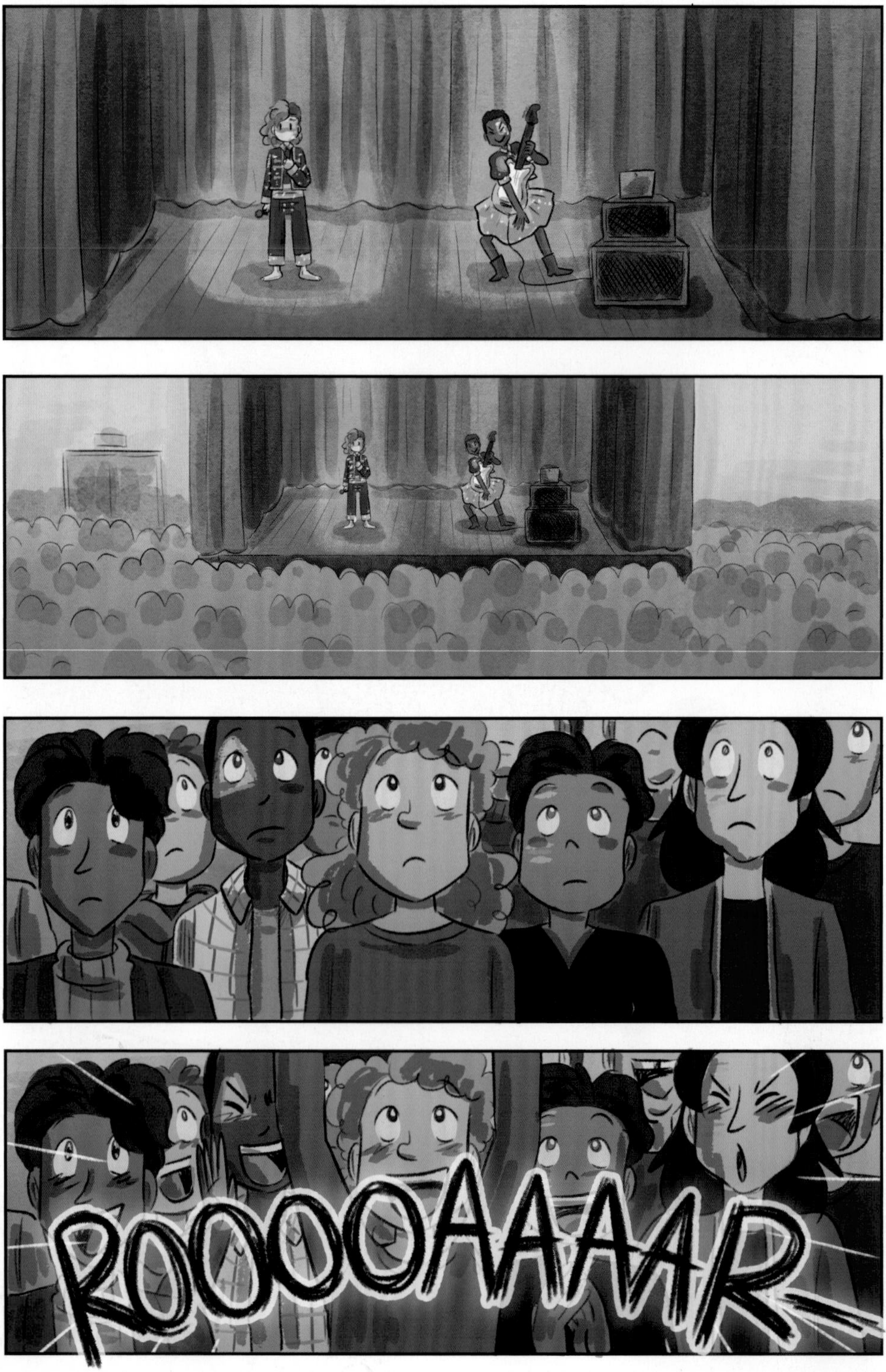
ROOOOAAAAR

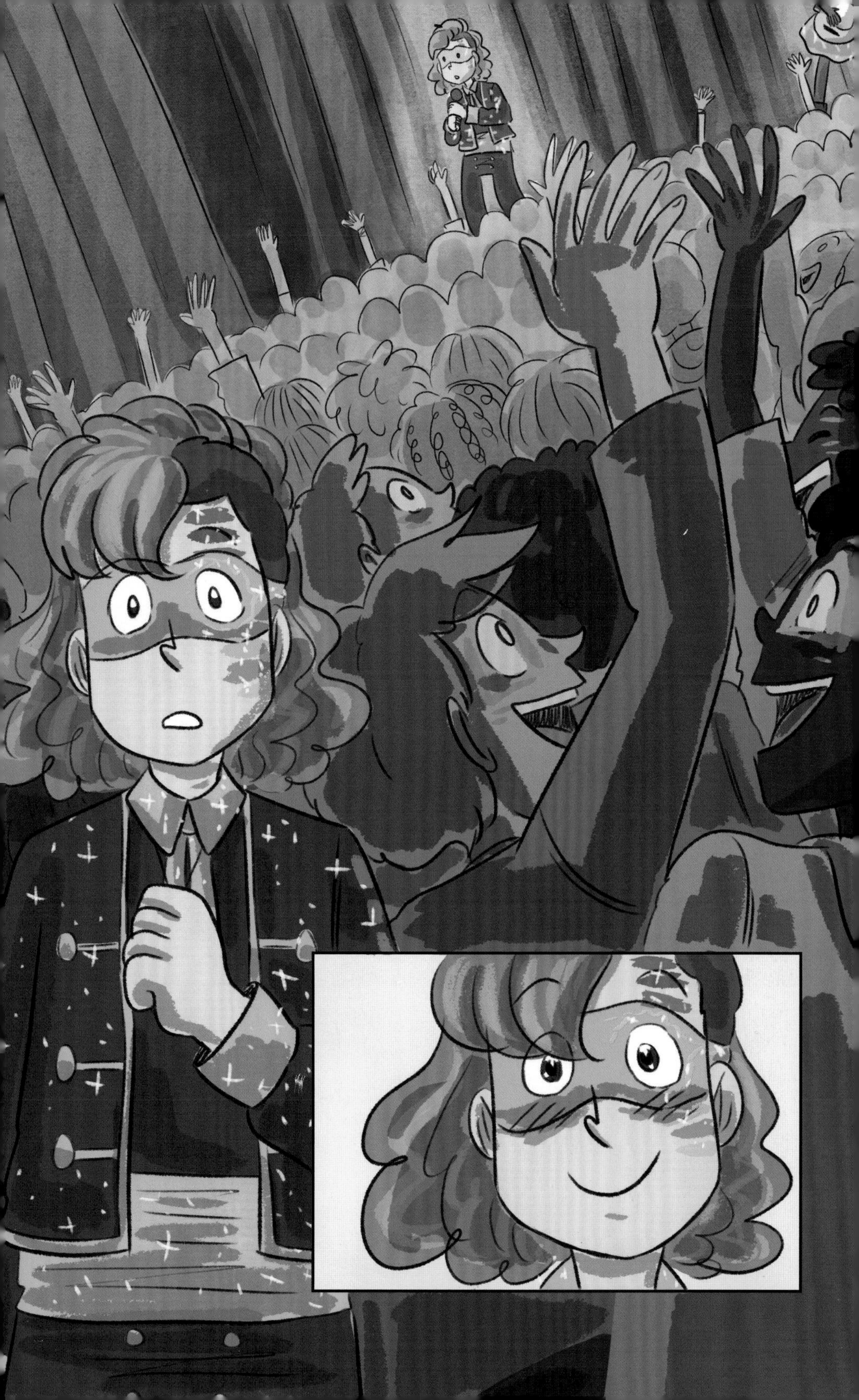

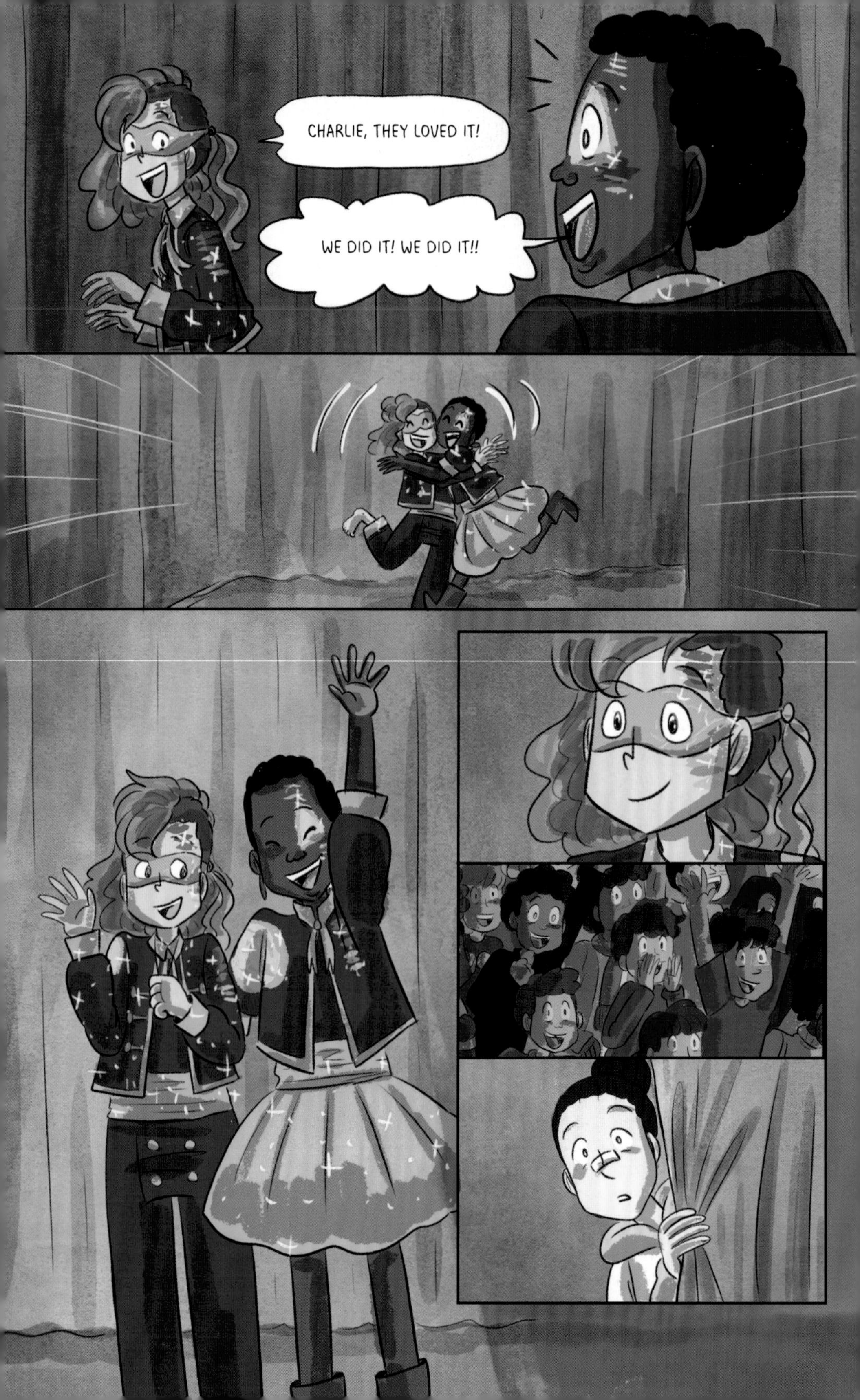
CHARLIE, THEY LOVED IT!
WE DID IT! WE DID IT!!

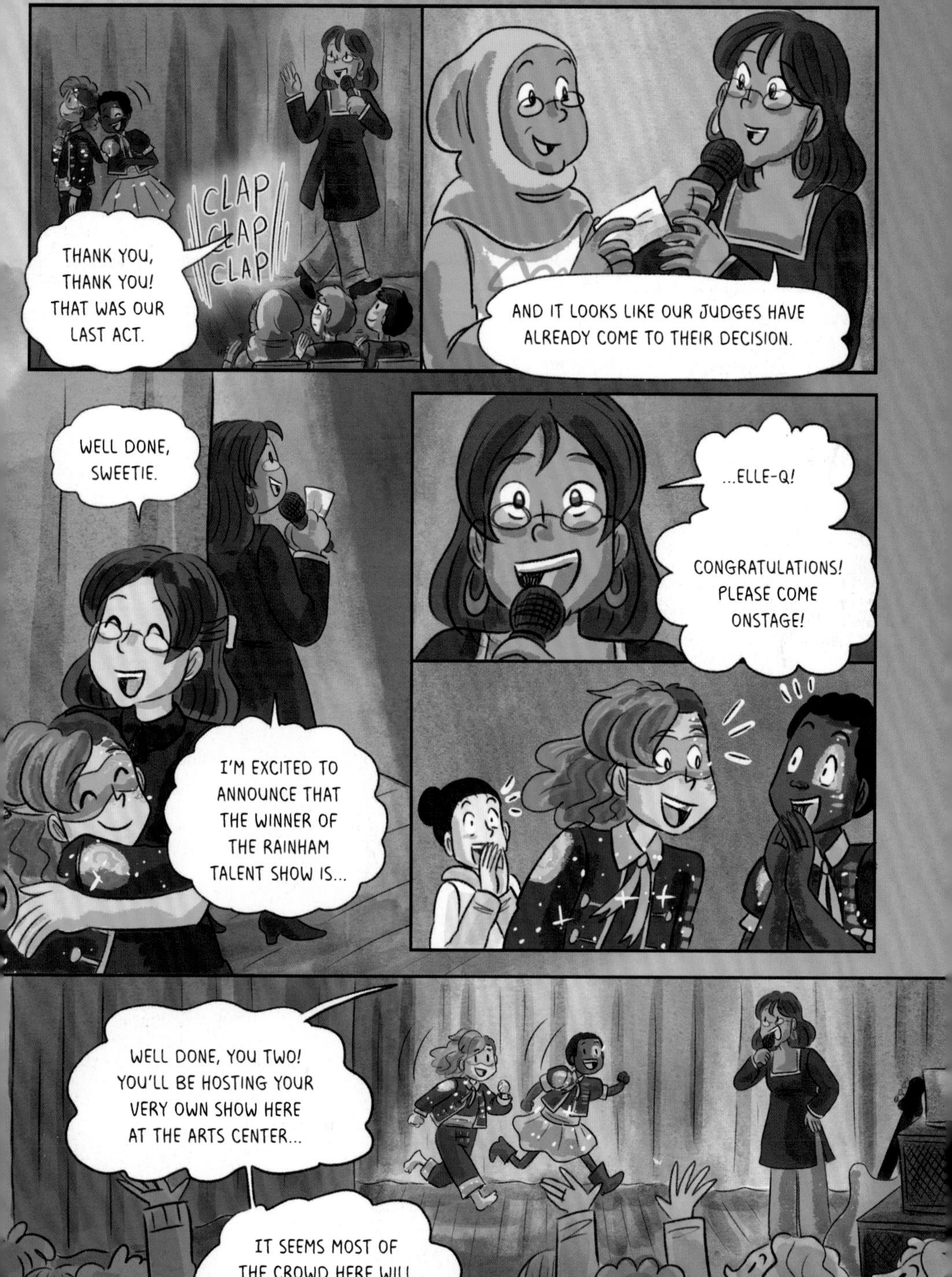
CLAP CLAP CLAP
THANK YOU, THANK YOU! THAT WAS OUR LAST ACT.
AND IT LOOKS LIKE OUR JUDGES HAVE ALREADY COME TO THEIR DECISION.
WELL DONE, SWEETIE.
I'M EXCITED TO ANNOUNCE THAT THE WINNER OF THE RAINHAM TALENT SHOW IS...
...ELLE-Q!
CONGRATULATIONS! PLEASE COME ONSTAGE!
WELL DONE, YOU TWO! YOU'LL BE HOSTING YOUR VERY OWN SHOW HERE AT THE ARTS CENTER...
IT SEEMS MOST OF THE CROWD HERE WILL BE PRETTY EXCITED ABOUT THAT!

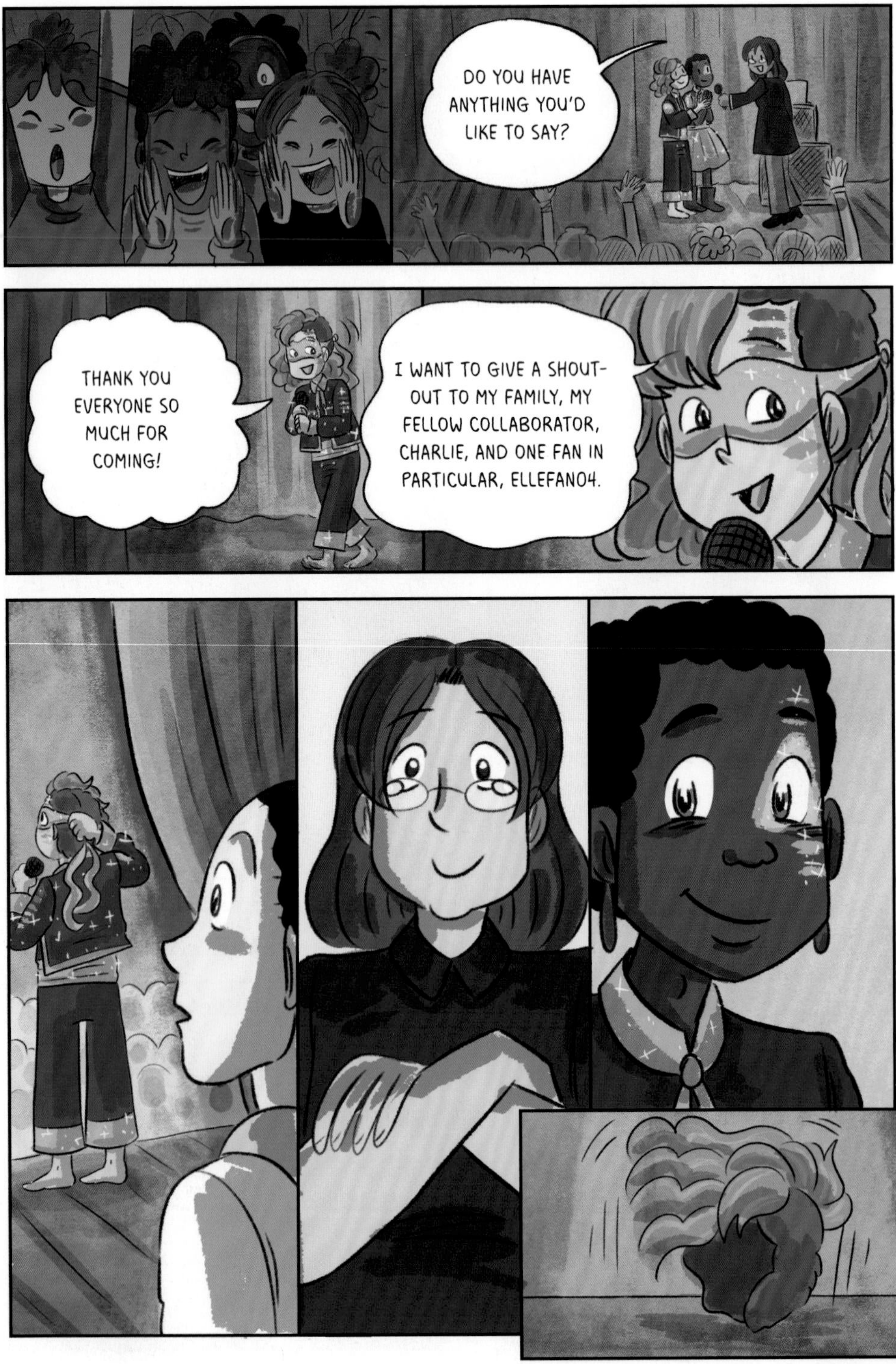
DO YOU HAVE ANYTHING YOU'D LIKE TO SAY?
THANK YOU EVERYONE SO MUCH FOR COMING!
I WANT TO GIVE A SHOUT-OUT TO MY FAMILY, MY FELLOW COLLABORATOR, CHARLIE, AND ONE FAN IN PARTICULAR, ELLEFAN04.

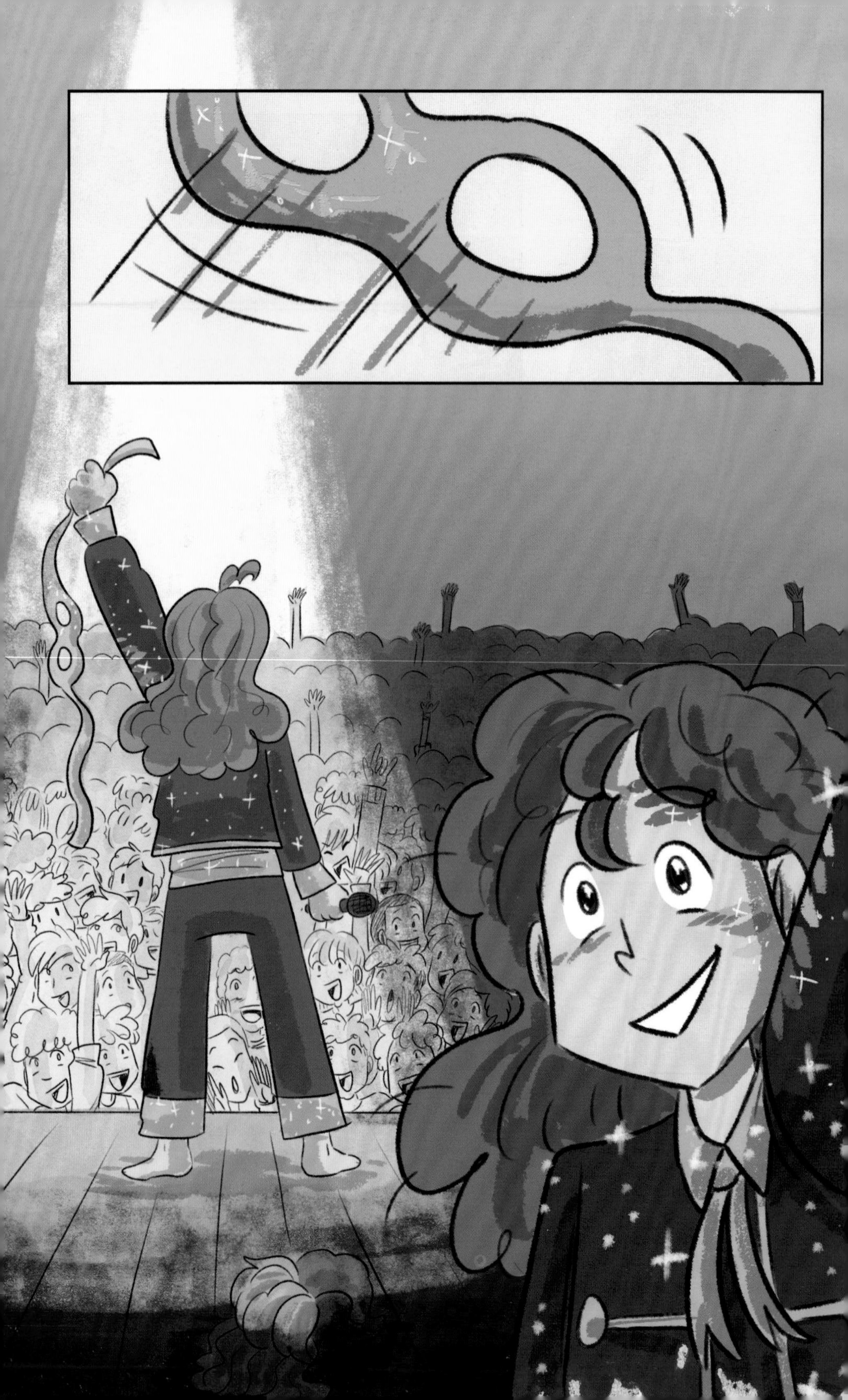